The Case is Busted

By

David M. Golden

Eloquent Books
New York, New York

Eloquent Books
An imprint of AEG Publishing Group
845 Third Avenue, 6th Floor - 6016
New York, NY 10022
www.eloquentbooks.com

ISBN: 978-1-60860-036-6
SKU: 1-60860-036-X

Printed in the United States of America

Book Design: Roger Hayes

Contents

6

CHAPTER ONE

No one in similar circumstances would ever have joined the Bar of England and Wales intending to qualify as a barrister-at-law.

It was just gone the seventies. In terms of age, well, if the life expectancy of the average working class male is to be measured by the hands of a clock face, I was not yet gone six. However, I was what was, and presumably still is, termed a mature student. My marriage was on the rocks. Betwixt espousal and estrangement, such period being fourteen and one half days inclusive of honeymoon, I had accumulated those sorts of debts that would do a third world country proud. In an attempt to avoid miscellaneous creditors my *modus operandi*, was to sleep for no more than a couple of nights in any one boarding house where I would not, under any circumstances, register as a guest by use of my true name of Izaak Gatehouse.

I'd spent all of my working life vegetating as a humble clerk in a solicitor's office. With the benefit of hindsight, I fancy that all prospect of elevation from the post room to my very own office had flown straight out of the sash windows on the day that I beat the senior partner to it by touching up the junior secretary-or was it a deed of conveyance? Well, anyway, I was evidently of the right calibre to be admitted as a student member of the Honorable Society of Gray's Inn.

For the uninitiated, I'd best explain that there are four Inns of Court, namely Lincoln's, Middle Temple, Inner Temple and, of course, Gray's. A prospective barrister must become a member of one of the Inns and (in those days) enroll with a college called The Council. The Inns are so called because in days of yore barristers would go there for the purposes of eating and drinking to excess, having unprotected sex and sleeping. Nowadays, it's unusual to attend an Inn to sleep.

The task of nominating Lincoln's, Middle Temple or what-have-you is down to the individual. The majority, it seemed to me, were influenced by whichever specialty happened to be associated with their respective Inn. Lincoln's, for example attracted those who aspired to practice law in the Courts of Chancery where it was traditional for probate disputes and suchlike to gather dust. A student might also select an Inn according to family history. I chose the Honorable Society of Gray's Inn because the name matched perfectly the color of my hair.

Incidentally, all of the Inns are blessed with Honorable by way of title but I never figured that one out. What remains for certain is that the four Honorables are conveniently situated between the City of London on the eastern side and Soho on the western side where, in one form or another, the unsuspecting are guaranteed of getting screwed.

In order to secure my place on the Council's training course it was necessary that I be examined as to my suitability and fitness. Academic achievements in a thus far undistinguished career had consisted of a certificate of merit in the subject of metalwork. Imagine my surprise when I was declared both suitable and fit.

In common with all other trainee barristers I was also required to attend my chosen Honorable, on twelve occasions, no less, to dine. Incredibly, before anyone can qualify as a barrister it is necessary to attend their respective Inn of Court and consume dinners.

I resolved that before removing myself altogether to London for the purpose of attending the law course I would make a day trip to the metropolis and chalk up one of the dinners. To this end I arrived ridiculously early and spent much of the day pounding the footpaths between the eastern screw and the western screw.

And so begins the tale of the legal career of Izaak Gatehouse as, for the umpteenth time, I slouched past the main entrance of Gray's Inn plucking up courage to enter while simultaneously ensuring that I didn't go stepping on the cracks between the paving slabs. There were moments, I concede, when I was tempted not to bother and to return home, tail between legs, and go work in the foundry; perhaps even the coal pit. But enter the Honorable Society of Gray's Inn I did, though not before harking back (only briefly, mind) to a lesson that I had had on the do's and the not to do's when dining at an Inn of Court.

Henry Sunderland was the name of my instructor and I had met him by prior appointment at The Whippet Inn in the Black Country town of Dudsall, such miserable place having played host to the firm of solicitors who were so pleased to see me off just weeks previous. I knew Henry just to say, "How goes it mate?" because on his way back from Dudsall Crown Court he often dropped by the office in pursuit of the junior secretary about whom I have and had already touched (Henry doing so, I would add, at an age when he should have been wishing life to be measured on a twenty-four hour digital clock). Now, by profession Henry was a barrister-at-law and Gray's was his Inn of Court. I reasoned that there was no person better qualified to teach me.

Tubby in frame, unmatching long in face and with a nose that exhibited expert knowledge of the insides of whisky tumblers, Henry squatted on the bar stool, feet dangling with free abandon. Having at my expense extended his field of expertise still further, Henry plonked the glass on the corner of the bar, stroked his henna hair, tweaked his unmatching moustache of grey and, in a typically toff, Oxbridge sort of a way, he proceeded to tell me all about the ancient tradition of dining in hall.

"Everyone must divide themselves into groups of four. Now, these groups are called messes. Each mess appoints a senior whose duty it is to divide out the nosh and propose a toast to the lower mess on the right. On the left of Mr. Senior sit the members of the upper mess and he, or she, proposes the return toast from members of the said upper mess. You see as far as the upper mess is concerned, the mess of which I speak is the lower mess."

Henry had rabbited on in like fashion for what seemed a lifetime, pausing only to revisit his specialty subject. I was none the wiser, other than for knowing beyond all doubt that the cost of sundry single malts vastly exceeded that of my own tipple, namely Tiptbury and Dudsall's finest mild ale.

Presently, and to the applause of my depleted wallet, he put his tumbler adjacent with the ceiling for the last time and slurred, "Be certain to obey the rules, old chap, because otherwise you may find yourself challenged."

"Challenged?" I had spluttered, very nearly choking on my Tiptbury and Dudsall's, "Challenged?"

"Yes, challenged. The wretched fellow who is challenged must acquit himself before all of Hall and in default he forfeits a bottle of

9

the very finest port. Good sport, what?"

"Oh yes, good sport," I lied as Henry clattered down from his bar stool. "Have you by chance any change for the bus?" I added.

Well, flashback done and dusted, I return now to where I left off.

From the outside, the grand hall looked civilized enough. I had approached it through a tunnel leading from High Holborn and in the process had to duck under the crash barrier next to a tiny porters lodge. Gray's Inn Hall nestled amid fine buildings of probable Georgian vintage, except that for its part, the hall was newer having apparently been rebuilt following an altercation with a rather large explosive device gifted by the Luftwaffe.

It was too early for dinner and, in any event, it was necessary to borrow a gown from somewhere or other because without one I would not be permitted to enter. There was a door in one of the passages next to the hall and a plaque read Robing Room, so in I went.

The robing room was an almost school cloakroom sort of an affair with coat pegs lining the wall each and every way. Since, in the far corner, there was a way through to the urinals I deduced, correctly as it happened, that these were facilities set aside for those members of the Inn who were of the male persuasion. Indeed, about fifteen or so individuals of the said persuasion were furiously rummaging through a great heap of thick black gowns on a center table. Occasionally two, maybe three, grabbed hold of the same garment and virtually wrestled each other for the prize. Well, compared with The Whippet Inn on a Saturday night in Dudsall this hubbub seemed like child's play. So, like a well seasoned veteran, I joined the affray and, with beginners luck, I fished out a garment that seemed less ragged and, mercifully, less smelly than some of the others.

In the manner of a hyena that has just nicked the prime joint of wildebeest from under the very noses of a pride of lions, I surreptitiously took my booty to one side and tried it on in front of a full-length mirror.

Not bad, I mused, *not too bad at all.*

Next, with both hands, I grasped the collars of my jacket. Looking around and, firstly satisfying myself that every other incumbent was still about his own business, I took a long, deliberate sort of a bow. Tell you something for nothing; I looked just like a barrister from one of those old films.

I was about to take a dive again, when along sidled another student. Scruffily dressed, ruddy cheeks and high cheekbones, all topped off with a mass of curly black hair, I instantly thought that here was the most unlikely looking of trainee barristers.

"Not long before I'm a fully fledged barrister too," he said in cheery manner and, from his accent, I imagined that he was of country stock. He was about my own age and, as such, a good bit older than the other students.

Contrast my own suit, all cleaned and pressed, his disclosed irrefutable evidence of breakfast having consisted of eggs and bacon, followed by coffee and chocolate biscuits for elevenses, with luncheon taking the form of beer and a smoke.

For some reason the fellow had clearly taken me to be a fully fledged barrister and, to give him his due, had I not known it to be the reflection of Izaak Gatehouse before me, I too might have been fooled.

I rather liked the idea of being mistaken for learned counsel, but on balance I reckoned that it was best to come clean.

"Actually," I began, and that is as far as my admission progressed because, with a strange wince and a shrug of the shoulders (such actions being, to my mind, symptomatic of some kind of nervous affliction) he took a glance at his wristwatch.

"Bar's open," he said anxiously, "should be time for a quick one before dinner."

And with another wince and a shrug, accompanied on this occasion by a chuckle, he spun round on his heels, and, knocking students to one side, he made for the exit.

Drinking facilities within the building were something of which I was unaware. And besides, I was already thinking that a pint of Tiptbury and Dudsall's, or its London equivalent, would hit the spot. So, without further ado, I parted the ever increasing throng of bodies and followed.

This unlikeliest of barristers-in-waiting had a walk about him that was as nervous looking as his winces and his shrugs. His paces were short, almost minute, but this did not hinder his getting about because his legs moved like little pistons. His general stature was odd too. He seemed all the time to be tilting stiffly backwards, but this similarly afforded no hindrances, as was apparent from the manner in which he motored-up a flight of aged wooden stairs. Indeed, so quick was his ascent that I was soon trailing and, by the time that I reached the landing and a pair of swing doors, he was gone.

I gingerly pushed open the doors and within discovered a large, rectangular room which positively reeked of tobacco smoke. Strewn about were easy chairs of varying style and vintage although, without exception, each and every one was exceedingly ropey. Most were occupied by equally ropey looking, cigarette-smoking students who, between puffs, had their noses stuck in reading matter which was as varied as *Hot Scandinavian Girls Monthly* to the very depths of the broadsheets.

The bar was straight ahead, obscured somewhat by all of the smoke, but open at least it was, and doing a very brisk trade. Unfortunately, brisk though trade was, the sole purveyor (an elderly lady, well past her prime, knocking on for eleven o'clock, I reckoned) simply could not keep up. Indeed, the queue must have been four or five deep and, although nervous and thirsty as I was, I was not so nervous, and, not so desperately thirsty, as to want to hang around for her clock to turn twelve. And so, by way of alternative pursuit, I decided on familiarizing myself with the entire goings on at Gray's Inn by casting a glance at a notice board.

The Gray's Inn library appealed for the return of law books, missing, presumed stolen. There was a formal report on disciplinary proceedings against a member of the Inn, Queen's Counsel, no less, who was guilty of having abandoned a client mid-trial on grounds of family bereavement. Unfortunately for him, the learned trial judge had switched on the television simultaneously with the Queen's Counsel leaping for joy at the sight of his nag in the winning enclosure at Sandown. The punishment handed down was six months suspension from practice and a ban on the use of dining facilities within the Inn. Bizarrely, the emphasis was on the ban, as opposed to the period of suspension, which would presumably result in severe loss of income.

On a tasteful postcard, with a silver crest, I also noted that a student sought a lodger for his Mayfair apartment. Unfortunately, there was a caveat that the successful candidate would be expected to be a female graduate of either Oxford or Cambridge Universities. On the basis of nothing ventured, I made a mental note of the contact number, though frankly held out modest hope, for my seat of learning in the art of spot welding had been at Dudsall Secondary School for Boys.

12

Just then, I heard a gaggle of females ascending the stairs and, quick as a flash, I pulled open wide one of the swing doors. I gestured to the first, a tall rather attractive blonde, that she and her companions could, and should, pass. I may only have been a graduate of Dudsall Secondary, but I at least had a sound knowledge of etiquette, even if the welding together of bits of stolen motors came more natural.

The girl, black gown folded about one arm, stopped and momentarily cast me an icy stare.

"No need for that," she snapped, in a manner altogether too hostile for my liking.

"Sorry," I replied meekly and, inwardly, I rebuked myself for so doing, but such was the indoctrination of Dudsall, and of Dudsall Secondary in particular, that when the lower orders were faced with altercation from the higher orders, it was assumed appropriate to know ones place and back down.

But back down I was not about to do when the second one came through.

"I have hands of my own!" this one barked.

"Well, pardon me I'm sure," I said, in a manner which I felt was appropriately sarcastic in the circumstances.

She was a good bit taller than me, and I like to think that I'm not exactly vertically challenged. She was wearing her gown and I recall thinking that it was just as well because it tended to hide, for the most part, a dreadful ensemble consisting of blue boiler suit, multi-colored cardigan and a bright green tie about her bare neck (for she wore no shirt). And talk about her head of hair, well. This was truly something to behold. It was short, spiky, and un-even and might easily have resembled an autumnal stubble field had it not been for liberal use of pink hair dye.

Perched on her unfortunate hooknose was a pair of the biggest spectacles that I had ever seen, other than in a practical joke shop. However, it was no joke when she scooted over to where I was standing and stuck her hands right in my face.

"I've already told you once," came the barking again, only the decibels were lower this time, and were more intimidating as a result, "I have hands of my own. Here, take a look if you don't believe me."

And what a pair of mitts she had. Frightening, they were huge,

13

with just about the longest fingernails that it had ever been my misfortune to clap eyes on. And they were varnished jet black.

With talons such as those, I jerked my head back. And who could have blamed me? But the things kept coming. So, back my head went, even further. Still no joy. She was plainly out to do me some serious bodily harm.

"Open a door and I suppose you think you can go to bed with me!"

Here was a fine kettle of fish. Five minutes into my first visitation at Gray's Inn, and about to get laid into. Accused of sexual harassment too, knowing my miserable luck. And all for doing the gentlemanly thing by opening a door for a lady. Well, perhaps I had, in truth, opened the door for her blonde mate. But that was a mere technicality. A noble act, I had performed and not a jot, nothing in return had I expected. Not even an excuse to strike-up a conversation and see where it might all end up had I anticipated.

I commenced contemplating with urgency whether to beat a hasty retreat or otherwise gift this irksome individual a swift kick in the shin. But my thought process was interrupted by a voice with a rustic twang, whose owner was possessed of winces and shrugs.

"Damned, daft feminist!"

Immediately, my assailant withdrew her talons from the proximity of my, somewhat thankful, right cheek and she turned towards the room.

"I might have known that Ian Prospect, the biggest sexist pig at the Bar, would have to stick his nose in."

Ian Prospect, being the name by which I shall henceforth refer to the rustic one, with all of his nervous-type winces and shrugs, was seated in a rather battered, leather armchair just a couple of paces away. Lodged between his teeth was a long and eccentric clay pipe. And lodged between his knees was the matter which he had evidently been reading. It was a pig keeping magazine.

Ian Prospect removed the pipe from his jaws and proceeded to peer deep into the bowl. Next, he sniffed at it and performed one of his winces, only this time in mock horror and not out of apparent nervousness.

Having, by accident or design, attracted the attention of the whole room, Ian Prospect returned the pipe to his mouth and clamped it tight.

He switched on the most mischievous of grins towards my assailant (guaranteed to wind her into a fair old frenzy) and then, to cap it all, he winked. "What you need is a man, and a jolly good spanking," he said. With the noticeable exception of my assailant and her brood, everyone thereabouts fell about laughing. For his part, Ian Prospect arose, as if to acknowledge the appreciation of his audience. He winced, shrugged, and chuckled. "Tell you what," he carried on, plainly not knowing when to draw stumps and call it a day, "let's kiss and make up."

Strangely, it seemed only to be Ian Prospect who at all was surprised when my assailant became his assailant.

"I'll give you a kiss," she snarled, in a manner which conveyed that she had no actual intention of conveying affection.

"Wrong time of the month, is it?" said Ian Prospect, ducking and weaving to avoid flying fists.

During the course of the ensuing mêlée, a gown became separated from one of the combatants and fluttered to my feet. During punch-ups at Dudsall Secondary, I had always been the one to hold the coats. Instinct therefore took hold and compelled me to gather-up the stray garment. This was not before Ian Prospect copped a hefty right hook.

As the boot joined up with the fist and also set about going in, I ran my hand nervously around the gown and, blow me down, realized that it had some kind of a square collar whereas my own, somewhat glittering prize, had not. No wonder that Ian Prospect had been confused earlier. I had only gone and selected myself the robes of a fully qualified barrister.

I decided to leave Ian Prospect to his fate and return downstairs snappily to swap gowns. I felt a twinge of guilt because he had, in fairness, saved my bacon. But on my maiden dinner, I was not about to get banged to rights for wrongful impersonation of a barrister.

I departed through the self-same swinging doors that were responsible for the fracas in the first place. As I did so, my eyes met with the most attractive of brunettes imaginable. She smiled the prettiest of smiles. But Izaak Gatehouse was not about to get caught out for a second time. So I barged through the door and then loosed my grip, making certain that it banged shut in her face. There followed quite the sweetest of yelps.

"Some people are so ignorant," she complained, rubbing her tiny snub nose.

As an aside, I make mention here that a barristers gown, as opposed to the gown of a student, has a piece of material dangling down the back. It's called a pocket, although, on the basis that the original incumbents of the Inns of Court were clerics, it seems fairly obvious that the pocket is actually no more than a hood. Over time, the hood has been scaled down to exhibition size. Well no wonder. Spotty-faced teenagers sporting hooded attire as they charge around shopping malls doing dreadful deeds is one thing. But a bunch of hooded barristers, rampaging around The Royal Courts of Justice, can of lager in one hand, can of spray paint in the other, would do little to instil public confidence in the legal profession.

And another thing. Such is the intransigence of the law, that a pocket it is called and so a pocket it shall be. Never mind the fact that, un-pocket like, the thing has no insides. The tale nevertheless goes that, in the good old days, cash would surreptitiously find itself slung in the pocket as an incentive for the wearer to perform great feats in advocacy by, for example, persuading the tribunal to show mercy and hand down a sentence of death by public hanging in lieu of transportation to Australia. And to cap it all, since the slinging of cash in the pocket thing was gratuitous in nature, there could be no legal contract. And no legal contract meant that it was not possible to sue the barrister, irrespective of the most monumental of cock-ups. Indeed, that anomaly has only recently been done away with.

Anyway, I thought I'd share that one with you.

Back now to my inaugural dinner and, having descended the wooden stairs, I found the robing room empty of persons and, worse, empty of gowns. There next came the pounding of hooves and I adjudged that it was a sure sign that dinner was fast approaching. I could not possibly enter Hall dolled-up like a barrister. But hang about. I still had the gown that had fallen at my feet. The misappropriation of property belonging to a fellow pupil ought to have been unthinkable. On the other hand, whoever the owner, whether it was Ian Prospect or my assailant turned his assailant, neither one of them should have been cavorting in the first place. And so nicking the gown was sort of like natural justice.

Stepping outside, sporting now the purloined garment, I lodged myself within a pack of noisy, chattering students. Indeed, so tight was the pack, that I was virtually lifted across the square right into the

16

vestibule of Gray's Inn Hall.

Here, an aged, almost Dickensian character stood behind a lift top desk. He was a servant. All employees of an Honorable are called servants. The tag presumably ensures that they never forget their place in the great scheme of things. Well, the job of this particular servant was to tick-off names in a whopping great ledger.

I was jostled through the lobby at such speed that I barely had time to identify myself to the old soul before being disgorged into the grand dining hall. Here, those students who intended to play by the rules dispersed in an orderly fashion and began searching for places at table. Those students who intended to breach the rules (not insignificant in number) simply did u-turns and went back out, the old soul at the desk being either oblivious or disinterested.

The hall was almost filled with five enormously long tables that shone with what must have been a decade's worth of beeswax. Indeed, so shiny were the tables that they were outshone only by the dozens of silver service settings neatly laid out. Just one of the tables went crossways. It was plainly the top table because it was at the top. And besides, it came equipped with plush red leather chairs, whereas the lengthways tables were surrounded by rows of hard benches, each and every one looking somewhat unforgiving.

The top table would be reserved for benchers of the Inn. Included within their ranks were judges, eminent barristers, academics and so on. It was, and still is, regarded as the highest of honors to be appointed a bencher, more so than elevation to judgeship.

In the manner of a non-bencher, I selected one of the lengthways tables. It was in the far left of Hall and, to my mind, sufficiently out of the way to ensure that I would steer clear of any trouble. However, before I could be seated, I was told to move on because the table was reserved for barristers only. Even newly qualified barristers are compelled to dine. It's pretty difficult to squeeze in the minimum number of dinners, what with lectures, exams and so on. Hence, the invariable need to carry them over, post qualification. Logically, one would expect fledglings to have to prove their worth before judge and jury. But not so, according to an Inn of Court, because gorging oneself to bursting point, drinking oneself into oblivion and, doubtless, throwing up in the rose garden and causing a general public nuisance are judged better attributes.

I nipped over smartly to a middle table and sat dead center of Hall. Here, I contented myself in the knowledge that I could bask in total obscurity and proceeded to take in the surroundings.

The rather plain exterior of the building had done no justice to what lay within. The impressive walls, all panelled in wood, were lined, for the most part, with portraits in oil. Most, I imagined, must have been pretty valuable, if only on account of being so ancient. Perched all along the higher reaches of the back wall was an elaborately carved balcony. The whole thing was fashioned out of the rear of a galleon. It was used as an overflow on especially busy nights and, sometimes, served as a gallery for spectators. They were most often students of the other Honorables. The bawdy behaviour at Gray's Inn was notorious and, on account of it, invariably worthy of a swift peep.

Presently, most of the fellow diners had organized themselves into the groups, or messes, of four. The only trouble was that, after all of this organising palaver was done with, I found myself sitting quite alone.

Meanwhile, over by the barristers table, a stocky, bearded individual had popped up, seemingly out of thin air. He was kitted out in a glorious medieval-looking costume, all blue and gold, finished off with long white stockings. He held a rather lengthy and rather vicious-looking stick which extended from floor level to shoulder height, where it ended with a silver tip. The apparition was either that of some dandy, who had come to grief with the galleon, the back end of which was, of course, dangling overhead, or otherwise he was the head porter. Since the pursuit of this individual appeared to be the swapping around of seating arrangements, I deduced that the odds of him having popped back from the sixteenth century were remote.

The head porter, which is the title by which I shall henceforth refer to the individual, appeared to be taking pleasure in upsetting the barristers as he manoeuvred them each way and every way. However, it seemed to me that he was in a bit of a quandary for one of the messes towards the top end of the table was one barrister short of a fully constituted mess. The head porter proceeded to correct the deficiency by plucking a barrister from the adjoining mess. Naturally, his actions served only to reduce that mess. And so the head porter took someone from the next mess down, and then the next mess down after that, and so on, until bottom table, he found himself still one barrister down. I swear that he would have tried to solve the conundrum by going all the way back up the table, had it not been for the timely intervention of a student.

The student, a latecomer, was called over and told to deposit himself in the vacant place setting. Apparently, it was common for students to be chosen to make up the numbers in this manner. Sometimes, they were even asked to sit at the top table with the benchers but, unless the student was attractive and female, the honor usually fell to a barrister.

Content in the knowledge that he had a full barristers table; the head porter finished this Gray's Inn version of musical chairs and turned his attention towards the seating arrangements of the students. He began a head count and, midway up the table, stopped. My three empty spaces seemed to be yawning as wide as a chasm. One did not have to be head porter of an Inn of Court to figure out that I should be ejected. Indeed, even the average physics teacher at Dudsall Secondary was capable of working out that, with me out the way, everyone could simply shuffle up a bit.

Swinging his cane, the head porter strutted over. In an attempt to adopt an aura of disinterested innocence, I rotated my head in the direction of the back end of the galleon and whistled a little tune.

"You'll have to move to the next table, young man," he said, in a Scottish accent which was harsh, but initially forgivable, on account of his usage of the expression young man.

"Why don't you tell the others to shove up and leave me where I am?"

"Because you, lad, are Mr. Junior. Move yourself."

Young man or not, forgiveness was now fast disappearing from the agenda but, forever the peacemaker, I beckoned the fellow to come within whispering distance.

"You don't understand. This is my first dinner. I really would rather stop where I am, if that's okay with you."

"Oh, I see," he said in a hush. "Now I understand. Well actually," he said, with the decibels rising, "I do mind, as it happens." And next, so that all of Hall could hear, he hollered, "First time diner coming through! Follow me, Mr. Junior!"

I dutifully traipsed off after the head porter and I did so to a weak ripple of applause from a number of the other students. At the tail end of the bottom table, I was instructed to cease complaining and to be seated.

I had no sooner obeyed, and slouched against one of the wall panels, when the head porter shouted out, "Silence! All stand!"

Everyone shot to their feet and, at the top end of Hall, a door swung open and out toddled a line of near octogenarians, some wearing fancy robes, others wearing none, fancy or otherwise.

"Must be benchers guest night," I heard one of the students whisper.

"Well, well," said another, in equally hushed tones, "If it isn't the Director of Public Prosecutions in person."

"Quiet!" snapped the head porter, in not such hushed tones, and I swear he brandished his big stick.

One of the benchers looked far more youthful than the others. I reckoned he was not a day over seventy five. He was blessed with a head of hair which, in terms of quantity, had more than all the others put together.

While all of the said others shuffled off to their places around the top table, the one with the hair veered off in the direction of the barristers table. Here, he bowed to one of the barristers. The barrister, dead chuffed by the look of him, bowed back. And with that little ceremony out of the way, he with the hair joined the others at the top table where he stood, dead in the middle.

He proceeded to mumble in Latin. My knowledge of Latin was strictly limited to that which the junior secretary had taught me on the office floor. I therefore had no idea what he was saying. It was presumably a prayer.

Anyway, when he was done, we all sat down and the chattering started up.

"Fancy a swig of sherry?" a voice said in an unmistakable rustic sort of way. "I'm Prospect, by the way. But you may call me Ian."

What with all of my flustering, I hadn't taken in my dining companions and Ian (by which name I shall now proceed to refer to him, for he told me to do so) was sat immediately to my right.

"Well, Ian, I'm delighted to make your acquaintance. And thanks for helping out earlier."

I offered to shake him by the hand and, in the process, very nearly took the skin off mine as I clumsily skidded my knuckles along the wood panelling.

He took a long swig from his sherry glass, almost draining it in the process. He winced, a now familiar wince, and then finished the thing off, wincing once more.

"Barristers do not shake hands with each other," he said. "We are all brethren and as such we are deemed to already know each other."

"I'm not actually a barrister yet."

"Yes, I see you've got yourself a new robe," he chuckled.

Ian was still wearing his gown. At least it was not his that I had made off with.

"I see that you managed to hang onto yours." I said, stating the obvious.

"That was the least of my problems," and glancing quickly into his lap, Ian winced and then chuckled, "she was out to kick me in the old family jewels."

At the very thought of it, we both had a wince.

A homely waitress, or rather servant of the Inn, appeared seemingly from out of the blue. She swiped the sherry decanter from under the very nose of Ian. Her actions were met with a look of disdain and two winces. However, she was vindicated when another servant came over and, in its place, deposited another decanter, only this time of red wine.

Ian looked directly at the student who was seated opposite to him. He was a pleasing to look at individual, with a round jolly face. Not at all like the one who was over the table from me. His face was definitely not jolly, but judging from the comb over hairdo, it was at least plain for all to see that his barber had a sense of humor.

"Do the honors then, mess senior," said Ian. "The sooner we do the toasting, the sooner we can relax."

"Far too soon," replied the jolly faced one, "and, in any event, Prospect, you're not even a member of this Inn."

Ian winced, shrugged, and chuckled.

"As it happens, I'm here on a mission of mercy. Your cousin is in desperate need of clocking up a dinner but is otherwise engaged tonight. So I agreed to stand in."

"Don't be so daft, Prospect. She's called Jasmin. Even the old duffer at the door would have seen through that one."

The comb-over opposite me turned a bit red and, indicating that his humor might after all be up there with the barber, he let out a stifled laugh.

"Well, he didn't notice a thing," said Ian, rather pompously, and, grasping the wine decanter, he proceeded to pour himself a glass to near overflow proportions.

Then the decanter got slid to me. I thought it to be gentlemanly and generally courteous to offer it first to the other two. But I was promptly admonished for lacking etiquette. Therefore, I too poured one to near to the brim, gulped the lot down in one and re-charged my glass. At this, the mess senior became not so jolly in face and, himself forgetting all etiquette; he swiped the decanter, thereby depriving me of any opportunity of a triple.

"Prospect," he said, as Ian appeared to steady himself for the decanters return journey, "I concede that we should start the toasting now whilst we still have liquid with which to toast."

"All very well and good," said the comb over, "but some of us have yet to partake of a single drop."

I was to find that most students spoke the Oxbridge way, all very upper crust, and the comb over was no exception to the general rule.

"Let's have your names," said the jolly faced one, ignoring him.

"Prospect, Ian Prospect."

"Yes, yes I know that," and then he glanced at me.

The jolly faced one jotted my name down on a piece of scrap paper.

"Damn strange name," said Ian. "Down from Brum are we?"

"Black Country, if you don't mind. I'm nowt to do with that hell hole."

"Pardon me, I'm sure."

We toasted each other and the food came shortly thereafter. Typical British fare, it was. Roast beef and Yorkshire pudding, preceded by brown Windsor soup, which had not sat at all well on all that red wine. The portions of food were modest though, for the reason stated, I was not in the least bit perturbed by that. Not so Ian, however.

"I always sit at the end table because, chances are, there will be an incomplete mess but the portions of grub and booze remain the same. But you've ruined that tonight."

"Pardon me, I'm sure," and I grabbed hold of the decanter on

22

grounds that I should numb my hurt feelings.

"Steady on," said Ian, and he regained control of the thing, no doubt to blot out his feelings of guilt at having hurt me so.

But my hurt was a more worthy cause than ever his guilt could be and I got it back.

In this fashion, the wine passed merrily between us and each time we each managed a guzzle or two.

As a direct consequence of our goings-on, the mess senior, who had transmuted from being the jolly-faced one to the angry faced one, decided that he too should get stuck in. And so, in an ever increasing state of inebriation, dinner progressed. For his part, the mess senior developed a lack of coordination and in particular found it to be quite impossible to serve our vegetables. Indeed, at least one slice of carrot and a lump of gravy found themselves attached to the portrait behind my right ear.

The favorite conversation of Ian Prospect was Ian Prospect and for much of dinner he indulged himself something rotten.

As I had already deduced, Ian was indeed a mature student, having previously worked as an estate agent before deciding to go straight. He once worked within the oil industry, but on closer examination, I ascertained that his job description was petrol pump attendant.

Ian hailed from rural Warwickshire. A small village called Prestwick, to be exact, where, along with Colin the cat, he occupied a tiny, half-timbered cottage within the grounds of his manor house owning landlord. The cottage was called, officially or otherwise, The Fly in the Ointment. I was given the distinct impression that his status at the cottage was more akin to squatter than bona fide tenant. According to Ian, he had wormed his way into vacant possession by befriending the landlord. He had paid not a penny in rent for three years or more and had managed to frustrate each and every attempt, lawful or otherwise, to evict him.

Ian had two basic ambitions.

The first, which he explained with, perhaps misplaced pride, was to bed each and every female who was ready, able and willing. His well thought out stratagem was to latch on to lonely and/or bored women, usually of a certain age, and most often wives of close friends. Ian admitted that his somewhat questionable pursuit was based on the deathbed declaration of the local blacksmith.

"Shag who you can, when you can," the fading farrier had apparently told the fledgling Ian, "or otherwise you'll be laying here like me one day, wishing you'd given Her Ladyship a damned good seeing-to when you had the chance."

The other ambition, some might argue, was marginally nobler in that Ian was desperate to qualify as a barrister-at-law. He had sat and failed the Bar finals on more occasions than any student in recent, living memory. Indeed, the Dean had reeled Ian into his office on a number of occasions and suggested that he really ought to call it a day.

"I shall pass one day," boasted Ian. "Just you wait and see."

Towards the end of dinner, I witnessed a performance that was played out with monotonous regularity. The head porter, stick swinging, strutted up the entire length of Hall towards the benchers. Hot on his heals came an embarrassed looking individual wearing a chef's hat. On arrival at the top table, one of the benchers handed the chef a glass of port.

Ian explained, "The old codgers are thanking Chef for infecting us with salmonella."

The port for our mess was presented by one of the waitresses. At this point, a *coup d'état* of miniscule proportions occurred when Ian assumed the role of mess senior and wrestled the decanter from the jolly faced, turned angry faced one.

"Don't want this little lot ending up with that piece of carrot," said Ian.

We commenced knocking back the stuff like there was no tomorrow. Even the comb over joined in.

"There are barrels of the jolly old stuff in the jolly old cellar," he said, downing his third in about as many minutes.

With the decanter empty, the mess senior decided that he should order a refill. He passed it around, though not before consuming half of the contents.

"Steady on, old chap," said Ian, "you're looking a little green in the gills."

Green in the gills he may have been but at least he was, once more, jolly in face.

For my part, I was beginning to warm to the evening when, all of a sudden, the benchers got up to leave.

"All rise!" bellowed the head porter.

Everyone did, with the notable exception of our mess. We were just too plain gone to be bothered and, besides, would not have wished the simple act of standing to eat into valuable drinking time.

As the last of the benchers hobbled through the door and was gone, so too went any hope that this dining at an Inn of Court palaver was not, after all, so hazardous a pursuit.

"Up junior!" called someone from somewhere.

"Up junior!" called someone from somewhere else, only louder this time.

There was a ripple-like effect as others joined in. And soon, virtually the whole of Hall rang to the cries of, "Up Junior!"

"Well, up you get," hissed Ian, and he winced, just a little.

"What in hell's name for?" I said.

Over on the barrister's table, the remnant of a bread roll was launched. I was right in the line of fire but, happily, the comb over chose that moment to lean sideways and grasp the port. The projectile hit him square on the bald patch from whence it veered off and smacked into the portrait.

"For pity's sake, stand on the bench." said Ian, shrugging as well as wincing.

"What for?"

Another missile, a box of matches, came hurtling over. Its trajectory was way off line and, on this occasion, the jolly faced one was to get it, straight in the ear.

"Stand on the bench," said Ian, once again, only adding, "and ask for permission to smoke."

"But, I don't smoke. Hate the habit."

"Just stand on the bench, face the senior of Hall; him over there."

Soon, the catcalling was accompanied by the sound of dozens of fists pounding on the table tops. There was jeering too, and I swear that the jolly faced one took it upon himself to call my parentage into question.

It was no good. This could not be allowed to continue. If the baying mob wanted me ridiculed, then ridiculed I must be. Thus, I took a mighty gulp of fine port, stood-up and climbed onto the bench. I proceeded to address the barrister in the far corner and I did so to a few muted cheers.

"Mr. Senior! I request permission to smoke!"

Not a word. Not so much as a nod of the head. Not even an indication that he was, perhaps, giving my enquiry due consideration. And there was no way that he could not have heard me. Someone with a hearing impediment who was stood at the far end of the Dudsall foundry going full pelt would have complained about my decibels.

"Mr. Senior!"

"In heaven's name, there's no need to shout!" shouted Mr. Senior at last, and he got to his feet. "Do you, Mr. Junior, happen to smoke yourself?"

"No I don't!"

"I don't either! It's a filthy habit and so no, you may not smoke!"

He sat back down. I did too. I was sheepish. Not so, Mr. Senior. He looked right, proper smug.

The catcalls started up again, only this time with more fervor than before.

"You'll have to get up and have another go," hissed Ian, and he shrugged and winced, just a little.

"Good sport this!" someone hollered from somewhere.

From an inside pocket that must have been bottomless, Ian proceeded to produce the, exceedingly long pipe. A wedge of Virginia followed and, bringing up the rear, came the most ridiculous of lighters imaginable. It was tubular and, beneath the scorch marks, was probably made of brass. There was a wick sticking out of the top. The thing stank of petrol and must surely have constituted a fire hazard.

Ian unwrapped the wedge and, with his thumbnail, he scraped some off the end and shoved it firmly in the pipe. He proceeded to bring the thing to nasal height. He sniffed and winced, just a little and shrugged, just a little.

The catcalls, from our immediate vicinity, at any rate, dried up as fellow students stared, almost transfixed, at the spectacle of Ian fiddling with his smoking accoutrements.

"Well," said Ian, when he was done fiddling, "the pompous old devil isn't about to ruin my smoke."

He brought the lighter level with his pipe and began to swizzle a little wheel which was next to the wick. He swizzled and swizzled but the swizzles produced no spark. However, with each swizzle, the smell of petrol intensified.

"Bloody hell," came an anxious voice from a few places up, "I hope the idiot doesn't intend lighting that thing."

And then, *whoosh*. The thing let loose a flame that shot halfway to the ceiling. And it took Ian's right eyebrow with it.

"That's it!" came a screeching that sounded horribly familiar. What with everything else, I had forgotten about my assailant, turned Ian's assailant. "I have witnessed enough and I challenge Mr. Junior!"

"Stand on the bench," said Ian with urgency and, in so doing, he winced and shrugged, just a little and rubbed his forehead, furiously.

I did as I was advised and stood overlooking a now baying mob.

The assailant approached. She was still kitted out as before, except that the hotchpotch was more noticeable than before owing to the absence of any robe.

"Mr. Senior!" her challenge began, and she proceeded to speak with clarity. "Not only has Mr. Junior made a fine mess of requesting permission for Hall to smoke; a tradition, I might add, with chauvinistic undertones."

"Get to the point!" someone interrupted.

"Here, here!" chipped in someone else.

The assailant re-started, "Not only has Mr. Junior made a fine mess of requesting permission to smoke but he, but he . . ."

She was again interrupted, only by a good dozen or more this time. They slung various abuses, the overall inference being that she should stop beating around the bush and get on with it. For my part, I remained statue-like on the bench. I felt my face going redder and redder.

"He, he stole my gown," she eventually spluttered.

Mr. Senior shot to his feet and the whole of Hall fell silent.

"Is that so, Mr. Junior? Have you stolen her gown?"

This was awkward. In a manner of speaking I had indeed pilfered her wretched robe, but I was not about to confess all. I cleared my throat.

"As I understand matters, no member of this, indeed any, Inn of Court should enter Hall improperly dressed and, most certainly, without a gown. As such this person has no right to be here, let alone issue a challenge."

"I say, nice one, Gatehouse, old chap," said Ian and he stopped rubbing his forehead, clamped the clay pipe firmly between his teeth and with a wince, shrug and a chuckle, he folded both arms and then leaned back casually against the wall.

I regret that my moment of glory was short lived because another student rose to her feet. It was only the brunette who had had the door slammed in her face.

"I too wish to challenge Mr. Junior!" she said, and, on ensuring that her sultry tones had got everyone's attention, she continued thus. "Mr. Junior is a member of a mess that has flouted most, if not all of the rules of the Inn. In particular, they failed to toast the members of their upper mess." She paused momentarily. "I've been keeping my eye on them."

"Explain yourself!" bawled Mr. Senior.

"You can't possibly blame me for the omissions of this mess," I said.

"And pray tell me why not?"

I pointed directly at the jolly faced one. It knocked the jolly look right off his face, I can tell you.

"He is the senior of our mess. It's hardly my fault that he failed to instruct us to honor the customs."

Ian attracted my attention with a swift tug on the robe.

"I say, nice one, Gatehouse, old chap," he said, once again.

I sensed that things were going my way and, buoyed up with confidence, I said, "Mr. Senior! I'll have two bottles of port! One a-piece from my challengers!"

"I say, nice one, Gatehouse, old chap," said Ian, only this time he winced, shrugged, and even taking trouble to remove the pipe from his mouth, he went on, "I shouldn't push it, if I were you. Perhaps it's best to sit down while the going's good."

The mob directed its attention towards our hapless mess senior.

I did as Ian had suggested and sat down, smartly.

Across the table the now stricken with fear faced one, hauled himself up and onto the bench. It was no mean feat considering that, by now, the fellow looked to me to be half-cut. His successful, if unsteady, ascent was greeted with many cheers and much clapping.

Wavering precariously, he went as if to talk when, from seemingly nowhere, the head porter appeared. He rapped his cane smartly on the floor.

"Quiet please!"

Once again, out trundled the benchers and, once again, everyone stood. But the sudden upwards movement took our mess senior by surprise because, with a shriek, he fell backwards. The swift, and untimely, descent was, to put it mildly, rather spectacular. With all limbs splayed, and rotating hopelessly, the now terrified, screaming faced one plunged towards the deck. In the event, serious bodily harm to his person was averted only by reason of the line of his trajectory being broken by an individual, hereinbefore referred to as my assailant, turned Ian's assailant. Both crashed to the ground and all eyes, including those of the benchers, became transfixed at the two writhing bodies.

It was the loyal head porter who had the presence of mind to sort things out. He firstly extrapolated the assailant from the horror stricken faced one and helped her to her place, though not before straightening her clothes with grateful gusto. Next, he grabbed our fallen comrade by the collar.

"Get this drunken idiot back to his seat," he growled, at no one in particular.

Someone assisted our mess senior to the bench from whence he had just flown and with everyone in Hall now stood silently still, except our mess senior who groaned and swayed, the bencher with a full head of hair coughed. We took our seats.

"Members of Hall," he said, in plain English as opposed to Latin, "tonight we are honored to be addressed by the Director of Public Prosecutions." The now distinctly poorly faced looking one, let out a further groan and followed it with a sigh. Undeterred, the bencher continued, "I expect that many of you will have read in the press that the Crown Prosecution Service has compiled a blacklist of overly defense-minded counsel. I envisage that our most welcome guest will throw some light on the matter."

The DPP arose and I clapped enthusiastically, but no one else did. Plainly it was not the done thing.

"Here, here," said our mess senior, supportively.

The DPP started his address.

"Tonight, I shall be describing the work of my department and the basis on which . . ." he stopped and looked agog. To my horror, our mess senior had begun to be violently ill. "Well, I have never had that effect on an audience before," and then the DPP carried on, almost dismissively.

29

Ian, who throughout had continued to have the pipe between his teeth, at last removed the thing and shoved it back in his inside pocket. He winced and shrugged and turned towards me.

"Gatehouse, old chap, I'm off before we find ourselves up before the benchers."

He rose to the melody of the positively green faced one sounding right proper poorly.

"Hang about, I'm coming too."

We tried not to disrupt the proceedings still further, by tiptoeing around the table. But, as luck would have it, a glass became entangled around Ian's robe. I looked on, horrified, as the thing wobbled this way and that and then toppled to the floor and shattered. The DPP, who was on the riveting bit about defense-minded barristers, once again stopped, mid flow. Ian winced and, with his backwards lean, he crossed, sylph-like, towards the door. For my part, I belted off after him and exited to the melody of retching and the DPP protesting that he had never ever, in the whole of his illustrious career, been so insulted.

Had there been any justice, the evening would have ended without further incident. But the offer of a ride and a bed for the night at Ian's cottage was too good an opportunity to miss.

"I park my old banger in Hanger Lane," said Ian, as we strolled toward the gates. "I catch the tube and, hey presto, I've avoided the traffic."

At the main road, Ian stopped and breathed in the toxic night air. He fetched out his smoking kit and I watched in wonderment as, with a deft twist of the wrist, the lighter let forth a flame like a howitzer. He winced, just a little, and sucked furiously on the pipe. It lit up for all of five seconds before the thing extinguished itself. Ian looked purposely, firstly into the pipe and then dangerously into the lighter, which was still spurting fire.

"Damned cheap tobacco," he murmured, and then said, "Come on, Gatehouse, old dear, Chancery Lane is just along the street."

At platform level, Ian found himself jostled by a bunch of boisterous youths. True, they were high-spirited but unlikely, in my estimation, to cause real trouble. Well, unlikely to cause real trouble until Ian decided to open his mouth.

"You bunch of louts!" he hollered. "A dashed good horse

whipping is what you need!"

One of the lads stopped. He must have been a good six inches taller than his mates and he looked to be a good six years older too. This led me to believe that he was in overall command. And besides, a tattoo across his left knuckle read BOSS.

"Are you talking to us?" he said, in a tone that sounded like razor blades being mangled.

"I most certainly am," said Ian, with authority. "Are you ragamuffins looking for trouble?"

The lad turned to his colleagues and conferred. After a moment or two, he proceeded to disclose that he had not come looking for trouble, but if it was trouble that Ian was after then trouble Ian would get, and he advanced.

"Police!" said Ian. "You hold them there, Gatehouse, old chap. I'll go and fetch the law."

And with that, Ian doubled back up the staircase and, in a thrice, was clean out of sight.

The lad proceeded to issue me with venomous ultimatums, all containing a plentiful array of adjectives. Many were brand spanking new, even to one such as I, who had known the streets of Dudsall. He then transported BOSS in the direction of my right eye and he did so at ever such a mighty speed.

I crashed to the floor, as would heavy metal in the Dudsall foundry, but before losing consciousness I heard Ian's tones drifting down from street level.

"You teach those yobs a jolly good lesson, Gatehouse, old boy!"

There could be no doubting it. Dining at an Inn of Court was a most hazardous pursuit.

CHAPTER TWO

My recollection of the journey on the underground is vague. I am given to understand that Ian, along with a couple of late night commuters, carted me onto the train where, for much of the ride, I lay spark out on a bench seat. However, by the time we reached our destination, I was *compos mentis* and even managed to hobble under my own steam to the side street where Ian had deposited his motor vehicle.

It was not only my ego that was bruised as a result of the scurrilous and felonious belting that had come my way. One eye was completely closed and vision through the other was a bit bleary. Even so, I could tell that Ian's earlier reference to his mode of transport as an old banger was no understatement.

It was a harlequin of a vehicle, consisting of spare parts cannibalised from motor cars of various makes, models, and vintage, chucked together and, seemingly, held together by rust. The medley most resembled an early MGB roadster and the dominant color was black. It had an open top, but the convertible top was noticeably absent. What with the weather beginning to look a bit grim, the omission ought to have been deemed a disadvantage. However, in my opinion most humble, a wet hairdo was a price well worth paying if it meant ducking out on a dose of carbon monoxide poisoning.

Stuck to the windscreen there were two pieces of paper, one informal and written in hand, the other printed, and therefore formal looking. On close inspection, I noted that the former read TAX APPLIED FOR. Ian opted to grasp the other, the printed document, for himself.

"We live in a police state, Gatehouse, old chap. The damnable local council are threatening to tow the old girl away and have her crushed."

He crumpled the piece of paper in his hand and then threw it over the hedge and into someone's front garden. Next, Ian began to tug at the offside door.

"Don't worry, Gatehouse, old dear; it'll give in a bit."

And with a nerve-shattering screech, the thing flew open.

He winced at the nauseous din, chuckled a bit and hopped aboard. Next, while I remained on the footpath awaiting embarkation instructions, Ian embedded himself firmly in the driver's seat and began tap, tapping at a row of glass dials. He seemed to be so engrossed that I dared not interrupt. But, with the minutes ticking by and there being no signs of termination of the infernal tapping, I gave a polite cough.

"Oh there you are, Gatehouse. I thought you'd gone behind the hedge. Hop over, old chap. You can't use the door because I had to get the blacksmith to weld it shut."

"What in heaven's name for?"

Ian proceeded not only to shrug and wince, but also to shake his head horizontally. All of this was simultaneous and looked odd on account of it.

"Blasted thing kept falling off its hinges," he complained, almost as if he had played no part in the clear-cut recklessness of the bodging together of this pile of scrap on wheels.

I scrambled over the wreck and I am compelled to state that it was no mean feat, for by now my joints were getting proper stiff. It was plainly a reaction to the before mentioned scurrilous and felonious conduct that I had so heroically endured.

I landed not on the passenger seat but on a pile of junk. I let forth a yelp and then proceeded to extract from my nether regions various items which included three empty beer cans, an old newspaper and a pig keepers magazine, one broken screwdriver, two rubber johnnies (one still in mint condition), and a rubber hose.

Ian appeared to notice my look of concern as I held the rubber hose aloft. The uses, or former uses, of the other items of *objet d'art* at least spoke for themselves. But as one who had been brought up to know that things most dodgy go on in the countryside, it seemed pretty obvious to me that a rubber hose which was horse whip length was not about to be used for watering the roses. To my immense relief, however, Ian explained, with a wince, shrug, and a chuckle, that it was merely an implement with which to siphon fuel from vehicles belonging to others.

Ian turned the ignition key a few times and, presently, his perseverance paid off when a great deal of grinding and chugging gave way to a roaring as the engine came to life. It was not a healthy roaring, mind. But at least it was a roaring and, with an almighty jolt, the car shot forward.

"I think it's coming on to rain," I said, slouching down in an endeavour to avoid the biting wind.

"Sorry, old chap! Can't hear a thing! Rosemary tends to get a bit noisy when she gets going! Typical of a woman, I say!"

We swung onto the main carriageway, heading out of town, and we did so to a cacophony of hooters and horns emanating from the vehicles of outraged drivers. Ian, apparently oblivious, quite simply chose to carve them up.

It was as if, in some previous existence, Ian was a chariot racer. Even at that time of night, traffic was not spartan. He nevertheless managed to negotiate the entire stretch to the open country without stopping once. Humming merrily above the entire racket, Ian snaked in and out of the vehicles of the said outraged drivers. His strategy appeared to be based on the simple principal that anyone with a half decent motor would swerve, brake, u-turn, in fact take any evasive action, to avoid being side swiped.

Whether it was gasoline fumes, carbon monoxide fumes, the effects of the scurrilous and felonious belting, the onset of hypothermia, or a combination of two or more of those things, I presently fell into a slumber. But it was one of those dreaded, restless sleeps in which a chap finds himself wrenched from the arms of Morpheus, far too frequently, by a succession of horrible dreams. In my case, the nightmares were in the form of summary disbarment for unruly conduct and flashbacks of the scurrilous and felonious belting, save that it was the head porter with his cane who was metering out the punishment.

I eventually came too, conscious that the dreadful roaring of the engine had gone. Gone too was Ian. I peered about and saw that we were parked, surrounded by huge juggernauts. In the distance, I could hear the sound of disco music coming from what I assumed was a jukebox. I thought about clambering out of the wreck and going in search of Ian. However, it was just too plain cold and dark and I couldn't be bothered. So I drifted off to sleep again, this time dreaming of being chased by someone with a flamethrower.

I awoke to the sound of yelps and to the sight of Ian beating out flames where the infernal lighter had set fire to his jacket.

"Ever thought of investing in a box of matches?" I said, as Ian rubbed furiously, firstly at his charred lapel, and secondly at what was left of his remaining eyebrow.

"Certainly not," he replied dismissively, and then he went on, "I always take a pit stop here. I've had a leak and a cuppa and half a smoke and so it's time for the open road once more. Hold tight, Gatehouse, old chap, I think it's coming onto rain."

And with a tap, tapping of the glass dials, a few turns of the ignition key and a screeching of brakes, we were soon roaring away again.

By the time that we reached the first bend in the road, the heavens had opened.

"Ever thought of investing in a top for this thing?" I said. "And a pair of wipers that work?" I added, as rainwater on the windscreen rendered visibility virtually nil.

Ian skewed the vehicle to a halt. He winced and chuckled and, reaching beneath the dashboard, he produced a potato that had been cut cleanly in two. "Always does the trick, old boy," he said and, with that, he leapt from the car and began to rub the vegetable with fury all over the windscreen. Soon, a thick creamy substance appeared. Then, amazingly, despite rain continuing to pelt down, the windscreen cleared and vision was restored. "There you go. What did I tell you?"

"Very impressive," I said, "but what about the top."

Ian climbed back in and he did his customary wince and shrug. "Blasted thing blew away in the gales. Still, never mind, Gatehouse, old dear. A spot of rainwater never did anyone any harm."

Presently, we arrived in Warwickshire, somewhat cold and extremely damp.

"How far is this Prestwick place?" I eagerly asked of him because, by now, I was simply desperate for a bath and warm bed.

"I know a smashing pub around here," he said and, with that, he yanked the steering wheel hard left and, with a squealing of rubber on tarmac, we shot up some back lane.

Touchdown occurred on a pothole riddled car park midway between a mucky pick-up truck and a Bentley Continental, vintage and in pristine condition. Ian duly switched off and, praise be, with a shudder and a jolt, the roaring ceased.

"You get all sorts in here, Gatehouse, old chap. Bit like the Inns of Court, I suppose. Come on, I think we have time for a quick one or two." Ian virtually leaped from the car and, with his peculiar backwards stance and with his legs going like pistons, he was across the car park and in a thrice. "Best pint in the county, here," he chirped, as he disappeared through the rear entrance.

My battered face hurt like hell and just about every joint and muscle, some which I didn't even know existed, had pretty much seized up. Add to that the fact that my suit was sodden, my feet were swimming in their respective shoes, I stank of engine oil and my nationality was Black Country, I submit that it was perfectly natural for me to be feeling negative, a bit.

Well, I managed eventually to disembark. Taking due account of my circumstances, it was no mean feat, I can tell you. What with struggling into a standing position, balancing myself, stepping onto the rear trunk, and then sliding down to car park level, it must have taken me a whole five minutes. And, in the interests of historical and geographic accuracy, it is right and proper to record that I took a while to hobble across the car park and all.

Through a tiny, mud splattered window I spied Ian. He was stood casually with an arm resting on the bar. He appeared to be engrossed in conversation with a small gathering and it was pretty clear that the reprobate had not missed me one jot.

Still, the close proximity of a red brick lavatory block, separate from the main building, was at least promising. Mark my words; it is an undisputable fact of life, along with night following day and other such *minutiae*, that a chap can always trust a boozer with an outside toilet.

There was just one other incumbent, an elderly, fairly well dressed gentleman, who seemed to be as unsteady on his feet as me. He gave the distinct impression that he had been in there for some time, without having any luck.

"Good evening," I said, sidling alongside. "What's the name of this place, then?"

My approach had clearly gone unnoticed because, upon enquiry of the appellation of this most promising of establishments, the prostatic pensioner duly jumped out of his skin, turned towards me and his luck changed.

"Why," he said, in a well-spoken and gentle sort of way, "we are at The Case, of course."

"The Case?"

"Yes, young man. The Case. Or to put it more fully, The Case Is Open." He proceeded to button his flies and spat in the urinal, either for luck or due to the onset of bronchial pneumonia. "And I don't mind telling you, young man, that The Case purveys the very best of ales in the whole of the county."

The pensioner spat once more, leading me to suppose that he was, indeed, in the first stages of bronchial pneumonia and then he hobbled off out.

"Dirty old devil," I said, under my breath.

Having myself done as nature commanded of me most urgently, I made my own, faltering, way towards the rear entrance of The Case. As I crossed the small corner of car park from the lavatory block, I heard a powerful, perfectly well tuned motorcar engine start up. Next, the vintage Bentley glided past and, from behind the steering wheel, the prostatic pensioner gave a cheery wave.

I duly ventured into The Case and could have been forgiven for assuming that I had gone into a time warp or, for that matter, another lavatory. Decorations were conspicuous by their absence, with just an ashtray or two here and three or more empty crisp packets there. The usual thingamajigs associated with the more upbeat of public houses were conspicuous by their absence. True, in the scruffier still lobby, there was one innovative trapping that I virtually fell over. It was a Russian billiards table. The thing worked on old sixpenny pieces that were obtainable from behind the bar for the modern day equivalent of half a bob.

The walls were yellowed by a combination of age and tobacco smoke. So too was the ceiling. Indeed, glancing ceiling wards, I noticed that some bright spark had had an aeroplane propeller hung there, precariously. Looking at the floor, I saw that the said bright spark, or some other bright spark, had done away with carpeting in favour of bare floorboards that were covered with a liberal sprinkling of sawdust.

There were a few cribbage tables dotted about but no persons were seated around the same and drinks lay abandoned. Everyone was gathered about Ian.

Unseen, I hobbled towards the throng and overheard Ian recounting tales of Gray's Inn.

"The DPP," said Ian, boldly, "told everyone in Hall that my response to the challenge was brilliant."

The congregation, as one, wowed and gasped at the embellished anecdote.

"You surely are a one, our Ian," said a husky voiced country girl.

She wore an outfit which was both too low and too short. The girl had a comely frame and it was positively bursting to come out.

Ian shrugged, winced, and then winked at her and he did so to the obvious alarm of a farm hand sort who was holding her hand.

"Of course," Ian went on, "the DPP would have asked me to share a pint or two of port with him, except that I promised to provide a lift to . . ."

I coughed.

"Gatehouse, old chap! Draw hither and partake of some excellent ale."

The throng surrounding Ian parted, thereby facilitating access to the bar.

"I suppose that I may as well have a pint, since I'm here anyway," said I, in a manner most sullen.

A landlady stood behind the bar. Well, she was presumably the landlady because, without in any way, shape or form intending to stereotype, the average barmaid sort would not have turned out in a knitted cardigan, beneath a flowery pinafore. Neither would she have gone to work sporting a particularly ill fitting, National Health Service wig. Further and additionally and, once again not wishing in any way, shape and so on, your typical barmaid was unlikely to be knocking on so much in terms of age. Indeed, by reverting to my clock face analogy, I reckoned she was liable to turn midnight and have her plug pulled before she could pull the next pint.

"I hopes you're not goin' to cause no trouble, like," said the landlady, no doubt influenced by my battered appearance.

"I can vouch for my friend and colleague," said Ian, butting in.

"Only I don't serve them yuppie, mod, teddy boy, rocker sorts,

38

our Ian. What would you like, my dear?" she proceeded to enquire of me.

There were four, maybe five, beer kegs, all in a row, sitting proudly on a trestle sort of a table that was in the back of the bar area. Beneath the tap of each keg, there were differently colored washing bowls, slops, for the use of.

"I'll have that one," I said, jabbing my finger in the general direction of the blue bowl.

It wasn't half a bad pint, I can tell you. And that's coming from someone who was weaned on Tiptbury and Dudsall's finest. After it was polished off, I thought it best to have another. Well, it would have been rude not to. So too would it have been rude to refuse the offer of a third from a homespun sort. He was dressed, and smelt, as if he had just walked in from cauliflower picking.

"You look like you've had a dust-up with one of them steamroller things," he said. "What you needs is another pint."

By way of respite from churning out yarns, Ian decided that it was high time for another smoke. He winced, shrugged, and fetched out his pipe and the ridiculous lighter. He swizzled, just once this time, and the howitzer shot a flame right up to the propeller and back. The landlady, the congregation, myself included, shied away. Ian, as daft as ever, was not so deft and, with a crackle, it was this time his forelock which went up in smoke. Undaunted, Ian pointed the source of the inferno towards his pipe and began suck, sucking with a fury. Next, having gotten ignition, he extinguished firstly the lighter and, next, his hair. He winced, shrugged and, rocking to and fro, chuckled, with pipe clamped firmly between the teeth.

"Do you know something, Gatehouse, old dear," he said at last, "I thought we might run into Mr. Justice Lancaster tonight. I could have sworn that I saw his old Bentley parked outside." He continued rocking on his feet and, after a few more moments of silence, he nodded in the direction of a row of bottles on a shelf above the bar. "See those up there, Gatehouse, old chap."

"Yes, I see them."

"There you have liquor from every country in the whole wide world."

"In which case," I said, as quick as a flash, for by now I was up for it, "I'm fed up of the fruits of the end barrel and I'm going to broaden my horizon."

"I say, welcome aboard, Gatehouse, old dear."

"You what?" said the puzzled homespun.

"Right then," I said to the equally puzzled landlady, "I'll kick off in Scotland and have that single malt in the middle, please."

"This be weird, if you ask me," said the homespun, who promptly lost all further interest and returned to his pint, a packet of pork scratchings and a game of cribbage.

As I knocked back my tot, Ian chuckled and announced, "Damnation, I fancy a trip around the globe and all." Having given each bottle the once-over, Ian beckoned to the landlady and admitted, "I've always wanted to visit Scandinavia, ever since I met that au pair from Malmo. Make it one large schnapps for me, please."

"Too cold for me in Sweden tonight," I said. "I think I'll travel south and have myself a gin and tonic."

Next, Ian tazzed off to Russia, where he proceeded to toss off a vodka. For my part, I caught the overnight ferry to France and tackled the cognac.

We bumped into each other in Holland and, on mutually agreeing that egg flip was as right sickly and boring as the very Dutchmen who produced the stuff, we took a hop and a skip and a jump and found ourselves in Portugal. Here, after a brief stop over, I left Ian to the port and made my way to Spain, for I was now so far gone as to develop a craving for sweet sherry.

"When in Portugal, do as the Portuguese do," said Ian, and, with that, he set sail intending to make mischief in the Americas, promptly ran aground in the West Indies and, on the basis that he was there anyway, he tried a tot of rum, said, "This is the fellow for me," and he made a night of it in Kingston, Jamaica.

Nearing closing time, and feeling really rotten poorly, we made our return to this green and pleasant land, finished off with an elderflower wine apiece, said our farewells and fell out the door.

We tore away in the wreck, leaving in our wake a shower of gravel and a cloud of exhaust fumes and a public house with its wet stock very much depleted.

We rounded the first bend at a pace far in excess of that which had been contemplated by the relevant highways authority. It was I who was the first to spot a rather large, inanimate object lying in the road, dead center. Regrettably, Ian was too busy engaged tap, tapping the glass dials.

At the point of no return, where failure to take evasive action was certain to result in mishap, I identified the object as a stag that had presumably jumped the fence only to come to grief under the wheels of some other motor vehicle.

When, to the accompaniment of inappropriate, albeit accurate, adjectives, Ian looked up from the dials it was too late for, as stated, the point of no return was passed. With a yank of the steering wheel hard left, Ian avoided actual contact with the carcass. But, looming up ahead, directly in our path, I spotted a further obstacle to the furtherance of our journey. It was the weapon that had presumably delivered the *coup-de-grace* to the stag, namely a vintage Bentley Continental. The vehicle could no longer be described with accuracy as superb in terms of looks, being as it was smashed up and abandoned, the driver having withdrawn, thereby averting the potential for conflict between the judiciary and the executive, in this particular instance, the relevant police authority. Or, putting it bluntly, His Lordship had legged it to avoid Old Bill.

It was high time, I reckoned, to commit mutiny. I leaned towards the driver's cockpit and gave the steering wheel a damned good yank to the right.

"Good grief, Gatehouse, you're going to kill us both, dead!"

We shot, bullet-like, towards a field. However, restricting free and uninterrupted access to the same was a five bar gate. And, travelling as we were at a voluminous rate of knots, it was rather impractical for either one of us to hop out to unlatch the thing. And so it was that the gate was instantaneously converted into matchwood.

The acreage, and all or any hereditaments attached thereto, into which we ploughed was not of the traditional greensward variety, consisting as it did of a crop of cauliflowers poking out of a one in five gradient.

As we plunged down the slope, I let out an almighty holler. Ian promptly issued me with a sharp rebuke, along the lines that such cowardly behaviour was simply not British. For good measure, he added that he was fully in control of the situation and that *prima facie* our chances of survival were fair to middling. And, with that, he yanked the steering wheel hard left, resulting in the vehicle spinning around and continuing the descent, only this time sideways and at a greatly enhanced speed.

Ian let out an almighty holler, screamed for divine intervention and blubbered that he was too young to die.

Through a shower of uprooted cauliflowers I saw, to my absolute horror, the silhouette of two enormous oak trees. Having already failed miserably in my attempt at mutiny, I thought it entirely appropriate to jump ship and leave Ian to it. I pushed, thumped, and shouldered the door but it would not shift. Some damn fool blacksmith had welded the thing shut. So, resigned to my fate, I closed my eyes and awaited the inevitable impact.

But there was no impact, inevitable or otherwise. I opened my eyes, just as the last cauliflower bounced off the bonnet, and, praise be, the motor car was lodged fairly and squarely between the oaks. Well, who would have thought that someone would plant two trees 387.9 centimeters apart, being the exact length of an MGB roadster, give or take a cauliflower or two stuck in the radiator?

We sat in silence for what seemed an age, though in actual fact was perhaps no more than a few seconds. For my part, I grasped the dashboard showing white knuckles. I hardly dared to breathe because, with darkness all around and perched at a dodgy angle, I had no idea whether we were at the actual bottom of the slope. For all I knew, one false move could dislodge the wreck from between the trees, sending us, once more, downwards.

Presently, Ian reached gingerly into his pocket and fetched out his smoking kit. Oblivious to the dripping, let alone fumes, coming from the general direction of the fuel tank, he began his swizzles at the howitzer. When the pipe was lit, he waited for the screeches of the screech owl to die down as it flew out of the branches above, with tail feathers singed.

Turning my way, with pipe clamped firmly in place, he calmly said, "Do you know what, Gatehouse, old chap?" he puffed, winced, and shrugged, just a little. "I know a fantastic pub, just a field or two from here. It sells a most unusual brand of tequila. Fancy a trip down Mexico way?"

CHAPTER THREE

I lay low at Ian's cottage, the appropriately named, The Fly in the Ointment, for about a fortnight. The interlude permitted me time in which to tend my battle wounds and to feel generally sorry for myself.

From the exterior, The Fly in the Ointment could have passed as the archetypal English country cottage. The roof was thatched and the walls were half-timbered. There were even red roses surrounding a large front door of stripped oak. They were attached to a trellis that looked to be hanging on for dear life.

Ian boasted that the manufacturers of a particular brand of biscuits had paid him handsomely for the dubious honor of having a picture of the cottage superimposed on their tins. They were those sorts of biscuit that multiply, like a plague of sugar-frosted Staffordshire knots around Christmastime. Enter the New Year and the supermarket shelves are devoid of the things. I often pondered over their mysterious disappearance. It was as if, come the first croak of "Auld Lang Syne," the whole lot got sucked down a black hole.

Well, at least that little mystery was solved and, in a manner of speaking, they were sucked down a black hole. It transpired that Ian had a dirty great stockpile in the cellar. Anyone daft enough to exhibit a mere fleeting interest in The Fly in the Ointment was guaranteed to be flogged a tin full.

In a manner akin to the biscuit tins, the attractive exterior of the cottage was a mere facade for the horrors that lay within.

The kitchen was comprised of bathroom, lavatory and work surface because a dividing wall had long since given way. A torn and tatty curtain was strung-up in a rather ingenious fashion and it screened the bathtub from the table and the cooking stove. There was no need to conceal the lavatory, however. Ian explained that, ever

43

since the collapse of the wall, the sole use put to that particular facility was for washing muddy boots and vegetables. The actual lavatory, to be used as such, was in a brick-built affair at the bottom of the garden.

"Whatever you do, Gatehouse, old dear, don't forget to take the toilet paper."

This being a one-bedroom cottage, I slept with Colin the cat at the bottom of the stairs. There, we shared a makeshift bed of scatter cushions. Nocturnal traffic to and from the bedroom was such that I felt as if I was laying my head to rest on the hard shoulder of a freeway. Putting matters another way. The turnaround of mature, presumably vulnerable, women on their way upstairs each night was such that Ian must have been super human or he too knew his Latin pretty well.

For completeness, I ought to concede that the sitting room was at least hospitable. It was dominated by an inglenook fireplace, with a built-in bread oven. The only furniture consisted of two battered, but extremely comfortable, leather chairs. Ian kept the fire going, day and night, with a plentiful supply of dead elm and garden furniture. I found it to be the most pleasurable of pursuits to commandeer one of the chairs and gaze sleepily into the glowing embers of next doors wicker table. However, while doing so, Ian was out and about the parish of Prestwick, doing things most odd.

On my first day at The Fly in the Ointment, Ian had risen with the lark and made his way to the scene of our altercation with the five bar gate. The gamekeeper was there before him but, undaunted by such opposition, Ian proceeded to lay claim to the remains of the wretched deer. Ian apparently submitted that, by virtue of ancient charter, he was entitled to first pickings on account of the beast having done harm to his chattel, to wit the MGB roadster, currently parked between the oak trees. For good measure, Ian followed through with a warning that if Amos (this being the name of the somewhat bamboozled gamekeeper) protested ownership then he, and his boss (Lord "somutt or other") would be sued in the very highest of all the courts in all the land. The rationale was that the beast ought to have been properly fenced in.

Having thus seen off Amos, Ian dragged the carcass single handed to the local butcher where the wretched creature (and I refer here to the stag) was prepared for human consumption. Ian described the procedures employed in the most intimate of detail, but I only half listened. Indeed, I stopped listening altogether when he got to the part

44

with hooks, hanging and buckets. Scoffing the likes of Bambi is one thing but, in the name of heaven, there is such a thing as too much information.

Anyway, for all his trouble, Benjamin (this being the name of the butcher) was rewarded with a crisp ten pound note and the promise of a tin of biscuits at a discounted cost. Being a man of simple taste, to match his presumable simple mind, Benjamin was happy, so much so that he gave Ian unrestricted use of his delivery bike until such time as the motor car was back on solid ground.

By midday the butcher's joy had turned to rage and it was I who answered the pounding of fists on the big oak door. Ian, meanwhile, legged it out back.

Over coffee (white, with bits floating in it) the peeved purveyor explained that his whole week's takings were effectively done for. Ian had apparently cycled around the entire village hawking overly fresh venison on the cheap.

Come lunchtime, the front door received another pummelling. It was the local farmer. Once more, Ian legged it out back.

I sat the aggrieved agronomist down in one of the comfortable chairs and, as I tipped milk with bits in it into his coffee, he poured out his heart. Arnold (this being the name of the farmer) was pretty cheesed-off, having been conned into recovering the stricken motor car. From what I could tell, for Arnold spoke in a very odd rustic way, Ian had promised remuneration for services rendered, in the form of a crisp ten pound note, which was not forthcoming. Further and additionally, during pre-contract negotiations Ian had failed to mention certain points of potential relevance, not least that the motor car was on a ruddy great slope that only the very biggest of tractors could get down, that it was buried up to the wheel arches in mud and it had done hundreds of pounds worth of damage to the cauliflowers. To cap things off, while the farmer was hard at it, pushing and pulling with the biggest of his tractors, Ian was hard at it, pushing and pulling with the farmer's wife.

"The swine even promised me a tin of biscuits," said Arnold, woefully.

Edging towards the end of my week of recuperation, there happened at the cottage a further visitation and, this time, Ian did not leg it out back.

Some may have said that Jane Jetty (Janie, apparently, to close friends) was not a "full on, in your face" beauty. If The Fly in the Ointment was your typical English cottage, then Janie Jetty was your typical English Rose. I was smitten from the moment she glided out of the little green Morris Minor that putt putted up the lane and stopped outside. She was tall and darkish, with a swan-like neck. Her eyes danced and smiled and were incredibly big. She wore clothes of linen; you know the classic sort that is never out of fashion. Just like her hair, in fact; shoulder length, curls, but not too many.

"I should close your gaping mouth, if I were you," said Ian, as I ogled from the front window.

He opened the big front door and Janie stepped into the front room and into my life. For a woman she was rather tall and she needed to duck, ever so slightly, to come in.

"It's lovely to see you, Ian."

Her voice was soft and pleasing, with no discernable accent.

"It's smashing to see you too, Janie."

Ian lunged forwards and Janie turned and offered her cheek, thereby avoiding any collision of the lips, accidental or otherwise. It was an expertly carried out manoeuvre that was guaranteed not to cause offense to the disappointed male of the species.

"I've heard that you have been involved in an accident and . . ." Janie stopped and, bending her beautiful neck forwards, she peered intently at Ian's face. "Goodness, me," she said, "your eyebrows are singed. Did the car catch fire?"

"Nothing I couldn't handle," said Ian, with a wince and a shrug, followed by a chuckle. Then, acknowledging me, at last. "Janie," he said, "permit me to introduce my friend and colleague, Izaak Gatehouse. And, as you can see, he's a bit battered and bruised."

I felt embarrassed that all I wore was Ian's dressing gown and absolutely nothing else, not even on my feet. At least the thing was full length, although the belt consisted of a piece of orange binder twine.

"Why, hallo friend and colleague," said Janie, and she put forth her hand.

We shook. Her hand felt at home in mine. It was soft and warm and just the touch sent shivers up and down.

"I'm delighted to make your acquaintance, Jane."

"Oh, call me Janie. Close friends always do."

46

Keeping her hand in mine, *This is going okay*, I thought and, with the sort of presence of mind which was usually a stranger to me, I gave her other hand the once over to see whether she wore an engagement, or worse still, a wedding ring. Neither was present, though interestingly an extremely glittery diamond ring adorned the hand which I held.

"Can I have my hand back, now?"

"Oh, so sorry," I said, feeling embarrassed and thinking that hopes of this going okay were perhaps premature.

Janie seated herself in one of the armchairs and, before darting off to make coffee; Ian reached into the inglenook and chucked the garden gate from next door onto the fire. Colin was contentedly snoozing in the other chair. I was having none of that. I sat myself down and, as soon as the hissing and spitting was done with, I wasted no time in letting rip with full particulars of my plight to date.

What a good listener she was; and an extraordinary good-looking woman to my mind. She was, quite simply, a classic and natural beauty and she had no need to cover her clear, pale skin with makeup. Indeed, all that she wore was lipstick and the very slightest amount of eye shadow.

"Poor thing, I'm so worried for you," said Janie, and without warning she reached forward to my arm and squeezed it, gently.

My heart did a somersault and I sensed my cheekbones beginning to burn. It was either bashfulness or the effect of the neighbor's gate which, during our chitchat, was going up in smoke as quick as a factory with unpaid judgment debts.

Ian returned all too soon and within his cupped hands were three steaming cups. Janie immediately pulled away from me.

"Ouch! Ouch!" said Ian and, with his peculiar backwards lean, he tore across the room and deposited the cups in front of the fire.

"Bless you, Ian," said Janie.

"Hope you kept yourselves amused while I was gone," he said, and he winced, shrugged, and chuckled in a knowing sort of a way.

Janie reached down and copped hold of one of the cups. She clasped it with both hands, almost as if in prayer and, between sips, proceeded to tell Ian that she knew all about our shenanigans. For my part, I could not keep my eyes off the woman. In her hands, even the simple act of drinking from a chipped coffee cup was graceful. Sometimes, she sipped a little too much and instinctively blinked. As she did so, the very tiniest of crow's feet became visible around her huge and wonderful eyes. These served only to add to her character and overall loveliness. Janie was younger than me, as anyone could tell. However, those lines suggested that the gap could not be much over ten years, meaning that no person could accuse me of being her father. True, she must have been brought up on a diet of The Bay City Rollers. But if that was the sort of piffle that she chatted about over candlelit suppers, I could always shut her up with a kiss.

"Gatehouse, old chap. Did you hear what Janie was saying?"

Ian's talking brought me back from where I had been.

"I said did you hear what Janie was saying?"

"Of course I did."

I was lying. But when all was said and done it was my intention to practice as a barrister. So of course I was lying. And a good job of lying I had done.

"You're lying, Gatehouse," said Ian, "It's written all over what's left of your face."

Having drunk her drink, Janie placed the cup on the floor. She sat back and her dark skirt rode above the knee. It was only slight, but nonetheless sensual.

"Is it agreed then, Izaak?" she said, straightening her skirt.

I swear that she had noticed me staring, and I felt stupid on account of it.

"Is what agreed?" I said.

"Aha!" said Ian, gleefully. "I said he was lying and that proves it."

He seized a poker that was leaning against the inside of the inglenook and, without warning, he gave the burning gate an almighty wallop. The flames, which had been settling down to a cozy sort of a glow, reacted to this unprovoked attack by leaping up and sending sparks flying everywhere.

The cat had apparently calmed his self by taking a therapeutic climb up the curtains. But at the sight of his lord and master wielding the poker, Colin leapt from the left finial right into Janie's lap where he dug his claws in.

Janie stood and, once more, there came the sounds of hissing and spitting. She gracefully wiped cat hair and embers from the designer fabric.

"You are simply the limit, Ian," she said. "The fire would burn

48

more effectively if you left the thing alone. And," she added, "it may improve our chances in the best kept village competition were you to stop ripping up gates and stealing garden furniture and purchase firewood, like everybody else."

Janie was indignant in the way that she had spoken. I found it extremely attractive. I also found attractive the way that her neck and chest turned the brightest of crimson. How I longed to know this woman, that I might stir the emotions and send her glorious neck and chest sunset red with passion.

Ian chuckled and winced, just a little. He replaced the poker and stood before the fire that he had whooped-up.

"As it happens, Gatehouse, old chap, Janie here has offered to drive all the way to this Dud place . . ."

"Dudsall," I interrupted.

"Yes, Dudsall," he said, "where she will attend upon the guesthouse and collect your worldly goods."

"Janie, I can't allow you to do that," I said, knowing that I jolly well could. "I simply couldn't allow it, not even in a month of Sundays."

In truth my physical condition no longer hampered travelling. The actual distance was no problem, either. I could easily catch a bus. Hitchhike, if I had to. Quite simply, the arrangement which Janie proposed meant that this, our first meeting, would not be the last.

"I insist," she said, and I was instantly relieved that I had not over-egged my protest.

Janie motioned towards the door and Ian pelted over for the purpose of opening the same. He puckered his lips for a kiss and, with expert precision; Janie once again engineered mouth to cheek contact. She waved at me and I could have sworn that our eyes lingered, momentarily.

Halfway up the path, Janie stopped, tutted, and spun round.

"How silly of me," she said. "I don't have Izaak's address."

Forgetting, for a moment, my alleged miscellaneous ailments, I darted through to the kitchen for the purpose of laying hands on pen and paper. As I mooched through a collection of old papers, shifting Colin from one pile to the next, imagine my surprise, delight in fact, when I sensed that Janie, having apparently returned to the house, was stood behind, so close as to be virtually touching.

I swiftly turned, our eyes met once more and our lips were so close that I could feel her sweet breath.

"I have pen and parchment here, old chap," said Ian, bursting through.

Janie immediately stepped back. She was all of a fluster. At that moment I could have cheerfully throttled Ian.

"One of you write the address down," Janie said, snappily and, just then, I noticed with immense satisfaction that the crimson rash was once more about her neck and chest.

I scribbled the details onto the document, described by Ian as parchment, which was actually a used envelope. Indeed, it was not just any old envelope. I could tell, from size, color and absence of any postage stamp that it had formerly contained a County Court Summons.

"There you are," I said, and I handed the note to Janie.

"Izaak," she said and I saw with astonished glee that, as she addressed me, the redness became even redder. Indeed, it spread to her face. "Izaak," she said again, "I have been thinking that you really should be getting rest. I know that it's terribly good of Ian to put you up, but. . ."

Janie faltered and glanced down.

"Yes?" I said, in anticipation.

"Stay at the hall," Janie spluttered. "We have plenty of room and I'm quite certain that my family will not object."

I was shocked, and that's no lie. There and then I wanted to throw myself at Janie's feet, declare my undying love and perhaps intimate that, if it was not considered impudent or overly forward, she may care to have a child by me. Regrettably, before I could say any of these things, let alone communicate a simple "Yes," Ian jumped in.

"Izaak will not hear of it," he advanced on my behalf, "and, besides which, I have to be at Lincoln's Inn for the whole of the next fortnight. Izaak can sleep in my bed."

Having so scuppered my designs, Ian winced and shrugged, just a little, and he returned to the sitting room. From there came the unmistakable sound of a metal poker belting the hell out of the remains of the gate.

"Well, Izaak," said Janie, softly, "if I can't accommodate you at the hall, I can at least take you to London one week on Monday. I have an appointment there."

"That's great. Thank you, Janie."

Our guest made her way once more towards the front door. In another attempt at a smooch, Ian lunged, only this time with poker in hand. Janie seized a cobwebby pint glass from off the window shelf and, quick as a flash, she handed the same to Ian. Her deft action had the desired effect of stopping Ian dead in his tracks.

Ian stood still for a moment, with an exceedingly puzzled look about his face. Poker in one hand, pint glass in the other and with the smouldering gate in dangerous proximity to the seat of his trousers, he looked a very sorry state. Janie put her lips towards his cheek, and she kissed, though in doing so she kissed fresh air. I advanced, only for Janie to shake me limply by the hand. I felt proper deflated, I can tell you. Talk about mixed signals.

Janie made her way down the little pathway, with me in the dressing gown, looking on mesmerised.

"A very tricky situation," murmured Ian, making certain that he was not overheard. "A very tricky situation," he said again.

I waved as the little green car putt putted down the lane.

As soon as Janie was gone, I turned to Ian and said, "Okay, so what do you mean with all this tricky situation nonsense? Is she spoken for, or what?"

"It's a case of or what I fear. Don't even think about it, old chap. She'll break your heart."

Ian closed the door too. He did it with a hefty kick.

"Whatever do you mean, Ian?"

"Here, take this," said Ian, and he handed me the pint glass. In a rare moment of sincerity, he placed his spare hand on my shoulder. "There never was so sweet a changeling as our Janie, old dear. Or should I call you Oberon?"

"Please explain, Ian."

But Ian had no intentions of explaining. He looked in the direction of the inglenook and, reverting to Jack the lad; he winced, shrugged, chuckled, and said, "Cripes, Gatehouse! The fire's going out! You'd best come out back and lend a hand chopping up the vicar's gazebo!"

In the days that followed, I made frequent enquiry as to Janie, her status, family and so on. Each and every question was evaded by Ian's constant flippancy. Janie therefore remained, in my eyes at any rate, a woman of mystery. My belongings did not materialize either. By the eve of Ian's going to London, I had virtually resigned myself to never ever seeing the captivating creature again. It was Sunday when Ian's motorcar was returned by a local handyman, in readiness for his going the following day.

"Great job," I said, as we gave the vehicle the once over, "it looks almost like a different car."

"Funny you should say that, Gatehouse, old chap. In a manner of speaking it is. The other day, I came across an abandoned vehicle and, by a remarkable coincidence, it was an MGB. Just like mine. The body on mine was pretty well shot, as you know. So I simply had the things swapped over." He breathed on the virtually brand, spanking new coach paint and then rubbed the area with his shirtsleeve. He thereby succeeded in the removal of a tiny smudge. "A damned piece of good luck, I call it."

"A damned piece of grand theft auto, I call it, Ian."

He shrugged, winced and chuckled. "Come on, Gatehouse," he said, "let's drive up to The Case for a celebratory noggin or three."

So that's what we did. It was my first night out after the accident, so I took it steady and, after a taste of the fruits from the end barrel (as before, I did not wish to appear rude), I restricted my foreign travel to within the boundaries of Northern Europe, with a schnapps from Germany here and a particularly foul concoction from Switzerland there (apparently popular with skiers, but we all know about their sorts). Ian did likewise. He planned to be leaving very early, next day.

On our way out, the landlady presented us with a mint humbug a piece.

"There's a police car in the lay bye, there be. Suck on your mints and they'll never suspect you've had a drink."

"Damned cheek," said Ian, and we stepped outside. "I'm perfectly fit to drive." He stopped and produced his smoking gear and, with the pipe hanging from his jaw, he added, "Perhaps we'll go back via Oakley Castle, just in case."

So, via the village of Oakley Castle we did go. It was a right posh place and all. I swear there wasn't a single habitation that didn't come with its own Corinthian pillars, big black metal gates and lamppost lit driveways.

About halfway through the village, near to a road sign, Prestwick

3 Miles, Ian slowed the car.

"What's the problem?" I asked, above the din of the engine.

"Bit low on fuel, old chap. Need to have enough for London. Best fill up."

"You'll never find a garage open at this time of night."

"There's one just around the corner, except . . ." Ian switched off the engine and, because he did not apply the brakes, the car freewheeled along the street. "We mustn't wake the residents," he said, with a chuckle.

On reaching a slight incline, our vehicle came to a perfect standstill. Ian applied the handbrake.

"Well, there's certainly no garage hereabouts," I said.

"Be a good chap and fetch the hose from out of the boot."

"I can't possibly. . ."

"Shush, Gatehouse, old chap. Keep it to a whisper."

"I can't possibly," I whispered. "I'm supposed to be training as a barrister. I have a reputation to maintain."

"Now, see here, Gatehouse, old dear, you lost any reputation when you decided to be suckled, nurtured or whatever in that Dudsall place."

"Are you serious, Ian?"

"Deadly serious, old chap. I, on the other hand was born an esquire. So I do have a reputation to lose, but I'm up for it." He paused for a moment, and then shaking his head, said "You plain Mr.'s of this world are so lucky . . ."

"Plain Mr. or not," I cut in, "I'm not doing it."

"In that case, Gatehouse, old chap, you'll be walking back to Prestwick because the old girl is very nearly empty."

"Right," said I, huffing. "I assume you have a container of some sort."

"Of course," said Ian and he winced and shrugged, just a little and, from the side of his seat, he produced two, rather large, plastic bottles. One was empty and he handed it to me. The other was half full of cider or something. He kept hold of that one. "Waste not, want not," and he glugged at the bottle until it was dry.

The wrought iron gates outside the house nearest to us were not locked. I discovered that fact only after I had clambered up the ruddy great things. Sitting astride one of them, in dangerous proximity to a spike, I had offered Ian a helping hand to haul him up. But, with one of his winces and shrugs, he simply turned the handle and hey presto the gates swung open. He strolled through and I found myself clinging on for dear life until I could cling no more and, with a yelp, I fell into the conifers.

"Stop messing about, Gatehouse!" hissed Ian. "Go see if the car at the front has a locking fuel cap. I'll concentrate on this four wheel drive monstrosity."

So, I crept up the driveway for the purpose of concentrating on a rather expensive looking sports car, Italian from all the curves and chrome, I would have said. I returned a few moments later with my bottle full of petrol.

"Here," I said.

Ian was now seated on the driveway, busily attempting to ram his rubber hose down the fuel pipe of a luxury jeep-type vehicle. "How did you get that without the hose?" he whispered.

"With this," I whispered back, and I produced a long screwdriver. "I found it in the back of your car. I simply rammed it through the bottom of the fuel tank, and the lot came pouring out. Good, aye?"

"No it's not good. I didn't tell you to go and commit criminal damage. And you look dashed foolish with that twig sticking out of your hair."

"Oh! So theft is okay, is it?"

"That's not the point in issue," said Ian. "You've gone and gotten sufficient fuel to get me barely beyond Oxford. The rest has simply gone to waste and I've managed only a drop from this monster. Tell you what, Gatehouse; they ought to ban these things." He fetched out his pipe and other smoking accoutrements. "I need to think this one through."

"Ian?" I said, as Ian swizzled the little wheel atop the howitzer. "Don't you think it's a little dangerous to smoke around all this petrol?"

"Stop being so meek and . . ." Ian broke off as a blue flame shot up the driveway. "Run for it, Gatehouse! The whole lot's going to blow!" We sprinted out of the gates and dived into Ian's car. "If I drive steady and slow, we may have enough fuel to make it to Prestwick!" Ian spluttered. And he promptly tore away at an unsteady and quick pace.

I glanced over my shoulder and was horrified by the sight of the inferno. The sports car was enveloped in fire and looked as if it was, indeed, ready to explode. There was an ominous red glow coming from the vicinity of the luxury jeep.

"The other one's alight too," I said, with appropriate urgency and concern. "Shall we go back and help?"

"Help with what, Gatehouse? Go the whole hog and burn the house down?"

"Well, there's no need to be sarcastic."

"Anyway," said Ian, with a shrug, and he braked the car to a slower pace, "those gas guzzlers should be banned from the roads. I reckon we've struck a blow for the environment."

I glanced behind, once more. I was greeted with the sight of lights going on all about the village and shadowy figures darting hither and dither.

"And I suppose, Ian, that it's striking a blow for the environment to burn down the whole blinking orchard and all?"

CHAPTER FOUR

We spent a restless night at The Fly in the Ointment. What did it was the infernal racket drifting across the fields from the vicinity of the village of Oakley Castle. All that shouting, all those sirens blaring were simply not conducive to a good night's kip. Concerns that Old Bill might at any time come crashing through the big front door didn't help, either.

Come the morning though and we had not had our collars felt. Ian came downstairs, reeking of petroleum and went to the kitchen for a bath. He reappeared a few moments later, raking a comb through his locks, and said that he would be leaving for London straight after breakfast.

"That disturbance last night was an utter disgrace," he said. "I have a good mind to write to the council. All that fuss over trivia."

"All that fuss? Ian. We damned near blew up the entire village. And now you're beetling off and very probably leaving me to face the music."

And beetle off he did, so I spent the majority of the ensuing week keeping my head down and, in particular, diving under the window each time a car passed by.

Throughout the week I heard not a dickey bird from Janie. All alone, living on knot-shape biscuits and growing fonder by the day of Colin, I was probably exhibiting the onset of cabin fever.

The day of my own departure for London loomed and I had still heard nothing. I assumed that I would have to travel with just the clothes I was wearing, namely a dark dining suit, formerly pressed and clean, but now stained with blood, grease, and petrol. I assumed also that I would have to hitchhike and the prospect of that was disappointing, to put it mildly. It had poured rain the whole previous day. It had bucketed down all night and it was still raining.

It was therefore much to my relief, not to mention heart pounding joy, that the little green car came putting along. The windscreen wipers, which were going ten to the dozen, stopped as the engine stopped. Janie got out. She wore a long, stylish and expensive-looking raincoat.

I opened the big front door. I fumbled a bit because I had been stroking Colin and telling him all my woes.

"Hallo, Janie!"

Her face was glum. She said not a word as she splish-splashed down the path. Janie ducked and came into the front room. She still said nothing. Her face remained glum. I recall thinking, glum or not, Janie was as beautiful as before, if not more so. She wiped her feet. Heaven only knows why. The ratio of dirt within and dirt without was such that it would have made more sense to wipe her feet on the way out.

"Izaak," she said at last. "I'm not happy with you. And furthermore, my family is not happy. Bruce in particular considers that your actions have been quite inappropriate."

She looked and sounded angry. I shuddered at the prospect of it having become known to her that I was a party in a conspiracy to commit arson and theft in the next village. But where her family fitted into the scheme of things was anyone's guess. I didn't know them from Adam and, so far as I was aware, Janie's home (the hall to which she had previously referred) was in Prestwick and not Oakley. Further and additionally, as they say in legal circles, the only Bruce that I knew of was an historical figure from Scotland who had a penchant for striking up relations with every passing arachnid.

"Whatever is it, Janie?"

"Go to the car and fetch your case in." She sounded angry, all right.

The coat covered much of her chest. But her graceful neck was visible. It was bright crimson and I was glad of it. I noticed too that as Janie got madder, her wonderful eyes sparkled. I knew then that if my chances were scuppered I would surely regret it, for even moments of conflict with this creature could be filled with passion. Indeed, were I to land her, I might very well wish there to be frequent fallings out?

On balance, I figured that I could lay all the blame on Ian. When all was said and done, it was he who had form in the pyromania stakes.

Anyone who had mislaid their gate, fence or gazebo could attest to that fact. I would surely be acquitted in Janie's eyes and, although a proposal of marriage there and then might have been considered compulsive (inappropriate even, to them up at the hall) I could always wait till the dust had settled which, by my reckoning, would be when we got to Oxford.

In lieu of going down on one knee, I therefore handed Janie care and control of the cat and went for my case. It was a red vinyl thing and represented one third of a set. The case also represented the sum total of my share of the split of marital assets.

"Phew," I said on my return, "You wouldn't put the cat out in this weather."

"Sit," said Janie and so I sat, smartly I can tell you. "Now then, Izaak," she carried on, "or do I call you Brian?" She flung Colin outside and off he shot with his customary hissing and spitting.

"Oh," I said.

"Yes. Oh," she said.

"I was going to explain."

And it was true. I had fully intended to explain that, due to personal circumstances, I may perhaps have led proprietors of certain guesthouses into believing that I was one Brian Smith and not Mr. Izaak Gatehouse, an intended barrister-at-law. It hadn't been a total lie; well, not a very big lie. More of a white lie, I suppose. I certainly had no intention of defrauding anyone. It was just that everywhere I went I was followed by those who were owed money as a consequence of my disastrous marriage. Quite why the creditors insisted on pursuing me was unfair in my mind's eye. Who, after all, goes by the name of Izaak and purchases, by means of credit cards, hundreds of pounds worth of face cream, body cream, perfume, and such, not to mention the bikini line waxing? But, Izaak was apparently the name on the credit cards. It was therefore resolved that it was Izaak who should be hunted. And Izaak was being hunted, and that was no word of a lie.

"I'm a respectable person," said Janie. "I was made to look foolish, asking for the goods of Izaak Gatehouse only to ascertain, by a process of illumination that you were, in fact, known as Brian Smith. I felt humiliated, Izaak."

I swear that Janie's eyes began to swell. I felt concerned, but for me not her. I was concerned that she may never again wish to clap those beautiful eyes on me. That aside, I felt elated that I, Izaak Gatehouse, a.k.a. Brian Smith, was capable of stirring her emotions so.

"I'm so, so sorry it's just that . . ."

"I don't want any excuses," she cut in, "it's quite apparent that you are in debt and avoiding your creditors, your obligations."

"No, I am not," I protested. I ensured that I sounded suitably indignant. It never fails.

"Then tell me, Izaak, Brian, whatever your name is, why you left the guesthouse without paying? I had to settle the bill to retrieve your clothing."

"I hadn't checked out, Janie. Don't you remember? I was involved in an accident and couldn't return. If I had no intention of returning, why do you think I left my belongings behind?" I sounded even more indignant than before.

"But, but . . ." Janie spluttered.

That stumped her, all right. A case in point, in fact, as to why it takes a lawyer to avert what might otherwise be a gross miscarriage of justice. She had failed to pursue the assumed, some may say false, name of Brian bit because she had distracted herself on the bilking of the hotel bill point. It was, in fairness, a common mistake to make. But she brought the charge and I answered the charge. I was acquitted of the charge. It was not for me to answer a charge with which I was not directly charged. If she chose to charge me with dodging credit card bailiffs then, and only then, would I defend myself. What's more, she'd clean forgotten the guesthouse tab.

"I'll pop upstairs and change," I said swiftly, lest she cottoned on to the actual points in issue.

"Izaak," said Janie, sternly. I had reached the landing in a flash. "If you ever, ever lie to me again, I shall not wish to see you. And," she added, after a pause, "You owe me seventy pounds."

"Thank you, Janie. And I promise. I shall never lie to you again."

And my solemn undertaking not to lie to Janie ever, ever again is the reason why I found myself three miles outside Prestwick, trying to thumb a lift to London in the pouring rain.

Everything went swimmingly at first. The little green car was as little on the inside as it was on the outside and it felt intimate. Our conversation was stilted and awkward. We spoke small talk. Things like the fact that it was raining cats and dogs and that there appeared to be no letting up in the weather. In truth, I was desperate to know more of Janie than her knowledge of the cumulus puffed up above. If we wanted to know how bad the weather was, we needed only to turn up the car radio. It was telling us that the rain was so bad that the river had burst its banks and that the Prestwick bridge was down. In fact, had Janie truly wanted to know how bad the rain was, she needed only to look to her right, where a man in a canoe was going by.

Suddenly, Janie lost interest in the weather and she turned-up the radio, cutting off my espousing that, whatever the weatherman said, it was all down to Saint Swithin, in any case.

The weatherman had handed over to the newsman. And the newsman was saying that no one was yet caught for the wanton act of vandalism that occurred, just a few days previous, in the village of Oakley Castle.

"I really do not know what is happening in our society," Janie had said, and she had sounded and looked deadly serious. She said nothing more for a few moments because with all the surface water, sufficiently deep at the edges to paddle a canoe, the little car began to skew a bit. Janie jiggled about with the gear lever and played around with the foot pedals. In no time at all, she regained full control of the vehicle and in the process snatched away any hope that we might spend the night together in a ditch. Safely on our way again, Janie continued, "It's a frightening prospect that such things can occur in a tiny village, so close to our own. Whoever did it should be locked away. What do you think, Izaak?"

Well, what I thought was, if there was any locking away to be done, it should be her and me, locked up in a room, four poster bed and nothing but the sound of gondoliers punting past the window and not, I hasten to add, the sound of jerks in anoraks canoeing by on their way to the newspaper shop. And, if our relationship was to progress from beyond discussing a bit of damp weather to the point of total intimacy, I knew that I could not lie. I therefore told Janie that, exceptionally, the perpetrators of the wrong doing over in Oakley did not need locking up. Discharging my undertaking never, ever to be untruthful again, I came completely clean about the whole episode.

And that, in a nutshell, is how I found myself three miles outside of Prestwick, trying to thumb a lift to London, in the pouring rain.

CHAPTER FIVE

I made it to London, no thanks to Janie. The journey was horrendous and, what with all of the flooding, it took hours before I eventually strolled into Highgate, clutching my red vinyl suitcase. I was totally, utterly wet. I swear that, even if I could have afforded the hotels in that location, I would have been refused accommodation solely on account of the aqueous cut to my outfit. Totally sodden, I was. Totally sodden.

I decided to make my way down hill to the rather less salubrious, Belsize Park. There, I was pounced on and searched by a uniformed policeman. Even in those days, they had the power to do that sort of thing in London. It's now, of course, as common as going to the supermarket; all in the name of terrorism and so forth. Terrorism? I'll go to the foot of our stairs! Mark my words. Give the state a power and, as sure as night follows day, the state will abuse the power.

On balance, I suppose that, what with holding the case so close to my chest, the officer would have been forgiven for assuming that I'd just broken into one of the posh houses up the hill. In the event, the case was so positioned because both locks were busted. The damage had come about as a direct result of wanton criminal damage on the part of Janie. Having firstly ordered me out of the little green car, she had gone up the flooded road in a strop, only to reverse down the flooded road, only to stop, step out onto the flooded road, reach into the trunk for my case, kick my case around the flooded road, and then sling the said case into a ditch. Flood, or no flood, she'd then sped off, though not before shouting something along the lines that if I ever approached her in the future she would consult solicitors and have me enjoined.

Sometime during the assault, on this my sole chattel, the lid pinged open. Hence it took a good hour to extract my smalls from out of a culvert. And now the self same smalls were being rummaged by a copper who, as he went along, chucked them over his shoulder. Apparently satisfied that I was neither a house-breaker or unlicensed hawker, the dutiful officer then congratulated me on my public spirited cooperation and left me to fish my Y- fronts from out of the gutter.

I arrived at a large, shabby, building. Victorian probably. There was a sign in the overgrown garden and it read: Bed and Breakfast £10.00 per night. It was just the ticket. I had about one hundred quid to my name, so I could stay for an entire week and still have change for beer and, if I went easy, fish-n-chips. Within the week, I reckoned on an education grant coming through. Failing that, I would simply get a job collecting glasses or something.

I strolled up the path, kicking broken glass and discarded beer cans as I went. The entrance door was wide open. I couldn't figure whether this was by design or due to the thing near hanging off its hinges. The smell of damp hit me just as soon as I entered the red-tiled lobby.

An exceedingly seedy-looking individual seemed to appear from nowhere. I think that he must have heard me coming from a clattering that I made on the tiles, most of which were either loose or broken. He wore denims and a leather jacket that looked pretty ridiculous because he was getting on in years. He was fast running out of the sixties, I reckoned. And talk about his hairstyle? It was jet black with a Beatle fringe. On one so old it must surely have been a syrup.

The character stated that he was the owner of the establishment and he demanded to know the nature of my business. I discovered, however, that the flashing of seventy pounds worth of rent did much to quell his thirst for the answer of who I was and what I was about.

My room contained no furniture other than a double bed and it had not been made-up from the night before. The sheets were simply filthy and the mattress emitted an odour the source of which was perhaps best left a secret. There was no carpet, just bare wooden floorboards. And the electrical fittings consisted of a bare bulb dangling from a cord that was of hanging by the neck length.

Lest there be monsters about, I checked beneath the bed. It was a habit from childhood and it had stood the test of time. And besides, there was no such thing as obsessive-compulsive disorder in those days. As it happened, there were no hobgoblins either, but I did discover a haversack and a pair of red stiletto shoes. The haversack was stuffed with female clothing of a sort that never sees the light of day. It was of a type usually worn at night and only then on street corners, on the right side of town. One did not have to be a barrister to deduce that the ten pounds per night, paid in good faith to the awful little man downstairs, did not entitle me to vacant possession, free from all encumbrances.

I could find no bathroom and so I took a stroll outside the door and went down a dimly-lit corridor. There, I found what I was looking for. It was a communal affair and, by the look of things, the whole commune had enjoyed usage without once bothering to wipe, scrub or flush. I pulled at the lavatory chain, intending to rid the bowl of its unmentionable contents. After a couple of goes, the water came flowing and, as it did, the levels rose till my feet were swimming in raw sewage and shredded newspaper.

I went back to my room, with sounds like "what the hell's just come through the ceiling," emanating from the floor below. The next day, I had to be at one of the Honorables, Lincoln's Inn to be exact. This was for the purpose of attending an inaugural address by The Lord Chancellor. I ought to have felt excited but I felt thoroughly dejected and was in half a mind to jack the whole lot and go back to Dudsall. I could cope with having weathered a near monsoon. I could manage the discomfort of my surroundings. It was only short term. But, I couldn't contemplate the loss of Janie, whether it be short or long term or, worse, for good.

I lay down and began to fantasize that Janie and I were still intended to be as one, contemplating also the inevitable return of Blondie, the wearer of the wig beneath my bed. I was just at the nice bit of a slumber, wherein Janie had burst into my room for the dual purposes of professing sorrow at having rejected me so and, while she was about it, making mad passionate love, when I heard voices raised in anger outside of my bedroom door. They were Irish voices. Wrong side of Dublin, I reckoned. Next, bursting into my room came, not Janie and all her expressions of regret and wanting, but a couple of navvies. They were snarling and cussing and generally going hammer and tong at one another.

Now don't get me wrong here. I have no axe to grind with the

Irish. Indeed, a more amenable bunch you could not find. But even I draw the line at a pair of boozed-up Gaelics gambolling about my billet at midnight. Well, as they bounced from one wall to another, crashed to the floor, got up, bounced about again and fell down again, I scampered under the bed.

It went on for ages and, praises, when the cavalry arrived. It came in the unlikely form of the sleazy guy who had ridded me of my seventy quid. He was evidently on first name terms with the drunken combatants and calmed them down in no time at all with a "what would your mother be thinking" here and a "shame on your whole family" there. Peeping out from between the stilettos and blonde wig, it was a remarkable sight to behold. They'd been gouging each other's eyes out one minute and in the next they were hugging and back-slapping. That's the Irish for you.

After they were gone, I extracted myself from beneath the bed and decided to take a constitutional. Besides which, I had yet to attend to my ablutions. Previous attempts in that department had, of course, met with failure when all that I had succeeded in doing was flooding the room below. I went in the direction of the tube station where, in someone's front garden, I was glad to relieve myself among the narcissi. My actions did not meet with the approval of the householder, who was watching all along. So, under threat of the law being called, I made my way back to the billet.

I felt my way along the darkened corridor and, on opening the bedroom door, flicked the light switch. Nothing happened. I flicked the switch for a second time and then a third. In total blackness, except for some occasional flashing of light from a distant neon sign, I therefore began to disrobe. And what an irksome exercise that proved to be. I crashed and banged about as I hopped from foot to foot removing my shoes and socks. I fell over twice, fetching off my trousers, one leg of which had insisted on wrapping itself around the bed.

Stark naked and feeling fair fagged; all I wanted to do was leap into the arms of Morpheus. Instead, I leapt into the arms of Blondie who, during my absence, had returned and slunk beneath the sheets. I at least had some idea how the three bears must have felt when they came home to find a squatter in their midst. But the flatulent addition to my boudoir was no Goldilocks. It was a six foot something merchant seaman who commonly went by the name of Doris.

And so, seventy quid the lighter, I made a hasty exit.

Now in those days, it was not too difficult for a homeless person such as me to find a perch for the night in Lincoln's Inn Fields. Nowadays, of course, there is too much hassle from the likes of investigative journalists and condescending politicians. Should your average down-and-out so much as hover by a park bench some ladle-bearing do-gooder will surely shove some chicken soup down his gullet.

In the vicinity of the cafeteria I, at any rate, found a delightful little tin table beneath which I could bivouac. But, whereas my fellow dossers were accustomed to visitations from members of the Inns of Court (it was quite the norm for students and barristers, even the odd judge, to stagger past and throw-up in the waste paper bins) I had the honor of being the first lawyer to take up residence. As such, I was eyed with much suspicion.

I fancy that my ingratiation into that exclusive community began when I made it known that I was privy to the finer points of homeless person legislation. It did not occur to my bretheren that how come I was such an expert if I was in the same boat as them. The same principle applies in prison where there's always some inmate who was once a solicitor and knows best. Knows best? He's banged-up for embezzlement and knows best?

Anyway, I was soon partaking in the passing about of a bottle and, whilst there was no way of knowing the pedigree, I was content in the knowledge that it could be no less harmful than the stuff lurking in the cellars of Gray's Inn.

Anyone who has suffered the indignity of sleeping rough will attest to the fact that one's biological clock adopts a propensity to go haywire. For that reason, and not by virtue of the methyl alcohol level swishing about my system, I did not stir until mid-morning. Even then, it took an alarm call in the form of a swift kick up the rump to get me to my feet. It was delivered by the cafe proprietor, a Cockney-sort of an individual, who intimated that I must either move along, make a purchase or, if neither of the two options were to my liking, await the arrival of the law.

I opted for the second choice and was soon perched at, as opposed to perched under, the little tin table where I merrily munched at buttered toast and slurped some coffee.

My companions from the night before were all gone, presumably to their respective shop doorways and underpasses. However, sitting at another table, separated from me by a bunch of pecking pigeons, was a group who could only have been law students. You see, there were seven. One was female and extremely attractive. The others were most definitely not females. They were rather like identical sextuplets, with short back and side hairdo's, buck teeth and spotty faces. They even wore near identical clothes of cordoroy trousers and chequered sports jackets. They had a leather briefcase apiece and each case was open and full to bursting point with law books. All were vying for the attention of the beauty. Neither one of them stood a chance. Yes; they were a bunch of law students, all right.

The little tin table did me proud. It bore the brunt of a fair amount of rainwater. But I have always considered it a bit slovenly to breakfast in ones bedroom and so I sidled over to where the students were.

"How do," I said. "Are you Bar students too?" knowing full well that they were.

"Dashed cheeky fellow," said the one who was nearest. He made a face at the female which I suppose he and his mates may have thought was grinning, though I would say it was more like gurning, and he carried on, "Come, Cwalaline. There are wuffians about. Let us make our way to Wincoln's Inn."

Caroline, all figure-hugging skirt and black stockings, unfolded her legs and, with one hand, she brushed a few golden strands from in front of her face. Then she got up and began to haughtily promenade across the lawns. She went towards Lincoln's Inn and was quickly followed by the sextuplets who, besides encircling her, persisted in looking over their shoulders at me. I remember thinking that the whole ensemble resembled a Happy short of a full Snow White and her dwarfs.

My origin being Dudsall, where the skin comes thick, I went in hot pursuit, though not before I returned to my own tin table where I finished off my drink and toast with gusto and grabbed the busted case.

When she was about half-way across the lawns, Caroline turned her pretty head. With a panic-stricken look about her porcelain face, she squeaked, "Oh, Jeremy! The vagrant fellow is behind us."

Jeremy was identifiable from the others only by his reaction to Caroline's whining. He was keen to put a plump, groping hand about her waist.

"I may not look it, but I'm a student too!" I said, "I am. Honestly I am!" The pace of the students quickened and, hampered by the need to clutch the busted case so tight to my chest, I found difficulty in keeping up. I gave up altogether when the others broke into a trot. "I've just remembered some shopping! See you later!" I called, as they sprinted away.

So I found a green-roofed public convenience where I was able to spruce-up. For the cost of two pints of beer, the attendant even agreed to take care of my case for a few hours. "I've got twenty feet of binder twine, governor. While you're gone I'll wrap it round your case a few times. That'll keep it nicely shut for you." And so, freshly scrubbed and brushed, I arrived at Lincoln's Inn Hall for The Lord Chancellor's address.

Every year, it was the practice of The Lord Chancellor to give a pep talk to the new students. He is, or was, the literal "big wig," namely the head of all the judiciary. In those days, it was he who laid down many of the rules that affected the public, such as the availability of legal aid. Appointments to the House of Lords, the Court of Appeal and to the offices of Lord Chief Justice and President of the Family Division were made only after consultation with him. He was also a member of the cabinet and the only Law Lord who was not obliged to abstain from politically controversial debate. He sat as a judge in the highest appellate court in the land, namely The House of Lords.

Blimey, and they told us that any suggestion of scope for political patronage and bias was scurrilous.

I arrived at Lincoln's Inn Hall and was surprised to find that it was much smaller than the one at Gray's. There were not many seats either and so, while the going was good, I nabbed a place at the very front. It was not every day that the likes of Izaak Gatehouse would find himself within spitting distance of a real live Lord Chancellor.

As the minute hand on the big clock above ticked along, I began to wonder why it was just me and a cleaning lady who had thus far bothered to turned up. When, for the umpteenth time, I had lifted my feet clear of a thrusting mop I enquired of the cleaner whether The Lord Chancellor was running late.

"Gawd blimey," she said, almost swallowing the lit fag hanging from her lower lip, "this is the old hall, this is dear. You wanta be in New Hall. It's just over on . . ." She broke off as I leaped to my feet, cursed and bolted for the exit. ". . . the other side of the square," she continued as I slammed the door behind me.

The new hall to which the cleaner alluded was an altogether different affair in terms of size of building and size of occupancy. The place was packed out with dozens and dozens of law students and every one of them turned towards the back of the room as I blustered in.

"Silence!" barked one of the servants. He wore a smart navy blue uniform.

I tiptoed down a central aisle and, as I did so, I looked left and right in search of an empty seat. I instinctively walked with a stoop, almost as if it was to be assumed that with reduced height I must surely go unnoticed. I naturally did not go unnoticed and, indeed, this was to the extent that The Lord Chancellor himself, who was stood behind a lectern, halted his speech and gave me a look as if say that he wished he could still hand down the death penalty.

I withered and dithered, up and down, as I went about my search, conscious of a deafening silence. I tried to muscle-in on a particular row of seats which contained the beautiful Caroline and two thirds of her following. They were having none of it, however.

Presently, the silence was broken by The Lord Chancellor, no less. "Over there," and he nodded to his left.

"Aye?"

"Over there," and he nodded, once more, to his left. "There is a spare place over there."

"Oh. Right. Cheers." I said.

I'm certain that my words were not the correct form of address; indeed I was perhaps in contempt. But, I think he got the message.

I shuffled along the row and each and every student who I passed was obliged to stand. The head of the judiciary had unfortunately selected a seat that was at the end, next to the wall.

"This is like being at the dashed cinema," carped someone, as I went by. Mind you, he stopped carping after I'd trod on his brogues and that's the truth.

After, I'd settled in, The Lord Chancellor (I shall henceforth refer to him as The LC) intimated to us all that, if it was not too much trouble, he would start up again. And that's what The LC did. He told us how he got about town by pushbike; how he'd chucked-in his title to go into politics, only to get another one after becoming The LC. That one got a laugh. It is an indisputable fact of life that any witticism coming from a judge be it good, bad or downright pathetic is guaranteed to bring the house down. The LC loved it, so much so, that he joined in all of the merriment and he did so with a wheezing sort of a noise that sounded more like a death rattle than a giggle.

The LC got serious when he told us that politics was a dirty old business. Heaven knows how long it had taken him to work that one out. Either way, he was dead happy to return to the apparently good and honorable life at the Bar.

At around this stage, some form of attention-deficit disorder kicked in and I became altogether more interested in the aeroplanes flying past the big high windows. The portraits were pretty impressive too, but not so a row of hunting trophies. Stags heads they were and, according to their brass plaques, they had generally been shot by the likes of Captain James Farquharson-Jones in Glen Coe or some such place, in 1911 or some such time. The biggest of the stags seemed to be staring at me in a manner that I found most menacing. It was as if he knew me. And then it dawned that we had, indeed, made each other's acquaintance. His plaque read: Ian Prospect. 1980. Prestwick.

CHAPTER SIX

At the conclusion of The LC's address, I left Lincoln's Inn and headed straight up to The Council.

The Council, I discovered, was equipped with just about everything that a student, such as I, could wish for.

The gentlemen's lavatory, for example, had plenty of hot and cold water on tap. Every day a caretaker checked and, if necessary, changed the soap and towels. The wall mirror was well lit and ideal for wet shaving on account of it.

The Council also had an impressive lecture room, but more about the lavatory. The toilet rolls were made of soft tissue and not that unmerciful government-issue stuff. The general decor was of a pleasing pastel green; a tad shabby but, on the whole, acceptable. On the backs of doors, I found the customary graffiti of a pornographic kind. However, this being a school for barristers, the author had at least shown breeding by his use of a fountain pen. His intellect was up there too, as evidenced by the intermingling of Latin and Anglo Saxon.

All in all, I figured that the facilities at The Council were so good that I resolved there and then that each morning, before the arrival of other students, I could nip in, douse down and change into respectable clothing.

Following a swift cup of coffee in the common room, I went along to the main lecture room where I was scheduled to listen to an address from a Home Office Pathologist. This was all part of the practical and forensic side to the training course.

The pathologist was a man of some eminence. He had a crack at breaking the ice with a selection of gruesome gags and anecdotes, each one of which was pretty well rehearsed. But they all hit the dust. His gallows humor may have gone down well with the minions in the mortuary but this fellow had failed to take into consideration that his audience, on this occasion, consisted of a bunch of insipid law students. The one about necrophilia in the workplace was especially unfortunate because, at that point, one of my co-students got to his feet, shouted abuse, burst into tears and rushed out. It transpired that his granny was dead that very day.

Undeterred, the pathologist ploughed on. Having done with the wise-cracks, he went on to explain that, as an expert witness in court, he was to be looked upon as independent; he was there to assist the court and not the party who had called him to give evidence in the first place. Next, we were told that what would follow was not for persons of a nervous or delicate disposition. However, there had already appeared on a big silver screen behind him the image of a male, Caucasian, mid-thirties and very definitely dead. Stripped of all dignity, the corpse looked to have landed on the mortician's slab from a great height.

"He didn't see that one coming," the learned one said cheerfully, as he referred to an apparent knife wound to the chest, "but I think he got the point," he added, mischievously.

A dozen or more students made a bolt for the exit. Every jack one of them looked as white as the cadaver on the screen. At least a half were holding one hand across their mouths and making the sort of noises that made me glad I'd not swallowed food for a while. Undeterred, the lecturer made a comment that those who left were best suited to a career in the civil courts and on he went, only this time explaining that the knife wound was not a knife wound at all. It was apparently the point of entry where a high pressure water hose had been fired at the deceased from point blank range.

The next slide flashed up and half of the class got up and went the same way as the others. The image was that of the insides of the deceased. For the purposes of unobstructed access, his chest had been totally slit open just like an envelope. Over the sound of groaning, sighing, and trampling of feet, we were told that the force of water had been so strong as to turn every bodily organ to pulp. Death was instantaneous.

My own personal constitution weathered fair even during a selection of drowning cases. The poor unfortunates were bloated and, in some instances, worm-eaten. But I was in danger of being written off as a civil lawyer myself after the learned one showed us his selection of snuff videos. It was explained that snuff videos were intended to gratify only the most depraved of individuals. We were told how victims, for the most part vulnerable, were kidnapped and taken to secret locations. Torture, murder, and mayhem followed, all of which was filmed for the gratification of those creatures in our society who masquerade as human. The slide show lingered around a wretch who had been disembowelled alive.

"Sometimes, the films fall into the hands of the police," said the learned one. His words were, of course, before the days of the internet. "It is my job," he went on, "to advise whether murder has been committed." Up popped the next slide, which was a close up of entrails. "In this case, I was satisfied that there had been a hoax. These things," he pointed at the entrails, "are from a pig."

At the end of the lecture those of us who were still left clapped politely. The learned one thanked us but, before leaving the rostrum, he announced that he had a message from the Dean. Each one of us was required to attend the reception where timetables for the whole of the term would be distributed.

Feeling distinctly nauseous and contemplating a career at the Civil Bar I trundled-off to reception. There, I found an exceedingly prudish-looking woman handing out pieces of A4 paper. On being requested so to do, I duly identified myself whereupon she gave me the once-over through her thick-rimmed spectacles. Next, in addition to a timetable sheet, I found myself presented with a brown envelope.

Now there is always something foreboding about brown envelopes. It is probably something to do with the fact that the things are invariably guilty of wanging about tax demands, summonses and so forth on an indiscriminate basis. I tore open the top and, true to form, this was just another manila-wrapped mugging. It took the form of a letter from the Dean who requested, or rather insisted, that I attend upon him first thing the following day and explain why my course fees were overdue. Apparently, correspondence forwarded to my last known address had been returned marked "not known, try Brian Smith."

Under normal circumstances, I might have found this latest obstacle to my intended barrister-hood disconcerting. Strangely, I felt philosophical about the whole thing. I could cope with being hungry, homeless and stone broke. But it was the loss of Janie, before I had even won her, which got to me. If my destiny was to never again gaze on her beauty; if never again could I laugh with her, argue with her, so that her chest and swan-like neck went crimson with passion, I figured that the Dean might as well do his very worst. So, on the basis that the morning held no fears for me, I decided that I might as well get a good night's sleep.

I awoke next morning to a tumultuous roaring in my ears. One could have been forgiven for assuming that an express train had gone through my bedroom. In fact, one just had. To be exact, it was the intercity from up north. You see, such was the drop in temperature the night before that even the pigeons had quit Lincoln's Inn Fields. I had followed them on foot to the railway station where a row of plastic bucket seats became my bed.

My sleep on the concourse was an unsatisfactory affair. Three times, I was interrupted by the railway police. Three times, I was asked for identification in the form of my driver's license. Three times, I said that I was not a loiterer and was simply waiting for a friend who was on the train from Inverness.

Following so restless a slumber, it would have been nice to have had a lay-in. Fat chance, once the first herd of commuters came crashing by.

As the bowler-hat wearing, brolly-wielding straphangers filed past, I gathered together my worldly goods and shoved them in my share of the marital assets, namely the red suitcase. Next, I set off for the exit whereupon, to my surprise and to his horror, Henry Sunderland and I spied each other. He was kitted-out in morning attire and was plainly bound for one of the London courts, most probably The Court of Appeal. By his side was a pinstripe-suited individual who could only have been a solicitor.

Now, as any barrister will confirm, solicitors are the most loathsome of creatures. However, it is unfortunately the case that they are a necessary evil in that they dole out the briefs. As such it is custom to buy these persons drinks and meals and even talk nice to them. Henry was obviously doing his bit by travelling down with his instructing solicitor. Poor Henry. Boring tripe in his ear on the way down, boring tripe in his other ear on the way home, interspersed only by boring and irrelevant tripe in both ears midway through closing submissions, no doubt. Believe me, there is nothing more irksome and off-putting than the constant tugging of one's gown, quickly followed by the whispering of twaddle, just at the important bit.

It was nevertheless important for Henry to keep up appearances. That is probably why his face went ashen on the realization that the prospective barrister to whom he had imparted Inn's of Court etiquette and the unkempt vagabond waving wildly, betwixt gent's toilet and smutty book stand, was, in fact, one and the same person. Henry had a go at averting a parley by knocking his solicitor off course and steering both his self and the solicitor towards a side exit. But I was having none of that and steered off course and all. I would have caught hold of them too, by the drinks machine on my reckoning, had a railway policeman not chosen that very moment to drag me off. As luck would have it, the officer had done his detective work and found that there was no train due in from Inverness. It therefore followed that I should have my collar felt since I could not possibly be going about my lawful purpose.

In the closed confines of the little police office I was quizzed as to my movements and, not for the first time, stood witness to my only asset being rummaged. I write of a time when there were troubles in Ireland. The troubles had spilled over to the mainland and it followed that anyone going around looking vaguely Gaelic was liable to be arrested for being Irish with intent. I was saved from incarceration without trial solely by an intervention which took the form of a dog handler and his intrusive hound. You see, when the overly excited Alsatian had gotten hold of my only clean pair of Y-fronts and had shaken them like a rat and then tossed them in a corner, I had concluded that enough was enough and I protested in my very best Dudsall way. Thereupon, the dog handler informed my arresting officer that it was Black Country I was talking in and not Blarney. He also imparted the fact that Inverness always used to be in Scotland and, to his understanding it still was, barring some miraculous move across The Irish Sea under cover of darkness. So, in lieu of internment, I was duly released.

Later that same day, I was due to attend my second dinner at Gray's Inn. But this was subject to the proviso that, in the interim, the Dean did not kick me off the course. Not a morsel of food had passed my lips for twenty-four hours, at least. My funds were dangerously low and instinct told me that what little I did have should be put away for a rainy day. It would be a long time till dinner if, indeed, there was to be any dinner at all. In my estimation, the rainy day had already arrived. And besides, it would have been ridiculous for the Dean and me to compete with my stomach rumblings whilst having our chitchat. I therefore reasoned that a breakfast of modest sorts might be entirely appropriate.

Now then. Up near Dudsall in those days the cafes of a greasy spoon variety were strictly the preserve of the workers and the odd former schoolmate who tended to choke to death on a sausage after one too many Tiptbury and Dudsall's finest mild ales. At least a bloke knew where he stood. Not so in the metropolis, however, especially around the law courts. There, it was perfectly normal for executive and lawyer-types to have their bacon sandwiches while cosseted up with the ordinary man. It may have been something to do with the fact that most of the establishments were Italian owned and operated. You know the score. A cry and a sigh like he's just performed a life-saving brain operation. Eye contact like he wants to shag you rigid. And all he's done is slap a banger onto a slice of bloomer with brown sauce. You hand over the cash; sit at a grotty table all dreamy-eyed. You look out the window and realize that's no Rialto up above. It's the Holborn Viaduct.

Well, the one that I wandered into was no exception to the general rule.

Having gone through all of the palaver as aforesaid, paid-up and looked big about it, I sat with my measly fare over in the window seat. Opposite, there was a distinguished looking geezer who could easily have been an ex-military type. He must have been in his sixties. His hair, slightly thinning, was slicked back. He sported long sideburns and an enormous handlebar moustache.

I gawked across the table and compared his full-house English breakfast with my round of toast and a sausage. The geezer's plate was positively groaning under the weight of mushrooms, bacon, two eggs, over easy. I'd swear he even had a slice of black pudding lurking on the side. He glanced up. Our eyes met momentarily and I swiftly turned away.

The geezer carried on eating and I returned my gaze upon him. He prodded at the eggs and, blow me, they were only resting on a pile of sautéed potatoes. He pierced one of the little beauties and transported his dining fork to moustache level. The geezer parted his lips only then to stop, look a little surprised and he returned the fork, with morsel intact, to his plate. Lubricated, no doubt by a bit of runny egg yolk, the potato proceeded to slip off the fork prongs and found a bit of crispy bacon to cuddle-up with.

I was just beginning to think that the little potato was giving me the evil eye when I realized that it was, in fact, the geezer who was so doing. I gave him the evil eye back, I can tell you. I was having none of that sort of thing. In a thrice, the geezer unhooked his stare and a Mexican standoff was thereby averted. He nodded, stood up, and walked out of the cafe.

Well, that taught him a lesson and to the victor the spoils and all that stuff. Quick as a flash, I swapped his plate for mine and got stuck-in. Never had a meal tasted so fine. I was so starving hungry that in no time at all the plate was almost empty. I was even tempted to have a go at the black pudding. Ruminating on that conundrum, I was quite oblivious to all of the comings and goings in the cafe. That is until I heard a cough and looked up to see who had now taken the seat opposite. It was only the geezer, who had come back from fetching his newspaper.

I don't mind telling you that the geezer looked horror stricken. And who could blame him? What I'd done was deserving of a punch in the face where I came from. But all he did was drop his lower jaw and stare. He may have been up for black pudding but, at heart, the geezer was plainly a Home Counties man. By way of contrition, I shoved what was left of his breakfast across the table. He was having none of it. I knew that sort, all right. Always carry a grudge, they do.

It was up to him. As for me, it was time to move on; closure, as they say. So, I reached across to recover my own, paltry, breakfast. But, thereupon the geezer only went and opened-up his broadsheet and he used it to envelope my plate.

I sat staring at the wall of newsprint before me and imagined that, at any moment, the geezer would snap, emerge from behind his newspaper and seize me by the throat. As a precautionary measure, I began to eye-up objects within arm's-length that could act as blunt instruments should the need arise. The brown sauce bottle was nearest. However, my own personal favourite happened to be the condiment set. It afforded an attackee, such as me, two chances, namely to chuck pepper in the assailants eyes and, if that didn't work, deck him with the salt pot. But the condiments were on the far side. Unless I took preemptory action, I would never have reached the things in time. And making the first move could easily ruin a chap's chance of running self-defense before the local magistrates. So, there was no option; the brown sauce it had to be.

After a moment or two's silence, the newspaper twitched a bit. Then I heard a chink of teacup on saucer which was followed by a slurp. The geezer plainly intended to wet his whistle before letting me have it. I made a move for the condiments. Self-defense or no self-defense; I figured I could always make out I'd had an aberration or a seizure or something or anything, in fact.

I was about to sling a handful of white pepper his way when I heard a crunching noise. I sat back. Out gunned, out manoeuvred. The geezer had got me back, good and proper, no word of a lie. The devil was at my toast.

I figured that I might just as well finish off the geezer's breakfast. So I did. The geezer, meanwhile, crunched away and, when all the crunches were done with, he folded his newspaper flat. Then, he took the teacup to his lips, eyeing me as he did so, and he gulped till the contents were drained.

The geezer coughed and got up. I closed my eyes and flinched as his right hand came straight at me. But there came no battering, just a wafting sort of a breeze. I opened my eyes only to see that the geezer was offering me his broadsheet.

"Thank you very much," I said, taking the newspaper from his hand.

"Don't mention it," said the geezer, snappily and, without as much as a by your leave, he marched out and slammed the cafe door. Bloody rude!

CHAPTER SEVEN

As was instructed, I arrived promptly at The Council. However, by way of prelude to the dressing down by the Dean, I made a beeline for the lavatories where I unwrapped the exceedingly long bit of twine from around my case. Next, I washed and shaved and bolted myself in a cubicle where I changed the clothes of a vagabond for those of a prospective barrister. It was an expertly carried out manoeuvre, I can tell you. I reckon that I demonstrated the skill and timing and all round panache of a Formula One racing team going about a tire change. While in there, I heard the cleaner giving an almighty cry and he cussed to himself that he wished he could get his hands on whomsoever it was that had blocked his sparkling washbasin with bristles.

When the coast was clear, I unbolted the door and, clutching the little red case, neatly parcelled up with the string again, I zoomed off in search of the Dean's office. I found a little cupboard on the way. It was under the stairs. It was not locked and therefore dead handy as a hiding place for my solitary asset and contents.

I came across the Dean's office on the first floor. Outside of the office, lined-up against the wall, were a collection of chairs. One of them, the nearest to the door, was occupied by a fellow student who sported a smart, black dining suit and a hangdog expression. He had a sallow complexion which, under a spiky blonde hairdo, was entirely within keeping.

"Morning," said the student, grumpily. His voice was deep and he spoke with no toff accent, a rarity in that environment. "Suppose you're for the chop too."

"I think I probably am," I said and I plonked myself in the adjoining chair.

"I'm Paul," said the student and he extended his hand, "almost Mr. Paul Black, barrister-at-law of Gray's Inn, but fell at the first hurdle."

I shook Paul firmly by the hand and introduced myself.

Someone's head popped out from behind the door. It was the Dean's secretary, you know, her with the spectacles.

"The Dean should be with you presently," she said, and then her head popped back in again.

"I don't like this, Paul," I said, shaking my head. "I don't think my fees have been paid. I thought I'd get a grant, or somutt."

"Snap," said Paul, "except that in my case, Izzy . . ."

"You what?"

"I said Izzy. You know, Izaak-Izzy. Good, aye?"

"Oh, right."

"Well, Izzy," Paul carried on, "my old man is self-made."

"Nowt wrong in that." I said, as if I knew or cared.

"Except that the old sod thinks I should make it on my own too. And the problem is that I can't get a grant. Dad's income is far too high. And he won't give me a dime."

"I'm sorry to hear that, Paul. Have you tried . . . ?"

I was cut off by the door opening and the secretary's head popping back out.

"Mr. Black. Mr. Gatehouse. Dean will see you now."

"Good morning, sir," said Paul, woefully. We had gone in together but he took the lead through an outer office and into the Dean's inner sanctum.

The Dean sat scribbling away at a large desk of oak. He appeared to be absorbed in whatever it was he was writing and he didn't bother to give us a glance.

I coughed and also said, "Good morning, sir."

The Dean raised his head. I could tell in an instant that he was in his sixties. His hair, slightly thinning, was slicked-back. He sported long sideburns and an enormous handlebar moustache. I grant that the Dean was distinguished looking and probably ex-military. But, Dean or no Dean, this was the devil who'd snaffled my toast!

"Which one of you is Gatehouse?" asked the Dean. He sounded very grumpy and rather matter-of-fact. You'd have thought he'd missed breakfast, or something.

"I am, sir."

"Well, somehow, I'm not surprised."

"And, sir, can I offer my apologies for any misunderstanding, only . . ."

"No misunderstanding from where I was sitting, Mr. Gatehouse," interrupted the Dean, "or is it Mr. Smith?" He picked-up an envelope from his desk and held it aloft. "Ah, yes," he said, waving the thing about, "Brian Smith, late of The Canal View Private Hotel."

"I apologise for my conduct earlier, it's just that . . ."

"My office has been in touch with your local education authority. It would appear that papers in respect of a grant were returned undelivered. The authority was referred to one Mr. Brian Smith." The Dean looked at the writing on the envelope. "All very strange, to my mind," he murmured.

"How very strange," I said. And it was very strange, I don't mind telling you. He was referring to the last but one guest house where I'd stayed, up in Dudsall. The Canal View was not the one that Janie had gone to; she had been to Hill Top B&B. I was one Jerry Jones when I'd stayed at Canal View so how come they'd cottoned on to Brian Smith? Like we'd both acknowledged, it was all very strange. "How very strange," I said again.

The Dean tweaked his moustache a bit and then sat back in his chair. "A new application form is on its way. On arrival, it will be placed in the appropriate pigeonhole downstairs. I am assured that if, on this occasion, you take the trouble to complete and return the thing your grant, including payment of course fees, will be processed."

"Yes, sir. Thank you, sir."

"And now, Mr. Black, do you have any objection to discussing your position in the presence of Mr. Smith."

"Gatehouse," I cut in.

"Oh really," said the Dean, disinterested.

"You can say anything in the presence of Brian," said Paul.

"Izaak," I said, cutting in again.

"Yeh, Izzy, Izaak,"

The Dean sat forward and hoisted himself up. He went over to one of the sash windows and, in the process Paul, who had hitherto stood casually with one hand in his pocket, was obliged to nip to one side. The Dean stood for a few moments gazing down at the nearby lawns

80

of Gray's Inn. Then he tweaked his moustache again and turned to address, a now rather peaky-looking, Paul.

"I am aware of your apparent personal circumstances, Mr. Black. Have you made enquiries about the possibility of a loan?"

"No, sir."

"No, sir," mimicked the Dean unkindly. "Then it's just as well that I have. Your local authority operates a scheme and the application forms are on the way. You will find the damned things in the pigeonhole too."

The Dean motored towards the door and, this time, both of us had to nip to one side. He ushered us out with a nod of his head.

"Thank you, Dean," I said, as I sidled past.

"Thank you," said Paul, as he slouched by.

"I shall expect your financial affairs to be addressed promptly," said the Dean. "If either of you experience complications kindly contact my office without delay. Good day to you both."

Paul and I went sheepishly down the corridor. After a few paces, we breathed a sigh of relief and were about to offer each other our hearty congratulation when the Dean called out.

"Gatehouse, Smith, or whatever your name is! Come back here!"

Paul shrugged his shoulders. "Bad luck Izzy."

I about turned and saw that the Dean was stood in the corridor. As I approached, he thrust one hand in his trouser pocket and produced a role of bank notes. In those days the possession of a large wedge was stylish and not, as it is today, an apparent sign of terrorist or criminal activity. The Dean counted out fifty.

"Here," he said, handing over the notes, "you can repay me when the grant comes through. Spend it wisely."

"I certainly will, sir," I said. "And, sir," I added, "I don't know what to say."

"Neither did I at breakfast. When one next visits Gino's, one would prefer not to have one's provender pilfered. It's simply not cricket, Gatehouse. Good day."

And, with that, the Dean went back inside and slammed the door behind him. Bloody rude!

"What was all that about?" said Paul, on my return. "And what's with the Brian Smith, Izzy?"

"It's a long story, Paul. I'll tell you all about it over coffee." Then

I gleefully rubbed the bank notes between my fingers. "Tell you what," I added, after a brief pause, "let's go to the pub instead. Fancy a trip down Mexico way?"

CHAPTER EIGHT

"It sounds as if you're an old hand at it," said Paul. "Perhaps I can sit next to you for my first dinner? The whole thing sounds very dubious to me, especially the Mr. Junior nonsense."

I curtailed fiddling around with my salt-frosted glass and, with customary misplaced authority, said, "My pleasure, Paul. Be my guest."

"I'll tell you what, Izzy . . ." Paul broke off momentarily as he took a swig from his own glass. He grimaced, slammed the thing down, making an almighty racket, declared, "I can take most things, Izzy, but tequila sunrise at actual sunrise is going too far," and he carried-on, "I'll tell you something for nothing, Izzy. If one of those toff types decides to challenge me." With another swig, he finished his tipple and grimaced, once more. "I shall, I shall . . . Well, I don't really know what I shall do." He again slammed the glass, only this time, with sufficient force to topple the table, sending my glass and a fully laden ashtray flying. "Do you fancy a double for the road, Izzy?"

"Come on, Paul. It's time for our lecture."

And little did I know that, when it came to being challenged at dinner at Gray's Inn, Paul would instinctively know what he should do. But first, there was our lecture. It was a lecture on the law of evidence.

The lecturer was an Oxbridge don, semi-retired, I think. His academic credentials were apparently second to none but this miserable, moon-faced individual delivered his address in a dull monotone. There was no spontaneity, ad-libbing, or so on. He simply read from notes (very possibly his own textbook on the subject) and barely took time to draw breath. Had the don, at any stage, bothered to drag his face from the tomes it might very well have occurred to him

83

that he was succeeding only in lulling the entire audience to sleep. "Testimony," he droned, "is the statement of a man; indeed a man or woman or, for that matter, certain competent children. It is offered as evidence of the truth of that which is stated."

Paul, who was seated next to me, had fought a gallant fight against slipping into a coma. He suddenly slammed shut his book with a bang that reverberated around the entire auditorium. The don actually looked up. It was only momentarily but was sufficiently long to enable him to caste an icy-steely stare straight in Paul's direction. To my mind, the old codger ought to have been grateful for the mighty bang had dragged half his audience back from the dead.

Paul turned his wearisome head in my direction. His blonde locks were all akimbo where he'd been rubbing, presumably in frustration or boredom or both. "What this silly old sod means to say is that witnesses are the ones who give evidence. Tell you what, Izzy. I can't take this for much longer."

Seemingly oblivious, even though Paul's voice had reverberated like the closing of the book or, indeed, the slamming of a liquor glass the don ploughed-on. "In general, a witness may only give evidence of matters which he, or indeed she, has perceived with one of the five senses of man, or indeed, woman."

Noisily, Paul scooped-up his books and papers. "That's it then now then! I've had enough of this twaddle! I'll see you tonight, Izzy!" And, with that, Paul, with an ear-piercing screech, dragged his chair across the floor and stood-up. As he stomped out there was absolutely no let-up in all of the don's droning.

I managed to stay the course (just) although all that droning, combined with the aftershock of Paul's "double for the road," did send me into an involuntary siesta somewhere around the don's revelation that an evidentiary fact can be an independent item of evidence because the witness's assertion may be perfectly true and yet the inference from the fact asserted to the fact in issue may be incorrect. In short, I nodded off when he got to the bit on circumstantial evidence.

I departed the auditorium feeling rather crestfallen. Other than having picked up a few handy tips on transcendental meditation, plus the odd practical pointer such as not mixing law lectures with tequilas, I had learned not a thing. I therefore resolved that, in future, I would nip into the lecture solely for the purpose of registration and then nip out through the fire exit with a view to boning up on the subject in the altogether more convivial surroundings of the pub. In the event, everything clicked upon the realization that evidence is nothing at all about the truth. It's only about a bunch of lawyers theorising on whether something or other is admissible in a court of law.

Later that day, I sauntered around to the Gray's Inn common room. There I met with Paul who was sprawled in one of the armchairs, reading one of the more colorful tabloids.

"There was no way I was going to sit through that lot, Izzy." He sounded, per normal, grumpy and his expression, per normal, was hangdog. "Come on; let's get down to the pub." He rolled-up the newspaper and slung it in the general direction of the nearest coffee table. He missed, and the thing unfurled and came to rest right where some unfortunate was likely to slip on it. He rubbed at his spiky hairdo. "There are far too many lawyer-types around here."

"I wouldn't disagree with that, Paul."

"Will you say that again, Izzy?" He had plainly failed to hear me above the yelping of some unfortunate who had come to grief and was carping on about the dangers of reading matter being strewn about. "I said say that again, will you?"

So, I said it again, only a bit louder.

"Good, well that's settled then, Izzy. My brother may be down the road tonight. He's an accountant, you know. Come on, it's too damned noisy in here with all that hollering going on."

There was hollering going on in the pub and all. It was audible even before we left the precincts of Gray's Inn. I went in front and held the frosted glass door ajar for my companion. I did so to the noise of shattering glass and to squeaks, coming from the ladies who were present.

"That's my brother, over there," said Paul. He pointed at the very core of the mêlée that was going on. A sports-jacketed individual, with spiky blonde hair, not dissimilar to Paul's, was exchanging very unpleasant conversation with a charcoal-suited individual who was weedy and much tinier in stature. The sports jacketed one had seized the tiny one by his throat and was lifting him clean off the floor. It looked a very dangerous thing to be doing but at least it meant that the chitchat was eye to eye, nose to nose. "I'm afraid that John sometimes has trouble holding his drink. Come on, Izzy." Paul tutted. "Let's sort out the idiot."

We duly crossed to where John was grappling. The tiny fellow, by this stage, had a very reddened and puffed-up look about his face. His contorted features were not dissimilar to those of the clients of that pathologist from the previous day and I was worried on account of it. "Come now, sir," or something similar, he appeared to be croaking, "violence is not called for."

"Go on you twerp! Admit it!" growled John. "Admit that you're a solicitor!" He looked and sounded menacing. Then Paul tapped his brother on the shoulder. John reacted by dropping the little fellow and he aggressively swung around. However, on the realization that it was nowt but his sibling, John's entire demeanour changed. "Why, hallo, bruv. How you keeping?" he said, pleasantly and softly. The little fellow, meanwhile, was quick to seize the opportunity. His feet had hit the floor running and he nimbly ducked beneath John's outstretched elbow and, straightening his jacket, he scurried towards the exit. "Who's this with you then, mate?"

"John, meet Izaak. Izaak, meet John."

I went to shake hands but checked myself, ever so slightly, as John half-growled, "You're not a solicitor too, are you? Only you look like a solicitor and I don't like solicitors, I don't."

Paul tugged me to one side. "He's had a bad experience with a solicitor."

"Well, you don't say."

Paul continued, "Him and his girlfriend have just bought a property up in Docklands, where all that new development is going on. Trouble is, they forgot to ask their solicitor for a quote and now they've been landed with a huge great bill."

"Well, tell him to insist on a fair remuneration certificate from The Law Society," I said. "Insist on a fair remuneration certificate from The Law Society!" I again said, only this time for John's benefit.

"A what certificate?" John pulled me back over. I have to say that he had a glazed look about his eyes that I did not like one tiny jot.

"Mind the cloth, mind the cloth," I said, removing John's grasping paw from the sleeve of my jacket. "All you have to do is insist that the solicitors have the bill assessed by their professional body. It's quick, simple and fair and is a far better alternative than beating up every solicitor in sight. And, as it happens," I added, by way of double indemnity, "I'm not myself a solicitor." I put my hand to my mouth, coughed slightly and mumbled, "Thank God, I ain't one."

Paul pulled me back over, again. "Do you see the glazed look about him, Izzy? It's always a sign that he's had one too many." He placed an arm about my shoulder and guided me towards the bar. "Just making out we're on our way to order a drink," he said. "We don't want John to think he's being talked about."

"I like you, I do!" called John. His limbs had gone all wobbly-like and I swear that he was about to collapse.

"Who does he like, Paul?"

"You, of course, Izzy."

"Yes! You, of course!" said John. Then, he also took a hand to his mouth. He also feigned a cough and he also mumbled. It was something along the lines that I was either hard of hearing, dense, or, both

I found that it was me in the chair and so I shelled out for three beers. Paul downed his before mine and John's was even pulled.

"That was good. I needed that," said Paul, wiping a jacket sleeve across his mouth. A sort of a glazed look appeared. "Think I'll have another," and, with that, he grappled a half-drawn glass from out of the very hands of the bartender.

John motored over and wrestled the half-full glass from Paul. He succeeded only in rendering the glass one quarter full by soaking my trousers with the rest. It was no way to treat best bitter. "Watch out," he said, grabbing me by the collar. He did so with the hand that held the glass and the consequence was that the quarter was reunited with the other quarter which had already made my nether regions its home for the night. "Be very wary of Paul when he has that glazed look. It's a sure sign of trouble."

"Thanks for the tip; I'll bear that in mind."

Next, John began winging his empty glass around in mid-air and, at no one particular person, he shouted, "Come on then! Buy me a drink you tight-fisted miserable morons! I'll bet you're all a bunch of robbing solicitors!" With everyone else in close proximity looking away and, wisely avoiding eye contact, or indeed any form of contact, he refocused his attentions on me. "You sure you're not a bleeding solicitor?" He lost his footing and wheeling backwards, he ended up half sitting on a small table at which sat a middle-aged business man and a girl who was young enough to be his niece, who most definitely was not his actual niece, but who, at some cheap hotel, was destined to be described as his niece if she allowed him to ply her any more with the cheap white wine. "You sure you're not a bleeding solicitor?" John persisted.

"Come on, Izzy," said Paul. All this time he had remained passive, awaiting the drawing of the next pint. "I reckon we ought to high-tail it out of here before the law turns up."

I agreed that high-tailing it out of there was eminently sensible. We left to the sounds of more shattering glass, the man at the table protesting that he was not and had never been a solicitor and the girl shrieking that if the man was not a solicitor, and, moreover not a divorce solicitor, then what was he doing at a solicitors office taking down things about her and her marriage, most intimate.

From the relative sanctuary of Gray's Inn, Paul and I watched as a police car, all wailing sirens and flashing blue lights, screeched to a halt. Out jumped two hefty rozzers who, truncheons drawn, belted into the pub. We turned our backs and walked in the direction of the student's common room. Even from there, we could hear the shrieking of John, "This is wrongful arrest! I need a solicitor! Get me my solicitor!"

CHAPTER NINE

I was surprised that on this, the occasion of my second dinner, there were fewer students about. The elderly porter, as before, sat at his high desk. Business was so slack that he apparently had time to chat.

"Why, hallo there, Mr. Gatehouse. I've got your name down." In common with most servants of the Inn, he spoke East London. "Are you just dining with us or are you also keeping term?"

"Oh, keeping term," I said. "You have a good memory for names and faces, Mr. . . . .?"

"Smiff."

"You've a good memory, Mr. Smith."

"Just Smiff, Mr. Gatehouse, sir. And I ain't likely to forget your last visit, am I, sir?" He smiled, knowingly. "I may not say too much, Mr. Gatehouse, but I clock all the faces and I never miss a trick; and you and Mr. Prospect, the other week. Well, me and the other servants ain't stopped talkin' about it."

"Oh dear. Were we that obvious?"

"Obvious? Obvious, sir? I should say so." He craned his neck. "Best hurry along, sir. There's a bit of a queue forming."

So, I hurried along. Paul was next. He anxiously fingered the knot of his tie.

"Are you keeping term as well, Mr. Black, sir?"

"You what?"

"Yes, he is, Mr. Smith." I volunteered on Paul's behalf.

"Just Smiff, sir."

"Yes, he is," I volunteered once more, "he's keeping term, er, Smith." I took hold of Paul by the sleeve and I pulled him, ever so slightly. He came forward with a jerk. You see, Paul was still fingering

89

his blasted Windsor knot and hadn't expected the man-handling. Well, either that or his coordination was on the blink. "Keeping term just means that you're chalking-up a dinner."

"Careful, careful," said Paul, with a bit of an edge.

"Hurry along you fellows!" came a toff-like voice from behind.

Paul swung around to see what was what but I managed to swing him back, full circle. "Didn't like his tone, Izzy. Let me loose 'cause I want a word with Lord Muck, here."

"Come on, leave it out, Paul."

"Well, well, well," said the toff, haughtily, and he turned to his mates who were following-up the rear. "If it ain't the vagrant fellow."

"Cwikey! So it is!" came an excitable reply, "These vagwant chaps scwub up well."

Paul broke loose. "Why you pair of stuck-up little . . ."

"Are you keeping term with us tonight, Mr. Walsingham-Parker?" Mr. Smith's intervention was timely, coming as it did just as Paul, I swear, was about to strike. I got hold of Paul, this time by his robe, and reeled him back in. In the process, I was certain that I heard one or two stitches give up the ghost.

Above Paul's determined threats of, "I'll have him, Izzy. I will. I'll have him," I overheard Walsingham-Parker telling Mr. Smith, "Of course I'm keeping term, you fool. Do you think I'd come here to dine just for the fun of it?"

"Ever so sorry, Mr. Walsingham-Parker, sir," and Mr. Smith wrote the said name in his ledger.

I'll tell you what. Had my card not already have been marked, then never mind Paul, it would have been me "having" Walsingham-Parker. In my book, Mr. Smith had been subjected to tasteless intimidation for which there was no excuse.

Having stepped into the main hall, I set about telling Paul all about the layout; where the barristers sat, where the benchers sat and so on. I was about to get to the bit about the tail-end of the Spanish galleon when Walsingham-Parker and his chums came barging through.

"Out of the way, you fellows!"

"Yeth. Out of the way you fellows."

Having been very nearly knocked to the ground, Paul lunged, fists at the ready. "That's it now then, Izzy! He's getting it!"

David M. Golden

Fortunately for all, the head porter chose that very moment to, seemingly, appear from nowhere. Like a jack-in-the-box, he sprang-up between the squared-up twosome.

"I want this impudent wretch reported," said, a rather ruffled, Walsingham-Parker.

"Yeth, weported," came a voice which I am compelled to state, for the purpose of the record, emanated from a suitably safe distance.

Addressing the head porter for the very first time, Paul chose his words un-wisely. "You keep out of this, Horatio, unless you're looking for a knuckle sandwich too!"

Addressing Paul, for the very first time, the head porter gasped, "Imbecile!" and he proceeded to extricate Paul from around his left epaulette. Next, he manhandled Paul to where I was. As it happened, I wasn't too far from where Walsingham-Parker's chum had been keeping a low profile. "Is this another one of your drunken mates?" said the head porter, in a manner which I found altogether disagreeable.

"I swear he's only had a couple of pints."

"Then the tosspot can't take his drink!"

"Who are you calling a tosspot, Horatio? I'll have you, Horatio, if you don't watch it."

The head porter sort of threw Paul and demanded that we be seated. "Keep your mate's mouth shut and keep yourself out of any further trouble," he said. "Or else."

We found ourselves deposited with two female students and, thankfully, Walsingham-Parker and his ensemble were put on a far table. The girls appeared friendly enough. One took a note of our names in preparation for the toasting palaver. She was seated in the place designated for mess senior. Her friend, meanwhile, engaged us in conversation concerning the latest proposals of The Law Reform Commission. It was a sly thing to do for, as she entertained us and, as we began to lose the will to live, she was simultaneously filling her and her mate's sherry glass.

"What's all this?" said Paul presently, giving me a nudge which brought me round. "Tell you what, Izzy. If we don't do something, she's going to have the lot away."

And so, not one to be slow at coming forward in such situations, I did do something. I leaned across and grappled the decanter from her

91

hand. "It's your first dinner, isn't it?"

"Well, yes, actually it is."

"Thought as much." I nodded and smiled, in a knowing-condescending sort of a way. It was enough to make your average observer feel sick. I proceeded to fill my water goblet with the foul stuff. Then I leaned across and, one by one, returned the contents of their glasses to the decanter. "You won't mind me telling you then, that it is the tradition for us, older hands, to administer the sherry."

The girls exchanged hasty glances and, in unison, said, "Sorry."

Sweet.

Shoulders hunched, eyes more glazed, Paul waved his own goblet under my nose. "Well done, Izzy." He said it in a very authoritative, almost stylish manner. I poured him an entire glass, whereupon, in an un-authoritative way and with about as much style as that which lurks in the summer wardrobe of your average British male, those from Solihull in particular, he polished off the lot. "Fill her up," he demanded, wafting the empty glass before my nose.

The benchers arrived, grace was said (in Latin, naturally, although Paul swore that it was Spanish) and then the red wine was placed before us.

"Come to daddy," said Paul, whereupon he lifted the decanter to his mouth and the whole lot went down to where his sherry was.

The girls seemed a little startled. "But, but we now have no wine with which to toast," said the one who was not mess senior.

I graced them with another, vomit-inducing, smile. "Problem is you hadn't finished the sherry by the time the wine came around. That means you forfeit the lot." I paused to take a shufty in Paul's direction. Empty decanter in one hand, his other hanging limply, he was slumped forward, head almost touching the tabletop. "It's the tradition, you see," I carried on. "Mind you," I added, "swigging it straight down is a little unconventional. But I think that he was just making a point."

"But you took the sherry." It was she who was the mess senior chucking a spanner in the works this time.

"Ah, but you should have been quicker. It's tradition, you see."

"Sorry."

Sweet.

A merry waitress arrived with a salver of meat, swimming in grease. She placed the thing before us. "You seem to be 'avin a good time gents. Makes a change around these parts, I can tell you."

The waitress was then approached by one of her colleagues. She was laden with a tray of vegetables. The woman looked all of a fluster and I feared that at any moment she was liable to drop the lot. "E's gawn an done it again, e as."

"Who's done what again?" said our waitress.

Paul suddenly sat bolt upright. "Yes!" he said, loudly. "Who's done what again?"

The waitress appeared pleasantly surprised by Paul's enquiry and she bent down, slightly, and, in his ear, she explained, "It's that Mr. Walsingham-Parker, it is sir. Just like e did the time with Marjorie, e's picked on Rosy e as. In front of all is mates, it were. And now poor Rosy as run off cryin', she as."

Paul smacked the empty decanter on the table and, springing to his feet, he head-butted the vegetable tray clean out of the waitress's hands.

Dripping with broccoli, peas, sweet corn and just a tad of cauliflower cheese, Paul said, "Right! That really, really is it, now then! He's having it!"

"For crying-out loud, sit down!" I said, and I gave Paul's gown a sharp tug. I discovered that I was bang-on when, the last time I had given the thing a jerk, I thought I'd heard stitches go. Everyone, benchers included, had already broken off their respective chitchat to witness Paul's fandango with the florets. Consequently, the tearing in two of Paul's gown was audible throughout Hall.

For a moment, Paul stood dumbstruck. One-half of the gown flapped around his shoulder blades. The other half of the said garment had wrapped itself around the neck of she who was mess senior. In haste, I had flung the thing in her general direction. Presently, Paul stared down, in disbelief. "Now don't you start, Izzy!" he said, "I've enough on my plate with Walsingham thingy, over there!"

From where I sat, it seemed as if Paul's eyes had moved on from their glazed look stage. The things were, kind-of, rotating in their respective sockets. I figured that the condition could have come about as a result of the collision with the vegetable tray. On the other hand, was it the case that Paul's metabolism was such that even diminutive proportions of alcohol were prone to induce symptoms of anti-social behaviour? On the balance of probabilities, I concluded that the head porter had been right about Paul all along.

The tosspot couldn't take his drink.

A skirmish or worse, summary ejection (with all that that might entail), was averted by the waitress. "Cor blimey, love," she said, "I felt that bang meself." With a napkin, the waitress set about cleaning our dinner from off Paul. "After a nasty shock like that, I'll bet you could do with a nice drink. Tell you what, young gentleman, I'll go and refill yer jug."

At the prospect of downing another litre of Merlot, Paul's demeanour immediately changed for the better. "Why, thank you very much. Don't mind if I do," he said, pleasantly, and he resumed his place at table.

Thankfully, the prattle around Hall recommenced and, as the vestiges of the vegetables were mopped-up from the deck, we got stuck-in to the replenished wine stock. Pudding was prompt to arrive and we promptly demolished it. By the time of the arrival of port, Paul had resumed his slumped-over pose.

I swiped the port from under the very nose of our mess senior. "You can't have this," I said. "It's not permitted because you didn't finish the wine."

"But we didn't have any wine in the first place."

"Well, that's your fault because you didn't drink the sherry. Remember?"

"Sorry."

Sweet.

Following the traditional acknowledgment of Chef's culinary cock-up, the benchers toddled off, thank goodness, and Mr. Junior, poor devil, got up to do his stuff. He was a right proper Smart Alec and he acquitted himself well. Above all the catcalling, he came out with a string of witticisms, and in no time at all Mr. Senior was telling him things like, "Haven't you done well and, of course, you can smoke when you like, as much as you like." From all over the shop there came applause and he sat back down.

When all was quiet, Mr. Senior got up and told us that, following a respectable smoking intermission, due in no small part to Mr. Junior's sterling work, we would have a debate on the proposals of The Law Reform Commission. The girls could barely contain themselves, I can tell you.

"Taking part," boasted Mr. Senior "is my old and dear friend and our guest tonight, Mr. Edwin Warley-Hill."

A murmur of approval went all around. You see, Mr. Edwin Warley-Hill was a young and up-and-coming Member of Parliament. He held a junior ministerial position and yet he was only a kid. Even I'd heard of him. I was well impressed. Well, I was until Paul stuck his oar in. "That's my bloody M P," he slurred and, once again, he sat bolt upright and seemingly came around. "He's the one behind all these cutbacks in student grants, he is." Paul placed both his knuckles atop the table and, with remarkable recapture of his faculties, he majestically arose and addressed all of Hall thus. "This charlatan has the brass-neck to show his face round here, in front of all us students, and yet he's the one who wants all grants to be replaced by loans! I've been keeping my eye on him and his creepy-crawly, backstabbing ascent up the greasy pole!" Paul looked down at me momentarily. "I have, Izzy. I've been keeping an eye on him, I have." He resumed his address to Hall. "Mr. Senior, sir! I wish to challenge Mr. Edwin What's His Face, right here and now!"

There followed a swift conference between Mr. Edwin Warley-Hill M P on the one part and Mr. Senior on the other part. It was plain from all of the body language that Mr. Senior was telling Mr. Edwin Warley-Hill M P that he didn't have to do it if he didn't want to do it. But it was equally plain that The Honorable Member wanted to do it. So, he proceeded to stand-up with a view to him and Paul going head-to-head. He straightened his black dinner jacket and adjusted his bowtie. "Pray tell me," said the parliamentarian, with a smirk, "what is it that causes such offense?"

"You mate, that's what!" and I don't mind saying that that put paid to the smirk, good and proper.

The Honorable Member went all sort of quivery. "Er. Are you perhaps able to elucidate on what, precisely, I have done to offend you so?"

"By being born, mate, for starters! And, and." Paul began to jab his forefinger at the hapless chalengee. "You're wearing a dinner jacket and dickey-bow, mate!" Paul, once again, looked down. I was chatting to her opposite, pretending to show interest in the latest proposals of The Law Reform Commission. "It's true, Izzy. He's improperly dressed, he is." I pretended not to hear. Paul recommenced his challenge. "You see, my mate Izzy, here, knows all about dining in

95

Hall and he told me that you only wear black tie on call nights! And, and!" Paul gave his forefinger a particularly forceful jab. "This ain't a call night mate! So, cough-up a bottle of port or bugger off back to that House of Commons place where all the other crooks come from!"

Crimson-faced, the M P replied, "As a mere guest, I was not to know that black tie is only worn on evenings when students are called to the Bar."

"Aha!" said Paul. "Got you! On call nights the dress code is white tie! My friend Izzy, here, told me that!" He once more pivoted his head down. "That's right isn't it, Izzy?"

"Paul, just don't involve me. Leave me out of it, mate."

It was inevitable that, at some stage, Walsingham-Parker would stick his oar in. That stage, I now impart, had been reached. The loathsome individual strode towards Paul and tapped him firmly on the shoulder. "I say you cad! I have been observing you from afar! You steal drink; you spill provender all over the place! In fact, you break just about every rule imaginable and now, to cap it all, you insult a distinguished guest! I tell you what, you dashed bounder," and he pulled himself up to his very biggest height; "I'm going to challenge you!" Walsingham-Parker looked right proper pleased with his self. But his face went sort of ashen and he stopped smiling as Paul grabbed him by the lapels. "I say, I say! Let me go this instant!"

Paul proceeded to drag the wretch to within inches of his face. "You challenge me," snarled Paul, "and I'll kick your teeth in!"

Gasps of horror and indignation erupted all about.

"Quick, sir! Over here!" The voice was that of Mr. Smith, the assistant porter. He beckoned, with a discrete nod of the head. I didn't need telling twice, I can tell you. I pried apart Paul's hands and thereby released his grip on Walsingham-Parker. Then, I grabbed Paul by what was left of his gown and effectively dragged him to Mr. Smith. "Follow me through the kitchens, Mr. Gatehouse, sir. I'll show you the back way out."

We were taken down a corridor and through a door which Mr. Smith gently closed behind us. He thereby shut out the din emanating from the grand hall. The said din consisted of miscellaneous demands calling for our appropriate punishment. By way of example, suggestions had included the imposition of a whopping great fine, a "dashed good flogging" and, worse still, in their estimation, a

96

prohibition from enjoying usage of the Inn's facilities until such time that we could act like right good and proper gents.

There was a smell of done-to-death cabbage that got stronger and stronger. Through another door we went and, from the silly big hats being worn, I realized that we were in the kitchens. We found ourselves greeted by a round of applause from the inhabitants. "Good on yer!" said one. "Bout time e were taught a lesson!" said another.

Chef, who only moments before had graciously accepted the customary millilitre of port, was leaning against his range with a drinking straw between his lips. The sight of a chef mainlining vintage port straight out the bottle was new, even to me, who knew the ways of Dudsall. Between slurps, "My old mate Smiff, 'ere," he said, "told me that there'd be fun-n-games tonight. And e wasn't wrong. It's bout time that Mr. Walsingham-Parker ad a taste of is own medicine." Chef proceeded to toast Paul by raising his bottle. "Cheers, mate." Then he pointed with the bottle towards the direction of the food mixer. "Take a butcher at poor Rosy, over there."

Rosy, small in stature, straggly dark hair and a complexion which perfectly matched her name, was sat crying into a paper tissue. "Nice of you kind gents to stick up for me," she said betwixt blubbers.

Paul, it seemed to me, was totally disoriented. However, as Chef approached, bottle in one hand, pint glass in the other, my companion appeared to shape up. "'Ere," said Chef, "'ave some of the decent stuff," and he poured a good measure into the glass and handed the same to Paul.

"Why, cheers, mate!" and down went the lot in one.

Paul presented his glass for a recharge, only to be thwarted by cries sounding like "tally ho!" and the pounding of feet coming down the corridor.

"No time for that," I said, anxiously and I grabbed Paul, once more, by the remnant of his gown.

"You're starting, Izzy, you're starting!" said Paul, thrashing about and, in the process, the glass went flying out of his hands. Gravity duly did its stuff and, with a crack, the thing landed on the stone flags, sending out splinters all over the road.

"Out you go here!" said Mr. Smith, all of a fluster and he unlatched the door to the outside world. "Make for the Gray's Inn Road gate, sir! It ought to be open!"

As it happened, the Gray's Inn Road gate was banged as tight shut as a solicitor's cheque book. We must have been well gone, however, because we managed to scramble over the wall at the second (maybe, twenty-second) attempt. Paul was first to crash-land and, when I joined him, he was lying spread-eagled on the footpath cursing that that really was it now then and he would be keeping his eye on Walsingham-Parker.

"Come on, Paul," I said. "I think we need a drink," and, as was fast becoming habit, I made as if to grab Paul by what little remained of his gown. To my surprise, nothing, in fact, remained and, glancing vertical, there the thing was, impaled on a spike atop the wall. And, for all I know, the thing might well be there to this very day, flapping around, as a salutary warning to those who might be guests of Gray's Inn.

In the smoke room, I deposited Paul at a corner table and went to the bar, leaving him staring into space. On my return, Paul garbled something or other about a woman. "Talk a bit slower, Paul. I can't make out what you're trying to say." I put a brace of beer down and joined him.

"I was simply saying, Izzy, that I think her," he pointed, "fancies me. While you were at the bar, she kept looking. Nice isn't she? I said, nice isn't she?" I had, in truth, heard Paul but I was too overwhelmed to give him my thoughts. "She's a true English Rose, isn't she Izzy? Shall we go over?" Paul gave me an almighty nudge which nearly sent me flying. "I said, shall we go over?"

Janie was seated in the middle of a mixed group. Those who were male appeared to be transfixed. Hanging on her every word, they were. And one of them was seated far too close to her for my liking. He was far too close to her in terms of age and all. Judging by the cut of his clothes, he must have been worth a few bob. Anyway, I saw him place an arm around her shoulder and then he leaned over and kissed her gently on the top of the head. Paul gave me another nudge. "You've gone a bit pale, Izzy. Are you okay?"

"Come on, Paul. Let's leave. I wouldn't like to find myself enjoined for being within fifty paces."

"Aye?"

"The lady to whom you refer ain't about to have any cotter with me. In fact, to coin your phrase, mate, 'That's it now then.'"

CHAPTER TEN

The next collection of dinners, in comparison, was fairly sedate. They were almost enjoyable and lacked only decent food, decent drink, and decent conversation.

The weeks slipped by and there was still no sign of my education grant. Every time that I went by reception, I feared the slapping into my palm of a letter either demanding that I see the Dean or, worse, conveying news that I had been summarily kicked off the course.

I got myself a job. It was in a pub, down by the river, three nights a week and Saturdays. Bar students were not supposed to take on the sort of work that might bring the profession into disrepute. So I spent many of my working hours sweating and hoping that no one who knew me would walk in. Collecting glasses and doing stints behind the bar was probably acceptable. However, I was worried about the Saturday exotic dancing show and the 'hallo governor, I can offer you something a bit extra' goings on. Well, I mean to say, the sale and consumption of alcoholic beverages outside permitted licensing hours was one thing. (Blimey, if everyone had been hauled in for that up my way, they might just as well have convened the Licensed Victuallers AGM in the Dudsall nick). But assistant to the local brothel keeper may have been deemed an unbecoming occupation too far.

The pay wasn't all that great, either. And, save and except for packets of crisps and the odd half a pint, I was not about to accept the fringe benefits. But at least I had sufficient for a square meal every other day. Mind you, I still couldn't stretch to the sort of money commanded by the bed and breakfast joints. And a rented apartment was clean out of the question. But, when all was said and done, roosting alfresco never did the pigeons any harm.

On my nights off, fellow students would sometimes invite me in

99

for a nightcap. But it soon became obvious that I was never one to return the compliment. For Pete's sake, I could hardly invite them back for a *tête-à-tête* and snifter of methyl alcohol under my little tin table.

For much of the term, I managed to retain an aura of respectability by frequent use of the Council's washroom. There were, naturally, one or two embarrassing moments, like the time I decided to give sleeping in the student's common room a whirl. It was a bit wet and windy that night and, having taken care to case the joint, I figured that I could get away with it so long as I kept my head down till the cleaners were gone. Dinner was to consist of a chocolate bar which I left on one side intending to consume the same on my return from the ablutions. As luck would have it, my intended cantonment turned out to be the venue for the furtherance of an illicit affair between one of the secretaries and a barrister. On my return from the washroom, I don't know who was more shocked, the two women on seeing me, or, me upon seeing the wholly inappropriate act being performed with my dinner.

Autumn turned to winter and things got hairy. Even the expeditious transfer of me and my sole asset, the busted suitcase, to the more equable regions of the tube station failed to afford adequate refuge.

On one particular morning, I awoke with Jack Frost, not so much nipping my nose, but belting me with his ice pick. One of the other vagabonds had keeled over. Just like the Beatle on all the news that day, the pathetic, baggage of a man appeared to have popped his clapped out clogs. As was customary on such occasions, the passersby just, well, passed on by, but not before tut-tutting at the inconvenience of having to step around the pitiable parcel lying prostrate on the walkway. I did likewise, until, half way to The Strand, I stopped, thought to myself, *Hang about, I'm turning native,* and spun round.

Back at the underground, I figured that this, a most solemn of occasions, warranted the observance of all due and proper respect. I therefore laid my jacket gently on the corpse. Thereupon, the not so dear, and, not yet departed, sat up and clonked me with his gin bottle. Head gushing with blood, I reeled back as the inebriated itinerant accused me of attempting to mug him. The commuters, no doubt in anticipation of a spot of bloodletting, stopped all of their tutting and formed a circle. I found myself weaving this way and that as the itinerant took swings at me with his bottle. I couldn't break the circle, so I ended up trotting around like a Lipizzaner at the autumn circus on Dudsall Common.

Amongst the ever-increasing crowd were familiar, albeit open mouthed, individuals in the form of fellow students. I'd have laid odds that one of them was that Walsingham-Parker. In fact, on the third time round, I knew for certain that even the law of evidence don had stopped for a butcher.

It was perhaps fortunate that, before going back to the tube, I'd taken the precaution of stopping at a phone booth for the purpose of requesting assistance from the emergency services. Two medics duly arrived, both out of breath, having sprinted through the underpass. As the itinerant charged at me clasping a waste paper basket, I revealed the extent of my knowledge of forensic medicine with the revelation that he was not, after all, dead. Having firstly apologised for the inconvenience, I proceeded to tell the miffed-off medics that all was not lost, and we lived in a funny old world, since it was now me, and not a corpse, who would very much appreciate a lift to the infirmary.

During the course of the journey, I began to experience a very peculiar feeling. Indeed, at the other end, I fumbled so much that I couldn't take hold of my case, despite having successfully carted the thing around the metropolis for the past umpteenth weeks.

"Oh dear," said one of the medics, as I got stretchered off. "Vasoconstriction has reduced the blood flow to the muscles and reduced their efficiency."

"Aye?"

"You've got the first signs of hypothermia, mate."

The other medic sighed. "Unless it's normal for him to go whooping round in a circle, with a wound to the head, I'd say it's concussion."

Well, they were both right. But, after a solitary night's stopover in men's surgical, and, sporting a solitary stitch to my forehead, me and my busted case decided to head off out of London for an early Christmas. I must have looked a poor soul struggling round the north circular 'cause, even before I had chance to stick my thumb out, a truck pulled over, and the driver told me that I could hop in. So, I duly hopped in and, as luck would have it, the truck was bound for Warwickshire. Consequently, it was barely gone opening time when me and my only asset struggled through the door of The Case is Open.

As normal, Ian was stood at the bar holding court with the locals. "Good heavens above! It's Gatehouse!" He shooed the gathering so that they made room for me. "I see you've been in the wars again Gatehouse, old chap." He turned towards the bar where a tearful man stood. Reverting to my clock analogy, the old landlady had apparently turned midnight and shuffled off her mortal coil. Indeed, it was her wake that I had stumbled into and everyone, except Ian, was dressed smartly in black. "A pint of your very best, for every jack man in the house! Our wearisome prodigal has returned!" He clamped the ever present pipe between his teeth and began to rummage in his trouser pockets. He wore a pair of filthy grey cords. "Damnation Gatehouse, old dear. I seem to have mislaid my purse. You'd best stump up the round."

We stepped aside of the stampede and sat at one of the cribbage tables. "Ian," I said. "It's been awful. . . ."

"Never mind about that," said Ian, cutting in. He leaned forward and whispered up close. I could tell from his breath that he'd been at it again in Kingston, Jamaica. "What on earth possessed you to spill the beans to Janie about your shenanigans in Oakley Castle?"

"My shenanigans? Mine?"

"Oh, very well then, Gatehouse. Our shenanigans." Ian leaned back and crossed his legs. He had on a pair of sandals. His toes were sticking out and they were absolutely filthy. Ian casually placed both hands at the back of his head. "Fortunately," he went on, "I have resolved the entire issue. There will be no action taken against either one of us."

"How did you manage that?"

"With my new found authority, Gatehouse, old chap, that's how." Ian uncrossed his legs and sat forward, again. He began tugging at his shirt. It was a tunic shirt, grubby white with no collar attached. He nodded, winced, and chuckled, just a little. "I've got through the re-sits, old chap."

"That's fantastic, Ian. How did you manage it?"

"War of attrition, Gatehouse, that's how." He broke off momentarily and summonsed one of the locals, with a wave of the hand. "Carry my drink over would you? There's a good chap." The local came across and dutifully handed over a drink. "Thanks, old boy.

Very good of you." He took one or two slurps and carried on. "I think that in the end the Dean reckoned that there was no point in persistently failing me." Ian had a few more slurps and wiped some froth from his mouth. He used the sleeve of his barrister-type shirt. "So the Dean, bless him, has deferred to the public in terms of assessing whether I have sufficient competence to practice at the Bar. He handed me down a pass."

"Congratulations, Ian! What grade did you get?"

"What sort of a question is that, Gatehouse, old dear?" He finished off his drink and looked towards the bar. "Two pints over here, if you please!" He refocused his attentions on me. "Show me a client, Gatehouse, old chap, who wants to know what grade his brief got at college. The only thing that the average criminal wants to know is whether his brief can sweet talk the court into letting him off with a slap across the knuckles."

"So you got a third, then?"

"Yes," said Ian, snappily. He paused as a fresh glass was placed before him. Then, with a wince and a chuckle, he said, "It's a gentleman's third, Gatehouse, old chap. Yes, that's what I have. A gentleman's third." Ian raised his glass. "Cheers!"

Ian gave me a guided tour through each and every examination paper and each and every question appertaining thereto. By the time that he was done, we had almost drunk ourselves halfway round the globe. When we arrived in the foothills of The Himalayas, Ian tried a right peculiar concoction which took his breath away. Seizing my opportunity to get a word in edgeways, I began again, "It's been awful," and I told him of my plight. I started from when Janie had putted up to the front door in her little green car and I ended at the bit with the itinerant and his remarkable strength, at having lobbed a waste paper basket from the escalators clean into the path of a train on the central line. There were no interruptions from Ian, save and except for when I had gotten to the bit about assistant to the brothel keeper. "That Michaela," he had chuckled, whilst biting hard on his pipe, "she's always been a minx."

When I was done, I nodded purposefully, just the once (as if to say, "And you think you've got problems, mate") and then I folded my arms. Ian sucked at his pipe for a moment and he looked upwards and pondered my plight. Well, it was either that or he was pondering whether the aeroplane propeller was about to come crashing down from the ceiling. I'd already noticed that each time someone went out to, or, came in from the lavatory, the thing swung about, just like it was still attached to the Focker that had once crash landed in the cauliflower field.

Without a word, Ian got up and, with his peculiar backwards lean, he scurried off to the other end. There, I saw him chatting momentarily to the tearful bartender and then he dived into the pockets of his cords and produced a coin, which he handed over. Thereupon, the tearful one bent beneath his bar, only to re-emerge a few seconds later clasping an old Bakelite telephone. He shoved the same in front of Ian who, almost immediately, began dialing.

From where I sat, I watched all of Ian's winces and shrugs and I heard him chuckle, far too frequently for my liking. When he was done, he replaced the receiver on its cradle and came scooting back to me. "It's all sorted, Gatehouse, old dear," and Ian winced and shrugged, just a little.

"What's all sorted?"

"Next term, Gatehouse, old dear, you will be housed at the abode of one Sandra Crowe and her husband Martin and their brood." Ian broke off for the purpose of prodding one of the locals with a rolled up order of service. The local had been outside and had chosen that very moment to come our way, presumably to avoid a collision with the swinging propeller and thereby negate the chances of his being the next funeral. "Be a good chap and get a couple of pints in. It's my round next." Ian sent the local on his way. "Sandra and Martin live in High Barnet, just up the northern line. Very handy for the Inns of Court and . . . Oops!" Ian broke off, again. "Almost forgot," and, calling across to the local, he said. "Best get a chaser to go with mine! A large rum will do nicely, thanks!" He winced, shrugged, and chuckled. "Martin works for an art gallery in the center of London. . ."

"Yes, yes," I said. It was now my turn to cut in. "But how does this stroke of luck come about and who pays for it?"

Ian fetched out the howitzer. A large space opened up as all of the locals backed off. "It's taken care of, and . . ." A flame shot halfway to the bar and back. It was a miracle that we didn't bear witness to the second cremation of the day. "If I disclose the source, you may feel disinclined to accept this most generous offer."

"It's simply fantastic, Ian. But I've got the course fees to pay."

"Goodness gracious, Gatehouse, old chap." He winced and shrugged. "Tell me, does everyone from Dudsall have their glasses permanently half empty?" Ian copped hold of his own, literal glass and gulped until it was down to half full. He once more employed the service of the shirtsleeve with which to wipe away foam. "The course fees are being taken care of," he said, with a chuckle. And, despite my very best endeavours, there was no prising from Ian any information pertaining to my remarkable upturn in fortune. I therefore resolved that I would cease badgering Ian, well for a short time at any rate.

Presently, we returned to Ian's favored topic of conversation which was, of course, Ian. Having passed the Bar finals, he had wasted no time in securing pupillage with a barrister up in Birmingham. For a whole twelve months he would be at the barrister's beck and call, all, supposedly, in the name of training. "At least I'm allowed to accept work after the first six months," said Ian.

"I still owe the Dean his fifty quid," I said, remembering that I had a half empty glass.

Ian winced and chuckled. "Crikey, Gatehouse, old dear, I trust that you're not hinting that the benefactor stumps up for that as well, only . . ."

"Not a bit of it, Ian."

"Only, I was going to say, old chap, that there are plenty of bars in High Barnet. And," Ian added with a smirk, "you won't find yourself dodging leather-clad High Court Judges on the landing."

Just then, the propeller swung rather violently as a fairly large group walked in. You could have knocked me down with a feather because there, dead center, was Janie.

"Come to pay their respects, I daresay," said Ian.

Janie, dressed in a tweed country jacket and long black skirt, was as tasteful and as lovely as ever. Her companions consisted of a mixed bunch, but one of them was the wretch whom I had seen her with in London. As before, he was all over Janie like a rash. But at least on that topic, I consoled myself that despite his close proximity, he hadn't made that swan-like neck go red with passion, as I had done.

Janie turned momentarily. Our eyes met. Her jaw dropped. The penny dropped and all. Janie Jetty, she whom I loved and adored, was my benefactor.

Janie swiftly looked away and began to chat with the others. I could tell, even from across the room, that her wonderful eyes were sparkling. But she wasn't fooling me. All that jollity was just an act, to my mind. I got up from my seat.

Ian yanked me down. He removed the pipe from his mouth. "Do you have a death wish, old chap? After you spilled the beans, Janie Jetty there, dobbed us right in it. And the crew she's with are her so-called family and friends. We, Gatehouse, are *personae non gratae* and I suggest that we leave right here and now."

"Ian, I have to go over, if only to say thanks."

"Listen, Gatehouse, old chap. Now, how do I put this?" He tapped the infernal pipe on an ashtray, peered into the bowl, sniffed (I had no idea why), then he winced and shrugged, just a little. "Let's put it this way. Should you in any way shape or form make reference to your improved circumstances you will very likely cause embarrassment to a certain party." Ian looked at me in a knowing sort of a fashion. "Do you get my drift, Gatehouse, old dear? Mum's the word."

I nodded, in a determined fashion. "Absolutely, Ian." It was almost too good to be true. I was on cloud nine, I can tell you. That was until I clocked the wretch getting even nearer. By the time he'd finished his move, the pair were closer than two coats of emulsion. "Ian," I said. "What's the score with young Pinstripe, over there?"

Ian pointed with his pipe. "Who? Him?"

"Ar, 'im. The one jetting like a crow in the gutter."

"That's Mr. William Anker, old chap. He's an up and coming lawyer in the city." Ian gave the wretch a quick once over. "Janie and the others have sold one of their business interests." He put the pipe to his mouth. "It would appear that Anker has more than a fat fee on his mind." Ian stood up. "Come on then, Gatehouse, old dear. We wouldn't wish the good folk from the hall to instruct our friend to issue injunction proceedings, would we?"

So we left. I tried to catch Janie's eye as we had sidled past. But she was having none of it. Janie simply looked away, as if I didn't exist. Talk about mixed signals? I hovered, a bit, to see whether her telltale signs of passion were there. However, I found myself unable to linger long because Ian took hold of my collar and dragged me out. Still, as I walked with him to the wreck, I contented myself in the knowledge that the wonderful creature had surreptitiously forked out sufficient to give me a leg up. And not a word was to be spoken on the subject until, presumably, I had become a respectable barrister. It was both practical and dead romantic. Perhaps Christmas wasn't going to be too bad after all?

CHAPTER ELEVEN

Well, you might know. Christmas at The Fly in the Ointment was, sort of, different.

I spent many a long night hoofing it around the parish. This was to facilitate Ian's private entertainment of multifarious, lonely women of that certain age. Ian thought he was performing a social service. With hindsight, I reckon he probably was. Whether it was borne of guilt, release of tension, everlasting shame at what they had done (a bit unlikely, that one), the married ones went home vowing to give their relationships another shot after Ian had given them, as he so succinctly put it, "A damned good seeing to."

At least I had company on these nocturnal hikes. You see, during my spell in London, another waif and stray had taken up residence at The Fly in the Ointment. Dave was a slavering, snarling and, for all I knew, rabid bulldog of questionable pedigree. Some friends, so called, had gifted the monster in the guise of an early Christmas present. But after expert cross examination, I got it out of Ian that the giving of this token had been nearer to Halloween than Yuletide. Further and additionally, the benefactors were not three kings from the Orient but the Shipsford-on-Avon chapter of The Hells Angels. Now then, I'm no expert when it comes to *Canis familiaris*, but I reckon that even I would have called into question the temperament of that four-legged fiend. Not so Ian. He had figured that a bulldog was just the ticket, a simply ripping status symbol for an up and coming barrister-at-law.

The landlady had apparently lain in state at The Case for two whole days. Barred for life for taking a chunk out of the coffin and, apparently, shagging the Russian billiards table, Dave spent most nights chained to the chair leg where Colin wound him up something rotten. But on Christmas Eve the consequences of a particularly gruelling session were injurious. You see, come the evening and, before departing once more unto The Case, Ian erroneously assumed that it was I who had shackled the crazed quadruped.

Whilst we unholy reprobates quaffed and yelled our selection of sea shanties, the members of the local congregation were about their saintly business, namely the crooning of carols on the miscellaneous doorsteps of Prestwick.

Ian and I roared up in the wreck just as the Godly gathering arrived at The Fly in the Ointment. It was a truly delightful sight to behold. The vicar and his choir were flanked by a chorus, all dressed in Victorian costume. Each held a candlelit lantern on a stick.

Barely had the assemblage struck up with its rendition of "The Holly and the Ivy" when Ian butted in. "Excuse me. If you'd let us squeeze past, I'll sling a pew, I mean . . ." He winced and shrugged, just a little. "I meant to say, I'll sling a Yule log on the fire and then set you up for midnight mass with a hot toddy."

"Oh, simply splendid," said the vicar. He was a strange looking one, all right. Long grey hair, a long nose and round spectacles, just like that dead Beatle, and a pair of denims under his frock. But, I'd heard he was an inoffensive sort. And, when all was said and done, he had an impossible job considering that the parishioners, being of Warwickshire stock, honestly, truly believed that the Christ child was born of white, middle class parents who came from the east, probably just outside Lowestoft. "Make way for the generous gentlemen," said the vicar. His arms were outstretched as he ushered the flock.

Ian stepped up to the big front door and, in the darkness; he groped around for the handle. One of the choirboys chirped up. "Do you want to borrow my candle to find the key, mister?"

"No thanks, old chap." Ian winced and chuckled. "I only lock up if the landlord's on the loose. I doubt very much that even he will be lurking about on Christmas Eve."

The vicar counted in the choir and, once again, they began belting forth their ditty.

At the bit where, by all accounts, the holly wears a crown, Ian found his handle and pushed the door wide open. There immediately came a rush of air about our lower limbs as something rocketed past. Ian winced and shrugged, more than just a little. "What the hell was that, Gatehouse?"

The singing came to an abrupt halt and, momentarily, the night sky became lit as a dozen or more Victorian lanterns were chucked into the air. Every one tazzed off, save except the vicar, who was left standing with just his collection tin for company. Dave did a swift circuit around the garden and, no doubt reasoning that anyone with half a brain must have been half way to Oxford, he homed in on the lonesome man of the cloth.

"Good heavens!" cried the frantic cleric and, without so much as a "Merry Christmas," he bounded down the path and cleared the hawthorn hedge.

"That was one hell of a jump," I said, as Dave tore off in hot pursuit.

"I wager you five pounds, Gatehouse, that he doesn't make it beyond the post box."

"You're on."

It was the swiftest fiver that I've ever expended but, more importantly, the villagers never quite forgave the vicar for missing his own midnight mass. I personally consider that they were too harsh. Well, I mean to say, it's pretty nigh impossible to deliver a sermon from the top of a chestnut tree with ones Saint Michael's hanging from a ruddy great rip in ones trousers.

Ian found himself excommunicated and, as for Dave, he was exterminated following an expedited destruction order on the part of the local magistrate's court. It was a sad end to the misunderstood mutt but I suppose that his earthly exit had been inevitable when it transpired that one of the terror-stricken choirboys had the chairman of the bench as his dad.

Christmas done and dusted, I returned once more to London only, this time around, I went via the abode of Sandra and Martin Crowe.

They lived in one of those nineteen twenties-type houses. You know the sort. They have bow windows and there's usually an archway where the dining room's been knocked through.

I put my busted case on the doorstep and went to ring the doorbell. But before I had chance to do any such thing, the front door opened and, walking backwards, a scruffy youth came out. A pair of knapsacks was quick to follow and, coming as they did at a hefty rate of knots, one caught the youth unawares and smacked him right in the face. The other flew clean over his head and landed in the flowerbed.

"And don't come back!" The voice was female and it came from within.

The youth gathered up his knapsacks and stood on the footpath. "I simply told my college that I considered that my bedroom was a little on the grubby side." He was assertive in the manner that he addressed the gap where the door had just been. Judging from the velocity of the knapsacks as they left the house, I doubted whether he would have been so cocky had there not been a small garden to act as a natural line of defense. You see, there could be no doubting it that, whomsoever it was that chucked those bags, had a bit of muscle.

"I have never been so insulted!" The owner of the voice emerged and showed herself as an auburn-haired woman, probably in her mid thirties. She had a pretty, freckly face. The woman stopped momentarily and she looked at me, as if to say, "And what have we here?" and then carried on with her journey. On reaching her destination, she prodded the youth and said, "I keep a clean house and will never, ever again offer accommodation to students from your college!" Although the woman was fairly short in terms of her height, she was broad and big built (without being obese). And she certainly packed a mighty punch, as was evident from the manner in which the nudge sent the youth staggering backwards into the road. It was perhaps fortunate that there was no vehicle coming. "Never darken my door again!" she shouted, as the youth scampered off.

"Don't you worry about that!" He spoke from the definite safety of the end of the block. "You live in a mad house, you do!"

The woman tugged at her sloppy jumper so that it covered much of the top part of her legs. She had on a pair of denims and the poor things were stretched to bursting point. The woman came back up the path and stopped where I was stood. "And what do you want?" she said officiously. I couldn't help but notice the woman's teeth. They were rather large and crooked. She was no oil painting but the woman nevertheless had a certain *je ne sais quoi*.

"I'm Izaak. I think I'm expected." I hoped that I didn't sound nervous. "If it's a bad time I can always call back."

"Izaak?" She was puzzled, I could tell. My heart sank at the prospect of, once more, sleeping alfresco. There was then a look of recognition. "Izaak! Of course." I felt a sense of relief. "I've been waiting for you," she lied, with all the skill of a barrister. "I'm so, so sorry. It's been an awful day. I'm Sandra." She held out a hand and we warmly shook. "It's not always like this," she added.

We stood in awkward silence for a few moments. I figured she was bound to invite me to step inside. But she didn't. Maybe the spat to which I had borne witness had gotten her all flummoxed. "Shall I, sort of, come in?" I said, since otherwise I had visions of being there till midnight.

"Good gracious me!" said Sandra. "I'm all flummoxed. You must think I'm crazy."

"Not at all," I laughed. She weren't the only one with back teeth through which to lie.

"Grab your case, Izaak," said Sandra in an all of a sudden, enthusiastic sort of a way. "I'll show you to your room." She entered the house and, just inside, there was a flight of stairs which she began to negotiate two steps at a time. Heaven only knows what prevented the denims from bursting apart at the seams. At about the half way point, Sandra turned her head slightly. "Mind you don't trip over Crackerjack, only. . . ."She stopped, as I let forth a yelp. "Oh. Too late," she said.

A rather large dog was snoozing at the bottom of the stairs. He was lying flat out, just where some idiot was likely to trip over him. That certain person was me and I had come a right cropper. The string snapped and my case busted wide open. This was not a good start. "Is he all right?" I asked with concern, since having an, albeit out of date, edition of *Stone's Justices Manual* land on your head is enough to stun an elephant.

Sandra bounded down the stairs saying, "Don't worry. He's had far worse," and she set about gathering up my belongings, removing even the pair of Y-fronts that the dog wore on his head.

In actual fact, Crackerjack was not a dog but a hound. A basset hound to be exact. He was long, brown and white, and he didn't half whiff.

Sandra lent a hand transporting my rummage upstairs. I don't mind admitting that I felt a proper chump. Well, I mean to say. I had only just met the woman and yet there she was mauling my smalls. To her credit, Sandra did not bat an eyelid. She was clearly a man of the world.

Having reached the landing, Sandra kicked open one of the

bedroom doors. "I've moved my eldest lad in with the other two," she said, cheerily.

"There's no need to go to any trouble on my account." I was simultaneously thanking the heavens that I was not expected to double up with one of her little devils. Now don't get me wrong. I had nothing against children in those days. Indeed, I confess that I used to be one myself. I simply knew when to smell a rat. And I did not, for one moment, like the look of the toy drum and trumpet, not to mention the replica sub-machine gun, lying abandoned on the carpet. "I don't mind sharing," I lied.

"It's no trouble." Sandra threw her share of my belongings onto a desk that was handily placed beneath the window. I threw the other half and my busted case onto a single bed. By way of an aside, Sandra advised, "I'd get a new case, if I were you; or at least get some new string and stop knotting the old." The duvet cover had a super hero printed all over it; it was him with the black rubber fetish, I think. "Jason doesn't mind sharing with his brothers," she said. "If things are too tight, he can always use the student's room." Sandra once more straightened her sloppy jumper. "I don't suppose I'll need that room again," she sighed, "the local college is so strict about cleanliness." On making that remark, Sandra squeezed her hand into the pocket of her denims and produced a rather tatty tissue. She blew her nose and then said, "Tell me honestly and truly. Does my home look dirty to you?"

"Good gracious no!" In truth I hadn't had time to case the joint, but I certainly had no intention of falling victim to one of her hefty prods.

"Anyway," she added with nonchalance, "I think he planted that cockroach in the bathroom." I took it upon myself to try out the firmness of the bed. I did it by simply sitting on the edge where I bounced about a bit. But on the third bounce there came a squealing from under the super hero and out from a flap popped a startled-looking tabby cat. "Oh," said Sandra, "I see you've found Tuppence." The cat dashed towards the door and in the process rebounded off the toy drum and then made it to the bottom of the stairs in one almighty leap. Sandra crossed her arms. "Tell me, Izaak. Don't you like animals, or something?"

"Yes, no, yes." I was flustered. "I love 'em. In fact, Ian has a cat called Colin." We laughed at that one. "He had a dog and all, Dave, but he's dead." I laughed. She didn't.

"How is that old rogue, Ian?" I swear that Sandra's eyes went all misty and she started staring into space. But after the briefest of moments, she returned to earth and gave her watch the once-over. "Goodness me, Izaak! I must collect the children from school." Sandra scurried off to another bedroom. It was just across the landing. She began peeling off the jumper and, in the process, she didn't bother to close the door. Always the gentleman, I averted my eyes, a bit. I'll tell you something for nothing. No word of a lie. She was a big girl. Sandra re-emerged. Over her womanly proportions, she was doing up the buttons of a smart white blouse. "Right then, Izaak. I won't be long. If you feel peckish just pop downstairs and help yourself. I've got plenty for you to get your teeth into. Please make yourself at home."

After Sandra was gone, I went straight downstairs. True to form, a wall had been knocked through between the dining room and the sitting room. Where the former once was, a large glass table sat proudly on a raised platform. However, I didn't hang about to admire the interior decor. I went straight to the kitchen, in search of the refrigerator.

I duly found the fridge. Mind you, it didn't take much hunting down. It was a huge, American thing. Rare in those days it was. Now you can't open a magazine without adverts for the things leaping out. The sound of the opening of the fridge door was followed by the sound of meowing, which was followed by the appearance of Tuppence. The appearance of Tuppence was followed by a horrible smell, which was followed by a sort of wheezing noise, which was followed by the appearance of Crackerjack.

I reached into the very back of the fridge and fetched out a huge black forest gateaux. Remembering that Sandra had asked me to make myself at home, I decided to accept the offer, and I went through to where the glass top table stood. There, I took my place at the head of table and ploughed into the cake. Both animals joined me and in no time all that we had left was a cake stand. To round off the feast I handed the thing to Crackerjack who licked it dry.

When we were all done, Crackerjack dragged his floor-hugging belly back to the staircase. Tuppence went out through the cat flap intending, no doubt to have a songbird or two by way of dessert. And, as for me, I decided that I must continue to take Sandra literally and, treating the place like my very own, I lay on the sofa snoozing and wondering how many years had it been since I'd last seen ceilings festooned with so many paper lanterns.

I was distracted from my contemplations at, I suppose, around about teatime when Sandra and her brood came crashing in. There followed, by all parties thereto, a disinterested sort of introduction and, when it was all done, Jason set about tormenting Crackerjack with an adjustable spanner. Ben, the youngest (whom I shall henceforth, for the purposes of identification only, refer to as "the nursling") crept upstairs where he demonstrated a remarkable degree of dexterity for one so young and hammered merry hell out of the toy drum. Thomas, the middle one (and by far the quieter) assisted Sandra by getting things ready for tea. However, arms. laden with plates, Sandra found herself obliged to shout a warning that Thomas must have a care not to trip up the raised platform, whereupon Thomas did trip up the raised platform and he hit his head on the glass top table with ever such a mighty thwack.

Sandra raced over and, on ascertaining that her prized glass table was not harmed, she attended to the bawling child. He had a lump coming up on his forehead that looked very nasty. So, on explaining, "It's not always like this!" Sandra dragged Thomas off to get medical attention, leaving me in *loco parentis*.

I tried my best to restore a semblance of order. But I failed miserably. Telling Jason to leave Crackerjack be, he turned his attentions on Tuppence and, while he was about it, he turned up his favourite cassette, consisting as it did of music from Adam Ant. And as for the nursling. Having tired of the drum, he decided to demonstrate that he was ambidextrous on top of everything else by blowing bruit out the trumpet in his one hand and rat-tatting the replica sub machine gun in his other.

Always one to know when he's licked, I decided to explore the back garden and I left the pair of horrors about their respective pursuits. I navigated my way through the long grass, tripping over lost or abandoned toys in the process, and ended up at a children's swing. Compared to inside, it was blissful. The only noise came from the sound of passenger jets dodging the chimney pots. With my head craned skywards, I failed to notice that someone else had hacked their

115

way up the garden, that is, until I received a sharp tap on the shoulder.

"What's going on?" His voice was aggressive and, in keeping with his general appearance, it was a bit rough and all. He was a shaven-haired individual and he wore round spectacles. They were not the small sort as formerly worn by the dead Beatle, but much bigger. He wore denims and one of those donkey jackets that were much in favour with construction site workers. In fact, slap a helmet on his head and he'd have been a dead ringer for him out of The Village People. "What's going on?" he demanded, once again.

"Are you Martin?" He plainly was. "Only, I'm Roger."

"You what?"

"You know? Roger, lodger. Roger the Lodger." I laughed. He didn't.

"If you're telling me that you're Izaak, I'm pleased to meet you," and he held out his hand, "but where the hell is Sandra?"

"At the hospital."

"The hospital?" He adjusted his spectacles at that one.

"Yes, the hospital."

I duly related to Martin the tribulations of teatime and convinced him that he too should scurry off to the infirmary. Martin thanked me for childminding, assured me, "It's not always like this," and he hacked his way back down the garden.

Martin had no sooner closed the side gate when Sandra, complete with bandaged bairn, appeared at the patio door. She beckoned me towards the house and, as I got within earshot, she said, "Sorry! It's not always like this!" We resumed tea and it took the form of cottage pie that, for a whole hour, had been left to its own devices in the hottest part of the oven. "I can't think what could have happened to Martin," said Sandra. "You may as well have his share, Izaak," and she proceeded to chisel away at the serving dish before presenting me with a second wedge of burnt offering.

The children, looking the worst for wear, sat through the meal in relative harmony. When we had finished, all three were sent to their respective berths and they went without a murmur.

"Right," said Sandra, as soon as all was quiet upstairs, "let's go down the pub, and I'll introduce you to the gang." She gathered together the dinner plates and placed each one of them on the floor. Tuppence and Crackerjack were there in a thrice and they soon licked the plates clean. Thereupon, Sandra put the things straight into a crockery cupboard.

"What about Martin?" I asked.

"Oh, don't worry about him." She gave her wristwatch a quick shufty. "He's probably working late. He'll know where to find us."

"What about the children?"

"Oh, don't worry about them. They go out like lights, although . . ." Sandra stopped and pondered.

"I don't mind staying to look after them," I said. And it was true it was. I didn't mind looking after them. It was a nice quiet night that I craved. Well, hold your horses and be fair and all that, I'd had three weeks of circumnavigating the globe and three weeks of hiking around Prestwick, at the dead of night, while Ian did his social service thing.

"Nah," said Sandra. She'd done with the pondering. "Next door won't mind popping in." Sandra opened a door. I made as if to follow but checked myself on the realization that it was a cupboard door that she'd opened. Sandra reached in and copped hold of a denim bomber-type jacket. She put it on. Sandra tried to button the thing. What with her womanly proportions, it must have been two sizes too small, at least. "Oh no, not again," sighed Sandra, as she tried to yank the two ends together. "That blasted washing machine has shrunk it."

At The Coach and Horses, I was duly introduced to the gang. And what a fascinating bunch they were. There was Ron. He was an accountant. And there was Dean. He was a computer programmer, but he was formerly an accountant. So too was Sally (a former accountant, I mean). She had given it up to have a child. She double accounted, however, and ended up with twins. There was also Justin. You might know, he was an accountant. But at least you could distinguish him from Ron and Dean. He was much bigger in build and had a shock of blonde hair and piercing blue eyes.

Sally was a tiny dark haired creature who fluttered her eyes each time that someone spoke to her. At the same time she would bury her chin deep in her chest. I supposed that she thought it was all very coy and endearing. It wasn't. It was all very annoying. Dean was married to Sally. Sandra told me on the side that he didn't care too much for Ron. You see, Dean had been told that his seed count was such that you didn't need to be an accountant to count it. It could be done on the fingers of one hand. Consequently, Dean suspected that Ron, and not him, was father to the twins. Mind you, when Sally had insisted on flashing around photographs of the children, I inwardly conceded that Sandra probably had a point in that the twosome did seem somewhat un-Dean-like. The little girl had remarkable blue eyes and, talk about the boy. His hair of gold was amazing on one so young. It was a veritable thatch.

Sandra also told me on the side that she loved each and every member of the gang. She also said that Martin could take them or leave them except that, in the case of Sally, he had come down on the side of leaving her. After that revelation Sandra went over to Sally and, gin and tonics in hand, giggling like schoolgirls, they had gotten up to play darts with the local rugby team.

While raucous laughter came from the area of the spotlit oche (it was something to do with penetration of light through cheesecloth), Dean looked daggers at Ron, and Ron looked at Dean as if to say, "Not guilty mate, let's have closure." In this manner, I found myself chatting with just Justin. The conversation started with promise. It was about him and his brother jointly and severally stripping Lizzie and then giving her a good going over. On hearing that one, even the rugby team stopped to earwig. But they soon returned to their game of spotting the pattern on silhouetted panties when Justin disclosed that Lizzie was no more than a rusting hulk of a shunting engine. Him and his twin were only the founder members of some steam engine preservation society!

It was very much to my relief when the doors swung open and Martin stormed in and he looked as if he had a right cob on him. Still, at least his forceful entry curtailed Justin's incessant talking about railroad tat.

Martin stormed straight over to Sandra and, ignoring all of the eye fluttering and chin burrowing of her soul mate Sally, he demanded of Sandra an explanation as to where she had been and what was her game.

"I've been here, of course, you daft ape." She said it with a laugh and then she turned her back on him and threw an arrow that bounced out of double top and hit the spot light. The sundry members of the rugby team sighed as one in disappointment as Sally's dress went opaque.

"Why wasn't you at the hospital, woman?" said Martin. His face was red with anger.

"Because I was at the doctor's surgery down the road, that's why." Sandra handed her two remaining darts to a six foot something individual with cauliflower ears and a crooked nose. Then she squared up to Martin and added, firmly, "And stop calling me woman."

For a moment, Martin appeared puzzled. So did Sally who, all this time, had stood in the foreground fluttering and burrowing and generally vying for attention, to no avail. "But you were supposed to be at the hospital, woman."

"Stop calling me woman!" Sandra's face had now gone red with anger and all. "I have no idea why you should think that I was up at the hospital!"

I turned to Justin. "So, tell me, mate. Who else works on this engine of yours?"

Martin now had his nose pressed right up against Sandra's. "Listen here, woman! The children are running riot and I've not been fed!"

"Oh, really?" said Sandra. "Anything else?" She now spoke in hushed tones and she sounded intimidating on account of it.

"Yes there is, actually," Martin stepped back a pace, "the dog's been sick all over the house! Some damn fool has fed him black forest gateaux!"

I turned again to Justin. "Who helps you out at weekends? **Who?** That Sally, over there?"

Sandra placed both hands on her hips. She thrust back her shoulders and, in the process, her front got thrust forwards. It had no business doing that and even the rugby team was shocked, I can tell you because, as hereinbefore stated, Sandra was a big girl. "I suggest that you go home, like a good little chap, and mop the house." Sandra had plainly adopted her stance as an outward sign of her defiance. Her defiance was similarly demonstrated when she picked-up someone's whole pint glass and chucked the entire contents into Martin's face.

Martin was quick to react. He motored towards Sandra and grabbed her by the scruff of the neck. "You're coming with me, woman!" He sounded assertive enough, but looked a bit daft with his face, donkey jacket, everything in fact, dripping with Startled Rat Celebratory Fine Ale.

"Get off me!" yelped Sandra, while scuffling to get free. And to be fair, she put up a gallant fight to break free. Indeed, she very nearly made it after landing a wallop on Martin's nose that sent his spectacles skew whiff. Sandra made a bolt towards me, but her escape was thwarted when she careened into my table, tipping everything turtle. "Here, Izaak!" she said urgently, and she handed me the empty glass.

Martin was quickly on her again and seizing his wife with one hand, he removed his spectacles with the other. "Here, Izaak!"

And then, before going down on the floor and rolling about, both stood before me and said, "Sorry! It's not always like this!"

CHAPTER TWELVE

A fair few things went bump in the night and I can tell you that the sounds coming from the master bedroom were of a sort temporal and not spiritual. Initially, I reckoned that Martin was ahead on points and I was tempted to go in there and arbitrate. However, come the small hours, I hearkened as the twosome made it up and, from thereon, it was Sandra who was well and truly on top.

Over breakfast, Martin sat foggy-eyed and, between mouthfuls, he dragged away at a cigarette. I had no idea what was on his plate, save and except that it resembled something that Tuppence had carted in.

Sandra, meanwhile, sang her heart out in the kitchen. There could be no doubting it that Martin had given a good account of himself. "Izaak!" she chirped. "Would you like yours sunny side up?"

"Nothing for me thanks, Sandra!"

She breezed in holding a saucepan. Lying in the bottom was an object resembling an egg. "You'd best have it then, Martin," and she began hammering away with a spatula. "It's starting to give," she said, optimistically. As an expert in the art of spot welding, I could have told her for nothing that only a dose of sandblasting would likely shift the thing.

"I've had my fill, woman." Martin sounded masterful. He took an extra long draw on his coffin nail and then extinguished the same in the dregs of a teacup. Next, he leaned back (thereby exposing a goodly portion of stomach) though not before he had slung his dining fork on a plate, empty, save for left over bits of bacon fat. On hearing the rattle of dining fork on Pyrex, Crackerjack came in, having been preceded firstly by the awful whiff and secondly by the wheezing noise. "I think it would be best if you hurried along a bit, woman." Martin uttered the opinion above the mixed sounds of the said wheezing and a spluttering and hissing coming from the drowning cigarette.

Every bit the dutiful wife, Sandra scurried around her prized table collecting cups, plates, dishes, and so forth. She hummed merrily to herself as she did so. "I'm driving Martin into town today," said Sandra, on coming to my bit of table, "would you care for a lift, Izaak?" I had to nudge forwards, away from the wall as she came by and she had to breathe in a bit. This was on account of her being such a big girl. "Only it's Sally's turn to take the children to school," Sandra volunteered, as she went past.

"Great. Thank you very much."

Sandra began lining up the plates on the floor, whereupon the front doorbell sounded. Martin enquired whether I had any objection to getting up and answering. In the event, I didn't mind a bit and I got to the door just ahead of the nursling and the other two and, I would add, I got there before whomsoever it was who wanted our attention could press the button and give us a second rendition of "Return to Sorrento."

It was Sally whom I found on the doorstep and, with all of her eye fluttering and chin burrowing, she said that she and her twins wanted to come in. If it had been anything to do with me, I'd have told the mawkish mare to be gone. There was something right fishy about her and, coming as I did from up Dudsall way, I had an instinct about those sorts of things. But in the matter of whether to permit her to come in or not to let her in I had no standing. It was apparently her job to take the nursling and the other two to school and I knew this to be true for I had been told as much. And so I adjudged that I had no choice but to let her in. So I let her in.

While the twins bounded off somewhere or other with Sandra's lot, Sally came through to where Martin was still being masterful. Without bothering to ask, she nabbed my chair and sat next to the head of household. And then, with the fluttering at near takeoff speed and with much chin burrowing, she proceeded to compete with the slobbering and licking noises coming from the region of Martin's feet. "I do hope there isn't an atmosphere," she said, succeeding only in creating one where there had not been one to begin with. Sally had a voice that sounded as sickly as treacle tastes. She wasn't one to stop to draw breath either which meant that she was of those who blarted off before she could think and that's assuming the woman was capable of having a thought in the first place. "Only it was such a dreadful fight that you had last night," she said, raking over the immediate past. "It was even worse than the time Sandra didn't come home from Sarah's hen party," she carried on, going into the cupboard, seizing a skeleton and giving it a right good rattling.

Whilst jabberwocking in the manner aforesaid, Sally had somehow managed to cozy up to Martin and, in the process, her skirt had risen to near indecent proportions. He weren't a blind bit interested though and he simply lit another cigarette and called to Sandra who was in the kitchen, "We have to go or I'll be late, woman!"

Sandra came breezing in and, as she did so, Sally speedily uncozied herself from Martin and, simultaneously, she yanked the hem of her skirt back to where her seamstress had envisaged it ought to have been all along. Sandra bent down and scooped the plates from the floor. "Oh, Crackerjack!" she said. "You've missed one," and she bent back down to the floor and put back the top plate. "Well, shift yourself, husband. I'm almost ready!" Sandra piled the licked clean plates into the cupboard. "Hi, Sally!" she said by way of afterthought, "I'll quickly change my top." Sandra began peeling off her jumper and, as she flew by Martin, she was down to her bra. "You naughty boy!" squealed Sandra, as Martin gave her a playful wallop across the bottom. Sally, meanwhile, called a halt to the fluttering and burrowing and, with both palms on either side of her cheeks, she placed her elbows on the table top and sulked.

Sandra belted off upstairs and she came back moments later trying to button her blouse. She swore it had shrunk in the wash. Soon, Sally was on her way with the children and Sandra was ushering me into the rear of the family Cortina.

Throughout the journey, Sandra and Martin laughed, teased, and joked like a pair of adolescents. Sprawled on the back seat, I don't mind telling you that I felt a right proper gooseberry. Hence, it was with a sense of relief when, coming into Camden Town, I saw a spiky-haired individual wearing his smart black suit and his hangdog expression.

I wound-down the window and shouted out to the lobbating figure, "Happy New Year, Paul!" Next, I leaned forward and came between husband and wife. "You can drop me here if you like; I see a friend of mine."

The Cortina slowed and, even before it came to a standstill, I opened the rear door and commenced disembarkation. By the time that the vehicle was parked, I was on the footpath and heading for the trunk for the purpose of extracting my plastic shopping bag of textbooks.

Paul stood with both hands plunged deep in his trouser pockets. "All right are you, Izzy?" he enquired, cheerlessly. Coming as it did from Paul that was about as good as it could get. Indeed, as I found common in all those that couldn't take their drink, conversation never flowed freely from out the lips until alcohol had been permitted to flow in.

Sandra clambered from the driver's seat. "I'll open the boot," she said, scurrying towards the rear of the vehicle. As she did so, the strain on her blouse was such that the buttons were positively popping. And at the spectacle, Paul's eyes were straining and positively popping and all. "There you are," said Sandra, reaching in and grabbing hold of my bag, and, "oops a daisy," she added as the top two buttons gave up the ghost.

All of this time, Martin had remained inside the Cortina with his arm resting casually on the windowsill. He hadn't seen the buttons pop open, but it would have been difficult for him to miss the popping open of Paul's mouth. "Got a problem, mate?" he said gruffly and then he rubbed the bristles atop his head.

Paul immediately stopped his ogling and bent down to the open window. "Who's asking?"

Martin removed his arm from the sill and, with urgency, he began pulling at the door lever. "I'll show you who I am." He sounded aggressive, but rather less so when the door didn't budge and he uttered the caveat, "I will in a bit." Martin tried a shoulder charge but still had no joy. Sandra seemed to sense that there was trouble afoot. She placed my bag on the roadside and scurried back to the vehicle. She clambered into the driver's side just as Martin was trying to clamber out that way. It was as if he had twigged that he had been doing battle with no ordinary nearside door but a Cortina nearside door and, as such, it was always liable to get stuck. "I'll have you next time!" called Martin as the motor car sped off with a backfire, thereby showing off to all of Camden an additional design fault of a Cortina Mk II.

That day we had to go through another of the practical exercises.

It was straightforward enough and entailed a visit to The Central Criminal Court, commonly known as The Old Bailey. That's where the more serious crimes tend to get dealt with and, as such, it's a much favored resort for the injudicious and indiscriminate locking up of innocent and guilty alike. Yes, yes, I know that on the face of it a statement such as that may appear an itsy bitsy sweeping, controversial even. But bear with me a mo' and hark at this.

Paul and I started our day with a swift visit to The Council where we checked our respective pigeon holes. There was nowt in mine and nowt in Paul's either, so, without further ado, we sauntered down to The Bailey.

It was a foreboding place. And the security to get in was a bit foreboding. The brisk rubdown at reception was no worse than in any other Crown Court building. But I wasn't reckoning on the police with flak jackets and machine guns. Either there was a very naughty villain on trial or there had been a tip-off that law students, and moreover law students of Gray's Inn, were intending to descend.

Paul, me, Walsingham-Parker his self ("I'll have him this time, Izzy") and nine others were taken through a couple of corridors. Then, outside one of the courtrooms, we were told that it was a rare old honor to be guests of a judge, and a High Court Judge to boot, and that what he would impart must be treated as strictly confidential. Accordingly, this account is between you and me.

On being escorted into the actual courtroom, we were told to take our places in the wings where some seats were set aside. The judge, a plump, surly individual, who much reminded me of a bumblebee only with a wig on, brought the proceedings to a halt. Another group sat opposite. There were twelve of them just like us. All bar one looked dog-tired and dead bored just like us. I figured they were the jury, 'cause we definitely weren't. In any case, the judge turned to this other lot and said, "Ladies, or rather lady and gentlemen of the jury." He paused while he rubbed his wig up and down and glanced slightly in our direction as if to say, "That other lot are the jury, they are," and then he looked back at them and explained, "The persons who have just entered are students of the Bar," which then rendered it official to them, coming as it did from a judge, that they still were and we weren't the jury. "In other words," he went on, ignoring their immense and obvious disappointment at not after all having been usurped.

"They are trainee barristers." The judge took another shufty at us and then the jury and proclaimed, "The students are my guests," whereupon he looked again at us, only knowingly this time, as if to say, "There you go, I told you they were the jury, I did."

With all or any confusion done away with, the judge said that the proceedings could, indeed, would continue. Only a judge could have done all that unconfusing. But as if to deliberately undo all the said unconfusing, some bright spark popped to his feet and said, "Me Lud! I'm sorry to confuse the issue but a point of law arises!" He looked not a day over fifteen and he was one of three barristers who, bewigged and gowned, had places in front of the dock.

The lady and the gentlemen opposite appeared surprised when the judge said that they must go for a cup of tea while he chatted about the point of law with the barristers. They left the room with a court usher and they did so in a clear and obvious state of confusion.

Perhaps I should mention hereabouts that it is standard practice for lawyers to insult the intelligence of the public by talking in code. In this instance, the expression "A point of law arises" was simply barrister-speak for the fact that while the jury were having their cuppa (and, if their ship had come in, a shortbread biscuit too) the lawyers would have an argument over whether a particular piece of evidence was admissible.

Just as soon as the brass-handled door had clicked shut behind the last of the departing jurors, a witness by the name of Audrey Barton was ordered to be brought into court. She was grey and middle-aged, scruffily dressed in denims and a tired, worn looking jacket that perfectly went with her tired, worn looking face. As the witness, in a clear and obvious state of confusion, shuffled across the well of the court she swiftly glanced in the direction of the dock. There sat two prisoners, one black, the other one white, and they both caste a steely stare.

The judged barked, "Hurry along, madam!" which served only to disorientate the woman even more and, indeed, she stumbled as she went into the witness box.

A card was held up to the woman and she was told to read out loud the words on the card, whereupon the woman swore that she intended to tell the truth, the whole truth, and, nothing but the truth. She did so in a faltering and stammering sort of a way. And while she did so, the judge sighed, tutted, and rapped his fingers smartly on his desktop. A judge he may have been but his skills in the art of judgeship didn't stretch to figuring it out that the witness, owing to accident of birth, and not owing to some malign intention to piss him off, had probably attended some run down East End school. This would have been at about the same time that Sandra and Martin's house was built and, even assuming that she was able to go and be learned to every day in the first place, the facilities at that school were possibly not on a par with those of Eton, Rugby, or, wheresoever it was that His Lordship had gone to mug up in the arts of arrogance, how to shag a young girl, or boy, if she's unable or unwilling, without your mistress finding out, impatience and rudeness (very probably a bit of the old sadomasochism, but to be fair, on an extracurricular basis, that one) and wolfing-down food-bearing hampers from Ma and Pa.

After finishing the oath, Audrey Barton confirmed that she was indeed Audrey Barton and she thereby served notice that here was a witness who had propensities to be truthful and consistent and she could identify persons (herself, at any rate) with accuracy.

The fifteen-year-old barrister opened his mouth, presumably to ask his first question, but he was thwarted by the judge. "Hurry along!" said His Lordship. "I have to complete this trial by Friday!"

Paul, next to whom I sat, leaned in and whispered, rather too loudly, "If the trial runs over, I suppose it will mess up his dirty weekend in Lowestoft."

"Don't be impertinent." The haughty admonishment came from behind and, naturally, it had flowed from the lips of Walsingham-Parker.

"Lowestoft?" said I.

"Right then," said Paul, "I told you I'd have him." He turned his head around. "I'm going to have you, Walsingham–Parson!"

"Parker!"

"Silence in court!" shouted an usher.

"Lowestoft?" I said, again.

Meanwhile, the other proceedings had also begun with Mrs. Barton starting her evidence. It would be the job of the judge to decide whether all or any of what Mrs. Barton intended to say could be heard later by the jury. So basically, while the jurors drank their tea, we would bear witness to their function being usurped after all. Judges and other toffs, in common with posh hookers, have tendencies to talk in Latin about anything that at best is left unsaid (other than between the two consenting parties, in which case fair do's) but at worst may, in certain instances, be regarded as perverse. And falling, as it does, in the latter category, judges have tended to call the procedure for usurping a jury the *voir dire*. Being normal, you would call it a trial within a trial, unless you're from up Dudsall way, in which case you'd call it a ruddy pantomime.

Mrs. Barton told the court that she was the widow of a fish-n-chip shop proprietor. It was alleged that he was murdered by the two defendants. "My Bert, God rest his soul," she sobbed, "rushed out of the shop even though he had been shot. He came back ten minutes later and he handed me a piece of paper and he'd made a note of a car registration number . . ."

She found herself interrupted by the fifteen-year-old whom I figured was the prosecutor. "Now this is of vital importance," he said, and he paused for effect.

"There's no jury," sighed His Lordship, "so just get on with it."

"Yes, Me Lud. Sorry, Me Lud." He was plainly embarrassed, but he ploughed on. "Mrs. Barton. What were the exact words spoken by the deceased?"

"Who?"

"You, know. The deceased, Bert."

"Oh! Sorry!"

"That is quite all right."

"Get on with it."

"Sorry, Me Lud."

Mrs. Barton wore out her jacket even more by wiping her nose on a sleeve. "My Bert, may God forgive those two devils, told me that the white man had shot him with a sawn-off . . ."

"A sawn what?" interrupted the judge. He plainly knew that Mrs. Barton was making reference to a shotgun that had been modified for sinister usage by means of the barrel, or barrels, being shortened in length. In other words, sawn-off.

"I believe," said the fifteen-year- old, haughtily, "that it is a colloquium for a shot gun that has been modified by having its barrel, or barrels, shortened."

David M. Golden

In common with the judge, he knew darned well what Mrs. Barton meant. It's simply that, in courts up and down the country, judges and barristers regularly play the same lofty game that the chattering classes do over their supper tables. ("Oh, Jeremy, while in Cannes we dined with a fellow, John something or other, who apparently appears in a soap opera. Can't think of his last name or the programme, but a nice fellow . . ."). Lying sods. Every jack one of 'em knows the name of the show as they sniff, sip and approve the corked crap that Sophie picked up at a supermarket in the wrong end of Calais. I'd wager they know the night of the week it's on. John's inside leg measurements too, I shouldn't wonder.

Anyway, Mrs. Barton was permitted to get on with it and this is how she got on, "Bert said that it was very lucky for him that the so-and-so couldn't shoot straight 'cause otherwise it would have been his head and not his arm what copped it." Having been passed a tissue by the usher she dabbed both eyes. "But he weren't so lucky, God bless him." She swivelled her head towards the dock and caste a steely stare right back. "They killed him dead, they did." Thereupon, Mrs. Barton burst into tears.

His Lordship sighed and then took a look at his wristwatch. "I suppose you had better sit down, madam."

"You're very kind and you're a gentleman," blubbered Mrs. Barton, thereby demonstrating that, on at least two counts, she was eminently unqualified as a witness to give any sort of expert opinion evidence on the character and demeanour of those who she encountered. She nevertheless accepted the invitation and took her seat.

"Thank you," said the fifteen-year–old. "Please remain standing, I mean seated, because my learned friends may have some questions."

"The only problem," Mrs. Barton carried on, "is that my Bert, may God rest him and bring them two, especially the black one, to book died of a heart attack on his way to hospital."

"I said, thank you, Mrs. Barton," said the fifteen-year-old and he joined his witness in being seated, smartish.

Up popped one of the other barristers. He was much older than the prosecutor. He wore a grey wig; always a dead giveaway for someone who's been round the block a few times. He wore a grey complexion and all; always a dead giveaway for someone who's been knocking back the port and inhaling the Havanas to the extent that he must

129

surely be on his last lap round the said block. He wore a pair of dead Beatle glasses right at the end of his nose. "I represent the defendant Mr. Sparks. Do you understand?" He half-turned and pointed at the dock. "He is the gentleman who is wearing a loud jacket and is, some may say, deficient in the region of his follicles." He nodded repeatedly, just like a toy dog on the back window ledge of an Austin Allegro, and he turned to his brethren and then full face to His Lordship for approval at that one.

"Do you mean the bald white man?" said Mrs. Barton.

"Quite so," said the barrister snappily. He was flustered, I can tell you, for members of the lower orders were not supposed to go round shooting the foxes of members of the upper orders like that. "Did you witness the actual shooting?" he asked.

"No, I was out the back peeling the spuds"

"Peeling the what?" sneered His Lordship.

"I believe, Me Lud, that the witness refers to a root vegetable."

"Tosser," said Paul.

"Don't be so damned impertinent!" said Walsingham-Parker and, just like defense counsel, he nodded at the judge for approval.

"Silence in court!" said the usher.

"Usher," said His Lordship, "I shall require the name of the disruptive student who is nodding at me like a toy dog. I intend to report him to the Dean."

The barrister, meanwhile, was shuffling his papers, as barristers do. He held one of the papers aloft. It was distinguishable from the other bits of paper because it had a tea stain, or maybe a coffee stain, or worse, all over it. "Did you observe the getaway vehicle, madam?"

"No, but. . ."

"And from the words spoken by your husband it was obvious, was it not, that he fully intended to see you again?"

"Aye?"

"Mrs. Barton." The barrister sighed. "Your husband did not think that he was going to die, did he?"

"No."

"Thank you." He sighed again, presumably for luck, and he sat down.

The last of the barristers took his feet. "Mrs. Barton." At least this one sounded more cheerful than the others. "I represent the defendant

Mr. Northam."

"The murdering black bastard," observed the witness.

"Madam!" said His Lordship, fit to bust. "I shall not tolerate behaviour of that sort! Kindly moderate your language or I shall be forced to hold you in contempt!"

"Aye?"

"I shall have you locked up."

"Thank you, Me Lud," said counsel. "Now then, Mrs. Barton, isn't it correct that Bert told you that he was shot by a white man?"

"Yes."

"Thank you, Mrs. Barton."

Now it was the turn of the prosecutor, you remember, the fifteen-year-old, and he hauled himself back up. "I have no re-examination," he declared. "Does your Lordship have any questions?"

"Yes, I jolly well do," and His Lordship sat eagerly forward. "Madam," he began, without bothering to look up from his notebook, "I gather that between the discharging of the unlawfully adapted firearm and . . ."

"Aye?"

"There was a gap of at least ten minutes between the firing of the sawn-off and your conversation with the party, now departed?"

"Aye?"

"You know? Bert."

"Oh! The deceased!"

Paul leaned in again. "By George, I think she's got it." He twizzled his head to the one and nines where Walsingham-Parker was sulking. "She has, you know. She's got it."

"Shut up, you gutter snipe!"

"Silence in court!" said the usher.

"Usher!" said His Lordship. "Remove that individual from my court!"

Paul did his leaning in, all over again. "Told you I'd have him."

"And! And!" said His Lordship. I reckoned he was fair fit to explode, let alone bust, "Take that smirk off your face, Mr. Black!"

"Sorry, Uncle Cess, I mean, Uncle Cecil, I mean, Your Lordship, I mean, Me Lud!"

"Usher!" said Uncle Cess. "I intend to adjourn for a few moments! Kindly inform the jury that we shall be a little longer than anticipated!"

"I reckon they'll be having biscuits," whispered Paul.

"And Usher!" added Uncle Cess. "Tell Paul, I mean, tell Mr. Black to see me in chambers, now!"

CHAPTER THIRTEEN

Nearing the end of the short adjournment, Paul returned to court looking contrite and a bit peaky. Mind you, I'd have sworn he had the crumbs of a chocolate digestive biscuit around his mouth. As for the loathsome Walsingham-Parker. The break had evidently permitted His Lordship suitable time to reflect since the usher passed a note conveying the news that, albeit subject to a final warning, Walsingham-Parker was permitted to remain.

We all stood as the judge came back in. Then, just as soon as he did it, we all did it too and sat down. "Now, then Mrs. Barton," he said, and I'd have sworn he wiped a bit of chocolate from around his mouth, "you stated earlier that there was a gap of some ten minutes between the shooting and your conversation with Bert."

"Yes, that's right."

"And during this period is it possible, probable even, that Bert spoke to other persons?"

"Well, I know for a fact he did. You see, when I left off peeling the root vegetables and waited in the shop, Bert came back with three other people. Total strangers, they were . . ."

"Thank you, madam," smiled His Lordship and, simultaneously, a smug grin was wiped clean off the face of the barrister representing Mr. Northam.

Counsel for Mr. Sparks half rose and, on looking at the judge and, on the judge nodding approval, he fully rose and submitted, "Me Lud. The entire testimony of this witness, as against my client, is inadmissible." He stopped, only for a second, as if he expected a hammering from on high. But his Lordship remained silent, so counsel carried on. "The witness did not herself write down the registration of the vehicle in question. Her statement is therefore hearsay."

His Lordship reclined in his chair. He rubbed his wig up and down his brow a few times and then he looked to the heavens.

"I reckon that Uncle Cess is waiting for divine intervention," I whispered.

"Nah," said Paul, "you don't wait for divine intervention if you think that you're the one who's divine." He pointed skywards. "See that, Izzy? Uncle Attila is giving the ceiling rose some judicial scrutiny. If we get many more vibrations from the construction site opposite, the whole lot's liable to come down and Me Lud will join Bert on his cloud and, more importantly, our family trust will kick in."

"At least Me Lud could ask Bert for a first hand, none hearsay account, Paul." We both chuckled at that one.

When His Lordship was done with inspecting the structure, he addressed the barrister who acted for Mr. Northam. "And where do you stand in all of this?" he asked. "I suppose that you wish the evidence to be admitted because it supports your client's defense?" he said, thereby effectively answering his own question. You had to hand it to Uncle Cess. He'd already usurped the jury. I'd figured that it was only a matter of time before defense counsel was sent away for a cuppa and all.

"It is my client's case," said Mr. Northam's barrister, "that he accepted a lift from the other defendant, sometime after the shooting." He might just as well have tried ordering a meal without chips in a Dudsall restaurant. It was plain to see that His Lordship was having none of it. "Me Lud," continued counsel, "if you're not with me on that . . ."

"Which I'm not," said His Lordship, stating the obvious, because where he stood in the matter was written all over his face. "And how do you intend to deal with the fact that your client made an admission?"

"Ah, yes," said counsel, "my client was induced to make the statement because he was told that he would be granted bail if he did. His wife, you see, was about to give birth."

His Lordship exhaled. "You know perfectly well that that is a matter of evidence. We can convene another *voir dire* if you wish, but," and he had a shufty at his wristwatch. "I have to complete this trial by Friday."

Paul mouthed, "Lowestoft," and he did so knowingly. And then, dispensing with any need on the part of his audience to be skilled in the art of lip reading, he said, "Mr. Northam's only crime is being born with the wrong colored skin."

"Do you know, Paul? For once I agree with you."

"Tell you what, Izzy. Me Lud is, and has always been, a bigot."

Walsingham-Parker, who had somehow managed thus far to heed Uncle Cess's final warning, felt obliged to come in on that one. "How can you possibly malign the character of your good and noble relation?" And, just as Uncle Cess had done, he proceeded to answer his own question with, "It's because you're a black sheep, rogue in the family," and he proceeded to follow through with a demonstration that he had the selfsame character traits as Uncle Cess. "Any one only has to look at his face to know he's guilty."

I don't know what stopped me from clambering over, right then and there, into the one and nines. "You'd look guilty if you'd been locked up on remand for weeks, you bigoted, stuck up, son of a . . ."

"Silence in Court!"

It was next the duty of the fifteen-year-old to have his say on behalf of the prosecution. At first he stood there playing a game of whist, happy families, or something or other, with his papers. He appeared oblivious to the fact that His Lordship was already scribbling down the ruling. He coughed and Uncle Cess stopped writing and looked up. "I submit," submitted the fifteen-year-old, "that this written note," and he held up a copy for all of court to see, "was handed to Mrs. Barton by the deceased. It identifies a motor vehicle that is owned by the defendant, Mr. Sparks. Indeed, he was apprehended in that selfsame vehicle having been observed exceeding the speed limit . . ."

"For pity's sake," said His Lordship, and he shook his noble head, "in my court the commission of an act of murder is not proved by the fact that an accused happens to be caught driving a motor vehicle at thirty five miles per hour in a restricted zone."

Laughter resounded from all around at that one, save and except for the area where the witness box was situated. From there, Mrs. Barton, who it seemed to me had been clean forgotten, sat with tears in her eyes, confused, and most probably frit to death.

The fifteen-year-old tried a different angle. "I submit that the note does not offend the rule against hearsay," and, as if to prove that I cannot be accused of uttering sweeping remarks especially on the subject of toffs, tarts and their use of Latin, he only went and told Uncle Cess, "It forms part of the *res gestae*, Me Lud." He looked dead chuffed at that one and he looked towards us students, especially the female one, for acknowledgment. Next, almost as if he had clocked the glazed looks coming right back at him, he explained, "In other words, the actions by the deceased were so spontaneous that it is inconceivable that he could have been mistaken, confused, or worse, telling an untruth." The barrister paused and, taking hold of a decanter, he poured himself some water. He put a glass to his lips and sipped until it was half-full. "Me Lud!" he carried on boldly and refreshed, "if you are against me on that . . ."

"Which I am," said His Lordship and, with that, the fifteen-year-old nearly coughed up the water that he had only just sipped from his glass, half-empty. "I should imagine," explained Uncle Cess, "that with a shotgun wound to the arm, it was very probable that the deceased was both mistaken and confused . . ."

"But," said the barrister, butting in.

"Do not interrupt!" barked His Lordship, and he looked right angry. "I suppose," he said, calming down a bit, "that you submit that the note was a dying declaration and that, as such, it forms another exception to the rule against hearsay."

"Why, yes I do," said the fifteen-year-old and he looked and sounded as pleased as punch at that one.

"Well that's nonsense," said Uncle Cess, looking and sounding as pleased as punch. He explained, "I have to be satisfied that the deceased was likely to have imparted the truth because he had a settled, hopeless expectation of death. I am informed that, far from anticipating his demise, this man assumed that he would be going to the hospital for the sole purpose of getting himself, I think the expression is . . ." It was his turn to pause for effect and, as sure as he knew the inside leg measurements of that soap actor, "Patched up," he said, knowing full well that, that was indeed, the right expression.

"As Your Lordship pleases," said the fifteen-year-old, with his voice beginning to trail-off. "Perhaps," he rallied, "I can address the court on the issue of the verbal statement?"

At that point, Mrs. Barton tried to assist. "My Bert would not have wanted to worry me because . . ."

His Lordship was quick off the mark and handed down a point of procedure by telling her, "Madam. You are a witness and, as such, it is your job to answer questions."

"Sorry, Your Honorable."

"The word is Honor."

"Aye?"

"It's Your Honor and not Your Honorable!" Uncle Cess, in my humble opinion, was about to go nuclear.

"Sorry, Your Honor."

"That's better, but no, no!" Uncle Cess slapped his forehead and sat back. "I'm My Lord and not Your Honor!"

"Aye?"

His Lordship once more brought the palm of his hand in contact with his brow. It was at a speed even mightier than before and, in the process, the wig nearly came off.

The fifteen-year-old had another crack at the verbal statement bit. "In my submission. . ." But his submitting went no further.

"It is my judgment," adjudged Uncle Cess, "that the statement of the deceased to the effect that he was shot by a white man is hearsay. I will not permit the jury to hear it."

From the region of the dock, Mr. Northam took a leaf out of the judge's book by bringing his palm in contact with his head at high speed. He simultaneously gasped in disbelief. His barrister got up, and cried out, "With respect, M'Lud!" Now then, permit me to interpret that one. You see, when a lawyer, any lawyer, resorts to "with respect" it is the surest indication possible that he is about to be just about as disrespectful as it is possible to get. And to prove that here was no exception to the rule, His Lordship was open-mouthed as the barrister disrespectfully suggested, "Any right-minded person would accept that the statement by the deceased is part of the *res gestae*. The deceased informed Mrs. Barton that he was shot by a white man." He pointed towards the dock. "I will not state the obvious but my client is, in fact, black," he said, stating the obvious.

From his body language, the face discoloration, and from his mouth opening and shutting fourteen to the dozen, I figured that Uncle Cess began shouting his head off. It was not possible to know that as a fact because, upon the barrister having stated the said obvious, a jackhammer had started up on the construction site.

By the time the jack hammering ceased, His Lordship appeared to have calmed down and, in fact, he appeared more concerned by the precarious state of the ceiling than ever he was about the identity of whomsoever it was that had killed Bert, dead.

"Look," said Uncle Cess, calmly, "what is the evidence?" And, as if to prove that old habits die hard, he again answered his own question, and he did so thus. "Before the deceased spoke to his wife, he whiled away the time by chatting with at least three persons, unknown. It follows that the statement to his wife was not spontaneous and, as such, it forms no part of the *res gestae*. The statement is hearsay, pure and simple, and I will not permit the jury to hear it."

"But, but, Me Lud!" protested the barrister, in vain, "the statement by the deceased that he was shot by a white man is probably true!"

His Lordship launched his hand and delivered a further forceful blow to the forehead. "Well of course it's probably true!" he said. "But that's not the evidence!"

The barristers looked blankly at each other whilst, for the purpose of the record, Uncle Cess read aloud the decision that he had already written down. He kept one eye on the stenographer whose job it was to make the record. When the judge was done and, on presumably being contented that the travesty had been fully and accurately recorded, he commanded, "Let the jury return!"

The eleven men of the jury came in, followed by the one woman of the jury who, as pointed out by Paul, appeared to be stroking away biscuit crumbs from the region of her mouth.

Just as soon as they were seated, His Lordship told them, "Thank you for your patience. Now, please do not speculate but for reasons that are none of your business we have found that there is insufficient evidence upon which you can safely convict the defendant, Mr. Sparks." He ran his keen legal eye over the jury and he eventually settled on the solitary female member. "You, madam." The female sat bolt upright, pointed at herself, as if to say, "who, me?" and Uncle Cess said, "Yes, you, madam. Please stand." The woman did as she had been told. "I daresay that you and the other members of the jury have yet to appoint a chairman."

"Actually," said the woman, and her tone was both clear and confident, "we have not appointed a chairman. However, we have taken the precaution of appointing a chairperson and I am that person."

His Lordship slung his fountain pen on the desk top. It rolled off

138

the edge and landed below on the stenographers head. "Ouch! Sorry, My Lord."

"Madam Chairperson," said Uncle Cess and he said it with sarcasm and I could tell, from the titters emanating, that it appealed only to the barristers present and to Walsingham-Parker, "you the jury have taken an oath to try the case according to the evidence. Only you, the jury, are empowered to acquit Mr. Sparks and I direct you so to do."

"I beg your pardon?" She was indignant, and that's the truth.

Uncle Cess flagellated the judicial brow once more. "Listen to me, Madam Chairwoman. . ."

"Person!"

"All right, all right!" His Lordship took a deep breath. "Madam Chairperson. On the charge of murder contrary to common law do the jury find the defendant Mr. Sparks not guilty?"

"What about the live cartridges found in his pocket?"

"Madam. Your duty is to judge this man according to the evidence and not the truth. You find this man not guilty, do you not?"

Madam Chairperson looked at her colleagues. The eleven men shrugged and nodded and thereby gave their consent to the bringing in of a not guilty verdict. "Not guilty, I suppose," she said.

In the dock, Mr. Sparks shot to his feet, punched thin air, and cried, "Yes!"

In the dock, Mr. Northam remained seated, placed his head in his hands, and cried, "No!"

From where we sat, much of the public gallery was obscured. However, there was no obscuring the ovation that emanated from it as the not guilty verdict was handed down. Amidst the clapping, cheering, and whistles, one voice was heard to say, "See yah outside Charlie, boy! Bill says we're goin' to 'ave a right old knees up tonight!" The statement, of course, was hearsay, pure and simple. A court would not have accepted that Bill, whomsoever he was, intended to organize a knees up and, moreover, a right old knees up, at that.

In the dock, meanwhile, I observed that Mr. Sparks was as magnanimous in victory as he had been when bestowing the contents of a shotgun cartridge upon Bert. He leapt around in circles, blowing kisses at learned counsel, the eleven men and one woman true and even the judge. It is fair to state that, momentarily, he had stopped and listened to the account of Bill's intention to convene the knees up. Indeed, he had responded by calling back, "I can't wait! I ain't had a drink in months!" which only went to prove that he, himself, was not averse to relying on the odd hearsay statement.

I also observed His Lordship mouthing something. His actual words were drowned out by a combination of the raucous behaviour in the gallery and a resumption of the jack hammering outside. So, Uncle Cess beckoned the usher and whispered something in his ear. The usher went to the fifteen-year-old and whispered something in his ear. The fifteen-year-old turned to his colleagues and said, "The judge has discharged the Defendant, Sparks! We are to reconvene at two o'clock!" Meanwhile, Uncle Cess had got up to leave, only going to prove that he personally was not averse to having statements uttered by him transmuted into hearsay and then relied on by others as truth of their content.

A prison guard escorted Mr. Northam below. Another guard escorted Mr. Sparks to a door and released him. "I'm suing the police for malicious prosecution!" he shouted, upon vacating the dock.

As the courtroom began to clear, the usher came across to us students. "If you would care to wait here, His Lordship says he will be out to join you in a few moments."

"Well, I'm leaving," said Paul. "Are you coming too, Izzy?"

Totally taken aback, the usher said, "But His Lordship says that he intends to answer all your questions. What shall I tell him?"

"Tell him what you like, mate. The statement that His Lordship said he'll be out soon is probably true but I don't believe it."

The usher was flummoxed. "But I don't understand."

Paul shrugged. "There's no evidence that he'll be out." He stood up. "Tell His Lordship that I'm taking a leaf out of his book and ignoring anything that's hearsay," and, with that, Paul left.

CHAPTER FOURTEEN

Later I alighted stiff legged at High Barnet.

It had been a funny old day; first the barmy goings-on at The Bailey, followed by a near race riot when news of the said barmy goings on had hit the street and then a feeling, almost of decadence, as I had entered the tube station with a view to the purchase of a ticket to ride, in lieu of the procurement of a bench upon which to doze. As I turned the street corner, brandishing my *Evening Standard*, two children who were happily at play, gouging plants from some unfortunate's garden, called time on their capers and came about.

"Awoe, Uncle Izaak," beamed young Jason Crowe and, thrusting a fistful of winter pansies in my hand, the over familiar sprog said, "me and Ben have picked these for you."

I instinctively reached forth and accepted the offering but, mindful of the law of theft and, in particular, that part which dictates that the purloining of cultivated foliage is improper, I passed the booty to little Ben. I reckoned that it was just and equitable that if anyone was going to have his collar felt for larceny, then the nursling might as well swing for it.

Just then, and as if to complete the triad, along bounded Thomas, still swathed in bandages. "Uncle Izaak! Uncle Izaak!" spluttered the hasty hoodlum. "Aunty Janie is here!"

"Who?"

"Jetty, Jetty! It's Aunty Janie Jetty, Uncle Izaak!"

I rested the palm of my hand on the youngsters head. "I think you're wrong, Thomas." I sounded contrite. "You see, Janie. I mean Aunty Janie is at her house and it's a long, long way away."

"Do you mean Prestwick, Uncle Izaak?" He was a bright one, all right.

"Yes, I do mean Prestwick, Thomas," and I muttered under my breath, "with young Pinstripe, I'll wager."

"Oh no, she's not in Prestwick, Uncle Izaak." Thomas raised his swathed head, looked me straight in the eyes and said, "Aunty Janie Jetty is here on business, she is," and then he nodded and said, "she told me so." He nodded a second time, and then added. "And there's no Uncle Pinstripe, either. But she did tell Mummy that she wanted to come here alone to meet someone special."

Now, from an evidential point of view, this was a tricky one. For starters, I had to consider whether, as a child, the witness was both competent and compellable. I reckoned that, on balance, Thomas was a good sort and, besides, he stuck firm to his story even after I had examined him on the dangers of impiety and falsehood. So, on the basis that my threat of a cuff round the ear didn't break him, I proceeded to cogitate on the dangers of admitting hearsay evidence.

Is it possible, I pondered, *that Janie's statement that she's here in High Barnet, alone, to meet someone special, is an admission against her own interests and that, as such, it constitutes one of the common law exceptions to the rule against hearsay?* I could have gone further and concluded that the statement was not an exception to the rule at all but, rather, was not hearsay in the first place. Listen up and I'll elucidate. The fact in issue happened to be whether there was any hanky-panky between Janie, my benefactor and she who I loved, of the one part, and young Pinstripe, the hotshot commercial lawyer, of the other part. My *ratio decidendi* was that the statement conveyed via the child merely contradicted my assertion that the said Janie, my benefactor (and so on and so forth) was surely, at that moment, stuck up in Prestwick with Pinstripe stuck to her like Artex.

It was no good. Bend the law of evidence as much as I liked, no High Court Judge would have accepted that Janie was within "taking in my loving arms distance." Though the statement that she had come down alone to High Barnet to see someone special was possibly true, having been made in the presence and earshot of Thomas, his imparting of the gem could not have been spontaneous. On his way up the street, the little blighter had gone via the grocery store. Of that I was certain for throughout our parley he had been slurping on a frozen Jubley. The statement was not therefore part of the *res gestae*, it could not be relied on, and so, right there and then, I might just as well have forgotten the love of my life.

I patted the tyke on the head, said, "I'll see you later," and ran down the street screaming, "bollocks to hearsay!"

"Is that you?" said Sandra, as I blustered through the front door. Her voice came from the region of the kitchen.

My intention had been to steal in unnoticed and frequent the bathroom for beautification purposes. Regrettably, such ambitions were thwarted by an unusual chain of events, kick-started by the simple act of scooping up Tuppence. She had been lying on the warm bonnet of the little green car that was parked outside the house. It was necessary to juggle with Tuppence while I searched my trouser pockets for the house keys. She took a distinct disliking to all of the manhandling and dealt me a blow with her claws which scratched me, left to right, from forehead to mouth. Upon eventual insertion of key in lock, I pushed against the door only to discover (upon the door rebounding in my face) that there was an obstruction. I therefore booted the door and it flew open and, in the process, Crackerjack who, it transpired, had been snoozing on the doormat, was sent skidding along the hallway.

"Hi, Sandra! Yes, it is I!" and I tumbled into the kitchen, whereupon Tuppence swiped a further blow across my face which, on this occasion, was from right to left. Having thereby formed a perfect cross, Tuppence leapt straight into Janie's lap. "Oh, what a surprise! Hi, Janie!"

Janie stood up from the tiny kitchen table at which she and my landlady had presumably been discussing a certain person. Janie handed Tuppence to me and coldly said, "I see that you have been in the wars again, Izaak. I suggest that you tend to those scratches before they turn septic."

Sandra followed Janie in rising, only she went to the fridge. She reached in and extracted a large chunk of raw meat. "Here," she said, "put this on your eye while you're about it. You look just as if you've walked into a door, or something." Regrettably, Tuppence snatched the morsel, wolfed it down in one, leapt from my arms and, with a growl, she made for the general direction of the cat flap. "Oh," said Sandra, "You'd best settle for some ice."

I went upstairs feeling rather ridiculous. I came back down a few moments later to find the girls seated under the paper lanterns in the rather more luxurious living area. Never mind about feeling ridiculous. I certainly looked it. For starters, my eye had definitely come off second best following its altercation with the front door. It was half closed and was going blacker by the minute. I'd tried hard to clean up the crisscross scratches, but it had been hopeless. Indeed, you could have hoisted me up the nearest pole and passed me off as Saint Patrick's flag.

As soon as I came in, Sandra got up from the sofa, said, "Oh dear, that looks really sore," and then announced that she would boil the kettle.

I nabbed the place that had been vacated and, as I did so, Janie uncurled her legs and nudged, as far as she could go without falling off, to the far end of the sofa. I thought to myself, *Aha, trying to play it cool are you?* So, on the basis that two could play that game, I nudged up to the other end.

There followed an awkward silence that, eventually, was broken by Janie. She coughed, ever so slightly, and undid the top button of her suit top. My heart leapt for joy at the sight of her reddened chest. She could play it as cool as she liked but, in my book, there was no disguising those telltale signs of passion. She coughed, again. "Izaak, I think you should know that I am here . . ."

"I think I know, Janie and I . . ."

"Do you? But how?"

We heard the front door bang open and the pattering of three pairs of little feet. I simply had to let it be known to Janie that I knew of her generosity and I had to be let it be known also of my good and honorable intentions towards her. I only got as far as, "I must thank you . . ." when the triad burst in.

"Awoe, Aunty Janie!"

"Why, hallo my little dears!" She hadn't spoken to me in such tender tones, and that's no word of a lie. Her eyes sparkled as she addressed the youngsters. "And what do we have here?"

"These are for you," said the nursling in a crystal clear tone. Until that moment, I had rather assumed that he had never, since arriving in this life, gotten around to talking. What a fine how-do-you-do. He'd only been invoking the Fifth Amendment.

"Why, thank you!" said Janie. Her wonderful eyes sparkled and she leaned forward.

The nursling presented Janie with the pilfered pansies. Well, to be exact, he handed over a bunch of stalks, for fate had dealt the bouquet a hardy blow betwixt the end of the street and the end of the sofa. I imagined that the catastrophe had befallen the nursling as late as his unwarranted intrusion into the front room. This proposition was based on evidence taking the form of a half a dozen or so petals protruding from Crackerjacks mouth.

Janie planted a kiss firmly on the nursling's cheek. I immediately reproached myself for having tried to frame him. You see, there would have been no mutilation of the flowers had they remained under my custody, care, and control. And if a fistful of mangled stalks from the likes of a nursling warranted a smackeroo of those proportions, I imagined what might have awaited he who presented Janie with unsullied blooms.

From the hallway, I heard the ringing of the telephone. The children made a dash to answer the thing, thereby leaving me alone with Janie, once again. Above the noise of chattering through the wall, I had a bash at starting from where I had left off. "Janie," I said, "I know that . . ."

We were interrupted by Sandra who breezed in holding a fully laden tray. "Tea up!" she chirped. "I'm not interrupting anything, I hope."

My landlady had no sooner placed the tray down when the triad burst back in. "Mummy!" cried the eldest, in a state of excitement. "Guess what?" And, as if not to be out done by a High Court Judge, he demonstrated that he too was skilled in the art of answering his own question. "Sally and the gang are coming round to have supper with Aunty Janie!"

"That's great," said Sandra, "isn't it, Izaak?"

"Simply great," I said, and I folded my arms and crossed my legs and thought, *this is great, this is.*

Janie focused her beautiful eyes on the watch upon her slender wrist. "I really ought to be thinking about checking into my hotel."

"Oh, but you must stay for a short while," pleaded Sandra, and she grabbed Janie by her wrist. "Please, please stay."

"Yes, yes, yes," came a chorus from the children and then, in the middle of it all, the nursling pointed straight at Janie's chest and said, "Aunty Janie Jetty has gone all red!"

Most middle class supper parties that I have had the misfortune to attend have been tortuous, tacky affairs. And this one proved to be no

145

exception. Sandra and Sally expended much time gossiping about celebrities. They professed to know personally singers, actors and minor royals which was simultaneously spooky and remarkable considering that at least three such persons had been absent from this life for nigh on ten years.

Sally took it on herself to organize the seating and I was as far away from Janie as it could get without being deposited on the garden swing. Each time that I looked up from my prawn cocktail I felt quite certain that Janie was in the swift process of looking away.

Now and again there was a lull in the conversation, at which stage, all eyes would be turned on me for the purpose of those present making enquiry as to my legal studies and how come that someone with a Black Country accent came to be studying at the Bar. I imagined that the enquires were really only made in the manner of conversational condescension, so I simply pretended I'd not heard, kept my head down, and got on with scoffing whatever it was that lurked under the bread crumbs.

Towards the end of the meal, at the Black Forest gateaux stage to be exact, there occurred a delightful incident when Dean (or was it Ron?) decided that it would be truly fun if the ladies changed places with a male. All giggly-like the girls thought that a change of company would be just the ticket. And so, I found myself sitting between Ron and Dean. And as for Janie. Well, despite having also changed places, she was still the farthest from me. There could be no doubting it that Janie was a cool cookie.

Justin found himself seated next to Sandra and, on the one (metaphoric) hand; he proceeded to feign interest in her mind. But with his other (literal) hand he demonstrated remarkable interest in her plentiful thigh. I deduced that Justin's mind had become fuddled with Black Tower because he had, you see, clean forgot that the tabletop was made of glass. "It's like gawping into an aquarium," said I, assuming that the heat would be taken out of a potentially tricky situation. Well, what a hullabaloo. Martin decked Justin; Sandra decked Martin; Ron and Dean decked each other; Janie, coldly, got up and departed; Sally fluttered her eyes, burrowed her chin, looked lustily at me; I looked lustily at the bottle of hock and spent a lonesome night on the garden swing.

CHAPTER FIFTEEN

The following day after lectures, we had to attend another one of those practical exercises. The subject matter was the art of advocacy and the venue was a place most grand, namely, The Royal Courts of Justice.

I met up with Paul at a prearranged spot in Chancery Lane. I caught him gazing into the window of a jewellers shop. "When I'm qualified, I shall get one of those things to swing around," and he pointed at a row of half hunters on chains. "Oh, how do, Izzy? You look a bit fed up," he added by way of afterthought.

"It's nowt I can't handle," I said, nonchalantly.

Paul gave me the once over. With his one hand he scratched and ruffled his spiky hairdo. He bent slightly and, with the other hand, he copped hold of his attaché case that he had laid to rest on the footpath, presumably so that he could admire the gold watches on display. "You even forgot to dodge those broken paving slabs on the way up the street. My guess is that it's woman trouble. Who is it, Izzy? Not the landlady, is it? What time is it, by the way?"

"Try looking in the window again," I said, "there's every type of timepiece known to man staring back at you."

"Oops! We'd best make a move." He began walking towards The Strand. "Only if it is the landlady, I can quite understand. She's a big girl, you know."

"Yes."

"Aha! So, I'm right."

"No! I mean, yes, she's a bigun, all right, but no. It's not her."

"Don't tell me, Izzy." He stopped and blocked my path. "Is it the Janie woman?" And, taking a leaf out of Uncle Cess's book, he answered his own question. "Yes it is," and he proceeded to offer the

147

advice, "Now see here, Izzy, this can't be permitted to go on. There are plenty more fish in the sea."

We arrived at the steps of the court. Business for the day had long since concluded and the only persons to be found milling around consisted of security staff, cleaners, and fellow law students. Most of the students were unknown to me. Due to the sheer volume of students, compared with the relatively small facilities, I imagined that the organising of the lectures and practical exercises was akin to despatching a whole army on manoeuvres. And at the end of it all, we all knew the score. Only a fraction of us would get a pupillage and then go on to practice at the Bar of England and Wales.

But, hang about, I thought. At least one of the students milling about had a familiar face. It was Caroline. She of porcelain features and formerly of Lincoln's Inn Fields. She had plainly gotten wise and rid herself of the sextuplets. Further and additionally, she had plainly gotten wise and realized that there was more than met the eye to your average vagabond who nestles under your average little tin table.

"Why, hallo there," she beamed.

"There you go, Izzy. I told you so. There's plenty more fish in the sea."

Caroline strode across the steps. There was a breeze that night, wafting down The Strand. Consequently, Caroline kept shaking her head, ever so slightly, and at the same time she was brushing golden strands of hair from in front of her face. "I haven't a clue where to go. I gather that I'm in the Vice Chancellors Court."

With a sharp, discreet nudge, Paul propelled me forwards. "Oh, er, I know the layout fairly well," I lied. "I'm happy to show you. We're in that court too," and at least on both of those counts I had actually stated the honest truth.

"Gosh, thanks awfully," said Caroline.

As we turned to go in the building, the breeze really took hold and Caroline's tresses were lifted up so that her entire face was obscured. "Here, allow me." I said, and I copped hold of the flyaway hair and kept it from in front of her eyes. I was obliged to hold her dark skirt down a bit. That was interesting, that was, but I let go just as soon as we were in the calm of the building.

"Gosh, thanks awfully."

It had been my pleasure, and that's a fact. My swift actions had been close up and personal and she hadn't minded a bit.

What with all the flapping around Caroline, it was hardly surprising that I'd clean forgot Paul who was following on. I'll bet you've seen on the TV news just how big the front doors are. And Paul didn't take kindly to me letting the things swing shut in his face.

"Gosh, thanks awfully." He could be downright sarcastic, could Paul, when he wanted to be.

I steered Caroline and Paul through the stone clad corridors. I felt just like a mountain guide.

"Gosh! It's like a rabbit warren," said Caroline, as we bombed along the acres of stone flags. "By the way, I'm Caroline. Caroline Hunter."

"I'm Izaak. Izaak Gatehouse."

"Oxford, was it, where we met?"

"I'm Paul. Paul Black." He was scurrying behind and sounded out of breath. It hadn't helped that, at one point, Paul had gone scooting down the wrong tunnel. But at least he'd caught up in time to save my embarrassment. It was unintentional on his part, of course.

Suddenly, Caroline skidded on the floor. You see, the stone flags had turned to tiles and she hadn't been expecting it. I caught her in my arms and just saved her from hitting the deck. "My saviour," said Caroline, and our eyes met and lingered a bit. I lifted her so that she was once more vertical. And, not the first time that night, I found myself custodian of her modesty by tugging at her skirt until the hem was back where it belonged. Caroline adjusted the skirt, then she tugged at it herself and gave it one more adjustment. "I don't really know you, Izaak, but . . ." she paused and smiled, "you have knowledge of me."

"Oh! I'm very sorry," and I held up both hands, as if in surrender.

"I did not mean it as criticism, Izaak." She smiled, and brushed away still more flyaway strands. Even close up, her complexion was flawless and she definitely wore no makeup. I figured that Caroline was technically more pretty than Janie. Small wonder that she was the beauty of the law course and was declared as such in the student magazine. "Izaak," said Caroline, "did you hear me?"

"Oh, er. Sorry. I was only thinking that we've passed our courtroom."

Caroline adjusted her skirt, for the third time. "I did not mean it as

149

a criticism," she repeated, only adding, this time, "and I found it rather intimate." The add-on was said in a whisper, presumably so Paul couldn't hear.

We did a double back, ploughing into Paul in the process. "Watch it, Izzy. And you, Caroline. These are brand new shoes, you know."

We retraced our steps only this time with Paul in the lead. It was very nearly time for the exercise to start and so we had to get a move on. Indeed, we very nearly broke into a trot. "Izaak," said Caroline, and she stopped and so I stopped. Paul didn't realize we'd stopped and he carried on. "You know that there is to be a cocktail party at Middle Temple?"

"Yes, I have heard," I said, and I was telling the truth. I had heard about that particular shindig. You'll recall that Middle Temple is one of the four Honorables. The knees up to which Caroline eluded was indeed at Middle Temple but, as I understood it, anyone could get tickets. I'd even heard they intended to let solicitors in.

"Gosh, you must think me very forward," said Caroline, "only I have two tickets, and should very much like you to have one." As Caroline spoke, she kept playing with her blouse. It was odd. She kept undoing the top button and then doing it up again. Her jacket was open all the time and I'd have been made of stone not to notice the womanly curves.

"I couldn't deprive you of a ticket, Caroline," I said. *And besides,* I thought, *I can't afford it.*

"I think you misunderstand, Izaak." She noticed me ogling at all the buttoning and unbuttoning and she stopped doing it. She did so at the unbuttoned stage. Her chest was as smooth and as pure white as milk. "Izaak? Can you hear me, Izaak?"

"Oh, er. Sorry. It's just that I realize that we're at our courtroom." And it was true. A varnished plaque was there, on the door, to prove it. Vice Chancellors Court is what it said.

I pushed open the door for Caroline to pass. "Can we go to the cocktail party as a couple, Izaak?" She and that unbuttoned blouse were pressed up against me, tight.

I swallowed hard. It was a fair old turn up for the book. "I'd like that very much," I said. And as we entered the courtroom, I was thinking, *Two can play that game, Janie.*

The room was like one of those Chinese puzzles. It was mostly wooden and there were little benches in little boxes all over. Each box slotted neatly into another box. The place for the judge was in a box, so too were the places for the barristers, the solicitors, everyone in fact had their own box. There was a box, naturally, for a witness, though that wasn't a surprise, 'cause where would the court, any court, be without its witness box? The only place in the whole room where the box builder had not built a box was on the sidewalls where there were dozens and dozens of law books. They were on shelves and not in boxes.

Caroline and I had to zigzag through and around the boxes to get to the front of the court. We took our places in the box usually reserved for counsel.

"Good of you to find time," said a smooth, raven-haired barrister. He was in the judge's box. I knew he was a barrister because beneath a smart, black jacket, he wore a stripy tunic shirt and it had no collar attached and the top was un-studded. He'd plainly come out of court earlier, taken off his stiff wing collar and left his neck bare. Barristers still do it to this day. They pathetically think it's rock-n-roll.

Caroline was seated next to Paul and I was seated, on the end, next to Caroline. Paul leaned forward and looked at me with the hangdog look. He next took a shufty at Caroline, and in particular at her unbuttoned blouse, and then he looked at me, again. "Yes," he said, "good of you to find time." He once more took a shufty at Caroline. "In fact, Izzie, I'm amazed you found time at all."

"I assume that you are Mr. Gatehouse," said the barrister, coldly. I nodded and thereby conveyed to him the fact that his assumption could not have been more accurate. He looked at Caroline, looked at the name sheet in front of him, looked at Caroline, again, and warmly said, "I suppose that you are Miss Hunter?"

"I jolly well am!"

"Jolly good. Well done," said the barrister, smarmily. He sat staring at her for a few moments, while he presumably took on board the full extent of the vision of loveliness before him. As the barrister did so, he affectionately stroked his thick head of hair. Here was someone who loved himself something rotten.

Paul coughed. "Shall we crack on, mate? I mean, shall we start, sir? I have a train to catch."

"Oh yes, of course." The barrister shuffled some bits of paper. He had another swift deco at Caroline and, on the basis that he was peering right down the very end of his own nose, I adjudged that the distraction came from the region of the unbuttoned blouse and a couple of areas of outstanding natural beauty. "My name is Patrick Dawe," said the barrister. "I practice in the criminal courts and I have chambers in The Temple." The atmosphere was strangely tense, and I put it down to the sight and smell of all that wood and all those leather books. "At the end of last term you were presented with three briefs in respect of fictional criminal cases. I propose to call each of you by name and nominate the case that will be presented by that individual."

Caroline exhaled. "Gosh, Izaak. I'm jolly glad that I read all three briefs."

Paul leaned forward. He looked at me, then took a swift look at the open blouse, looked at me again, and said, "Gosh, Izzy. I thought we could select our own case and I've only read one." He paused, just a bit, while he had another gander. "At least I have a one in three chance of striking it lucky."

Well, my chances of striking it lucky were exactly nil. I hadn't been around at the end of term to collect any of this coursework. You may recall that I'd gone home with early Christmas gifts, in the form of hypothermia and a gin bottle shape gash to the forehead.

Our instructor looked towards Caroline. Indeed, it would be fair to state that he'd hardly stopped looking at her throughout. "Miss Hunter," he said, presently, "you may proceed first and I wish you to present mitigation in the case of the police against Mr. Speedy."

Caroline uncurled her legs and arose. While she was doing so, I leaned across to Paul, "Phish," I went, "Sling us your papers so I can take a butchers." Paul duly obliged. "Cheers, mate."

"Silence!" said Patrick Dawe, "You're being grossly discourteous towards Miss Hunter."

Caroline swished her hair. With one hand she took hold of her notes. The other hand, meanwhile, recommenced the buttoning and unbuttoning only, this time, she was at it two buttons at a time. Hers was one nervous habit that I didn't find in the tiniest bit annoying. Indeed, had the occasion arose, I'd have happily paid any therapist of hers to make the condition worse rather than better.

"Gosh, right," said Caroline, "you did say the mitigation part, yah?"

"Oh, yah," said the barrister, transfixed.

Caroline commenced her mitigation and, to the immense disappointment of all those present, she did so at a stage where the buttons were done up. "My chap, this Mr. Speedy fellow, shouldn't lose his driving license." She turned a page of her notes. "Talk about dashed rotten hard luck. He's not a bad old stick, you know . . ."

The vision of loveliness droned on in like fashion for all of one minute. When she was done, Patrick Dawe sighed, "That was wonderful, quite wonderful." But, just as soon as Caroline was seated, he appeared to pull himself together and snappily said, "Gatehouse! It's the shoplifting case for you."

"I'd rather do the speeding case."

"I cannot hear you, Gatehouse."

"I'd rather do the speeding case!"

"No, no, Gatehouse!" said the barrister. "I cannot hear you because this is a court of law and you have not exhibited the courtesy of rising to your feet to address me."

"Aye?"

"Oh, for pity's sake!" He looked right racked off, I can tell you. "When I say I cannot hear you, I actually mean that I will not hear you."

"I'd rather do the speeding case," I said rising.

"Yes, I heard you the first time," said the barrister, "and I have decided that you will do the shoplifting case. Let me see, now," and he began rummaging through the papers before him, "ah, yes," he carried on, upon locating what he was after, "it's the case against Mr. Pilfer before the Apprehendum Magistrates Court."

I did my own rummaging and extracted the relevant papers from the pile that Paul had given me. I opened the pretend brief and a dozen or so sheets slid out and fluttered onto Caroline's lap. I didn't have time to retrieve them, even though it would have been my pleasure so to do. Mind you, I did have time to notice that she was at it with the buttons, again.

"Your Worships," I began, boldly, and that's as far as I got before the illustrious Mr. Dawe stuck his oar in.

"No, no, no," he said, "no. Only solicitors and police officers address the magistrates in that fashion." He stroked his hair, and checked out the score with the blouse. Caroline was at a midway stage.

153

"We barristers," he said, after his eyes had popped back in, "rise above that sort of thing. It is appropriate to address the chair and only then by the title of sir or, as the case may be, madam."

I started again. "Madam," I said, and I could see the barrister wasn't amused because he only went and wrote a cross on his score sheet. "As you are aware, my client Mr. Pilfer has a hitherto exemplary background. . ."

"Izaak," whispered Caroline with urgency, "you dropped this," and she handed me one of the flyaway papers. It consisted of a list of the previous criminal convictions belonging to my fictional client.

"I propose to start again," I proposed, after I had given the list a quick once-over.

"Well, I propose that you will do no such thing," said Patrick Dawe, smugly. "You are supposed to be in a court of law, and . . ." he glanced at Caroline, gulped, and dropped his lower jaw, for she'd only gone and started on the third button down. He blinked, shook his head rapidly as if he hadn't believed what he was seeing, and carried on having his pop at me. "You do not get second chances in a court of law. It's not like playing charades, you know." He wrote another cross.

Off I went, again. "He has, of course, led an exemplary life since becoming a reformed bank robber . . ."

"What about the conviction for arson, Gatehouse?"

"Well, all right, there was the arson incident . . ."

"And don't forget the burglary."

"Oh, absolutely, sir, but let's face it, sir, he hasn't been in trouble for five years."

"Five days," said the barrister.

"Aye?"

"He committed a string of shoplifting offenses while he was on police bail. You will find the details on page five, which I assume is laying on Miss Hunter's lap."

"Lucky old page five is what I say!" The barrister awarded me another cross.

I struggled on in like fashion for what seemed an age. When it was done, I plonked myself down in the box.

"Bad luck," said Caroline, "an attack of nerves can happen to the best of us," and she squeezed my arm, ever so slightly.

Paul had his go and was well pleased when the barrister

announced what case he would be doing. "My one in three has come up, Izzy. I must bet on a horse this weekend." He proceeded to present his case and he did so without hesitation or indeed interruption from Patrick Dawe.

When we were done, the barrister proceeded to outline the basis on which he proposed to assess our respective performances. It is proper to state that he relished his role. He reminded us that failure to pass the practical exercises would result in the degree of utter barrister being withheld. He also opted to remind us that only an utter barrister was empowered to practice at the Bar. Next, he told us how we had got on. "Miss Hunter is top," he said, "and I must say that she gave an excellent speech in mitigation."

"Gosh, thank you very much," and, with four buttons undone, she beamed at the barrister.

"Gatehouse!" he said, after he had done with beaming straight back at Caroline. "You did by far the worst, but. . ." Continuing to relish our discomfort, he opted to pause. "I suppose that I will give you the bare minimum pass."

"Gosh, thank you sir."

"And, Gatehouse."

"Yes, sir?"

"I suggest that next time you're in a hole, stop digging."

"Yes, sir."

We began collecting our belongings and were in the process of exiting when Patrick Dawe called out, "Miss Hunter! I wonder if I could have a word."

"Oh! Right, yah!" And then in hushed tones, she said, "what do you think he wants, Izaak? I won't be a tick."

Caroline zigzagged her way round the Chinese puzzle until she reached the very front of the court. A conversation ensued between her and the barrister. Once, he looked over her shoulders at me. Twice she looked over her own shoulders at me, while he looked at the front of her blouse.

"Don't wish to state the obvious," said Paul, "but," and he proceeded to state the obvious, "I think they're talking about you."

After a giggle or two, Caroline unzigzagged her way back to where I had so patiently remained. She seemed a bit embarrassed. "Izaak," she said, "this is a little embarrassing. Paddy, I mean Patrick, has invited me to the cocktail party. Members of his chambers will be present and he feels certain that they will accept me as a pupil." She swished her hair and glanced momentarily in the direction of the eager barrister. "Tell you what," she said, "you can jolly well have both of my tickets for free."

"Ha!" laughed Paul. "That's a good one, that is."

"Whatever do you mean?" said Caroline.

"Possibility of pupillage? Barrister's equivalent of the casting couch, that is," said Paul, "oh, and by the way," he added, "in the name of heaven, button your blouse, woman."

"Look here, Caroline," I said, as she hastily made herself decent, "It really isn't a problem." And it was true. It wasn't a problem. The most beautiful female on the course she may have been but, when all was said and done, Caroline Hunter was simply not Janie Jetty.

CHAPTER SIXTEEN

The drudgery of practical exercises and lectures continued and, for that matter, so did the drunken dinners.

To cap it all, there was no respite in the Crowe's habitation. On more than one occasion I came close to upping sticks and reverting to sleeping alfresco. The problem, you see, was that the murder of Crowe's had irrepressible tendencies to lurch from one crisis to another.

I enjoyed some evenings gainfully employed at The Coach and Horses. Sandra and Martin enjoyed most other evenings with the gang also at The Coach and Horses and I would find myself ungainfully employed looking after their triad.

I regret that I was a negligent sort of a childminder. I frequently found myself having to interrupt research into the most abominable of subjects, such as revenue law, for the purpose of researching the most abominable of screams emanating from the kitchen, the airing cupboard, or whatever. The nursling, in particular, was adept at sticking household utensils into places where no household utensil ought really to have been stuck.

I swear that the odds were even that on my hosts return from their night out, one of them would have to belt off to the infirmary for the purpose of signing parental consent so that some infernal object could be retrieved by either pushing, sucking, pulling and, once, even by cutting.

Of Janie, I heard nothing. But I consoled myself that hers was a waiting game and that when the time was right she would declare her intentions. I consoled myself also that it would not be long before I became a respectable barrister-at-law. I reasoned that that was when Janie's declaration would come. There could be no other explanation for her having so generously sponsored me. And it was the thought of being as one with Janie that drove me on.

The day of the cocktail party dawned and, courtesy of Caroline, I had the two free tickets. I thought about taking Sandra, but that might have sent out the wrong signal. A strong hint had come from Sally's direction. I'd rather have danced on hot coals. I contemplated getting in touch with Janie. I could easily have got the number from Sandra, even if it meant rummaging through her handbag, or her dressing table drawers. On balance, I concluded that I must respect Janie's wishes and bide the time before I could show her off.

I therefore resolved that I would go alone. But at teatime, while dodging the cracks between the paving stones in Fleet Street, I happened on Michaela. Now, Michaela worked at the pub along the river. Ian had described her as a minx and, granted she and the other barmaids had a propensity to dress innovatively. You know the sort of gear to which I refer. Granted also, she and the others had a propensity to go upstairs quite a lot, especially with the mature clientele. But I'd always found her rather amiable. And, as it happened, she was better spoken than me. Mind you, coming as I did from Dudsall, that weren't saying a lot.

Well, Michaela jumped at the opportunity of being my squeeze for the night. I had no sooner put the proposition to her than she had shot off to get changed and cajole her mate Sharon into covering the night shift.

We arranged to meet at around seven o'clock next to one of the Cleopatra needles down on the embankment. From where I stood, I could see some couples strolling towards The Temple. The men were kitted out in dark lounge suits and their ladies were in their cocktail dresses. Little black numbers seemed to be the order of the day, though some had gone dressed in greens and blues. But, either way, it was all very discreetly and tastefully done.

I halted my observations when a sudden blaring of hooters came from the rush hour traffic. As usual the cars and other vehicles wanting to leave town were bumper to bumper that day. And it was normal for the occasional hothead to be sounding his horn to inform fellow motorists that it was him, and not they, who knew the Highway Code and that it was they, and not him, who should never ever have been granted a license to drive. However, it was not the norm for every vehicle in the street to be blasting away in an altogether unruly fashion.

There next came the noise of whistling and shouting. I even heard those sorts of suggestions that no gentleman would ever propose to a lady, well not in public, at any rate. I craned my neck to see what was afoot and, to my horror, saw Michaela weaving her way around the near stationary traffic. It was her orange hair that I noticed first. She was formerly blonde with black roots but something horrible must have happened during the bleaching process. I noticed, as she came closer, that as a vehicle slowed or stopped, Michaela would pounce and pin some sort of leaflet under the windshield wipers. From her mode of dress (black leather skirt, red blouse, low cut) I reasoned that her leaflets were not advertising some sort of accountancy service.

Michaela stepped up the curb and tottered over to where I was stood. The stepping up was no mean feat because she wore high heel shoes that were, as the name implies, high. They were patented and red and as such went with the blouse. She tottered on account of the said shoes being, not just high, but extraordinarily high. "I've made it in time!" She shouted so as to be heard above the crunching of metal and breaking of glass as a motor car ploughed into the rear of a white pick-up. "Brrrr. It's bit cold though," she shivered, "I'm almost freezing," she added, but her observation was wholly unnecessary. The fact that Michaela was feeling the cold was plain for all to see by reason of her having nothing on beneath the blouse. Further and additionally, the skirt was so short that it revealed the very tops of her black, fishnet stockings. Indeed, that particular fashion statement was very likely to have been the cause of the car going into the rear of the pick-up in the first place.

Michaela was a good sort. She had three tiny mouths to feed and she had no help at all from the three fathers. In fact she had often said that, even if she knew for certain who the fathers were, she was too proud to claim their support. So I didn't have the heart to back out of our date. I'd invited her to the cocktail party. She'd been sufficiently gracious to accept. So who was I to judge?

"You look stunning," I said. My increasing propensity to lie like all the other lawyers was troublesome. "Best hurry along." But there was no rushing the girl. "Michaela," I said, presently, "Do you have to insert a leaflet in every damned telephone box?"

"Izaak, deary," she replied. "Do you have to skirt around every one of the broken pavement slabs just to avoid walking on the cracks? There ain't no crocodiles round here what will gobble you up, only sharks."

The shindig was being held in one of the grand buildings within Middle Temple. There was a tented tunnel leading towards the entrance. "Cor, this is posh, Izaak! I've never walked on a red carpet before!" We joined a small queue of couples waiting to get through the door. "Mind you," Michaela added, whispering in my ear, "in my time, I've frolicked on a few red carpets."

The man at the door took my tickets. He looked at me, then Michaela, then the tickets, then Michaela, again. "Wait just a moment," he said. The man went inside and came back out, moments later, with another man.

This other man looked at me, then Michaela, then the tickets, then Michaela, again. He also said, "Wait just a moment," and the two of them went inside.

"Come on, Michaela," I said, "this could go on all night. Let's nip inside."

We duly entered and Michaela held on tight. Indeed, had she not done so, she might very well have teetered over; such was the height of her heels. The corridor was packed tight with guffawing lawyers and hence, once in, the chances of the two men copping hold of us was, in my estimation, low. "Coming through! Shift yourselves!" shrieked Michaela, as we went through, all the time being banged and buffeted. "Don't you dare spill that on my new blouse," she warned a champagne quaffing gentleman, who'd stepped backwards. He was pretty sophisticated, I can tell you, and he was certain to have been a Law Lord.

We came to a largish room where I managed to attract the attention of a passing waitress and I nabbed two glasses of bubbly from her tray. I handed one glass to Michaela, then chinked it with my own glass and, above the hubbub, said, "Cheers!"

I hadn't noticed a rather large open space developing around us until Michaela commented something along the lines that one or both of us must have been using the wrong type of soap. It appeared that Michaela was fast becoming the focus of attention. It appeared also that she was the reason for apparent discord between various couples who were stood around. You see, every time a male looked our way, or rather, looked Michaela's way, he tended to stare, transfixed, and, in most instances, open-mouthed. The female partner of the relevant male also stared, only scornfully, and not open-mouthed and then turned on their relevant male with all manner of accusations, such as, "So that's what turns you on these days," and, "Now we know why you're always late home on Thursdays," and, I swear, from one quarter came, "I recognise that cheap perfume, you beast."

There next came a booming voice from behind. "Ah! Vanmen, is the name!" He was addressing Michaela, of course, but I reckoned I might just as well cash in on her apparent popularity.

"I'm Gatehouse." I turned and immediately realized that I was addressing none other than Jeffrey Vanmen QC. He was perhaps the most famous advocate of his day and a pupillage in his set of chambers was guaranteed to establish a barrister for life. Well, I mean to say, hardly a week went by without news of Jeffrey Vanmen QC winning on behalf of a film star, sports star, the odd politician, and so forth. Small wonder that he had a whole flock in tow, all vying for his attention. But it was me, or rather my companion, who had his attention at that particular moment and it was too good an opportunity to miss.

"And what brings you here, my dear?" The devil had only gone and blanked me.

"Cor, you're ever so short," said my companion, "you don't even reach my boobs."

"She's a one, she is," I laughed, but Vanmen was having none of it. In common with the majority of Queen's Counsel he clearly had an ego that bruised very easily. He made as if he was about to weigh anchor and join a group that I reckoned were comprised of High Court Judges and their wives. "Napoleon was a titch and it didn't do him any harm, and he could pull the birds." My historical observation did not appear to have the desired effect. "And have you seen the size of Michaela's heels?" That seemed to make him think twice, but I had to be quick if I was to prevent his skedaddle to the judges. Then I remembered reading somewhere that he had a passion for birds of the feathered variety as well as the other sort. "I understand that the ospreys are back," I said.

"What was that you said?"

Phew, I thought to myself, *got him.* Then, I repeated above all the noise, "I understand that the ospreys are back!"

"Ah," said Vanmen, "a twitcher too are you?"

"No, just a bit of eye strain," I said.

"No, no. I mean, you're a bird watcher too."

"Yes, I know," I lied, "just a joke." And, following the principle, in for a penny in for a pound, I proceeded to boast, "Actually, I was an ornithologist in another life."

"I say, were you really?" That got his attention, all right. "Tell me, er it's Gatehouse, isn't it?" I nodded. "Tell me, Gatehouse, where did you study?"

That wasn't supposed to happen. "Oh, here and there," I said.

"Yes, but where in particular?" he pressed. I'd read about his cross examination technique. "Well, come on," he said. "I'm waiting." He had a reputation for never giving up until he'd broken down his witness.

I was saved by Michaela ploughing in. "You've got lovely eyes, you have," she said to my pint-sized inquisitor. You could tell, straight away, that he mellowed. As hereinbefore stated, Ian had said she was a minx, and he'd told the God's honest truth.

"Well, that's very kind of you to say so. Tell me, Miss . . .?"

"Michaela will do."

"Tell me, Michaela. Are you and Gatehouse an item?"

Well! I thought. *Don't mind me, mate.*

"Nah!" said Michaela. "Gatehouse and me are just good friends." She looked my way for approval. "We are, aren't we, Izaak?" The minx bent her knees so that she no longer towered over the little blighter.

I duly acknowledged, with a nod, that Michaela's assertion that we were just good friends was entirely correct. Then, as if to prove that I was, perhaps, cut out for a career at the Bar, a suitable spiel sprang to mind. "Open University, it was. That's where it were," I spluttered. That was a good one that was. There was no way that even the dreaded Vanmen could crack that one. "Couldn't afford anything else," I added. He'd have to give credit for my dedication. After all, orno-whatever was his passion. And, I was convincing him it was my passion and all, so much so that, like all those distance learning types, I'd burnt the midnight oil mugging up on the stuff, watched late night

TV and so forth. I could even tell him I'd read an *I-Spy* book.

Vanmen removed his attentions from Michaela for a mo'. My ploy had worked and I'd reeled him back in. "And where do you usually twitch, Gatehouse?"

I could have told him it was usually my right eye after too much reading under a strip light but I weren't about to fall for that one again. "Down in the West Country," I said. And I felt certain that it was, indeed, somewhere in the West Country. A camping holiday it had been and a man dressed in tweed had overheard me swear that, if it was the last thing I did, I'd have for garters the albatross that had swiped a pasty clean out of my hands. The man had said that it was no albatross that had made off with supper. He said it was definitely a black headed gull but, either way, be it an albatross or a black headed gull, I shouldn't be cussing and threatening our feathered friends so and that if I insisted on dangling a pasty over the harbour wall then what could I expect?

"Precisely where in the West Country, Gatehouse?"

I knew his game. The little devil wasn't about to give up till I'd cracked and told him I'd never, ever been bird watching in my whole life and that I was nothing but an impostor trying to get a short cut to pupillage. "I hope you're not accusing me of being an impostor trying to get pupillage," I said.

Vanmen looked agog and stepped back. "I beg your pardon?" He didn't half sound indignant.

"Oh, Izaak! What a thing to say," said Michaela. She sounded indignant and all.

"Michaela needs a lift home later," I said. I sensed my pupillage slipping away and I was desperate. And besides, if promoting Michaela was good enough for the licensee of the pub down on the river then it was good enough for me. "Now see here, like," I added, "precisely where it is in the West Country has slipped my mind for a mo' but I go there ever such a lot. And just as soon as I remember where it is I'll tell you and then you'll know I'm a twitcher too and not an impostor."

Jeffrey Vanmen QC smiled at Michaela, and addressing her red blouse, she was still feeling the cold you see, he said, "I'll meet you by the door at nine thirty," and then he set sail across the open space and joined the judges and their ladies. His entourage who'd been listening in, with mixed looks of confusion and horror, followed.

"Well, thanks a lot, Michaela!" It was my turn to sound indignant. "You made a right mess of that, you did!"

"Gatehouse!" It was a voice that was horribly familiar.

A couple, probably in their sixties, strolled over. She was one of those attractive women whom you'd call handsome. He was a distinguished looking geezer who could easily have been an ex-military type. His hair, slightly thinning, was slicked back. He sported long side burns and a handlebar moustache.

"Good evening, Dean," I said, nervously. "Good evening, Mrs. Dean," I said flippantly.

"Where is my fifty pounds?" said the Dean.

"And where is my fifty pounds, George?" All eyes turned on Michaela. "You legged it during that police raid without paying me a penny, you did."

The Dean took an almighty gulp. "Bubbles! I didn't recognise you!"

"I've gone ginger, I have!" Michaela nudged the Dean and sent him reeling. "Not everywhere, though," she added, with a bit of a smirk.

"Who is this woman, Richard?" Mrs. Dean sounded not best pleased. "And," she added, after a pause, presumably for thought, "Who is George, Richard?"

Michaela looked flummoxed. "Who's Richard, George?"

I was flummoxed and all. "Who's Bubbles, Michaela?"

The Dean had regained his step snappily, not least because I'd managed to grab his sleeve before he'd landed on a woman with a tray full of *vol-au-vent*. "Who's Michaela, Bubbles?" he asked.

Mrs. Dean cuffed the Dean. It was right on the left ear and it must have hurt something rotten. "I'll give you Bubbles, Richard, George, whatever your name is. Father was right about you all along!"

"There is a perfectly simple explanation, Maud! You must let me explain!" While he made the submission the Dean rubbed the ear with fury for, as I'd deduced, the cuffing had hurt him something rotten.

Mrs. Dean, Maud, whatever her name was, proceeded to nudge her husband and she did so with a force even mightier than Michaela. I tried to save him, but it was no good. George, Richard, or whatever his name was, went straight in the *vol-au-vent*. What's more, he took me with him.

After we had gotten up, both dripping in puff pastry and Rosemarie sauce, Mrs. Dean, Maud, whatever her name was, grabbed her husband by the scruff of the neck and marched him through startled onlookers to the exit. "I'll see you in my study, Smith, Jones, Gatehouse, whatever your name is!"

Before disappearing, Mrs. Dean, Maud, whatever her name was, stared scornfully at Michaela. "Slapper!" she hollered.

Mr. and Mrs. Dean departed without as much as a "Goodnight, thanks for having us," to anyone. Bloody rude!

"Slapper?" I said, after they had gone.

"Don't worry, Izaak. I've been called far worse. But more importantly," said Michaela, brushing a prawn from my lapel, "you're going to have a nasty black eye, after a bang like that from a silver tray."

"Slapper?" I said, again.

"You what?" said Michaela.

"That's it," I said, while simultaneously rubbing my injured eye. "It was at Slapton, it were."

"What was at Slapton?" said Michaela.

"It's where a perishing pterodactyl nicked me Cornish Pasty. Come on, Michaela," I said excitedly, "let's find Mr. Vanmen."

We barged our way through the partygoers, me in front, Michaela tottering behind. My badly bruised eye was fast closing. And Michaela looked as if she was in imminent danger of falling out of the red blouse. We consequently became the focus for much attention.

As Michaela had already observed, Jeffrey Vanmen QC was a short fellow and consequently it was difficult at first to pick him out in the crowd. But I hunted him down in the end. He was chatting to another bunch of influential looking types. Vanmen had his back to me so I neatly rapped his shoulder. "Slapton!" I said. "That's where I go, Slapton in the County of Devon!"

He looked at me in a very disagreeable manner. "I beg your pardon?" He sounded disagreeable and all. "Can't you see I'm in conversation?"

A familiar voice came from within his group. "I see that you have, once more, been in the wars, Izaak." It was Janie! And she was only with that Anker individual. You know, young Pinstripe.

"Oh! Er! Hallo, Janie! I've had an altercation with some *vol-au-vent*."

"Izaak, it seems to me that you are always having an altercation with something or someone."

Michaela barged in. "You've found him then, Izaak?"

Pinstripe's beady eyes gave Michaela the once over. "And who have we here?" I had never before heard talk young Pinstripe, Anker or whatever his name was. He spoke with an upper crust accent that was contrived and basically put-on. In short, he had a quid in his gob.

"She," said Vanmen, "is Michaela . . ."

"And she," interrupted Pinstripe, looking at me, "is presumably with him?"

"Oh, Izaak," gasped Janie.

"Oh, Janie," gasped I.

CHAPTER SEVENTEEN

Dear Gatehouse,

That's how the letter started. It was as simple as that.

I refer to your recent application for pupillage.
Please telephone my clerk who will be pleased to arrange
an interview.
Yours sincerely,
Walter Tweed.
Head of Globe Chambers,
Birmingham

"Sandra!" I hollered from the region of the doormat. "I've got an interview!"

My landlady came bounding down the stairs and I thrust the communiqué under her nose. "But the letter's from Birmingham," she said. "I thought you were aiming to get into one of those posh chambers down by the law courts."

Trust her to put the dampener on things. It was true, I had flirted with the idea of making a proper and formal application to one of the upmarket sets of chambers. But I was only Izaak Gatehouse of Dudsall. You had to be either a stunningly beautiful female, like Caroline, or an arrogant toff, like Walsingham-Parker, to get beyond a first interview with that lot down in The Temple. And, at the end of the day, did I really want to see out my days pretending that I was living in the nineteenth century?

I walked through to grab some breakfast. The finals were not far away and I reckoned that I ought to keep my strength up for all those lectures, practical exercises, and drunken dinners. The triad were at the glass top table before me. I had no sooner taken my place at table than I caught the nursling devouring Walter Tweed's esteemed epistle of 30th ultimo. You see, in the seconds between sitting down and turning, only slightly mind, to grab the cornflakes, the nursling had only gone and snaffled the letter, buttered the thing, and liberally coated it with strawberry jam.

I seized the letter from the nursling. "Thank you, that's mine, I think," I said, in an altogether hoity-toity sort of way. Then, as the nursling's eyes filled with tears, I poured him a bowl of cornflakes. And, as I did so, a plastic object came tumbling out of the packet and landed in the child's bowl with a clink. His tears of sorrow instantaneously turned to tears of joy.

"Wow!" said Jason, from the jug of milk end of the table, "It's the toy submarine!"

I plunged my hand in the bowl and managed to cop hold of Nautilus by its conning tower. The tears of joy became tears of sorrow, once more. "Look here," I told the nursling, "you'll only go and swallow the thing, and we haven't got time to go to the hospital today." And it was the case that we hadn't the time, for Sandra had promised to drive me into town. But the nursling was not about to exhibit reason and understanding. With outstretched mitts, he came at me and grappled for the submarine. In the ensuing struggle I dropped the toy. "Now, see what you've made me do!"

The nursling made as if to clamber down but he was beaten to it by Crackerjack. And so it came to pass that on its maiden voyage, Nautilus ended up in the dark depths where previously thereto had gone Martin's fountain pen, the odd sanitary towel, and Joey the pet cockatiel, the pleasure of whose company I never had.

"Mummy!" hollered Jason, "The dogs choking again!"

"Don't worry, Sandra!" I said. "I'll look after the children while you go to the vets! I can spend the time fixing a date for my interview!" By this time, the nursling had called time on the blubbering and was chomping on my letter, again.

"Mummy!" hollered Jason, once more, "Ben's choking too!"

"Don't worry, Sandra!" I said, as she came rushing in with the sick bucket, "The submarine's just surfaced! You take the babby to hospital and I'll stop here and hold the fort!"

I brought the flat of my hand into contact with the roof of the Mini Clubman on six, maybe seven, occasions in quick succession. It was no more than an acknowledgement to the driver that I very much appreciated the lift that he had given me on the last stretch of my journey to Birmingham. From the deco he gave me, however, I concluded that the driver didn't much appreciate his motor car doubling up as a pair of bongos. He sped off, apparently to report to his boss on how many widgets he'd flogged to the "puffta" southerners. I made my way towards the area of the city that housed Globe Chambers.

It was Thursday evening, traditionally known as "little Friday" in that part of the world, and it was consequently naive of me to presume, for one tiny moment, that I could negotiate the whole quarter mile walk without once falling victim to Brummagem road rage. Then, as now, faced with the choice of either running over a child or being late by fifteen seconds for the curry house, your average Brummie driver will invariably opt for saving the quarter minute. Consequently my whole life passed before me as my career at the Bar almost came to an abrupt end because I foolishly stepped off the footpath, assuming that the driver of an Allegro would stop on red. As I picked myself up from the curb the gentleman driver stuck his tattooed arm out of the car window and saluted. His shaven head was as bright red as the traffic light he'd decided to ignore. He very much looked as if he was about to succumb to a smoking, drinking, saturated fat, and stress induced seizure, traditional amongst very many of his ilk.

At least I was saved from him stopping and getting out and subjecting me to a thorough beating, or, worse still, the nerve-shattering Brummie accent, by another gentleman driver who poked the front of his Ford Corsair out of a car park exit. I thereupon bore witness to that most traditional of Brummagem dances, namely the Sparkhill Shuffle. The steps are simple. The driver, who is in the right, drives right up to the offending vehicle and, with arms flaying in mock panic, pretends that he has had to perform an emergency stop. A master in this craft might even manage a skid, but a wobble of the steering wheel, just to feign preventative action, is generally deemed acceptable. Meanwhile, the driver of the offending vehicle will slowly shake his head, thereby demonstrating to the other driver, and indeed to all or any passing Brummies, that he has secured the moral high ground by thus far remaining passive. But the passiveness never lasts for long and, in most cases, the courtship is seen out with both vehicles revving their respective engines and nudging forwards at each other, and then braking, then nudging a bit more, and so on.

As it happened, I hadn't seen a "Welcome to Birmingham" road sign before being dropped off. But it didn't much matter, for there was no doubting it. I was in Brummagem all right and Brummie was about his business.

I found the chambers of Mr. Walter Tweed, barrister-at-law, in that part of town that had somehow survived the pernicious attention of the Luftwaffe and the City of Birmingham Planning Department. To be exact, the chambers were situated on the second floor of a building known to most as Globe House which, in turn, once played host to a defunct newspaper, *The Globe*. For a guess, Walter Tweed and his associates had not had to do too much soul-searching and midnight oil burning before coming up with Globe Chambers by way of their trade name.

Contrast the solid oak doors of the chambers in The Temple, the door of Globe Chambers was half frosted glass and half plywood. Contrast the brass nameplates of all those chambers in The Temple, Globe Chambers was written in black, on white plastic. And contrast the names of the posh barristers from The Temple, all painted on shiny wooden plaques, the names of those who practiced at Globe Chambers was written in blue ballpoint on a piece of paper that was Cello taped to the frosted glass.

I delicately tapped the glass, not wishing to shatter the same such was its fragile appearance, and I entered.

An overweight individual was seated on a plywood desktop. He wore no jacket or tie and his shirtsleeves were rolled up. The man was talking into a huge contraption that was wedged under miscellaneous chins. "Yow get the brief to court in the morning, and oil meck shooer Mista Tweed am there." The individual gestured by means of the use of his free hand that I should enter and be seated on a brown plastic chair. "Allo! Allo!" He proceeded to shout into the device. "Am yow still there?" Then he addressed me, astonished. "Thems only hung up on we, them have."

"What the hell is it?" I said.

"What's, what?"

"That thing that you're talking into, that's what."

"This," said the individual proudly, "am a mobile telephone."

"Ha!" I said. "Them ruddy toys will never catch on!"

"Oi think yow 'ave a pint there," said the man, and he proceeded to chuck the device into a waste bin. "Right then," he carried on, after some flashes and sparks had subsided, "what can we do for yow?"

"I'm here for the interview with Mr. Tweed."

The man slid off the desktop. The tails of the grimy white shirt were flapping outside his trousers. The said trousers were at half-mast and, as such, his pair of shocking pink socks was in plain view for all to admire. "Yow talk funny for a barrister yow does. Am yow a yam-yam or sommut?"

"Ar," I replied, "I am from the Black Country. Dudsall, to be exact."

"Ar knew it!" said the man. "Ar knew it!" he said again. "Yow am a yam-yam and not a Brummie!"

Far be it for me to have told the individual, but he didn't sound himself as if he had been born within the sound of the bells of St Martin's Church in The Bull Ring. Neither was he possessed of the whinging, whining tongue usually associated with those unfortunate enough to have come from Solihull. His tone was actually gentle on the ear and, moreover, he looked only half-suicidal. And in my day, every one from Dudsall knew that all them Brummies wore faces as long as Livery Street. I reckoned that on balance he was probably suffering from Birmingham-by-Proxy Syndrome. You know, a victim of the government's boundary changes. One minute he'd been a Staffordshire man and the next minute he'd become a Brummie by virtue of statute. Small wonder the poor devil wore a confused look.

The individual bent down and examined a diary that lay on the self same desktop that he'd just vacated. "Oi am a bit confused we am," he said, "yow am supposed to be 'ere on Thursday, yow am."

"But it is Thursday."

"Blimey, yow will have to forgive we, only it's bin real busy round 'ere of late." He closed the diary. "Oil be forgetting the day of the week next, we will. But it aye a problem though, cus Mista Tweed am just back. Yow stay 'ere a mo' an 'ave a chat with we till he am ready. Fancy a brew do ya? Oil use sum new instant tea we 'ave."

I duly interrogated the individual and ascertained that he was the clerk of chambers, responsible for all administration. In common with all barrister's clerks it was his job to organize which barrister would cover what court. His name was Damian Barker and he told me to call him Damian, so I did, and henceforth I propose to refer to him as just that, "Damian."

There were eight other barristers who practiced law from Globe Chambers. However, it seemed apparent from what Damian said that Walter Tweed was by far the busiest. Indeed, I got the distinct impression that the others lived off Mr. Tweed's returns; that in other words, they did the court appearances that their Head of Chambers could not do because of his clashing commitments.

I had barely finished the tea when a side door opened. There in front of me stood Mr. Walter Tweed and my lower jaw dropped wide open.

"You are, Gatehouse, I assume?" He spoke clearly and in a relaxed style, almost a drawl.

"Why, yes. I most certainly am." I stood to attention.

"You appear to be surprised, Gatehouse. Is it because I am black?"

"Not at all," I stammered. "It's because you're dressed in full fox hunting attire. North Warwickshire hunt ain't it?"

And, no word of a lie. Mr. Tweed was kitted out in the full works. Pink jacket, jodhpurs, and, knee length boots. Why, he even had a top hat.

"You seem to be very well informed, Gatehouse." His drawl was very pleasing on the ear.

"I've a friend at the Bar, here in Brum, I mean Birmingham, and he knows a few things about the countryside."

"And who is this friend, Gatehouse?"

"He's called Ian Prospect, Mr. Tweed."

"Ha!" cried Mr. Tweed, and he slapped the side of one of the riding boots with a crop. I hadn't seen him holding the thing behind his back. "My God you're a friend of Prospect!" Mr. Tweed removed the top hat and shook his head, as if in despair. His was a noble looking head, bald, save for black wisps either side. He sat himself on the same desktop where I had first found Damian. "You may call me Walter," he said. "And I shall call you Izaak. Now then, Izaak," and Walter proceeded to stare. He had big, piercing eyes. His cheekbones were high. His was one of those faces the age of which would be anyone's guess. I guessed that he was in his mid forties but it could have been more, it could have been less. "Do you envisage any problem were you to become the pupil of a black man?"

"So long as yow don't mind having a pupil from Dudsall," I laughed, "but what's with the master of the hounds palaver?"

"Don't you worry," drawled Walter, and he got up, came over, and gave me a friendly slap across the back. "I have recently had a riding lesson and the assumption appears to be that I therefore have a desire to hunt."

"Ar," I said, "that's the horsey brigade for you, that is."

"Well," said Walter, "I was tempted, so much so, that I borrowed this little lot from the leader of the circuit. He's been known to hunt, you know . . ."

"I had heard."

"Well, as it happens, I am quite fond of animals, and besides," drawled Walter, "I do not much relish being paraded as a token black man. Come, Izaak!" He slapped my back, once again. "I shall get out of this ridiculous costume and we shall go somewhere for tea." He glared at Damian. "And I mean real tea."

In the event, the real tea was made by the proprietor of a sports shop. It was situated on the opposite side of the road to Globe Chambers. Its front door was right next to the big entrance of The Regal Knight Insurance Company whose offices were on both sides of the little shop and on top of it.

We had entered the shop, both resembling barristers. I was in my dark dining suit, by now looking a bit the worse for wear but on balance, still presentable, and Walter had swapped the hunter gear for a black jacket and stripy trousers. But on finishing off the real tea, my lower jaw had once again dropped as Walter emerged from behind some changing room curtains. This time, my interviewer was kitted out in full cricket whites, complete with leg pads. He held a bat over one shoulder.

"Now then, Izaak," drawled Walter, "I shall stand in the corner, over by mountaineering apparatus, whilst you bowl me a googly. Here!" he suddenly barked, "Catch this!" and he threw a hard ball in my direction. I naturally ducked and the thing hit a tennis playing manikin and knocked its head clean off. "Butter fingers," drawled

Walter. "You had better bat."

While the shop proprietor fumbled with his decapitated manikin, Walter took a long run. "What attracted you to a career at the Bar?" gasped Walter, as he let go a screamer. I had no intention of ending up headless so I nimbly leapt to one side. The ball crashed into a load of survival rations that were done up in metal foil and had been in a neat pile.

It was necessary for me to get down on my hands and knees and gather up the parcels. "I suppose that I'll fail the interview if I say that I have a wig-n-gown fetish?" The particular ration pack that had been clean bowled was split right open. There was an unmistakable odour of icing sugar. I reached inside and plucked out some Kendall Mint Cake. I held what was left of the bar aloft. "That's one less climber who'll succumb to a sugar induced coma!" We both laughed. Two heads in his hands, his own and the tennis player's, the shop proprietor wept.

Walter approached the proprietor. "Your goods are faulty, my man. Here, kindly observe," and Walter showed a red mark on the otherwise brilliant white trousers. Anyone could have told the learned Head of Chambers that it was fairly obvious that he'd made the mark by furiously rubbing the cricket ball up and down immediately prior to his run-up. "It simply is not good enough," and, with that, Walter strode towards the changing room, stopping briefly at the soccer section.

"Do not move until I have struck the ball," said Walter, and he tore down the aisle dressed in the home colors of Aston Villa FC. I, meanwhile, stood between a pair of makeshift goalposts, comprising a hat stand to my left and the weeping shop proprietor to my right. "Do you. . ." Walter struck the leather football, "intend to practice," he carried on, as the ball rocketed towards me, "criminal law?" And he completed his enquiry just as the ball struck the left post, which promptly toppled over and hit the right post on his head. Walter sauntered towards the right post. "This shop is a death trap, my fellow," he drawled, casually. "And do stop weeping."

"I think I'm cut out for a career at the Criminal Bar," I said, lifting the hat stand off the proprietor's chest. He was, you see, lying prostrate on the carpet.

Whilst the learned Head of Chambers returned to the changing room I brewed the proprietor a cup of real tea with extra sugar and a

174

chunk of mint cake which, Walter assured me, prevented the onset of shock. Upon Walter emerging, this time in barrister's kit, he handed over some cash in exchange for a quantity of squash balls. "Was it not for your establishment being conveniently close to Chambers, I would take my business elsewhere," he said. "And," he added, as we departed, "you are extremely lucky that I do not have you reported on health and safety grounds."

My interview recommenced as we crossed the road heading back to Globe Chambers. Walter asked me what I would say if I'd actually witnessed a crime and the perpetrator wanted me to act for him. I was prevented from answering that one because a Renault and a Hillman Imp were doing the Sparkhill Shuffle. The driver of the Hillman leapt from his vehicle and I stupidly made eye contact. "Can yow help we? Oil pay yow to confirm it were him what deliberately hit we, like."

"Sorry, no can do, mate."

"A not incorrect answer to my question," drawled Walter. "Rather interesting, actually."

Damian was, once more, perched on his desktop when we returned. Walter told me to sit in the brown plastic chair. He selected for himself a swivel chair that was behind the desk and hence, momentarily, Walter was out of view. "Kindly refrain, my learned clerk, from depositing yourself on top of the furniture."

"Sorry, Mista Tweed. It woe 'appen again, like."

"That is better. Now, whilst I talk to our friend Izaak, here. You, my learned clerk, go to the next office and collect together The Court of Appeal material that I require for next week."

"Ar, okay." And then, addressing me, Damian said, "Ta-ra a bit."

After Damian had closed the door behind him, Walter leaned back in his swivel chair and he casually placed both feet on the desktop and crossed the same. "Izaak," he drawled, and I gulped in anticipation. "I intend to offer you pupillage . . ."

"Cor, great, great . . ."

"The offer, my friend, is subject to you attaining a pass in the forthcoming Bar final examinations."

"That's reasonable, Walter, except . . ."

"Except, what, my friend?"

"What happens if I only get a third?"

"A what?" Walter uncrossed his legs, removed them from the

table, and sat eagerly forward.

"A gentleman's third, like. Only, I ain't a great scholar and I've had a few setbacks and . . ."

"Izaak!" interrupted Walter, and he stood up and walked towards the window. He gazed out at the Regal Knight on the other side of the street. After a moment's silence, he turned. "Izaak," he said again, only this time in his casual drawl. "My father came to this country in a mode of transport that is frequently referred to as the banana boat . . ."

"I wouldn't say any such . . ."

"Silence, please," said Walter, sternly, "I am talking," and so I shut up, smartish. "My father," he continued, having reverted to the drawl, "was obliged to travel third class." Walter came over and sat on the desktop, staring right at me. "Even though he traveled third class, my father docked in Southampton at the exact same time as those who had gone first class and, in some cases, second class."

"So, a gentleman's third will do then?"

Walter laughed. "It will be quite sufficient, my friend," and he thrust forth his arm. "First and only time, Izaak. First and only time."

"First and only time," I laughed, and we warmly shook each other's hand.

CHAPTER EIGHTEEN

At the Crowe habitation the chaotic conduct continued with unabashed fervor right up to the last few days before the finals. It was then that I became conscious of a marked decrease in decibels and, indeed, hostilities. It was my belief that Martin, as head of the household, had impressed upon the clan that its continuing state of health, thus far fair (save and except for the odd trip up to the infirmary), was wholly dependent on there being a bit of hush about the place.

The fragile peace held firm until a couple of days before the examinations when, to my horror, Martin broke news that he must travel to Scotland on business. I suppose the pressure of so much goodly behaviour had been too much to bear and, as such, Martin and his knapsack had barely gotten out of the house before battle lines were redrawn.

Even as Martin was walking down the garden path, Jason and the nursling, who were playing marbles on a chummy basis, began to bicker. By the time Martin had clambered into the family Cortina, a war was raging.

Up in the bedroom, I slammed shut my 1974 edition of *The County Court Practice* (otherwise called "The Green Book" to those in the know) and it was a silly act to perform on such a dated volume for it promptly fell to bits. Be that as it may, I stormed down the stairs.

"He's swiped my marley!" cried Jason, and I proceeded to separate the little bruisers.

"Now see here, Jason," I said, "It's only a marble and you've got dozens more upstairs."

"But I must have the one he's stolen off me!" And, with that, Jason stomped his foot in anger.

"Don't be so silly and selfish!" I looked angrily at Jason.

The eyes of Sandra's eldest began to swell with tears. "But he's taken my shiner, Uncle Izaak!"

With that, I confronted the nursling. "Hand it back, right here and now!" I knew from my youth what a rare and wondrous item a shiner was.

At my rebuke the nursling proceeded to blubber. So I sat him on me knee and calmly explained that it was wrong, even for the likes of a nursling, to contravene section 1 of The Theft Act, 1968. "So that's clear is it, Ben?" I had calmly concluded, "You must not go round purloining other people's property, especially Jason's."

"Purloin?" said the nursling, and he began to wriggle about a bit. "That's what Daddy has with his chips, that is."

"No, no," I said, and I scooped the youngster up by his armpits and deposited him on the floor. "It means stealing. You know? Nick. Swipe. Pilfer." A wet patch appeared on the carpet right where the nursling was stood. I knew that the wriggling had meant something was up, and I was right. You see, even Crackerjack was better house trained than the young 'un.

"I was going to give it back, Uncle Izaak."

Now, that was a fine kettle of fish that was. The half-inching nursling was only submitting that he had no intention of permanently depriving the owner, namely Jason, of his property, to wit the marble, otherwise known as the shiner.

If that's true, I pondered, *the nursling's not guilty of theft*. So I next cogitated whether it was right and proper to enter into without prejudice negotiations with a mere nursling. But that conundrum became inconsequential after the nursling imparted the revelation that, before he could negotiate the return of the marble, it must first negotiate his alimentary canal.

"Cough, it up you little blighter!" And I grasped the nursling by the ankles, upended him, and jangled him about a bit. But, my attempt at disgorging the marble from the youngster's gullet was unfortunate, indeed, some might have said criminally negligent. You see, the shaking and rattling succeeded only in lodging the shiner firmly in the nursling's windpipe.

I had neither the heart nor the mettle to phone up Sandra at the gym, or some such place, and disclose that one third of her lineal descent was in mortal peril. With reluctance, I therefore popped the blue-faced babby on my shoulders and trotted up to the hospital.

Following a bit of sucking from a big rubber pipe, and an almighty slap on the back, the shiner eventually shot out and spun round the operating theatre a few times until it came to rest at the surgeon's feet. "What idiot, in the name of heaven, permitted a toddler to play with a ball bearing?"

Well, in the fashion above-mentioned, a whole half day's study got scuppered. But, I'll tell you something for nothing, on the eve of the finals an eruption occurred of such proportions that, in comparison, Vesuvius was but a roman candle, and a damp one!

The day started well enough. Martin was still north of the border doing whatever employees of London art galleries do in Scotland. And as for Sandra, she was out with her brood. So I spent the majority of the day up in my bedroom where I mugged up on the finer points of civil law. You could have heard the proverbial pin drop. Well, that was until about teatime when Crackerjack and Tuppence decided that it was feeding time. For a whole half hour I put up with the yapping of Crackerjack and the mewing of Tuppence. Eventually my nerves could take not a minute more. With the benefit of hindsight, I suppose that I could simply have gone downstairs and fed 'em both. But I wasn't thinking straight and, on reaching the bottom of the stairs, I nudged Crackerjack out the front door with my feet and I slung out Tuppence to keep him company.

I returned to harmony of the bedroom but the peace was short lived as, indeed, was Tuppence. I had no sooner begun to pour over the finer points of injunctive relief (having the likes of me enjoined, as Janie might have put it) when from outside there came a screech of brakes, quickly followed by an awful squealing. I leapt to the window and there, laying dead center in the road was Tuppence, dead.

I abandoned the studies and bounded down the stairs. Once outside, I asked a small crowd who had gathered to give us a bit of room and I set about unsticking Tuppence from the tarmac.

A middle aged man, who told me he had been driving the car, came over. He was your typical Rover driver, you know, raincoat and flat cap even though the sun had been out for a week. "A dog chased her into the road," he garbled. I have to say, the man looked pale and shocked and generally under par. "There was nothing I could do."

As I held Tuppence, she twitched a bit. "Quick!" I said. "She might still be alive! Drive us up to the vets!"

"Right! Hop in!"

I hopped in with Tuppence on my lap. But we had barely gotten round the corner when she wheezed and went limp and I realized that the local songbirds could rest easy. Tuppence had definitely snuffed it this time.

Down at the animal hospital, a veterinarian said, "What a dreadful agonizing way to go." He put an arm about my shoulder, and assured me, "I'll dispose of her remains in a fitting and respectful way."

The car driver looked on, cap in his hand. "I'm so sorry, I'm so sorry," is all he could say and, all the time, he was shaking his bald head.

"You stop here and pay the bill," I told him, "and I'll walk home."

"It will be no trouble to drop you off."

"Nah. I need time to think what I'm going to tell the owner. I wouldn't wish you to feel guilty," I said, "but she loved that cat she did just like it were a child."

I reckon that it was the longest three quarters of a mile of my whole life. But by the time I arrived at the house I'd worked out a suitable spiel. It went something along the lines that it was the God's honest truth that Tuppence had not felt a thing and that she was in a far, far better place (not to say she hadn't been happy while on this Earth, 'cause she'd had a better life than most moggies) but, either way, she could now chase little cherub songbirds to her heart's content.

I entered the kitchen in trepidation and, to my horror, I found Sandra about to open a can of cat food. It was the one with salmon in it. Too good for a ruddy cat, I'll have you know, when there are all them starving people out there. Anyway, I had a lump in my throat 'cause it was Tuppence's personal favourite.

"Hi, Izaak!" said Sandra, and she went to the back door and starting calling, "Tuppence! Here, Tuppence!"

I steadied myself for the spiel, above mentioned. "Don't bother 'cause the cat's dead," I garbled, and I made off up the stairs.

Sandra caught up with me by the newel post and she pinned me to the banisters. It was a strange experience, it was. You see, as I've already tried to explain, Sandra was a big girl, all right, and I'd have happily challenged anyone to say different. "What do you mean, the cat's dead?"

"It weren't my fault," I pleaded. "That road's treacherous, it is."

Sandra held me tight. "I'll never forgive myself," she sobbed, "I know not to let the animals out…"

"Or the children," I interrupted.

"Okay. Okay. I know not to let the animals *or* the children, right?"

"Right."

"Out the front."

"There, there, we all make mistakes." My voluminous landlady swiveled up her face and we made eye contact. "Here," I said, gently, "blow your nose."

"Okay," and, Sandra cuddled up even closer.

"Good grief, woman!" I cried. "I meant blow your nose on this tissue and not on me perishing shirt sleeve!"

Sandra stepped back. She waved the flat of her hands at me and said, all confused like, "Sorry, sorry. Oh, my word, I'm so confused."

"Well," I said. "Look on the bright side. You've still got the dog." Sandra smiled, a bit. That'd done the trick. "You've always said you couldn't live if anything happened to Crackerjack."

"I know, I know," said Sandra, and she sniffed, so I decided it was my turn to step back. "I love that dog so very . . ." Sandra was interrupted. It was another screeching of brakes, only this time it was followed by yapping, and not squealing.

Pray tell me the identity of the clever Dick who coined the phrase "Lightning never strikes twice"? I'll tell you what. If I get my hands on him, I'll shove a sheet of the sizzling stuff right up the place where, according to tradition, anthropoids dispose of their kernels.

I once more bounded down the stairs and went out to see what was what. Moments later, I came back in and found Sandra sitting on the stairs. Arms folded, she was rocking back and forth. I reckoned she'd gone and flipped her lid.

"Izaak," she sobbed, "please tell me the worst."

So I gave Sandra the worst-case scenario. "The dog's dead," I told her, and she promptly keeled over and clattered down the stairs.

Sandra landed right in the middle of the hallway where she appeared to blackout. Now the hallway, in common with the majority of hallways, was a main shipping lane and it followed that, stretched out on the floor as she was, my landlady constituted a hazard to navigation. So I tugged Sandra by the hair a few times and somehow manhandled her so that she became slumped against the wall. It was no mean feat, I can tell you, 'cause, if I've said it once I've said it a dozen times, Sandra was a big girl.

I mopped Sandra's brow with the bit of tissue that I still had handy but it did no good. I therefore slapped her about the face a bit. That seemed to do the trick and Sandra's eyes flickered open. But then she began mumbling to herself that she must go back to a beach some place hot where sweet music played all day. I was about to panic, thinking she'd gone dangerously delirious, when I realized that someone was playing "Return to Sorrento" on the doorbell.

I gave Sandra another good slap, just for luck, and sprang to my feet. On the doorstep was another hapless car driver, only this one bore Crackerjack in his outstretched arms. "I think he's still alive!" said the driver, with urgency.

"Quick!" I said. "Let's get down to the vets."

The driver returned to his vehicle. It was a bit posher than the Rover that had done in Tuppence. It was a Jaguar Sovereign, or something like that. As such, it wasn't so much a car, more a limousine really. He, the driver that is, was posher than the other one. This one wore a blazer and slacks to go with the weather. And, on the basis he was driving and not walking, he wore no hat, either. Anyway, the man placed Crackerjack on the front seat and then he returned to the house 'cause he could see I was having problems shifting Sandra.

Our joint efforts enabled us to hoist Sandra to her feet. "My God!" gasped the man, when we were done. "She's a big . . ."

"Yes, I know she is," I said. "Now then, you get her to the car and I'll round up the children. I know they're about 'cause I can hear that blasted Ant music blaring from somewhere."

Moments later, we were all piled in the limo and heading for the animal hospital. Typically, I drew the short straw and found myself sitting in the front with Crackerjack on my lap.

The driver put his foot down hard. "I'm so, so sorry," he said, presently, "there was nothing I could do." He stopped talking for a mo' because some old lady appeared from nowhere and plonked her Zimmer right in our path. "Phew!" said the man, "that was close," and he continued, "you see, the dog was chasing a cat and he ran straight out in front of me."

"What happened to the cat?" I enquired.

"Killed outright, I'm afraid," said the man. "Oops! That was close too. Is there an old folk's home around here or something?"

From the rear seat, center left, Jason chipped in. "It looked to me like it was a ginger cat." The driver confirmed that the lad's observational skills were spot-on and, thereupon, the boy offered testimony along the lines that it was next door's cat that had gone to join Tuppence.

"Are you quite certain?" I said, because anyone knows that identification evidence is notoriously dodgy.

"Oh, I'm certain, Uncle Izaak. The man opposite told me."

Ha! I thought to myself. *Blooming hearsay, again.*

"And besides," the boy added, "I saw for myself that he was wearing the blue collar with a bell that Ben gave him for Christmas."

That seemed to clinch it. "Ginger's dead too!" bawled the nursling, whereupon Sandra fainted, again.

When we got to the vets, Sandra was still comatose but the rest of us made a surge for the surgery.

"It's not your day," came the veterinarian's diagnosis, as I handed over custody, care, and control of the spark-out hound. He placed Crackerjack on a table and commenced poking and prodding.

"Will he live?" I asked, anxiously.

After a few minutes silence, and after more poking and prodding, the veterinarian nonchalantly said, "I think he'll live to fight another day. He's just stunned."

I breathed a huge sigh of relief. "Thank goodness," I said, "I don't think Sandra could have taken any more." And, on mentioning her name, I remembered that Sandra was still stretched out on the back seat of the limo. "Can you, by chance, sort out the owner for us, only she's fainted?"

I returned to the limo in the company of the driver and, after much heaving and shoving, we somehow managed to extract my inanimate landlady and we manhandled her into the surgery. Once in, the veterinarian told us to put Sandra on a seat in the far corner. He could see we were having a fair old struggle. "Here," he said, "I'll lend a hand," and he proceeded to cop hold of her by the waist. "Good gracious!" he said. "She's a. . ."

"Yes, we know," said the driver and I, as one.

After Sandra was safely deposited, the veterinarian felt her pulse. Then he fetched out a tiny flashlight and began shining it in her eyes which, incidentally, were persistently rolling and flickering.

"What do you think?" I asked.

"I think she's got lovely eyes," said the veterinarian.

"No, no," I said. "Will she be all right?"

The veterinarian stepped back and rested a hand under his chin. "Mmm," he went, "I don't really know. What do you reckon?"

"Well, how the hell do you expect me to know?"

"Well, excuse me," he said, all indignant like, "I'm a vet, so how the hell do you expect me to know?" He stepped forward and shone his flashlight again, only this time down Sandra's front. "We could loosen her clothing a bit, I suppose."

"That sounds sensible," said the driver.

I should record hereabouts that during all this time, the triad were wreaking havoc. Indeed, it would be fair to state that they were wholly oblivious to the state of health of she who had given unto them life. Jason and Thomas blustered about playing a game of blind man's bluff. The blindfold was in the form of a used bandage found in the waste bin. The one who's turn it was to be "it" (I can't remember whether it was Jason or the other one) kept tripping over anything, or any one, that happened to be in his path. The nursling, meanwhile, had his paws stuck in a drawer that contained a collection of particularly gruesome looking instruments.

Fetching his eyes off Sandra for a mo', the veterinarian advised, "He'll do himself a nasty injury if he keeps sticking that up there."

On the basis that Sandra was showing few signs of coming round, the veterinarian decided to give her a few slaps. I, meanwhile, took down particulars of the driver for insurance purposes. "Benjamin," he said.

"Benjamin, what?" I said.

"No. John Benjamin," he said.

"Oh! Sorry," I said, "so it's Mr. Benjamin?"

"No," he said, "it's Doctor Benjamin."

"Well, why the ruddy hell didn't you tell us you're a doctor?"

"Because no one ruddy asked me, that's why."

With that, whomsoever it was who was "it" (Thomas or the other one) came bombing past and the veterinarian found himself obliged to shout a warning, "Don't hit your head on that open drawer!" and thereupon he who was "it" did hit his head on the drawer and the drawer together with its contents went flying.

Now, a drawer full of vicious gizmos with serrated edges landing on a hard floor makes the sort of racket that would wake the dead. And, at that particular crescendo, Crackerjack twitched a bit, broke wind a bit, and sat up. He jumped, or rather fell, off the table and dragged himself over to Sandra where he proceeded to lick her heartily. Joyously, with all of that slobbering going on, Sandra came too, so the veterinarian stopped knocking her about.

Sandra stood up, teetered a little and, holding her face, she remarked that sometime soon she had to see a doctor 'cause her cheeks were feeling proper tingly. She brushed away the hands of the veterinarian. "What on earth are you doing with my buttons?"

The veterinarian stated, all sheepish-like, that it would be sensible if he kept Crackerjack overnight for observational purposes. We concurred that it was an eminently sensible suggestion, though his further suggestion that Sandra return after surgery hours the next day did seem a little strange and led me to wonder whether it was more than Crackerjack that he intended to observe. Anyway, his parting shot was, "It's quicker if you leave by the back door," and so that's the way we went.

Always the gent, I invited Sandra to go first and it was regrettably an invitation that she chose to accept. On stepping outside, Sandra stopped dead in her tracks, gasped, and screamed. The veterinarian, you see, had failed to discharge his undertaking to dispose of Tuppence in a fitting and respectful way. In lieu thereof he had slung the mangled moggie out back where she was left hanging, half in, half out, of the incinerator. Sandra fainted.

After a bit more slapping about we all found ourselves back home. There, I returned to the bedroom and resumed my attempts to comprehend civil law and The Civil Evidence Act in particular. But the triad were having none of it. Indeed, their behaviour was so riotous that even Sandra could take no more and she departed the abode stating that it was her intention to seek comfort from her soul mate, Sally.

Now then. After a whole half hour of Jason and Thomas tripping

185

up and the nursling sticking things up, I was at breaking point. I stormed out of the bedroom and screamed, "Jason and Thomas! If the pair of you don't stop tripping up whatever it is you're tripping up, I shall stick whatever it is right up where Ben keeps sticking that knitting needle!"

"I'm telling my mum!" bawled Jason.

"And social services!" said Thomas

But ignoring the attractive proposition of both children, of their own volition, being taken into care, I next focused on the nursling.

"Ben!"

"Yes, Uncle Izaak?"

"If you don't stop sticking that knitting needle up there, I shall shove it up sidewards! And don't look at me with them big tearful eyes!"

Well, that seemed to do the trick. Not a single sob, snivel, or boohoo did I hear after that. Mind you, I'd have sworn one of their number whispered to another one of their number, "He'd be disbarred if he dared do that."

I carried on with me revision and, at around section 4 (being the bit where a statement contained in a document was admissible if made by a person with a duty to compile the same) I heard another screech of brakes. I did not, as it happened, consider it at all necessary to either leap up to the window or bound down the stairs to see what was what. There was, you see, no further room for mischance. But, I know you don't believe me, so cast your eyes over the following statement of fact that, as sure as eggs is eggs, would have been admissible in any civil court pursuant to Section 4 of the before mentioned Act of Parliament:

Landlady x 1. Well clear of the danger zone, presumably swilling gin with soul mate Sally.

Landlord (you know, Martin) x1. Still driving around Scotland in the family Cortina.

Sprogs x 3. Across the landing, frit to death lest I jab 'em. Possibly compiling a formal complaint to go before the Disciplinary Committee of the Bar Council.

Quadrupeds x 2. At the animal hospital, one in a considerably better state of health than the other.

Feathered friend x1. Got out of his cage weeks before I'd even gone to live at the mad house. Already dead.

Moments later, and as if to prove that section 4 was nonsense, Martin came bursting in. "What's going on, Izaak?" Behind the big spectacles, his eyes were full of fury.

"Why, hallo, Martin. I thought you were in that part of the U.K. where a defendant cannot be convicted of a crime on his own admission without corroborative evidence."

"Don't get smart with me, you little shit. Where's Sandra?"

"With Sally."

"Why?"

"She's upset."

"Why?"

"The dog's injured."

"How?"

"Chasing cats in the road."

"Where are the children?"

"In bed."

"Why?"

"They're upset."

"Why?"

"I didn't threaten to do 'em harm, honest."

"I asked, why?"

"Tuppence is, sort of, dead."

"Why? How?"

"She was one of the ones that the dog kept chasing in the road."

"I knew I shouldn't have gone anywhere!"

And, without so much as "I'm sorry for disturbing you on this, the most important day in your life, thus far, Izaak, old chap," Martin spun on his heels and left. Moments later, with a squealing of tires, the Cortina tore off.

For the umpteenth time, I nose-dived into the Civil Evidence Act. But at section 5 (it was all about computerized records and thereby rendered null and void all my efforts pertaining to section 4) there came a little tapping at my door.

In toddled the nursling. "Was that my daddy?" I saw that he was clutching Bluey. Now, Bluey was a bear. Moreover, Bluey was actually brown in color and not blue. Bluey had been gifted to the nursling by Santa Claus. He knew that as a fact for Sandra and Martin had uttered it to him. It was a spontaneous utterance made at one o'clock on Christmas morning. It was a joint and several utterance made in the heat of the moment when there could have been no time for falsification. It was *res gestae*, all right and the nursling was therefore right to accept as a fact that which others may have regarded as hearsay, namely the account of a man with a white beard parking his flying sled on the roof and gaining access to the property by means of clambering down the chimney, which was bricked up two years earlier when the new central heating went in, or so I was led to believe. The man who had the flying sled proceeded to abandon Bluey inside a stripey sock, along with a tangerine, a walnut, and a chocolate bell wrapped up in silver foil. The nursling was right also to ignore the Made in Korea label, stuck right where one might usually expect to find a bear's privy members, for that was a mere section 4 record and, as such, could be regarded as bollocks. "Oh dear, Bluey," said the nursling. "Uncle Izaak looks so tired."

"Ben," I said. "Come to me a moment." The nursling trundled over. "Do you remember what you were doing with that horrible nasty sharp thing at the vets? Well . . ." I didn't wait for a response, but I copped hold of The Civil Evidence Act and wafted it about a bit.

"Yes, Uncle Izaak?"

It was no good. I hadn't got it in me to do harm to a mere nursling. "Nothing, Ben," I said. "It's nothing at all."

"Night night then, Uncle Izaak."

"Yes, night night, Ben."

"And night night to Bluey, Uncle Izaak," and the child waved the bear under my nose.

I made as if to kiss Bluey goodnight on his blind side. He was, permit me to explain, a single eyed bear, the other one having been consumed by the nursling. The mutilation had occurred on Christmas morning and Bluey had not even been fully extracted from the stripey sock. When, on Boxing Day, the nursling was discharged from hospital the consultant swore that he intended to sue Bluey's importer. The eye that was extracted from the nursling's windpipe was apparently attached to a dagger-like pin that was capable of piercing anything, including a surgeon's glove. It was an empty threat, of course, since whomsoever it was who had imported Bluey, the factory in Korea or the man with a flying sled, were both, in some form or another, beyond the jurisdiction of the court. "Oh, my God!" I cried. "I'm blinded!" As I had puckered for the kiss, the nursling had only gone and turned Bluey to his good side. And the nursling had only been working on the eye since December. And the eye, with it's dagger-like pin, had only chosen that moment to pop out. I belted off to the bathroom for bandages and antiseptic.

The nursling and his bear, now rendered totally without sight, returned to bed. I returned to my own room and lay upon the bed bathing my eye. Thereupon, I heard the Cortina roaring down the street and it skidded to a halt right outside.

The doors opened and then, one after the other, slammed shut. "You bitch! You whore!" I heard Martin holler, as the spouses came up the path.

"I'm sorry, Martin! I'm so sorry!" Sandra cried.

"You unfaithful trollop!"

"Please forgive me, Martin! I know we can work things out!"

"You tart! You slag! You hussy!" I deduced that my landlord had been wound up by something or other. "You shrew!" Well, at least he was running low on expletives.

I cringed as, with a shrilly scrape, a key somehow found its way in the front door and the twosome tumbled inside and began negotiating the stairs.

Martin booted in my bedroom door. I sat bolt upright whereupon I saw that Martin had hold of Sandra by her hair. He was twizzling her about and, to keep herself from falling, she had hold of Martin by his donkey jacket. Sandra tried very hard to break free but, the harder she tried, the more he twizzled her about. "Go on!" shouted Martin, presently. "Tell Izaak what you've been up to!"

"Ouch!" said Sandra, as her husband gave the auburn locks a good tugging. "I've been with another man!"

"Tell him the rest!" demanded Martin. "You scarlet woman!" he added, and I thereupon deduced that his expletives had totally run out. Martin proceeded to administer a particularly callous yank, and he once more demanded Sandra to tell me the rest.

The rest consisted of Sandra admitting, "I've been having an affair with the captain of the rugby team! And Martin's just caught me at it!"

Well, what a fine how do you do. Sandra, a respectable wife and mother of three, caught red-handed, *flagrante delicto*, with some aria

189

chortling prop forward. I was shocked and that's the truth for I'd naturally assumed that all rugby players were overly in touch with their feminine side. Well, I mean to say, communal bathing, and all that sort of thing. In my day, the old rub-a-dub was an appointment most sacrosanct; an effect into which a fellow and his loofah could wallow without fear of some homoerotic hooker landing a jockstrap on his top post. "Are you listening, Izaak? I want Sandra to tell you what position I found her in!"

"In a scrum, I'll wager," I quipped.

Sandra managed to cop hold of Martin's hand. She pried it open and released herself from his grip. "Trust you men to stick together," she said, nastily.

"Hold your horses!" I said, getting up from the bed. "Just hold your horses and listen!" A hush descended, so, quietly this time I told the pair of them what was what. "Firstly," I began, "I'm sorry you've got problems.. But it aye no fault of mine. Secondly," I carried on, "It ain't my place to take sides. And thirdly," I was on a roll, I was, "I'm supposed to be sitting me exams in the morning and this pantomime ain't on. Is it?"

"Oh, right. Sorry," said Sandra, meekly. "We'll leave you in peace, then."

"We'll leave you in peace," concurred her husband, equally as meek, and the pair departed.

I immediately dived into my criminal law book and looked up the bit on homicide. It was my considered judgment that had Martin, there and then, fetched out the bread knife he stood a good chance of getting just a few years on the inside for manslaughter on the grounds of provocation. But all was ominously quiet downstairs and, the longer he waited before his strike, the more likely it was that he'd be adjudged to have begun cooling off. And the more cooling off he did, the more likely it was that he'd get potted for murder. I began to think that, taking everything into account, a mandatory life sentence was too harsh on even one such as Martin, when the doorbell went. It brought me to my senses. Hooking up a doorbell with chimes from "Return to Sorrento" was so wilful and wanton that life imprisonment was too soft a sentence. There was no doubting it that Martin was possessed of malice aforethought, all right, and he deserved to swing.

"Hi guys!" It was soul mate Sally and the rest of the gang. It was a sad, yet predictable fact, that come a drama, any drama, be it a wedding, funeral, or act of domestic violence, the gang would show up for the party.

After a few token recriminations all round, I heard the chinking of glasses. And soon, the record player began to blare out Martin's selection of hits from the sixties. The party was in full swing.

I lay on the bed and hastily thumbed my volume to see what sort of sentences were usually handed down to serial killers who went about bumping off a bunch of noisy, middle aged swingers by means of the use of a blunt instrument, namely, a huge book on criminal law. Suddenly, there came the sound of gasps from the gang, followed by a shrilly scrape of a needle sliding across a recording of "Bits and Pieces" by The Dave Clark Five. It was no way to treat a record but, to be fair, that particular piece of vicious vinyl had had it coming.

I next heard Sandra's voice. She screamed, hysterically, "You two-faced treacherous, evil monster!"

Hallo, I thought, *this is an interesting one, this is.*

Then it was Martin's turn. "Please forgive me, Sandra! She did all the chasing, she did!"

Then Sally's. "But you said we would leave it all behind and start again in Holland!"

Holland? I thought to myself. *Holland? Jab her with your bread knife, mate, but for pity's sake, Martin. Even the Sally's of this world don't deserve Holland.*

"Martin!" It was Sandra, again. "Get yourself up those stairs!" And, moments later, my bedroom door found itself kicked open, again. This time, it was Sandra who had Martin. She had him by the ear, presumably because he hadn't enough hair to cop hold of. "Go on! Tell Izaak what you've been up to!" Martin managed to wrench himself free. "Damn and blast it!" Sandra seemed annoyed at losing her catch. "You wouldn't wriggle free if you had a decent head of hair to hold onto, you fat, bald, little. . .!"

"I admit it, Izaak!" Martin fell on his hands and knees. "I swear it's all over, but I've been having an affair with Sally!"

"But, Martin. You hate her even more than me."

"It was all an act," said Martin. "A big act to throw everyone off the scent."

Well. I felt cheated, I did.

"Right!" I said. "That's it now, then!" I jumped off the bed and, reaching under the said bed, I pulled out my still busted, yet reliable, red suitcase.

"What, what?" said Martin, looking up. He sounded confused and silly. He looked it and all, on his hands and knees, like that.

"Izaak?" said Sandra, sounding as equally silly and confused. "Where are you going?"

"I'll tell you where. I'll tell you where, all right." I was impressing even myself with how intimidating I could sound if I put a mind to it. "I am returning to where I can be guaranteed of peace and quiet, among people who have more style than you pair and your mates."

"Where?" said Martin.

"Yes. Where?" said his spouse.

"During the next two weeks," I said, "I shall be living under a little tin table that I know. It's a bit bijou, but very handy for Central London."

I began stuffing the case with law books, socks and shirts, undergarments, and more law books. When I was done I shut the lid and secured it with binder twine done up in a granny knot. Martin had removed himself from the floor and was seated on the bed. Sandra stood in the doorway. She was totally blocking my path, on account of her being a big girl, so I barged through.

I struggled down the stairs, clasping the busted case close to my chest. Regrettably, I lost a bit of dignity half way down 'cause I missed a step, fell flat on my back, and came down the rest like I was on a luge. "Whoops! Ouch! Sod it!"

I reached for the door handle but before departing forever the Crowe habitation I turned around. At the top of the stairs I saw Sandra, with Martin's face poking out above her shoulder. Downstairs, each and every member of the gang had congregated. I stepped out into the cold and walked down the path. I did so to the chorus, "Sorry! It's not always like this!"

CHAPTER NINETEEN

Well, during the hours of daylight I did the exams. During the hours of darkness I slept contentedly under the little tin table in Lincoln's Inn Fields. Except for time spent in a small pizza restaurant, all you can eat and a soft drink thrown in, that's how I spent the next fortnight.

It was with a feeling of immense relief that, with the whole nightmare of London done and dusted, I found myself hammering away at the big oak door of The Fly in the Ointment.

But there came no response from within. So I hammered again. And again. I knew that Ian was somewhere about. His black sports car was parked right outside. And he was always too drunk to go anywhere on foot.

I swore that I heard heavy breathing coming from within. Then I heard scratching and more heavy breathing. *Oh heck!* I thought. *He's had a seizure or sommut.* And to be fair. It was only a matter of time before all those trips around the globe caught up with him.

I turned the handle and barged in fully expecting to find Ian collapsed on the floor. As I entered, an object came at me. "What in the name of . . .!" A reddish thing it was. A blasted pig it was. Having successfully sent me tumbling, the creature set about gnawing at the binder twine around my busted case. Now, the binder twine and the busted case had been inseparable companions for many months. It therefore followed that, in common with the busted case, the twine was both well travelled and a bit worn. Further and additionally, the creature was no ordinary rampaging pig but a huge monster of a rampaging pig. The natural consequences of these things meant that, within seconds, I was bearing witness to the creature chewing up my law books and running amok with a pair of Y- fronts on its head.

"Gatehouse, old dear!" Ian strolled casually in from the kitchen. It was necessary for him to shout so that he could be heard above the grunting and squealing as an under garment went by. "I see that you and The General have already met!"

I picked myself up and brushed myself down. "So, I'm berthing with that thing, am I?"

"Shush," said Ian, and he began rounding up the creature. "I'll have you know, Gatehouse, old chap, that pigs are highly sensitive and intelligent creatures." Well, that particular highly sensitive and intelligent creature had no intentions of being brought to heel. Ian still walked, and in the immediate instance trotted, with his peculiar backwards lean and it was a comical sight to see him scooting around in ever-increasing circles. In fact, The General was much quicker than Ian was and, consequently, it was difficult to make out which one was doing the actual chasing. Eventually, the animal tried to overtake, whereupon Ian managed to corner it inside the big inglenook. "Here," he said, with a wince and a chuckle and Ian removed my Y- fronts from the ears of The General and he threw them over. "Now then," said Ian, with another wince, "you stand guard, while I fetch a stick and a board. She'll have to go outside for a while." The General let out a particularly loud, ear-piercing squeal. "You've quite upset her, Gatehouse, old dear! I told you that pigs are highly sensitive and intelligent! And The General's a purebred Tamworth so, in my estimation, she's more sensitive and intelligent than most!"

Ian darted out and I dragged one of the leather armchairs over to the inglenook. With the armchair on one side of The General and with me on the other side she had nowhere to go, or so I assumed. Regrettably, the creature decided to head for the chink of daylight between my legs. Sensitive and intelligent or not, it was plain that physics wasn't The General's strong point. You see, she was higher off the ground than my crutch was and she was wider than my legs could stretch. Consequently, as the creature made its break for freedom, I found myself taken with her for the ride.

Ian returned with a large oblong board and a stick. He was just in time to witness The General's second lap around the sitting room with me riding her, not only bareback, but back to front. "Do stop messing about, Gatehouse, old chap!" On the third lap, The General decided that enough was enough. She swerved and bucked and sent me flying.

194

Ian shrugged, winced, and chuckled. "I trust that you haven't caused her unnecessary stress, Gatehouse, old dear. I'm showing her and the litter at The Prestwick Show tomorrow."

For the second time, I picked myself up and brushed myself down. "What do you mean the lit. . .?" I had intended to make enquiry as to Ian's reference to a litter but all became self-explanatory as six, seven, possibly more, piglets came trotting through. *Her so-called intelligence, I thought to myself, don't stretch to birth control, either.* Anyway, the piglets made straight for their mum who promptly lay down in the inglenook and showed her undercarriage. Now Colin the cat, I would add, had witnessed the entire proceedings from beneath a coffee table. But at the prospect of free milk, he shot out and got stuck in with the sucklings.

Ian put down his board and stick. He shrugged, winced, chuckled. "A timely intervention," he said.

"First there's Dave. Now, The General. In the name of heaven, Ian, what's going on this time?"

"Self sufficiency, Gatehouse, old chap." Ian retrieved the chair that I'd used as a corral and he plonked himself down. Ian crossed his legs and I noticed that he wore his customary corduroy trousers and sandals without socks. "I'll have you know, Gatehouse, old dear, that the local solicitors are fascinated that a barrister should also be a pig breeder . . ."

"Ha!" I said. "Self sufficiency? More like touting for work."

Ian uncrossed his legs and got up from the chair. He reached under the inglenook and copped hold of his clay pipe from a small stone shelf. "Don't be so cynical." Ian produced the infernal lighter from his pocket. "Anyway," he said, and he paused so that he could twirl the wheel atop the thing. His actions resulted in no flames at all, just a sickly stench of petrol. He sniffed the lighter, shrugged, winced, and carried on, "It's important for The General to look her best tomorrow which is why," he then chuckled, "she sleeps in here tonight and you sleep in the outhouse." Without warning the lighter combusted and shot fire straight into the inglenook where it proceeded to singe Colin on the bottom. The startled cat squealed and exited at an almighty pace. "Oh," said Ian, undaunted, "that reminds me. The General won't go anywhere without Colin, which is why. . ." As the inferno died down, Ian paused to light the pipe. After a few puffs he clamped the thing firmly between his teeth and plunged both hands deep into his trouser pockets. Ian rode up and down on the balls of his feet looking every inch the picture of contentment. "Which is why," he smirked, "you can come and keep your eye on Colin."

"I'll do no such thing, Ian."

Ian stopped going up and down, removed the pipe from his mouth, and tapped it gently on the side of the inglenook. The bowl proceeded to snap off. It fell headlong onto the stone flags, where it smashed into a thousand pieces. "Damnation," said Ian, "that was my favourite clay. Anyway," he went on, with a shrug, a wince, and a chuckle, "you may find that a certain lady of this parish is judging the best kept pet competition . . ."

"Where's the grooming gear?" I said. "We want Colin to look his best, don't we?"

I was greeted the following morning by your archetypal English summer's day. It was cold and damp and misty. The weather report stated that the sun would burn off the mist and that, as a consequence, we could expect fine weather around noon; the fine weather would precede a deep depression and by the afternoon heavy rain was likely, with flash flooding in parts. Yes, it was country show weather all right, and, from my makeshift quarters in the outhouse, I'd heard Ian and a bunch of local yokels loading The General and her litter and setting off for the showground at an hour that most would consider wholly indecent. It was evident from the squeals, the grunting, and an awful lot of pushing and pulling that, in terms of her involvement in the annual Prestwick Show, The General was an unwilling party. From squeals and grunting in the night, no doubt accompanied by a fair amount of pushing and pulling, it had been equally evident that Ian's houseguest on that particular occasion was also an unwilling party, of sorts. She had banged the front door behind her at two in the morning and clattered up the road in high heels grumbling, "Think you can seduce me with a bottle of cider and a packet of pork scratchings, do you?" Whomsoever she was, and I truly believe that it was the policeman's wife (or someone who sounded very much like her), I was glad that I had swapped places with The General because the ruckus in the cottage sounded very nasty, especially on Ian declaring, "Very well, you win. I'll crack open the Black Tower."

I arrived at the showground during the sunny slot, so it must have been around about twelve. In lieu of the customary red suitcase, I clasped a cardboard box to my chest and it contained another unwilling party, namely, Colin.

I found Ian holding court over by the unused railway track. He was wearing a long white coat. It was meant to be a stockman's coat except his had Shipsford Cottage Hospital printed on it's top pocket. The General and the piglets were penned in the very corner of the field behind a row of wooden pallets. As me and Colin approached, Ian dismissed a bunch of country-looking types. They all looked the same to me and you probably know the sort I'm talking about. In their fifties to sixties, a greasy ratting cap, a matching sports coat, yellow trousers (very handy for disguising the consequences of a prostrate problem) and, a ridiculously oversized shepherds crook. "Gatehouse, old chap!" Ian wafted a can of lager. "The General has come first, as I knew she would! Best pig, best pure bred, best litter! In fact, Gatehouse, old dear! Best everything!"

"Well, that's great, Ian. Congratulations." I placed the cardboard box at Ian's feet. "Where's the competition, like? Only on the way in, I saw sheep, goats, cattle, like. I even saw a llama, for heaven's sake, but I aye seen no pigs."

Ian shrugged and winced, just a little. "There were no others," he said quickly and quietly.

"You what?"

"You heard me, Gatehouse. There were no other entrants."

I decided to shelter from the sun at the side of a horse trailer. You see, it was still only twelve fifteen and so summer hadn't yet passed us by. "Let's get this right then, Ian." I sat on the mudguard and casually folded my legs. "So, if you were the only entrant, it could also be said that you were worst pig, worst pure bred and worst litter." I laughed aloud at that one, I did.

"Typical Brummie!" said Ian, snappily.

"Yam-yam!" I snapped back.

"Whatever!" said Ian. "Why, Gatehouse, old chap, is that glass of yours always half empty?"

Further discord was averted by reason of a sudden clap of thunder. Summer done with, I told Ian that I proposed to take shelter at the small animal competition. So I scooped up the box containing Colin and headed off for the marquee.

By the time that I had gotten to the other side of the field, it was pouring hard and there was a gale blowing. Any responsible show organizer would have abandoned the whole thing right there and then. But it was the annual Prestwick show. Never mind that if you wandered too far from a duckboard, you'd need air sea rescue to haul you safely back to the marrow competition. The annual Prestwick show was an English country show and the show had to go on.

I skidded through the entrance, narrowly missing the guinea pig stand. The usual folk were milling around. They were indistinguishable from the lot I'd left with Ian, only some were female (possibly). They were all laughing and joking about the weather and remarking that, come rain or shine, nothing would stop them from having a good day out. *Wait till you have to pay twenty quid to have your motor sucked out of the car park by a tractor,* I thought to myself.

At the far end of the tent, I caught sight of Janie and experienced an instant change of heart about all them homespuns for on balance, come rain or shine, a good day out had suddenly become entirely possible.

She stood out from all the rest. For starters, Janie was as tall as and, in some instances, taller than the men were. She wore a strange, green jacket. It had a wax-like finish, the likes of which I had never seen before. Janie even had on a pair of green Wellington boots. I figured that the man who sold her the outfit must have laughed all the way to the bank 'cause tat like that wasn't about to catch on. The ensemble, especially the green Wellington boots for Pete's sake, was a total fashion disaster and it was just as well that I adored the woman.

By the looks of things, Janie was alone. She did not appear to be in the company of her friends or relations to whom she was generally joined at the hip. Neither could I see young Pinstripe lurking. It was a perfect opportunity to steal up to her unnoticed, tell her that it was fate that brought me to the tent 'cause I was entering Colin in a pet competition that, it turned out she was judging, but, on the basis I was there any way, I'd like to say that I knew it was her who had sponsored my studies and that it was about time she stopped beating around the bush and, in no particular order, agree to run away, get wed, have a child, live in a cottage (no pigs, mind), and, generally, live happily ever after. Alternatively, I reckoned I could play it safe and ask if she'd like tea and a bit of cake at the WI stand.

I placed the cardboard box on a trestle table, intending to slick back my rain sodden hair. Colin, who had thus far been as good as gold, chose that moment to poke his head out. By an unfortunate twist of fate, the trestle table onto which I had placed the box was host to the entrants in the cuddliest bunny rabbit competition. Now, of all the furry and feathered friends who hung around The Fly in the Ointment, rabbit was Colin's personal favorite dish of the day.

They do say that the human brain has a knack of blocking out upsetting and tragic goings-on. Well, I think that's what happened to me. It was either that or it was the punch in the face from the father of Jake who, in turn was the father of Mr. Squiggles, a long haired dwarf, who hightailed it down the railway track and was never seen again.

After I'd picked myself up from the turf and, pausing only to count the stars, I set off down the full length of the trestle table in pursuit of Colin. He was slower than normal, but that was probably on account of his insistence on stopping along the way to seize the odd bunny around the throat and give it a good shaking.

It was possibly the screams of horror or the insults being hurled, or a combination of the two that caused Janie to turn and look my way. Either way, she appeared very surprised, especially when Colin took it on himself to leap into her arms. I think it was his assault on an angora that was a bunny too far. It was the biggest and most vicious rabbit that I'd ever seen, not to say, incidentally, that rabbit sightings, and sightings of long hair angora's in particular, was a common occurrence down Dudsall High Road.

Janie instinctively stroked and patted Colin and that seemed to calm him down a bit. I dodged the last few owners. They were hastily returning pet bunnies, though, in some instances, what was left of their bunnies, back to their respective cages. Janie focused her huge beautiful eyes straight at me. She was as lovely as ever despite being kitted out in the strange waxen jacket and funny colored Wellies. But Janie didn't maintain eye contact for nearly as long as I'd have like. In lieu thereof, she stared beyond at the scenes of carnage atop the trestle table. "I see, Izaak," she said calmly and coolly, "that, once again, you have experienced an altercation."

She may have sounded dispassionate but I noticed that, beneath the jacket, her chest and swan-like neck had turned the very brightest of crimson. "It weren't my fault, Janie," I said. "Some bloke just took a swing at me." Janie handed over Colin. As soon as I had hold of him, he proceeded to hiss and spit, and he stuck his claws straight in my cheek. "Ouch!" I went, and I dropped Colin who proceeded to skedaddle somewhere or other.

"Izaak," said Janie. She fixed me again with her huge and beautiful, bright eyes, but she still sounded calm and cool. "I am aware that your wholly inappropriate behaviour has resulted in the near wrecking of the Crowe family . . ."

"It weren't down to me . . ."

"Be quiet!" barked Janie. Her eyes were ablaze. Her chest and neck blazed red with passion. She was wonderful. "And I suppose, Izaak," she carried on, "that the scene of mayhem before my eyes is nothing to do with you, either?"

"But, Janie!"

"But nothing, Izaak." She was having none of it. "I am concerned that you and disaster walk hand in hand. I am concerned that you walk hand in hand with dubious company . . ."

"Oh, I can explain about Michaela, sort of . . ."

"I said be quiet, Izaak." Now Janie sounded menacing. "I am concerned about a lot of things, including your criminal conduct." But, her eyes still sparkled and those crimson signs of passion were still there. Once together, I figured, even our rows would be sensuous affairs. "Izaak?" said Janie, "Are you listening to a single word that I say?"

"Of course I am."

"Good. Well listen to this. Most of all I, and my family," (*them again*, I thought). "Listen to me, Izaak. I am concerned that our paths keep crossing and I wish to draw a line. If you approach me again I shall consult my solicitor."

"But . . ."

"I'll have no excuses," said Janie. I think she was about to add a bit more but she was interrupted by some little tyke who seemed to pop out of nowhere and was plainly of a mind that it were open season and that I was the subject matter of the said opening.

"You need shooting," said the tyke. He was a miniature version of the other country types, right down to his flat cap. "I've counted two dead rabbits! I'll be surprised if one lasts the night! Three have run away! And! And!" he finished off, "the vicar's fainted!"

Janie turned to leave. "Oh, Izaak," she said.

"Oh, Janie," I said.

CHAPTER TWENTY

"Gatehouse!" said Ian. It was after the show. "I had to rescue Colin from a marauding mob of rabbit fanciers." I'd left soon after Janie had put me in my place. It was early evening and Ian had just walked through the door. "I have to take my hat off to you, Gatehouse, old chap." He shrugged, winced, and chuckled. "The show committee has barred you for life. There's a lynch mob on it's way . . ."

"A what?"

"It's comprised of local members of The Rabbit Breeders Association . . ."

"Phew! That's all right, then!"

"And, to cap it all, Gatehouse, old dear. One Mr. William Anker is reputed to be applying, at this very moment, for an *ex parte* interlocutory injunction."

"He'll have a job," I said. And I wasn't far off the mark, for anyone knew that in order to obtain a temporary injunction without notice it was necessary to demonstrate that there was physical harm or a threat of physical harm. "Young Pinstripe'll have a job proving I constitute a danger to any one, not least Janie."

"Gatehouse!" said Ian. "There are independent witnesses who will state, on oath, that you ran towards her, sporting a black eye, having firstly been directly responsible for miscellaneous acts of murder and mayhem on participants in the rabbit competition one of whom was Miss Flopsey-Whatsey, owned by Janie's niece, who is missing, (Miss Flopsey-Whatsey, that is) and is presumed dead or, alternatively, has been shagged rotten by the mixymitosis riddled inhabitants of the warren along the disued Shipsford to Downton Line, in which case, she might just as well be dead!"

"Well, I'll grant you that, Ian. However . . ."

"However, nothing, Gatehouse, old chap. After Janie fled in floods of tears, you gave chase, cornered her by the hoopla stall, extolled the virtues of Battenberg cake, and begged her to resolve all outstanding issues over a cup of real tea the likes of which she would find nowhere else other than in a bedroom at The Vine Guesthouse, the proprietor of which, I might add, is Mrs. Roberts whose son, Edward, is currently serving six months for voyeurism by use of a two-way mirror."

"Now, see here, Ian." I was indignant, and he knew it. "Don't you get all technical on me, like?" There came a sudden knocking on the door. As a precautionary measure, and not by way of any attempt to frustrate due process of law, I exited the cottage via the rear entrance, though not before instructing Ian, "Tell 'em I've gone to a faraway place where they'll be beaten up if they try serving anything vaguely official, let alone an injunction."

Ian shrugged and winced. "Don't be daft, Gatehouse, old dear. No one will believe you've gone to Glasgow."

I had no sooner shut myself in than I heard a knocking on the door of the outhouse. I seized hold of a chunk of kindling wood with which to crown young Pinstripe should he dare slap due process into my palm. I raised the wood, ready to strike. The door opened and in stepped Ian. "What are you doing, Ian?"

"Be quiet, Gatehouse. And do put Mrs. Horsham-Smith's house sign down. You won't knock the skin off a rice pudding with that thing. Here," Ian dragged out of the blackness a rather long and cumbersome object. "Try her bird table, instead."

After closing the door, Ian joined me in being seated on an old and tatty, and exceedingly wobbly pine table. "I'd rather leave Pinstripe's forehead with an everlasting impression of Fossip Cottage," I whispered, only to add, "Careful, Ian. This table's dangerous."

"Well, you can rest easy, Gatehouse. It's Police Constable Stringer who's come knocking and he's after my blood."

"So it was Mrs. Stringer storming off up the road last night, was it?"

"Staff Nurse Stringer," said Ian, "is a disgrace to her profession. She appears to have succumbed to interrogation and in consequence has committed a gross breach of confidentiality."

"Aye?"

"In short, Gatehouse, old dear, she's spilt the proverbial beans and last Tuesday's beans, in particular. But shush a moment. I hear footsteps. . ."

Ian was right for there came the sound of footsteps outside. We huddled on the pine tabletop, both nervously fingering Mrs. Horsham-Smith's bird table. At first, the footsteps went by. But, halfway up the garden, they seemed to stop, return, and then stop again, only directly outside the door.

Suddenly, the door flew open. Ian jumped to his feet, leaving me pinned down. "This is police brutality and I'll sue!" And then, "Oh," said Ian, as The General nosed her way in.

"Remove Mrs. Horsham-Smith's bird table from my lap, Ian!"

"Shush, Gatehouse. The law may still be about." Ian shrugged and winced.

"Well, if he is," I said, "I'm certain that both he and the whole of the village know our whereabouts by now. After all, Ian. . ." I paused while I did the job of removing the bird table myself and, while I was about it, I shooed three or four piglets from around my feet. It was as well I did 'cause a leg promptly snapped clean off the pine table and the whole thing collapsed. "Let's face it," I said, on recovering from the shock, "hollering an accusation of misfeasance in public office ain't quite the same as complaining about the noisy church bells . . ." I paused again, only this time so I could wipe wood bark from my trousers. "Especially when the threat to commence proceedings, and no doubt invoke Section 69 of The Supreme Court Act, is hollered from an outhouse in Prestwick on Saturday teatime."

"Gatehouse, old chap." Ian poked his nose outside. "Providence has intervened and sent Stringer on his travels. I can see him walking in the direction of Fossip Cottage." He winced, shrugged, and this time chuckled. "I fancy he's gone off to report on progress in detecting the crime wave." Ian bent down and copped hold of the bird table. "You barricade The General with this thing while I go for my stick and board." Next, Ian scooted back to the house, though not before chuckling, "Of course, I blame it all on the gypsies."

It didn't take long to steer The General back to the sitting room where she lay down, showed her undercarriage and the hungry litter proceeded to get stuck in. Colin joined in too, presumably for the purpose of washing down his hearty meal.

203

"Bless you," I said, as Ian passed to me an old jam jar brimming with real tea. A few broken cups were the penalty for admitting a clumsy, yet pure bred, Tamworth into the household. And, fair do's, it could have been worse for I once had a neighbour who had employed a pure-bred Brummie to fix her electric toaster. She ended up with no saucers, no plates, and no nothing in fact, not even a house. But at least she salvaged an empty cup. It was the one the Brummie had used to douse the fuse box.

"Gatehouse, old chap." Ian took his place in the other comfortable chair. He slurped a few times from a rose bowl in which his own tea steamed merrily. "When, as a young lad, the local farrier bounced me on his knee he told me tales of gladiators, Vikings, cowboys, and yet more gladiators . . ."

"Oh, ah?"

"I'm being serious, Gatehouse."

"Sorry," and I swished my jam jar a bit and then finished off its contents.

"Anyway," continued Ian, with a shrug and a wince, "he also told me of the time that, as a mere lad, he had crawled through the undergrowth atop Breeve Hill and witnessed a crow's court."

"A what?" I sat eagerly forward.

"A crow's court," said Ian. "Ha! I thought that would get your attention." Ian removed himself from the chair and tootled over to the inglenook where he nudged a pair of piglets out of harm's way. Next, Ian fetched out the howitzer, and, after half a dozen swizzles, he had the fire going. Ian returned to his seat with one sideburn singed, though not before chucking a No Parking sign into the fire. Having thereby provided an explanation as to why it was that someone always managed to obstruct the vicar's driveway, Ian proceeded to provide an explanation as to his reference to the crow's court.

"It was the cawing that first attracted his attention," said Ian. "And, as he crawled nearer, he saw a flock of crows . . ."

"Murder," I said.

"Exactly, Gatehouse. Because that's precisely what they intended to do to the poor chap in the middle."

"Aye?"

"The crows, you see, were stood in a near perfect circle. And in the center of the circle was a single solitary fellow who was plainly on trial. And . . ." Ian paused to pick up the rose bowl, had a swig, complained something rotten that his real tea had gone cold, and continued, "when the trial was done, the whole flock, the whole damned murder of crows, began pecking the defendant like fury."

"That's amazing, Ian." I sat back agog. "And now you consider that you are the crow in the center of the circle? Yes, I see it all now. You're the subject of a crow's court, you're being victimised and . . ."

"Whatever are you talking about, Gatehouse, old chap?" Ian got up and poured what remained of his real tea over the fire. The consequential hissing and spitting sent The General scurrying into the kitchen and she was followed by the litter and Colin, who perfectly imitated the fire.

"You know?" I said. "The point about the crow's court . . ."

"Gatehouse!" said Ian, and he said it scornfully, "Your overactive imagination is troublesome. The young whippersnapper, who was later to become the farrier of this parish, was simply crawling around Breeve Hill for the sole purpose of spying into the bedroom window of the police house." Ian winced, shrugged, and chuckled. "He was nabbed because the crows weren't reckoning on their court being open to the public. So, rising and cawing, our feathered friends madly swept the sky."

"So what happened, Ian?"

"You may well ask, Gatehouse, old chap . . ."

"I just, sort of, did."

"Quite. Well," said Ian. "The court of law, now airborne, sounded like an alarm going off and consequently the whippersnapper found himself arrested for voyeurism."

"That's shameful behaviour, that is."

Ian returned to his chair, and he chuckled. "He who was to become the farrier had no qualms about the peeping tom rap. He knew it was a fair cop. It was the charge of contravening the Protection of Birds Act, 1954 that was unfortunate. Indeed his widow, Mrs. Roberts of The Vine Guesthouse, still carries the shame of having been married to a molester of wild birds."

"The what? But how?"

"Gatehouse, old dear. Having been caught in possession of a mangled crow, you try convincing a magistrate that he was injured by reason of having been indicted to stand trial before his peers!"

"Okay, then, Ian." I was totally confused by now. "So, what's the relevance of all this and the going's on with the flame-haired Nurse Stringer?"

Ian shook his head in disbelief. "Must I spell out everything, Gatehouse? Having told Nurse Stringer that he would be on garden furniture watch all Tuesday night, PC Stringer went up Breeve Hill, crawled through the self same undergrowth, and spied into the self same bedroom window of the self same police house. Gatehouse, old chap." He again shook his head. "PC Stringer's behaviour is unbecoming of an officer of the law."

"But, Ian," I submitted, "you can't get arrested for spying into your own bedroom window."

"No, No!" said Ian. "Once again you entirely miss the point in issue . . ."

"Which is what?"

"Which happens to be the imminent risk of me being arrested, or worse, for having been observed enjoying one of PC Stringer's Havanas."

"Well," I said. "It's a bit cheeky, but . . ."

"Gatehouse, old chap." Ian shrugged and winced. "I fear that at the relevant time I happened to be prancing around PC Stringer's bedroom wearing little more than a smile." Ian got up from his chair and went over to the inglenook. He reached down, copped hold of some wood, and placed it next to the no parking sign that was burning very nicely.

I also got up, and I did so for the purpose of making more real tea. As I walked to the kitchen, "Why the sudden propensity to pilfer signs?" I enquired, on realizing that it was information pertaining to the police house, namely that access for members of the public was through a side door that was also going up in smoke.

Ian winced and shrugged. "The residents of Prestwick have taken to locking away their garden furniture at night." He once again shook his head. "These are cynical times, Gatehouse, old dear. No one seems to trust anyone anymore."

"I reckon you can do with that," I said on my return, handing to Ian a royal wedding commemorative cup. Even the pig had found that one too distasteful to go near. I joined Ian, standing by the blaze and warmed my backside. "How come," I said, eventually, "that you discovered that PC Stringer was spying on you and Nurse Stringer?"

"I'll tell you how come, Gatehouse." Ian swigged some real tea, grimaced, shrugged, and winced, and said, "While I was in the shower, the damnable fellow returned to the house and sat himself down at the table upon which District Nurse Stringer had laid our candlelit supper." Ian looked me pitiably in the eyes. "He's a rum'n, he is."

"Good grief, Ian!" I was mortified. "Where, how, what did you do?"

"Where, how, what, you may ask, Gatehouse, old dear." Ian returned to his chair. On being seated, he immediately leapt up, saying, "Ouch! The seat of my trousers is damned hot!" Thereupon, he spilt what remained of the real tea down his front. "Ouch! You've scalded me, Gatehouse!" After a bit of fussing and wiping, Ian settled back down, and he continued thus. "For what seemed hours, although it was probably no more than five minutes, I hung around in the shower room." Ian winced, a little. "My clothes, you see, were still deposited where I'd left them . . ."

"Where?"

"Next to the table."

I was mortified all over again for Ian cared not one iota that he alluded to having had a tryst on a surface intended for the preparation and consumption of food within premises that were not solely domestic for the purposes of the Health and Safety at Work Act, 1974. It was small wonder that PC Stringer was miffed. As the occupier of the premises he was strictly responsible and a breach of the said Act rendered him liable to a fine, imprisonment, or both. But it didn't stop there. District Nurse Stringer was a big girl. She was not, I grant you, as big a girl as ever Sandra was, but a big girl she technically was. It followed that there had been a further breach of the said Act for which the officer was liable. You see, the table had been a danger to any person or persons who might come into contact with the thing. It was old and tatty and wobbly and liable to collapse. I knew that as a fact because some writing on the wreckage in the outhouse told me that it was once the property of Warwickshire Constabulary.

"Gatehouse?" said Ian. "Are you listening to me? Anyway," he continued, wholly oblivious to the full criminal ramifications, let alone the potential for an action in the civil court for breach of statutory duty. "I couldn't stay in the shower room all night so, I finished shaving . . .”

“What?”

“Gatehouse. Even you must have noticed that PC Stringer sports no facial hair. And, moreover, he leaves his wet shaving kit lying around.” Ian shrugged, winced, and chuckled. “He can have no qualms if it's put to use by third parties . . .”

“But . . .”

“But, nothing, Gatehouse, old chap. As I was saying, I finished shaving, and ventured downstairs . . .”

“What? Starkers, like?”

“Good heavens no, Gatehouse. I have standards, you know. I donned his dressing gown, of course.”

“What?” The guile of the reprobate never ceased to amaze. I went to the other chair and, after also carping that my backside was scorched through having stood so close to the fire, I too plonked myself down.

“Gatehouse, old chap. I can only describe the events that ensued as troublesome.”

“Frankly, Ian, I ain't surprised.”

“I entered the kitchen and, you'll never believe it, Gatehouse. PC Stringer requested my presence at table.”

“What? Do you mean he asked you to dine? Straight out the shower and in the man's dressing gown having sort of already been at it at the table, if you get my drift?”

“Precisely, Gatehouse.” Ian once more left his chair for the purpose of attending the fire. This time he copped hold of the poker and prodded the timber because the signs were showing signs of fizzling out. “Damned cheap wood,” muttered Ian. “Anyway, Gatehouse,” he resumed, after he was done, “I partook of provender with the pair of them, and, after the plates were polished clean, I got dressed in the downstairs toilet and left.”

“What? Just like that?”

“Just like that, Gatehouse.” Ian reached beneath the inglenook and from a wooden box he plucked an exceedingly long Havana cigar. He rolled the thing between his fingers, sniffed it, winced, and produced the howitzer from his trouser pocket. “Not a word passed between the three of us, other than for District Nurse Stringer to enquire whether the lamb chops were too pink, and for PC Stringer to remark that pink is how lamb chops ought to be . . ." Ian paused while he swizzled the wheel atop the howitzer. After the Havana was lit, and, after Ian had dashed the entire length of the room for the purpose of extinguishing the curtains, he completed his tale with the revelation that he'd returned the following day to see whether either one of the spouses had done the other one in. "The place was deserted, Gatehouse. Very strange. Anyone could have strolled in, you know."

"Yes, Ian. So I see."

"Any way, Gatehouse, old chap." Ian popped the Havana between his lips and sucked like fury. Then, between puffs, he said, "The fellow has been all over the parish asking questions about me. Gatehouse!" Ian stuffed his hands deep inside his trouser pockets. "I reckon he's compiled a dossier on my known movements and now he's out to get me." He had spoken through gritted teeth.

"Ian, I reckon it's delayed shock or sommut and, now it's sunk in, he's after your blood. If he killed you he'd say it were provocation, you know."

"Thank you very much, Gatehouse!"

"Don't go getting shirty with me," I said, "Look at the evidence, Ian." I proceeded to reel off the said evidence in support of my proposition that Ian was in imminent danger of being bumped off by the local copper. By way of visual aid to my presentation, I casually held a closed fist aloft with the intention of popping up a finger for each point of evidence and a thumb should the issues stretch beyond four. "One," I said, and, at the same time my forefinger flipped up, "you were starkers and alone with his wife and, while I accept she's a nurse, you ain't no doctor. Two," and up popped the middle finger, "you showered and shaved in the man's bathroom." Ian shrugged and chuckled at that one. Assisted by a showing of the ring finger, "Three," I said, "you donned his dressing gown, and four," I said, with the little finger, "that was at least better than prancing around, displaying yourself, while puffing on his Havanas." I was on a roll, but Ian just shrugged and chuckled some more, and so, bringing out my thumb in reserve, "five," I said, "I suppose you were at his single malt and all . . ."

"I most certainly was not!" Ian was mortally offended by that one. "What in hell's name do you take me for? How dare . . .!"

He was interrupted by a knocking on the front door.

"Pinstripe!" I said, and I rolled over the arm of the chair and crawled under the window.

"Stringer!" cried Ian, and he too ducked beneath the window.

But it was neither Pinstripe nor PC Stringer. As we crouched beneath the window we heard footsteps going round to the back of the house. It was followed by the noise of the rear door opening.

"Damned cheek of it," said Ian. "Fancy walking in uninvited?"

"Yoo-hoo!" The voice was female. "Is there any one at home?"

"Janie?" said Ian.

"Janie?" I said, and I leapt up to greet our visitor. I cared not a jot that she had just as likely turned litigant in person and was reckoning on gifting me due process. Where I'd come from, we admired women with spirit. "Now then, about earlier," I said, as Janie came through. At her feet was The General. Colin was there too, and he was clawing to get up, mad jealous that in her loving arms, Janie bore two piglets.

"I'll have no excuses," said Janie. She still hadn't rid herself of the strange jacket of wax and the funny Wellington boots, but she was stunningly beautiful, nonetheless. "I am here, out of courtesy, because I found these," and she glanced at the two squirming creatures before her, "in the road, where they might come to harm."

Ian had remained beneath the windowsill. With a shrug and a wince, he said, "Thanks, Janie! You're a brick!"

"Ian," said Janie. "You look extremely foolish, squirming on the floor. Here," and she bent forwards, "take these." Janie passed the piglets to Ian. Colin was quick to seize his chance and clambered his way up for affection. "Colin, how could you have been so cruel?" Her beautiful eyes swelled and moistened, as she spoke.

"It weren't his fault, Janie," I said. "It was a dreadful accident, sort of thing . . ."

"Izaak!" said Janie. She was simply stunning when she was aroused. "Izaak! Listen to me! I said that I'll have no excuses!"

"Now, listen here, Janie," said Ian, and he placed the piglets before The General because she was getting a little fretful. Then, Ian removed himself from the floor. "Now listen here, Janie," he repeated. I'd not heard Ian talk with such authority before, and I didn't think Janie had either, because she started listening. "I think that you are being a little too harsh on Gatehouse, here." They both looked my way, and I was thrilled beyond all measure that, for her part, Janie

210

blushed; indeed her chest glowed the reddest of red with passion. "Gatehouse is a good egg, Janie, and he's simply had a run of bad luck. It's as if the whole world is picking on him . . ."

"Yes," said Janie, and her voice had mellowed. She gulped, and I was ecstatic to see that the redness had spread to her swanlike neck. "I suppose that Izaak's ever present facial injuries are testimony to his having been victimized. After all," and she actually smiled, "no one could be the aggressor on so many occasions."

"Precisely," said Ian, with a shrug and a wince. "Indeed, it could be said that, by reason of some hidden and mysterious force beyond his control, Gatehouse finds himself indicted before a crow's court."

"Now, hang about, Ian!" I said, for I couldn't be having any of that. "I ain't been peeping into anyone's bedroom window, especially not Janie's!"

"Oh! Izaak!" said Janie, and she threw Colin in my face and strode to the front door.

I followed behind. "Oh! Janie!" I said, and the door slammed shut in my face.

CHAPTER TWENTY-ONE

During the next few weeks I took a leaf out of Ian's book and obtained temporary employment in the oil industry. In those days there were still petrol pump attendants about, especially in rural Warwickshire. The pay wasn't too good but there were great tips for cleaning windshields and doing other jobs like changing oil or water.

Of Janie I saw nothing, save, and except for fleeting glances, when her little green car putted and rattled down the Prestwick to Shipsford Road. By a remarkable phenomenon, the Morris Minor would always hop the twig as it passed the garage forecourt where I worked. It was a further phenomenon that the little car never ran out of fuel for not once did it pull over. At the end of the six weeks, I'd concluded that either Janie had discovered the secret of perpetual motion or she had decided to take her car fifteen miles out of the way to a garage on the other side of Shipsford.

On a fine morning, I had my employment summarily terminated for gross misconduct. It was as well that, with the exam results looming, I'd have been off the following week, in any event.

Anybody could have made the same mistake. The customer in the red Italian sports car had simply said that he wanted a top up of oil should I, within my discretion, consider that a top up was necessary, and indeed, desirable. "While you're about it, check the water level," said the customer, who plainly had no inkling that my knowledge of mechanics was limited to participation in metalwork classes when, as lads, we had welded together the front end of a Mk I Cortina with the back end of a Mk II. And that exercise required, not skill, but hope, namely that the back end of the former and the front end of the latter did not break surface in the Dudsall Canal, the fate that had befallen the class of '69 when a barge laden with nutty slack went down. The customer was a big, oafish individual, in his mid sixties, I reckoned. He had a loud, chequered suit of the sort worn by a used car salesman and a postcard stuck to the windshield gave notice that the vehicle was for sale if the price was right. But, with his bushy beard and wild hairdo, the man didn't look like a salesman of any product, let alone a salesman of used motorcars and of sleek Italian motor cars, in particular.

"I can't believe it! I simply can't believe it!" said my erstwhile employer as the sports car was winched onto a trailer belonging to an automobile recovery company. "Didn't you suspect that water shouldn't go in the engine after the oil you'd put in the radiator spewed out and struck a motorcyclist?"

"He was lucky to survive," I said. And it was true, he was very lucky, indeed. His bike had skidded on the oil, landed under the sports car, and caught fire. Providence had smiled on the biker that day for I had been on hand to pull him clear of the flames as they engulfed the motor car. I reckoned that I was deserved of a medal for bravery and not the sack. But at least it was a Friday, and I'd received my pay, in cash, the night before on little Friday.

One week later I was to be found milling around the grounds of Gray's Inn where, with dozens of other students, I awaited formal publication of the results by the ancient tradition of Cello taping lists of names on windows.

At the appointed hour I found myself flattened in the charge. But that weren't a real problem. For an entire academic year I'd gotten used to hitting the deck at Gray's Inn. It was at either the hands or fists of others or at my own hand; assisted for the most part with one too many glasses of the stuff lurking within the cellars. Anyway, I crawled and bashed my way through a forest of legs pausing only to glance up and apologise profusely to those owners of legs who wore rah-rah skirts and I eventually reached the windows, though not before crawling and bashing my way back through the said forest for the sole purpose of obtaining assurances that the owners of the before mentioned legs with rah-rahs honestly and truly accepted my apologies. Next, and ignoring the contemptuous cries of, "Pervert, you need locking up," and, "Oh my God, I think I've come out the house commando," I crawled up the windows and looked for Izaak Gatehouse on the lists. The lists were long and, optimistically, I began

213

my quest at the top of the lists. Presently, I abandoned all hope of having been awarded a first class honors, "It's a High Court Judgeship just around the corner for you, my lad, providing you marry right and don't hang around bordellos but, if you must, don't get caught" sort of a pass. Consequently, I started my search afresh, only from the bottom up and, in that fashion, I instantaneously came across my name. Succeeding (almost) in banishing Janie Jetty from my thoughts, I reeled backwards, screamed like a judge dressed up like a schoolboy being flogged something rotten, and decided to hightail it back to Warwickshire, though not before cautioning one of the owners of the legs above mentioned that, if I were her, I'd see a gynecologist, soon.

"The drinks are on me!" I cried, careering through the door of The Case is Open. It was a reckless thing to do for I found myself flattened once more by another mob who were similarly anxious to get to the bar. However, there was a sole, solitary, incumbent who did not make a rush for the bar. He remained seated at one of the cribbage tables, still wearing his loud chequered suit and still sporting his bushy beard and wild hair-do.

"How do," I said, "I didn't see your motor outside."

"Well, you wouldn't would you? It's burned to buggery."

"I ain't seen you in here before," I said, nervously.

"No," he said, "I don't come here often and I'm only here now because I was hoping to bump into you."

"Ta-ra a bit," I said.

"Come back and pay for this lot!" cried the bartender.

I returned to The Fly in the Ointment by way of the back lane, and through the river 'cause the bridge was still down, and through the vicar's garden that was shamefully void of furniture for one who hosted more barbecues than the whole population of Solihull.

"Ian, if anyone asks, I've gone to Glasgow," I said, as I burst in, tripping over The General, twelve hours to the minute I'd tripped over The General bursting out.

"Congratulations!" said Ian

"No cliental be bothered where my name was on the list," I said.

"No," said Ian, with a shrug and a wince, "I mean congratulations for fording the river without getting washed up in Bristol."

"But I've passed the exams, Ian."

"I know," said Ian, with a chuckle, as well as a shrug and a wince,

"I could have told you that earlier had you not left the house at an indecent hour."

"But how?"

Ian shooed The General into the kitchen. "The Dean's secretary told me last week," he said, adding, "She's started to sleep on the armchairs and it won't do."

"Who? The Dean's secretary?"

"No, The General, you clot! Sharon sleeps with me, if she sleeps at all." The caveat was said in a chuckle, and Ian had shrugged and winced, just a little.

I next proceeded to demand of Ian an explanation as to how come he'd permitted me to fret over the exams for an entire week, sweating, tossing and turning, and getting no sleep, when, all along, he'd had in his boudoir the resources with which to cure my malady but he'd chosen to imitate the symptoms of my malady. Ian was prohibited from providing his explanation because there came a loud knocking at the door, followed by an opening of the door.

"Damned cheek!" said Ian.

"Aha! Caught you!" said the man in the loud chequered suit.

"Why, hallo, Harry," said Ian casually, with a shrug and a wince. "I thought that you may have been the law or, worse, my landlord."

"I've been looking for you," said the man, addressing me. He sounded formal, but not as formal as I'd anticipated taking into account the fact that I'd burnt to a frazzle his Italian sports car. Even so, when the man reached into the inside pocket of his loud suit I reckoned that it was best to air on caution's side and leg it. And I was about to till he pulled out, not a weapon, but a bulging white envelope.

"Here," he said, with a smile, "take this with my thanks."

I tore open the top and peeped inside. "But it's stuffed full of bank notes!" I said.

Ian shrugged and winced, a lot. Indeed, the nervous affliction, habit, call it what you may, was so exaggerated that I thought Ian would involuntarily flip over the armchair, somehow. "That wasn't your motor that went up in smoke, was it, Harry?"

Harry scratched his beard and beamed. "It certainly was, Ian. And had I known before now that young Pit Stop lived under your roof, I'd have popped some cash round sooner, just like the last time."

Ian chuckled. "Well, I'll be dashed!"

215

"Who, what, when, how?" I said, and I fell back into one of the armchairs.

"Gatehouse," said Ian. "It appears that you have come of age and that the identity of your benefactor should be revealed."

"Aye?"

Harry made it to the other chair ahead of Ian and settled himself down. "Do you mean he don't know a thing, Ian?"

Ian stood over us. "Harry, I deemed it appropriate to say nothing for his own protection. Indeed, I deemed it appropriate for everyone's protection." He proceeded to shrug, wince, and chuckle.

"Well, Pit Stop, it's like this," and Harry budged his bulky frame forwards to the very edge of his seat. "When those two motors of mine blew up last year, I couldn't believe my luck. I'm in the business, you see, and I'd really caught a cold. I couldn't shift either one of them and then, like a gift from the gods, you pair of clowns happen along and, bingo! Top book I got from the insurance company, I did, and it's all thanks to you."

"So you see," said Ian, excitedly, "after Janie Jetty had done the honorable thing by grassing on us, Harry, here, came straight round to express his gratitude."

"He surely didn't pay you, did he?"

At this juncture, Harry coughed. "I am still here, you know."

"Oh. Er, sorry, like," I said. "I was simply . . ."

"We know you were," said Ian, with a wince and a shrug, "and, as explained, there was a certain amount of cash that exchanged hands. And don't knock it, Gatehouse, old dear, because it helped to pay for your studies and it put, not just a roof above your head, but the roof of the voluptuous Sandra." He then had a chuckle.

"But this is dreadful," I said. And it was true. This was dreadful for my benefactor had turned out to be not Janie but some car dealer turned insurance fraudster.

For my part, I was in a broken-hearted daze but, for his part, Ian simply juggled with the law to justify why no crime had been committed. "Well, perhaps a bit of attempted theft of fuel by means of siphoning, Gatehouse, old dear. . ."

"And what about the criminal damage?" I said, for any one knew that, but for our intoxication, we would not have made the mistake of incinerating Harry's motors. That meant we'd been reckless in law and had therefore contravened the Criminal Damage Act, 1971!

Harry coughed. "No charges pressed by me as lawful owner," he said, thereby implying that we had the defense of lawful excuse. For good measure, Harry even intimated that we were not guilty of fraud because the barbequing of his motors was done with no dishonest intent. Harry stated that if anyone was guilty of dishonesty, it was The Council of Legal Education for charging such exorbitant course fees. "I'd have thought that, with your half share," he had concluded, "you could even have stretched to a weekend in a country house hotel, or something, maybe even the Costa del Sol! I'll tell you something for nothing," and he began telling it with a laugh, "It's no wonder The Regal Knight Insurance Company charge such high premiums with you pair on the loose!"

"Harry?" I said. "Ian?" I said. "How much money in total was handed over, sort of thing?"

"Damnation, Gatehouse," said Ian. "I'm talking, Harry," he also said, as Harry had tried to have his six penneth. Ian shrugged and winced. "Very well, Gatehouse. You keep everything that Harry's contributed on this auspicious occasion."

I pulled myself up from the chair. "I ain't touching no laundered money," I said, and I went through to the kitchen. As I did so, I threw the envelope stuffed with cash straight into Harry's startled face.

"Fetch me a jam jar of tea while you're in there, old dear!" chuckled Ian. "Oh! And by the way," he added, "there's post for you next to the sink."

I bypassed the kettle and went straight to the sink. *Make your own flamin' brew,* I thought to myself, and then, *Hallo,* I thought to myself again, on perusing the post, *It's from Globe Chambers.*

As before:

Gatehouse,

That's how Walter addressed me.

Prospect has informed me of the good news. Congratulations. Please attend Chambers one week on Monday at no later than 8.30 am. My learned clerk will hand

*to you a spare brief in respect of a trial that starts at not
before 11.00 am. Prepare the case as if it were your own.
Regards,
Walter Tweed.*

I next noticed a note. It was folded in two.

*The Orient Express leaves on the second Friday of next
month. I look forward to seeing you in London on that day.*

I eyed the signature. Twice I eyed it, three times, in case my eyes
were performing tricks.

Janie Jetty

That was the signature, I swear it was!

I strode back to the sitting room. I was elated. I may have been
wrong about Janie sponsoring me. And who would really have wanted
to have been her kept man, in any event? But I wasn't wrong about her
waiting till I'd qualified to come clean about her feelings. She'd
played a cool game all right, but she couldn't hide all that blushing and
passion. Now she could jettison her baggage and make a fresh start
with me.

From the sink to Harry's chair it was only a three second hop,
even taking account of the additional time taken to bump into The
General and accidentally step on a piglet. But three seconds is all that
it took to think through my strategy. *Call to the Bar next week, start
pupillage, meet Janie in London. Propose in Venice. Come Christmas
of next year it'll be Mr. Izaak Gatehouse, barrister of Gray's Inn
kissing his wife Mrs. Janie Gatehouse under the mistletoe and a little
Gatehouse scampering about our feet, if I'm quick about it, and not a
pig, pure bred Tamworth, or otherwise in sight.*

As I came through, Ian was handing a cigar to Harry. "Gracious
me, Ian! These things cost a small fortune!"

"Harry," I said. "You're quite right and no law has been broken."
And it was quite true 'cause in the same three seconds I'd concluded
that when I set off the chain of events that cremated Harry's motor, I'd
had no inkling that my actions had enabled him to claim top wack

value in a recession hit economy in which he'd have had a job flogging anything, let alone a motor that was worth more than a house (three, maybe four houses with inside toilets, if the houses were from up Dudsall way). You see, at the time, my mind was innocent of any insurance claim, fraudulent or otherwise. And, if by some quirk, I was somehow or other guilty of goings on after the fact it was only money from The Regal Knight I'd gotten so I'd simply pop down the church on Sunday for a dash of atonement. Let me explain: it was a well known fact that The Regal Knight was holy as well as just plain regal for come hail, thunder, earthquakes, locusts, hurricanes, you name the disaster, and The Regal Knight had a knack of knowing about it in advance, as evidenced by their low claims record and consequential healthy profits. Well, it was either having a direct line to the Almighty that accounted for the popping of champagne corks at the annual meeting of shareholders or they charged premiums that were so high as to be criminal, and that would have been a scandalous accusation for one such as I to make.

"I apologise for my earlier rudeness, Harry," and I held out my hand, "I'll have that envelope back, if I may be so bold."

CHAPTER TWENTY-TWO

Dinner on call night was a sell-out. Typically, my long awaited call to the Bar of England and Wales was as an anticlimax. We all stood in a line that stretched from the front of Hall to the back and beyond, down the steps, through the kitchens, and in the cellars. It was a white tie do and I'd hired my clobber from an outfitters just around the corner from Chancery Lane. And what's more I was entitled to wear the robes of a fully-fledged barrister.

It took the best part of an hour to get to the front. By the time I was there I knew precisely what the crack was 'cause, by that stage, I'd heard the same spiel dozens of times over. A big wig told the student whose turn it was next that he had powers vested in him and was intending to use these self same powers to call that student to the Bar. Then, with a shake of the hand, and the handing over of a certificate the big wig was ready for the next one.

I acknowledge that, as I'd neared the front, I had one or two reservations that someone might leap out and exclaim that it was a dreadful mistake that one such as Izaak Gatehouse was being called to the Bar. But, no such person leapt out, and so, the big wig duly exercised the power vested in him and, as a real barrister, I took my place at table.

"Well, if it's not, Mr. Izzy Gatehouse, barrister-at-law!"

"How do, Paul." His expression was hangdog as ever, and, as ever, he sat slumped over.

"You know my bird, don't you?" Paul nodded his head and thereby directed my attention to the person who sat opposite.

"Why, hallo, Caroline!" I said. She was as radiant as ever and the sight of her provided an immediate explanation for the slight hold up in the proceedings when the big wig had apparently decided to discuss life history with one of the students.

"Gosh, Izaak," beamed Caroline. "Who would have thought that Paul and I would become a couple, yah?"

"Yah," I said, and then I turned to Paul. "You seem a bit fed up, mate. Is there sommut up?"

"Nah!" said Paul. "It's just that, you know what it's like? You wait months for the moment and then when it comes, it's all over in a flash and you're left wondering what all the fuss was about in the first place."

I nodded, knowingly. "What, the sex, sort of thing, like?"

"You what?" said Paul, sitting up straight. "I mean qualifying for the Bar, you dim wit. Shall I tell you something, Izzy?" And he didn't bother to wait for my answer. "You've got a problem, mate, you have."

Now, dinner on call night was generally a riotous affair. But not for me for, come the spotted dick, I was off. It was not some aversion to wet cement posing as pudding to which I'd succumbed. You see, I had a grand plan to execute.

From Gray's Inn, I went to the underground station, and sixty or so minutes later, I was to be found at the front of a check-in desk at Heathrow Airport. It was a foolproof grand plan and it was guaranteed to knock Janie clean off her feet. It was the big push. And, in common with most, if not all, brilliant plans it was dead simple. In fact, on reflection, it was more a case of parachuting behind the lines than a big push.

I'd best explain. You see, with a portion of the cash that I had so deservingly acquired from Harry, I'd booked a late night flight to Venice. Once there, I didn't intend to hang about. All I needed was the time to find a suitable spot where, in a few days, I would take Janie for the purpose of popping the question. And upon Janie bursting into tears of happiness and giving an answer in the affirmative, I'd fish out a bottle of something really special from a secret hidey hole and we'd celebrate. Besides, I couldn't be having her think I'd got complacent just because she'd said yes. *There ain't nowt,* I had figured, *that can possibly go wrong.*

"This case is busted," said the lady behind the check-in desk. "If the string breaks, the entire contents will fall out."

"Well it aye happened to me before," I assured her, so, without further ado the red suitcase (my hereinbefore-mentioned sole asset)

221

shot along a conveyor belt and disappeared through some rubber flaps.

A couple of hours later, the said sole asset popped out from behind the rubber flaps at the Venetian end. Its lid was open and half the contents were trailing behind. Even to Italian standards, it was too embarrassing by half to go trotting round the carrousel in pursuit of various unmentionables. So, I copped hold of the case, tutted at my fellow passengers as if to say, "Who'd board a plane in this day and age with a pair of them in his luggage?" and followed the signs for the water bus, all the time thanking my lucky stars that I'd purchased my bottle of bubbly on the plane.

At the vaporetto station I hastily tied a few knots in the broken binder twine and wrapped it round the case. Bowline knots I tied. I'd learned how to do them by watching the bargemen down on the Dudsall cut. My personal favorite knots were granny knots but I think Venice had brought out the sailor in me. Next, I handed over a few hundred thousand lire (like everything else, even inflation was done with style in Italy) and I stumbled onto the waterbus bound for St Marks.

I stood, with the wind and salt in my face, staring dreamily as the pointed end of the boat cut into the morning fog. The odour of diesel oil and cheap cigarette tobacco hung everywhere. It was the sort of smell that I associated with the top deck of a Dudsall corporation bus and, as such, I should have found it loathsome. But in Venice, everything seemed romantic. It was probably the water that did it. Dudsall buses had wheels (unless it was match day with the Baggies, in which case their axles had tendencies to be found stood on piles of bricks, with no wheels at all) but, either way, they didn't go on water. Well, save and except the No. 6, and only then after the aqueduct had flooded, and, on such occasions, it tended to break down, meaning that everyone had to hitch up their trousers and get out and walk, and that definitely weren't romantic.

"San Michele!" came an excitable voice from the region of the wheelhouse. Like everyone else in those parts he shouted as if he was serving notice that the Russians had just dropped the bomb.

I looked up, and, looming from out of the fog, I saw an island. And it was a strange island and all. Dead straight walls it had, with tall trees sprouting all over the shop. "What's this place, then?" I enquired of a fellow passenger. I reckoned that he must be local. And my assumption was entirely correct. He was Italian, all right and, as such, he spoke better English than me.

"Why, it's Isola di San Michele," said the local. "It's where the Venetians bury their dead," he added by way of clarification

Bostin! I thought. "How far away is the city?" I asked of the local.

He shrugged. "Piazza San Marco? About the same as from Dudsall to Darlesbury. We'll do it in fifteen minutes, mate, providing him at the tiller gets a move on."

The vaporetto chugged along the landing stage of the island of the dead and, clutching my sole asset (naturally), I disembarked. The grand plan was getting better and better. True, I'd have to juggle around a bit for a whole night in Venice before taking Janie on the dawn run to San Michele. *Ha!* I figured, *Harry's Bar; very ironic considering the source of my wealth. That'll keep us awake half the night and away from the temptations of the old four poster!* It was tricky I grant you 'cause even on the Orient Express I'd have to feign a headache or something. You see, I'd learned my lesson and I weren't about to have Janie harbor thoughts that my intentions towards her were anything other than of love, devotion, and commitment.

Well, after dropping me, and a few mourners, the vaporetto spluttered away. I'd had another great idea and this one was better than the last. And, as soon as the last of the mourners had, mourned off sort of a thing, I set about unwinding the twine from around my sole asset. Come on now, and be fair! Anyone who's watched *The Guns of Navarone* on Christmas morning knows that all grand plans need a bit of an overhaul now and again. Well, be honest; who'd have thought him with the squint, concealed radio, and swastika tattooed on his left buttock weren't a member of the Blues and Royals? True, I'd figured on conveniently fishing the bubbly from out of a giant flower pot on some piazza or something, but this was twice as good this was. After declaring my love, devotion, and commitment as aforesaid, I'd cop hold of the binder twine and haul the bottle out of the Adriatic. Tell you what, there was no way young Pinstripe could top that one. And it would make a great anecdote for the supper parties that I assumed Janie would force me to endure, before I popped off upstairs to change little Gatehouse's nappy and fetch out a good book, *War and Peace* or something, while Janie did the social chitchat thing. Well, you know give and take and all that? Even the likes of Izaak Gatehouse couldn't expect to have Janie all to his self for the next thirty years, forty if I laid off the grappa for a while. So; in exchange for her lifelong commitment I was prepared to be sociable, a bit.

I proceeded to tie a granny knot around the neck of the bottle. I hadn't been at all happy with the bowline and had been tempted by a slipknot, much favored by the hangman and Morris dancers, but a granny knot meant that, after my proposal, I wouldn't have to spend the remainder of the weekend gnawing at the twine like a demented timber wolf. Next, I began swinging the twine around my head. Around and around it went. I'd seen gauchos do the same thing on the tele', only they didn't have Asti Spumanti, or indeed any form of beverage, alcoholic or otherwise, on the end of their rope. The trick was to sling the bottle into the very depths of the lagoon where no vaporetto, water taxi, dredging, sort of thingamabob, not even a stray gondola, could wash it back to shore.

On the fifth swing, I heard a twanging sort of a noise and the string went limp. *That weren't supposed to happen,* I thought, *I knew it should have been the slipknot.* I had no sooner started pulling in the string, wondering where the Asti had gone, when my curiosity was satisfied. You see there came an almighty crashing off glass, quickly followed by a lot of shouting, and a roaring of an engine. Next, out of the fog, came a vaporetto that was packed to the gunwalls with mourners. It had a broken windshield and an unconscious skipper at the helm and the thing was coming straight at me. There was no way that I intended to hang around, so I grabbed my case and made a bolt for it. But the vaporetto was travelling at a fair old rate of knots and, before I had chance to leg it, the thing smacked straight into the landing stage. Well, the force of it all knocked me clean off my feet, but then things began to go wrong.

A well-meaning passenger held out a helping hand as the craft skidded and bumped along. I instinctively reached out, but the vaporetto, on coming to the end of the landing stage, decided to head straight out to sea. Now, in my opinion most humble, the local lingo made about as much sense as section 1 of the Criminal Law Act, 1977, and so, assuming that the face at the other end of the arm was Venetian, I had no means of imparting the fact that, whilst I greatly appreciated the gesture, I would really rather him let go before I was drowned, dead. So, as I found myself dragged off the jetty and dragged out to sea, I screamed. But that only made the helping hand grip tighter and I swear that I'd have been skimmed all the way to Beirut, or worse, The Lido, had I not careened into a low-lying marker post. The face on the other end of the helping hand grimaced, as if to say, "Cripes! Mamma Mia! I felt that!" Thereupon, he released the vice-like grip and, as the boat disappeared into the fog, I was left doing the doggy-paddle, thinking, *That's put the conception of little Gatehouse back a bit, that has.*

CHAPTER TWENTY-THREE

"Gatehouse, you look dreadful," said Ian. It was Monday morning and I'd just got back from the airport. "I thought you said that you were going to get yourself called to the Bar and then go some place quiet to relax?"

Relax? I thought to myself. The shenanigans in the lagoon were bad enough and, as I shall hereinafter describe, I'd unquestionably done myself serious and embarrassing injury. But to cap it all they'd sat me next to someone with attention-deficit disorder on the return flight. It was as well obsessive-compulsive disorder didn't exist in those days else I'd have deemed it essential to count every one of his five hundred and nineteen paces up and down the aisle. I was consequently shattered as well as hurting something rotten by the time that I landed at Heathrow. "Ian," I said. "I've done myself a bit of harm, like," and I pointed in a southerly direction.

"What? How?" Ian's enquiry was accompanied with a shrug, and a wince, quickly followed by a chuckle.

"It's private, and I'd rather not say," and too right it was private, and I wasn't about to broadcast the fact that I'd been to Venice, let alone that the causative effect of a collision with some half submerged marker post had been nasty; very nasty, indeed. But it really would be a pity if I went and spoiled things and reduced this belles-lettres to the level of a lavatorial lament. So, I'll tell you what. Taking it as read that soubriquets along the lines of "chopper," "exocet," "Percy," "the old man," constitute the language of the gutter and of the barristers robing room, I shall henceforth, and in the interests of good all round taste and prose, refer to the subject matter of my malady as "the old block and tackle" with which, I must now declare, I was having a spot of bother.

"Well, please yourself," chuckled Ian, and he scooted over to the inglenook where The General and the piglets were happily snoozing. He took hold of the stick and board that were leaning up against a woodpile and he began rattling the first named object against the second named. "Come on, Gatehouse, old chap!" He needed to shout for the purpose of making himself heard above the self-induced racket. "If you still want that lift up to Globe Chambers you'd best get yourself ready while I get this little lot outdoors!"

So, spruced-up and looking the part, we were soon tearing away in the wreck leaving The General, the piglets, and Colin mooching around in the garden.

"It's no good, Ian!" I found it necessary to shout so that I could be heard above the noise of the wind and the rattling of the car. "I have to go again!"

"But you only went ten minutes ago!" The vehicle skewed to a halt and Ian turned off the ignition. "Very well then, Gatehouse, old dear, if you really must, then you'd best go behind the hedge."

"Sorry!" I said, another ten minutes later. We'd just left the countryside. "I have to go again!"

The car pulled over. There came the screeching of brakes and sounding of hooters from behind. Ian had failed to use his indicators, not that it mattered because the indicators, in common with the majority of the visual and audible warning devices scattered about the car, never worked. "Good heavens above, Gatehouse, old chap! I simply can't imagine where it's all coming from!"

"That's the problem, Ian. I can hardly go at all, and I'm desperate, I am."

Ian grasped the steering wheel in both his hands and he winced, not once, but twice. "I don't know what you've been up to, Gatehouse, but I only hope that it was worthwhile." He proceeded to shrug, wince for a third time, and chuckle.

We arrived in Birmingham ahead of the rush-hour traffic and thereby avoided the road rage, almost. There was just the one kafuffle. A driver appeared to be edging her motor car from a parking bay into the mainstream of traffic. It meant that a driver in the mainstream had to either slow, ever so slightly, to let her out, go round her, ever so slightly, thereby letting her out with the added bonus of not losing the two seconds that would be wasted were he to have gone for the first

227

option. Or thirdly, being the option that he actually went for, rev the engine to cooking point, drive straight at her, smash into the front of her car, spin round, narrowly missing a group of schoolchildren, and end up facing the oncoming traffic. The stratagem adopted had resulted in a multi-car pileup. "Yow 'ave med we late fur work, missus, yow 'ave!" came the cries from the crumpled Austin Allegro. "Oh! Why does it 'ave ta 'appen ta we!"

Ian edged the wreck around all of the twisted metal and broken glass. He ignored various enquires as to whether we were both feeling okay. Passersby could naturally be forgiven for assuming that our car had been a participant in the pile-up; indeed those motor cars that were actually involved were in far better shape than ever the wreck was. You see, it had only taken Ian a few trips to break in the brand spanking new bodywork of his motor.

Ian drove a few hundred yards more and then began to slow.

"What? Why are we stopping?"

"Because there's a gentlemen's lavatory opposite and if, on the first day in Chambers, you persist in trotting off to the loo every ten minutes, there will be rumours circulating by lunchtime."

Well, in the main foyer of Globe House I went straight to an appropriate room where I stared at the names of those makers of fine porcelain, Mr. Armitage and Mr. Shanks. I did so for nigh on fifteen minutes during which time I passed but a driblet, and the pain coming from the old block and tackle was excruciating.

And so it was, that as a barrister with a stoop, I entered Chambers and began my pupillage.

Damian was sat astride his desk. Having naively assumed that mobile telephones might after all catch on Damian had evidently retrieved his own breezeblock sized model from the wastebasket. As before, I found him jabberwocking into the same, fifteen to the dozen. "Oil meck shooer Mista Tweed am aware of the hearing and oil meck shooer that if the brief am returned yow approve Counsel Mista Tweed suggests, like." Damian motioned with his head that I should be seated in the plastic bucket chair, so I did as I was bade. Meanwhile, Damian continued with his chitchat. "Yeh, mate, yow can depend on us not to let yow down. Okay, okay. Ta-ra, mate." Damian removed the device from his ear and placed it on the desktop and then he removed himself from the desktop. "Oh, blimey, Mista Gateouse . . ."

"Call me Izaak,"

"Oh, blimey, Mista Izaak, oil be fur it now cus Mista Tweed ain't gonna' trust a Regal Knight case with one of the tenants in Chambers, lyke." Damian slapped the back of an outstretched hand against his forehead. "Oh, blimey Ol' Riley, what shall oi do? Oil be in a fix if oi car sort this thing out."

"My dear, learned clerk, I suggest that you step this way."

"Oi day see yow there, Mista Tweed." Walter had popped his head round the door leading off from the clerk's office.

Damian scurried towards the door and, simultaneously, the remaining parts of Walter united with his head in the clerk's office. He wore a smart black jacket with grey stripy trousers. "Good morning, Gatehouse," drawled my pupil master. "Here is the brief for you to prepare." I was handed a large pile of papers all done up in pink ribbon. "We shall go to court presently, my friend, but first I must attend to Chambers business."

I did a nosedive into the papers. The client, Mr. Jack Tish, was charged with just one count on an indictment of conspiracy to steal. It was said that on dates, that I'm blowed if I can now recall, Mr. Tish along with another had conspired to steal motorcars, had changed their identities, and gone and shipped them overseas.

As I read how Mr. Tish had exercised his right of silence I could hear from the raised voices coming from the next office that Damian had opted to do no such thing. "Oil tell 'em ta send the brief to another set of chambers shall I then, Mista Tweed?" In response thereto, my learned pupil master appeared to be insisting that Damian should stay cool and that, since the case under discussion was not due to be heard until 2.00 p.m. the following day, something would turn-up.

Presently, the door opened. "Very well, Izaak," drawled Walter, "let us depart." I vacated the bucket seat. "Gatehouse?" said Walter. "Where are your robes?" He looked and sounded astonished.

"I aye got none. I mean I don't own any robes yet," and too right I didn't posses robes of my own. Granted, my benefactor Harry had been fairly generous but the cost of a wig-n-gown, not to mention the rest of the fancy dress, wing collar, and so on was pretty extortionate. Indeed, it was generally accepted that only the likes of them such as Walsingham-Parker could stretch to the price of robes during pupillage.

"Damian, my learned clerk."

"Yes, Mista Tweed?"

"How tall are you, my learned pupil?" Walter drawled casually as he spoke, whilst simultaneously eying me up and down. "Damian, my learned clerk," he said again, "bring me the robes of Patterson," and he proceeded to waft Damian away.

While the clerk was out of the room, Walter explained that it was not essential for a pupil to be robed for court. However, he considered that it was good experience. Further and additionally, it would mean that I could be seated at the front, with all the other barristers, and I could also assist Walter by reading out long passages thereby affording him the odd breather.

Moments later, Damian made a blustering return. He held forth a large blue bag. It was the same color as the pump bags that we carried fags-n-booze in at Dudsall School sports day. It was the same shape and all. The bag that Damian held was bigger, but, taking it as read that the average barrister was nought but a big school kid, and a smutty one at that, the bag could be said to have been perfectly scaled up. "Doe let 'im lose 'em, Mista Tweed," said Damian. "If yow do, Mista Patterson will goo mad at we he will. Look," he said, focussing on me, "Mista Patterson's initials am on the bag so there aye no reason to mix 'em up."

"Have no worries, my learned clerk," drawled Walter, "should you experience any problems, kindly refer Patterson to me." My pupil master copped hold of the bag from Damian and he proceeded to transport the same to me. "You heard my learned clerk, Izaak. Take good care of these," and he grinned, just a little. "Take good care of that also," and he nodded in the direction a large black briefcase.

Now, to anyone's standards, the short walk from Globe Chambers to the Crown Court would have taken three minutes at most. It took us all of fifteen minutes, and it weren't because of road rage, or, for that matter, the before mentioned spot of bother. It was simply the case that everyone we encountered along the way were simply desperate to enquire after the health of my pupil master.

"Mista Tweed!" exclaimed the road sweeper. "I trust that yow am well today!"

Walter nodded, as if to impart the news that he was perfectly hunky dory, and then he grinned, just a little.

"Morning to you, Tweed. Trust you're well?" The greeting and enquiry came from someone with a blue bag slung over his shoulder. He was too snooty to be a schoolboy, so I figured he was a barrister.

"Good day to you, Jones," said Walter, "I assume that your trial is in its fifth week?" and Walter thereby confirmed that the character was, indeed, just another barrister.

As we crossed the road, there came a tooting of a car horn. "Hope you're feeling okay, Mr. Tweed!"

Walter waved at the taxicab and, naturally, he grinned, just a little.

"Good morning. Good morning. Good morning." This one was an elderly gent, and he wore a bowler hat, which was a rare site, especially in Birmingham. In fact it was a miracle he'd not been strung up the minute he'd stepped out. "I do trust that you are feeling quite well, Walter?"

"I am very well, thank you, Judge."

"And how are Mrs. Tweed and the children?" pursued the judge, by way of variation to the general theme.

By the time that we arrived at the grand, gothic, entrance of the court, time was running short. It was as well that the security staff waved us through, ahead of everyone else in the queue, though not before obtaining assurances from Walter that he was definitely feeling fit and well.

Amid the traditional blue bank of cigarette smoke and blue language of the robing room, Walter kitted himself out in next to no time. Meanwhile, I struggled like crazy with the tunic shirt and winged collar that I'd found at the bottom of Patterson's blue bag.

"It must be over starched," said Walter, generously, and he came over, captured the flaying ends, and by use of a pearly stud, he snappily fixed the collar around my neck. Next, and to the apparent amusement of other barristers present, Walter assisted in securing the pair of white bibs (or bands) around the collar. From thereon, the dressing up was plain sailing, well, almost. I clambered into the black gown at the second attempt, the first bash having been aborted after Walter had remarked that it was not traditional to wear the thing inside out. At least I managed to plonk the wig atop of my head without the need for assistance or advice, even though I hadn't a clue how I'd keep it in situ.

Walter, cool, calm, and collected, bewigged and gowned, glided out of the robing room. I scampered behind, jiggling with the briefcase and my own set of papers, all the while checking that the wig and me had not parted company. I understood that in the fullness of time I would forget all about the headdress; that the chances of the wig plopping on the floor were remote and that, in time, I'd have the nerve to wear the same at a rakish angle.

We came to a big, metal door. It was grey, heavy looking, and basically would have been more at home in the bowels of a battle cruiser. Walter pressed a big doorbell, and, after an electronic kind of crackling, a voice was heard to enquire who we were and what our business was. "Counsel to see Jack Tish," drawled Walter. "And be quick about it, my fellow."

Through the electronic crackling I heard the voice go something like, "I'll give him be quick, I will," and, a few moments later, there came the jangling of keys followed by the heaving open of the huge chunk of metal. Before us stood a blue suited prison warden. "Well, if it's not, Mr. Tweed!" *He is plump and fairly young,* I thought, *for a prison officer,* not that I had any experience of prison officers, you understand. "How are you feeling today, sir?"

Now, at this stage, I feel bound to impart that, endearing though it was, the constant concern for the state of health of my pupil master, was a total mystery. You see, Walter looked to me to be in fine fettle. Indeed, he appeared to be the very picture of health, happiness, and, I would add, wealth.

"I am quite well, thank you," drawled Walter. "Which cell is he in, please?"

The door was opened wider, and I trailed Walter as he strode inside. "He's in cell number three, sir. And," added the turnkey, "the solicitor is already with him."

"Well, let us hope he hasn't shot my fox," mumbled Walter, as he glided off in the direction of cell number three.

"Is that a toilet?" I enquired of the officer, knowing perfectly well that the porcelain object stood behind a blue door was most probably a toilet. Indeed, it fitted the profile of a jankhole because it was connected by a pipe to an overhead tank and a chain.

"Oh no," said the warden, "that's no toilet."

"Well, if it ain't a toilet, then the wooden thing sitting on it can't be a seat, so it must be the biggest ruddy horseshoe ever!" I never meant to sound rude, but the old block and tackle had continued to nag throughout, and, keep it to yourself, I was simply desperate to have another crack, even though the spot of bother was restricting flow to just the odd driblet.

"There's no need for sarcasm," said the officer.

"My belief," said Walter, "is that the facility is for staff use only. I suggest, my learned pupil, that you address the convenience within the cell. I feel quite certain that our client will not mind . . ."

"But what about the solicitor?"

"My friend, he probably had the sense to go before he came out."

As we entered cell number three, the instructing solicitor got up from a wooden bench. "Morning, Mr. Tweed." His tone was effeminate. "I do hope that you're feeling well." He was plainly not to be outdone by all those others who had showed such remarkable interest in Walter's state of health. "You'll be pleased to hear that I've been through the statements and I think that Chummy, here, may change his plea to guilty." His whole body language was effeminate, especially because while, one arm rested casually on his hip, the other arm was deployed at head height for the purposes of providing a visual demonstration of the topics on which he spoke. For example, on making reference to Chummy, he had twizzled his wrist and pointed in the direction of the occupant of cell number three. On referring to the possibility of Chummy changing his plea, the arm had pointed straight down, as if to signify that an imminent term of imprisonment was in the offing. The pose very much reminded me of a teapot with a spout that had sprung to life.

Walter went around the teapot and he sat next to the client. "Good morning, Mr. Tish," he said. "I trust that you feel well, especially considering that you have been remanded in custody for ten weeks, awaiting trial."

Mr. Tish was sixty-four. Indeed, at midnight, he would turn sixty-five. I'd read it in the brief, you see. "I didn't realize you were from foreign parts too," smiled the client, who didn't sound in the least bit Welsh, but I knew he was 'cause I'd read that. "Any one can tell that you're feeling very fit and healthy, Mr. Tweed," and the client, thereby showed that he had grasped the very point that was missed by everyone else who we'd thus far encountered.

"You apparently wish to plead guilty," drawled my pupil master.

"Please explain why that is so."

"Well, it's simple, Mr. Tweed." The client got to his feet and then bent, slightly, and rubbed the greasy trousers of an awful brown suit that he wore. I recall thinking that he might have been better to go to court in a prison issue boiler suit. "You see, firstly, Mr. Tweed . . ."

"Kindly do not stand over me," said Walter, and he sounded cross. But then he started patting the vacated part of the bench saying, in his casual drawl, this time, "Be seated next to me, my friend."

The client was quick to obey. "Firstly, Mr. Tweed," he went again, "I'm told that the man who I'm supposed to have made plans with was an undercover copper . . ." He paused, as if awaiting comment.

"I am aware of that," said Walter. I was too, 'cause like I've said, I'd read the brief.

"Secondly, Mr. Tweed," and the clients sallow eyes began to swell with tears, "I'm homeless and probably best off in prison. It's why I didn't bother to apply for bail, you see."

Walter looked towards the instructing solicitor who, on hearing the second reason for the proposed change of plea, had shuffled awkwardly.

"Mr. Tish," said Walter, after a brief pause, "I suggest that you put your trust in me and we shall have this trial. Then, if all goes well, we shall direct you to those who are able to assist homeless persons."

Blimey, I thought. *I could have done with Walter when I were sleeping alfresco.*

The client nodded his approval to the course of action proposed. The solicitor did a bit more shuffling and Walter said, "My learned pupil, Mr. Gatehouse, here, will advise you on the right of pre-emptory challenge, but," and then Walter grinned, a little, and went on, "after he has, with your permission, answered a call of nature."

"You what?" said the client.

"He apparently needs to use your toilet," said Walter.

I was taught that it was rude, indeed very rude, to conduct a conference with a client and solicitor in any manner other than on a face to face basis, all the time maintaining eye contact. Well, I conducted the next bit of the conference with my back turned, standing over a stainless steel toilet, with only the gown I'd borrowed from Patterson shielding the old block and tackle from view. "Each and every member of the jury," I said, between gasps and groans, "will be asked to swear an oath to judge you according to the evidence. If you're acquainted with one of the members of the jury, or you wish to object to that person, please indicate that fact when, and only when, the person comes to the book to be sworn."

"You what?" said the client.

Walter took the helm, again. "If you know one of the jury," he drawled, "let Mr. Gatehouse know. Otherwise, leave everything to me."

We left the client banged up in his cell and went up some winding stone steps. From there, I followed Walter and the solicitor through gothic archways until we came to the courtroom. It was necessary to pass through some swing doors and, when it came to my turn, I got the briefcase stuck. Walter leaned over at that point, having firstly extracted me from the vice-like grip of the doors, and, ensuring that he could not be overheard by the solicitor, said, "Do not carry the case into court next time, my friend. Only solicitors do that."

"Okay. Sorry," I said, and then, to Walter's immense surprise, I added, "I think I'd best pop off to the toilet before we start, just in case, like."

When I returned, having had no luck at all, the court was in session. Walter was none too amused, especially since I had to ask him to stand so that I could come by. Anyway, I shuffled along, all the while smiling at the judge and I found a suitable place on the front bench. The said place was equidistant between Walter and prosecuting counsel. Next, I politely bowed to the judge, and sat down. Walter leaned in. "Next time you enter court, my friend, I suggest that you ensure that your trouser flies are done up."

The judge was a Circuit Judge and not a High Court Judge and, as such, he was "Your Honor" and not "My Lord" and he was dressed in black and purple and not crimson. But, if nowt else, his face was crimson; well it was when Walter shot to his feet just as soon as the twelfth juryman was sworn and stated that a point of law had arisen.

"We have not even commenced the evidence," said His Honor. "Under no circumstances will I send the jury out. Say what you want to say."

"Very well, Your Honor," said Walter. "My client has been charged with conspiracy and for the charge to be made out he must have agreed to enter into unlawful conduct with another . . ."

His Honor rolled his eyes. "Mr. Tweed. The allegation is that your client, Mr. Tish, entered into an agreement with a Mr. Trapham." The judge looked at the jury. "And the jury will be told that he is not on trial today . . ."

"Because he was an undercover police officer. . ."

"And the point, Mr. Tweed, is precisely what?"

"The precise point, Your Honor, is that the police officer can hardly be said to have had any intention of committing the planned offense . . ."

"But, Mr. Tweed, it was committed."

"But, Your Honor, that's not the point. The charge is conspiracy, not theft. And for the offense to be made out there must be shown to have been a meeting of two guilty minds. The officer had no intention of stealing motor cars . . ."

The judge cut in at that point. "I think we had better continue in the absence of the jury," he said, turning more crimson by the second.

"Too late," said the prosecutor, rising. I'd forgotten about him. "A new jury must be sworn."

"Very well!" said His Honor, shooting to his feet, so fast that his wig nearly flew off. "I'll adjourn while a new jury panel is assembled!"

A new jury was selected after which His Honor told them that they had to go out and have a cup of tea, if they were lucky, perhaps a biscuit, if they were very lucky. It was explained that a point of law had arisen.

A juryman, front row, far left, got to his feet, and bravely said, "But the trial hasn't even started yet."

"It is none of your concern," said His Honor. He hadn't liked that, not one tiny bit. In common with all lawyers, judges prefer non-lawyers, especially jurors, to be seen and not heard, and certainly, not to spoil things by thinking for themselves. "You will retire and return when I say so," His Honor went on. He had to retain control of the trial. Otherwise, who knows where it would all end? Jurors considering the truth and not the evidence if he weren't careful!

Anyway. The uprising suppressed, the jury gone, His Honor told Walter that he intended to hear the prosecution evidence and then listen to defense submissions.

"But it will take two days," said Walter, "and I shall be making the same, straightforward, point."

His Honor was having none of it. "You know quite well, Mr. Tweed, that it is only fair to permit the Crown to present its case. And besides," he added with a sly smile in the direction of Crown counsel, "the prosecution may decide to apply to amend the indictment to read that the conspiracy was also with others unknown."

"I am in no doubt that he will now," drawled Walter, casually, "but better that than wait until the conclusion of the Crown's case, make the self same submission and stand accused by this court of presenting an ambush defense."

The judge coughed and spluttered at that one but waiving Walter aside, he directed that the jury should return, but not before granting the prosecution's application to amend the indictment in the manner that he had predicted.

Moments later, the judge was telling the jury that Mr. Tish was charged with conspiracy. He told them that they were the sole judges of the facts.

"You could have fooled me," said the brave juryman.

His Honor told them that he was the sole judge of the law.

"You can say that again," said the self same juror.

After a brief opening the prosecutor told the jury that, with His Honor's permission, and His Honor indicated, with a grimace, that such permission was given, he would call the first witness. "And this witness," he explained, haughtily, "was the owner of a very expensive car that was stolen at the dead of night, in a village where the residents live in fear of criminals such as this defendant. Call Mr. Empots!" he then called.

The witness was brought into court. The first thing that I observed about the witness who, apparently lived in fear, was the bushy beard and wild hairdo. He wore a loud, chequered suit and all.

I tapped Walter on the shoulder. "I think that I may know this witness."

"What?" drawled Walter "What?" He said again, on the penny evidently dropping. "But I gave you the papers to read. I had better inform the judge."

Before Walter could rise to his feet, Harry was handed the testament and he duly swore to tell the truth the whole truth and

237

nothing but the truth. On handing the good book back to a court usher, Harry look across. "Hallo, Pit Stop!"

"Who? What?" said His Honor, who, simultaneously, did the impossible by going even more crimson in the face. "Did he say Pit Stop?"

Walter managed to get to his feet, without His Honor having a total seizure. "I regret to inform, Your Honor, that the witness appears to be acquainted with my pupil who sits beside me."

His Honor sat back, agog. "But didn't Mr. Pit Stop read the papers?"

"No, Your Honor. It is his first day in pupillage."

One of His Honor's hands slapped the judicial forehead. "A couple of hours into his pupillage and Mr. Pit Stop, here, has aborted the second trial of the day? Very well," said His Honor, with a sigh, "I shall adjourn for a moment to enable the court staff to assemble another jury panel . . ." The judge was prevented from saying more because the clerk of the court got up from his lowly place and whispered into one of the judicial ears. "I am informed," said His Honor, after the whispering was concluded, "that there are no further jurors available today. I am therefore obliged to adjourn until tomorrow morning."

"Court adjourned!" said the court clerk. "All rise!"

His Honor again left his seat. "Pit Stop," he mumbled. "I intend to remember that name."

CHAPTER TWENTY-FOUR

Following the abandonment of the second trial, Walter decided to attend to Chambers business. He told me to take the rest of the day off, but it was not out of kindness. You see, he explained, with due respect of course, that it would be altogether better if I absented myself rather than serve as a reminder of the goings on in court. "I shall expect you in Chambers first thing, Gatehouse, by which time I will have decided on an appropriate course of action."

Ian was somewhere or other attending to his own business, so I decided to attend to my own business and get the old block and tackle checked out at Shipsford Cottage Hospital.

"Dear God!" said the doctor. With a face as fresh as his white coat, he appeared to be not a day over twelve. "How the hell did that happen?" So, relying on doctor/patient privilege I told him all. "Ha!" he cried. "Come over here, nurse, and listen to this!"

A nurse approached the trolley on which I lay with a gown lifted indiscreetly around the waist. She had flaming red hair that was done up in an endearing neat bunch. "Dear God!" She copped hold of a teaspoon that had lain with an empty cup on a saucer on a table next to me. The nurse proceeded to examine my nether regions. The spoon was pretty cold but, on noticing evidence that that part of the appendages called the old block had seen action in Dudsall bus shelters on freezing December nights and had acquitted his self fine, she nonchalantly rapped the spoon on top of the hero, stared me full on in my screaming face, and, with a puzzled look, said, "Just a minute. You're Ian Prospect's mate, aren't you?"

"I ain't never heard of him, Nurse Stringer."

"Then how do you know my name?" She may have come across all coy and innocent and untouchable done up in her starched green and white striped pinafore, but she was a sly and naughty one, all right.

"He's going to have to have an emergency circumcision," said the doctor to the nurse.

"I'll tell them to prepare the operating room then," said the nurse to the doctor.

"Will I be out by morning?" I said to both the doctor and the nurse. "Only, I'm working tomorrow and then I'm having a few days off." I then lifted up my head and told them both, sincerely, "I'm going for a romantic journey on the Orient Express with my fiancée."

The pair of medics stared at each other. They proceeded to point at the old block and tackle, after which they stared at each other again, and both cried, "Ha!" and they fell about laughing.

"Look, here," I said, interrupting the jollity, "I'm being serious here. Can I have a temporary job done, like, so I can leave tonight?"

"He's being serious," said the doctor to the nurse, whilst simultaneously wiping away tears of laughter.

"We have no choice then," said the nurse to the doctor, whilst simultaneously wiping away green eye shadow that was streaming down her cheeks. "I'll see if we still have those rods."

After a brief interlude, during which period I gave the doctor my solemn undertaking that I'd be back in a fortnight to say cheerio for good to the little fella's top hat, Nurse Stringer returned baring an oblong-shaped box.

"Right," said the doctor. He reached into the box that nestled contentedly atop Nurse Stringer's bosom and he produced a thin silver tube. "It may not work but it's worth a go."

"What's worth a go?" I asked, nervously.

"I intend," said the doctor. And then he took a deep breath. "I intend to insert rods through the foreskin in varying sizes upwards." His stratagem was spoken with youthful enthusiasm.

My head collapsed back on the pillow. "Can't I just have a few tablets for it, sort of thing?"

"Not possible," said Nurse Stringer, and she stood right over me and she wore a smile that was cruel, very cruel.

"Don't alarm yourself," said the doctor, waving the tube around. "By the time I get to rod number nine you should have a gap through which you can effectively and proficiently pass water."

"What about sex?"

240

"My God!" said the flame haired Nurse Stringer. "He's as bad as his mate Ian Prospect. Here you go, Doctor," and she plucked a tube from out of the box. "If he's in such a hurry, then start the procedure with this."

The doctor swapped tubes, he took some deep breaths, and, before blacking out, I heard him say, "We'll start with number six then."

CHAPTER TWENTY-FIVE

Next day, I had an eventful journey up to Birmingham. I had no lift from Ian because he was expecting a delegation from members of a pig breeding association. There was apparently grave concern in the pig world that the piglets were not pure bred Tamworth's. You see, the said members were hyperventilating over the fact that it had taken generations for a particular breed to be bred out and then, along came Ian, who had bred the breed back in.

Anyway, that's another story. As for me, I had to chance my arm that I'd be able to thumb a lift in sufficient time for the *tête-à-tête* with Walter. I strolled half a mile, at least, down the main road with no joy and I was getting anxious. As usual, there was a back up of traffic at the diversion around the Prestwick Bridge. So, desperate, like, I opened the passenger's door of the first car that I came to and I hopped aboard. "This is an emergency," I told the driver. "Take this car to Birmingham."

"No problem at all, young Pit Stop," said the driver.

"Harry!" I said. "I must be gone!"

"Nonsense," said Harry as he nudged the motor forwards a bit. "I won't tell anyone if you won't." He placed a huge fist on the gearshift and I noticed that his little finger, though it was actually bigger than the biggest of my fingers, bore a chunky sovereign ring. It matched almost perfectly the gold medallion that proudly dangled from his neck. I remember thinking that, subject to clearing court security with all those troy ounces about his person, he'd certainly cut a fine figure before a jury comprised of Brummies. "Traffic's clearing," he smiled, and he accelerated away. "We should get you to court on time, young Pit Stop."

Too right he would get me to court on time for Harry's mode of conveyance was a growling, low-slung sports car of Teutonic manufacture that was much favoured by the Yuppies who hung around Sloane Square.

"Listen here, Harry!" I shouted, not through anger, but because I was competing with the huge engine that was weirdly in the back where, in normal cars, people put their luggage. "On no account can we discuss the case in hand! If I'd known it involved you and another one of your insurance scams, I would have told my pupil master. . ."

"A what?"

"I would have told my boss that I couldn't take part in the trial!"

With that, the huge hand flicked a stick, a lever, or something, and the cars tick tock told me that Harry was turning left. And the only left turn was the entrance to a farm which is where Harry stopped. "Now listen here, Pit Stop." Harry didn't shout. He had no need to having turned off the engine. He paused, and during the interlude he gave his bushy beard a few scratches. "What we have here is a prime example as to why folk, like me, should be judged on the evidence and not on their so called propensity to do wrongful things." Harry grasped the lapels of his chequered jacket and leaned towards me. It was very intimidating, it was. "Call yourself a defense lawyer?" He said those words in a sneering sort of a way.

"I have no idea what you're talking about," I said, and I sounded suitably hoity-toity, just like a barrister. "But I know your game, mate," I added.

"Well," said Harry, and he leaned towards me even closer, so, in actual fact, he had said 'well' at such close quarters that our noses were very nearly doing an Eskimo snog. "Well," he said again, "as it happens, I don't know this Jack Tish character from Adam. And furthermore," he furthermore said, only moving his face away from mine, which came as a relief 'cause the smell of stale tobacco smoke at that time of day was very unpleasant, "the evidence that I had nothing to do with the theft is that I never had the car insured, so I could hardly have been wanting to commit insurance fraud. So, you see, Mr. la-di-da Pit Stop, such are the dangers of failing to judge people solely on the evidence." Harry concluded his submission with a sharp jerk of his head, as if to say, "up yours, sunshine," though not before he had declared, "I heard that in Court Two after yesterday's cock-up, I did."

"Well, all right," I shrugged, "I suppose that makes it okay for me to accept a lift from you. But, but," I added, 'cause I was hardly about to capitulate totally, "I'm still telling my boss, I am"

"Damian!" I said, bursting into Chambers. "As soon as I've been to the lavatory, I must see Mr. Tweed!" I needed to tell Walter that I had been in conversation with a Crown witness. I needed the lavatory because rod numbers six to nine inclusive had not done the trick.

"Where am they?" said Damian. "Oh, pray tell we they ain't lost." The blustering clerk had made his enquiry whilst simultaneously tucking in the tails of his shirt. He had said the prayer, in prayer-like fashion, namely by joining the tips of the fingers of both hands and looking towards the heavens or, rather, the hole that was left where a polystyrene ceiling tile had fallen from grace.

"Where are what, Damian?" I said, and I made the enquiry because I hadn't the foggiest notion what the learned clerk was rabbiting about.

"The robes," he said, "the robes. Please, God doe tell we that Mista Patterson's robes am lost?"

"Oh! The robes," I said. "No problem, Damian. I left them in the robing room."

"Oh, my God! Oh, my good God!" Damian proceeded to take the Almighty's name in vain a third, maybe four times, and he staggered back, collided with the desk, and lay in a dramatic pose atop the same. "They am lost," he said in a groan, with the forearm that was not crushed beneath him, to his brow. "They am lost," he repeated, only adding, "forever they am gone."

"I can't see what all the fuss is about . . ."

"Izaak, my friend." What with the kafuffle, I hadn't noticed Walter come in. "The reason for the fuss, though overly dramatic, I concede, is that the Crown Court robing room is like a thieves kitchen."

"But, Walter," I said. "But, Walter," I said again, only we'd been distracted by the sound of Damian sobbing like a babby, "why should any barrister steal from another barrister? What's the point?"

"The point, my friend," drawled Walter, "is that our client Mr. Tish is said to steal motor cars at midnight and by morning the self same motor cars have been transported to the Republic of Ireland sporting new registration numbers."

"But I still don't get the point, Walter."

"Very well," drawled Walter. He proceeded to lift Damian's head by his hair. "Have you no dignity, my good fellow?" He thereby made a good bit of room for himself on the desktop. "Putting things bluntly, Izaak, the robes of Igor Patterson, having no doubt had new name tags inserted are, as we speak, being flaunted around The Old Bailey, or, some such place, or, worse, Stoke on Trent County Court."

"But there's no evidence of that," I submitted.

"My friend," said Walter in his drawl, and, this time with a grin, "I am not talking evidence, here. You must learn to see beyond the evidence and at a person's propensity to act in a certain manner if you wish to be a successful defense lawyer."

Damian sat up at this juncture. If it hadn't been for the fact that he was a Brummie by proxy, I'd have sworn he'd regained some self control and dignity. "What shall oi do when Mista Patterson asks we for his robes, Mista Tweed?"

Walter grinned. "You leave Patterson to me, my learned clerk." My pupil master next directed his attentions towards me. "I cannot even recall when Patterson last appeared before a higher court. I could not help but notice that his wig is as pure white as the driven snow. It is a sure sign that the thing spends more time in a tin box than ever it does in a court of law. I doubt very much whether he will miss the things until next Michaelmas. Damian!" he proceeded to bark. "Kindly bring to me the Regal Knight papers in respect of this afternoon's inquisition."

With Damian out of the room, I thought it best to come clean with Walter. "Walter," I said, "this witness Harry . . ."

"Ah! Thank you, my learned clerk." Walter cut me off because Damian had blustered back in. "My dear learned pupil," drawled Walter, "by unfortunate circumstances beyond anyone's control, I consider that your further input in the case Regina v Jack Tish is compromised."

"Compromised?" I said.

"You heard, my friend, compromised. I have therefore made suitably enquiry and you have been granted exemption to appear before Her Majesty's Coroner for the District of Southbridge at 2.00 p.m. There you will represent the interests of the Regal Knight Insurance Company in a matter touching the death, including the cause of death, of one, Mr. Medway."

"I don't know what to say, Walter."

"As little as possible, I suggest," drawled Walter. "Never ask a question solely to justify your presence at an inquest. It is tempting so to do but the consequences are generally catastrophic. Only solicitors and certain members of the Bar who were educated at English boarding schools make those kinds of mistakes. The former know no better. The latter simply like the sound of their own voices."

Walter proceeded to gather up the set of papers in the case of Regina v Jack Tish. "What should I be aiming to achieve?" I eagerly asked of him.

"Ensure that you keep a full and adequate note of the evidence, my friend. It may be admissible in proceedings brought against she who was insured by the Regal Knight."

"Who'll bring the proceedings, Walter?"

"Why, the relatives of the deceased and his estate of course." My pupil master tried to insert his voluminous papers within a loop of pink ribbon. He had no joy 'cause every time he got the ones on top within the loop, the bottom ones popped out.

"Mista Tweed," said Damian, "oil get yow a ring binder. We am always tellin' yower instructing solicitors to use ring binders and not pink ribbon, we am."

"My learned clerk," drawled Walter, "that infernal mobile telephone of yours will be in common usage before solicitors employ the use of ring binders in lieu of damnable pink ribbon. Here!" Walter had shouted because the papers on the top as well as the papers on the bottom had simultaneously popped out thereby leaving him holding nowt but the draft of a submission of no case to answer and his electricity bill. "Go and fetch that ring binder, now!"

"Righty ho, Mista Tweed. Consider it done."

"And now, my friend," said Walter, with the learned clerk having, once again, departed, "what was it that you wished to address with me?"

"It weren't important," I lied with the sincerity of a barrister.

It was a train ride and a bus ride over to Southbridge. The train ride came first and, seeing as reading on buses made me feel ill, and seeing as reading on trains did no such thing, I adjudged that it would be entirely rational to read on the train.

Now then, I am in no doubt that, once upon a time, activities along the lines of trial by combat, burning of witches and the ransacking of seaside towns by marauding Scandinavians in silly hats, all calling themselves Eric, had a part to play in the development of our constitutional and administrative law. But, whereas Lancelot and her in Wookey Hole and all them Eric's are extinct, Her Majesty's Coroners are alive and kicking.

I hereby undertake not to deride the ancient and noble office of coroner by harping on about its activities such as the occasional need to act in place of sheriffs, being the descendants of those who imposed income tax at the higher rate on the peoples of Nottingham whilst engaging in tomfoolery with men sporting feathers in their silly hats and who had propensities to fire off arrows from crossbows at 'em, and not, I hasten to add, those gentlemen from the Americas who wore tin stars on their chest and who had propensities to fire off bullets from six shooters, straight at any man, with or without a hat, let alone a man who was so unwise as to sport a feather in a silly hat. Neither would it be fair to take the rise and spill the beans about a coroner's duty to hold inquests on treasure trove; in other words, adjudicate on whether the likes of Eric, while sprinting across Scarborough Sands with King Alfred pointing a sword up his jaxy, had either lost his gold and silver, meaning that the Crown could keep it, or whether he had hidden it with the express intention of the same being unearthed by a berk in a bobble hat and a metal detector, meaning that the berk might keep it, all such gold and silver having been nicked from Lindisfarne in the first place.

But in the matter of Bartholomew Medway, deceased for nigh on six months, the facts seemed easy enough. The Regal Knight insured a Ford Capri, driven by Ms. Shirley Stoser, and it had knocked Bartholomew Medway clean off his motorbike. At two o'clock sharp, the coroner for the District of Southbridge and a jury of seven would decide whether Bartholomew Medway, deceased, as I say, for six months, no more, no less, had met his maker by any one of a number of verdicts including, but not necessarily restricted to, accidental death (Whoops! All part of life's rich pattern, sort of thing), unlawful killing (I knew that bitch in a Capri, in common with most, if not all, drivers of Capri's, both male and female, were nowt but a homicidal maniac), sometimes even suicide (Oh blimey Ol' Riley! Wished I'd not told him I'd faked all them orgasms throughout our fifteen year marriage before he tore off on his bike, screaming, "I ain't never been a real man, yow frigid and heartless cowbag!")

247

It took the best part of an hour to complete the second leg of the journey by means of an ancient bus. On the top deck, right at the very front, affording splendid views of the river running alongside, I folded my arms, crossed my legs and cogitated on what questions I ought to ask, as opposed to those questions that I ought not to ask, and, without wishing to put her on the spot, whether Janie might care for a pair of little Gatehouses, as opposed to just the one. I was long overdue for a driblet by the time that I reached Southbridge. So, just as soon as the bus pulled up to the town hall, the Southbridge Town Hall, you see, being the venue for the inquest, I rushed in and made a bolt for the conveniences.

I duly addressed Mr. Armitage and Mr. Shanks and instantaneously experienced the bit of trouble. It seemed somehow right and proper to moan and groan and pummel the wall a bit and, in doing so, I barely managed a driblet. "No! Please, no! Ah!" I cried.

A hand suddenly came from nowhere and rested on my shoulder. "There, there," went a voice that was consolatory in tone, "be strong, mate. It happens to us all, you know."

"What?" I said, "a bit of trouble with the old block and tackle?"

"No, the loss of a loved one."

"Well, I ain't lost a loved one," I said, sounding suitably indignant, though I did at that point glance down, and add, "well not yet I haven't."

"Are you in the right place, mate? Only I'm the coroner's officer."

"Well, of course I know who you are." I put the old block away and turned my back on Messrs Armitage and Shanks.

The coroner's officer, in common with most, if not all, coroner's officers, looked a typical retired policeman sort. Everything he wore was blue, except for his tweed jacket. He had a moustache that was as thin as the sort of straight line made by an HB pencil. In terms of coloration, it was in its natural state, namely grey, but, his head of hair, quite thick for someone in his sixty-something year, had a weirdly orangey glow 'cause then, as now, hair dye on men simply made 'em look as if Reynard the Fox had crawled up there.

"It's just that you sounded stricken with grief," said the officer.

"I'm perfectly well, thank you," I lied. "I'm counsel and I'm here to represent the interest of Ms. Stoser."

"Are you sure?"

"Yes, I've never felt better. I couldn't be more bostin."

"No, no," said the officer. He looked right proper puzzled. "Are you sure you're counsel?"

"Yes, quite sure."

"Then you'd best follow me and I'll point the lady out to you, sir," and the officer strode to the exit and I followed him out to the corridor, though not before he had turned to face me. And, thereupon, he had casually remarked, "They are responsible for more deaths than ever motorcycles are, sir."

"Aye?"

"Bacteria, sir. You forgot to wash your hands, sir."

"Good afternoon, Ms. Stoser," I said, extending my hand to the lady who sat on a bench, with her back to the wall. "Don't worry about dying from a nasty disease," I smiled, "my hands are only wet 'cause I've just washed them."

"I beg your pardon?" Ms. Stoser sounded as indignant as a bent solicitor caught with his hand in the till.

"Only a joke to break the tension," I said, creating tension. "You were meant to think I'd got wet hands 'cause I'd just left the lavatory."

"Well you had," said Ms. Stoser. She was plainly a stickler for detail.

"I know I have, but my hands aren't wet because they have somutt unmentionable on them, you see."

"I should jolly well think not!"

"I've washed my hands, you see."

"I should jolly well hope so."

"Any way," I said, having done with the usual preliminaries. "Shall we discuss the case?"

"Who are you?" said Ms. Stoser.

"Shall I start again?"

"I think you better had."

So, I did. Start again, that is. And, second time around, Ms. Stoser didn't display half as much confusion. Six months previous, she was driving her Ford Capri when a motorcycle carrying Bartholomew Medway, about to be declared deceased, came around a bend on the wrong side of the road.

"It was a tragic accident," said Ms. Stoser. She was pleasant enough once she got off her high horse. About forty, I'd have said, with flecks of grey in her brown hair that, in common with half the female population at that time, was done in a smart pageboy cut. She was probably worth a few bob and I based the opinion, not on the cashmere suit, and, neither did I base it on the diamond earrings and gold Rolex watch. My estimation of the size of her bank balance was based on common knowledge that she felt able to be fully comprehensively insured by the likes of The Regal Knight. "I truly believe that they detest me," Ms. Stoser went on, and she jerked her head, quick like, and, by so doing, she drew my attention to a group of leather-clad individuals who were milling around just outside the door of the council chamber. "Mr. Gatehouse," she said, quietly, indeed, so quietly that I had difficulty hearing her, even though she was sat not nine inches away, "they are members of a local motorcycle gang and the deceased was a member. I am fearful that they may wish to do us harm."

"Who, me?" I said, pointing at the chest of me, myself. "It weren't me who killed him, stone dead." I waved and waggled my fingers at one of the gang members. Save for a droopy moustache he had not a hair on his face, or indeed, head. He was taller than the others were. Six foot something, probably, though from where I was sat, he might just as well have been ten foot something. Anyway, he chose to snub my attempts at being matey and he turned his back and I thereby found myself facing a skull and crossbones. "Any trouble from that lot and just tell me," I told Ms. Stoser. "Now you go into the court while I pay a call."

"What, again?"

"Yes, again."

But before I had chance to go, the coroner's officer came over. "Court's about to start, sir."

"I have to pay a visit first."

"What, again, sir?"

"Now don't you go fretting, mate," I told him sternly. "I'll be certain to wash my hands."

I entered the court, having effectively wasted my time on account of the spot of bother, and I found that the coroner had already started. A coroner's court is relatively laid back, or as laid back as the coroner wants it to be. It transpired that Her Majesty's Coroner for the District of Southbridge relished his roll, for, just as soon as I entered, he snapped, "When I directed that this court would be sitting at two o'clock I did not mean two minutes past two!" Coroners were either lawyers or doctors. This one was a lawyer. Indeed, he was a partner in a Southbridge firm of solicitors who went by the name "Shaftice, Shaftice and Shaftice." The coroner was one of the Shaftice's but I weren't made privy as to whether he was the Shaftice at the beginning, the middle or the end so, I'll tell you what. I shall avoid all room for confusion and shall henceforth refer to Her Majesty's Coroner for the District of Southbridge as just plain old "HMC."

"I regret that I am a few moments late, sir." In truth, I had no such regrets. I'd told the officer that I needed to pay a visit and a couple of minutes either way was neither here nor there, *and besides,* I thought to myself, as I scurried to the front, *the subject matter of your inquisition won't give a hoot, mate, because he's a dead'n.* I nabbed a place at a large table that was plainly used for meetings of the local council. "I represent the interests of Ms. Stoser, sir."

"Well," said HMC, in a tone that was too sarcastic by half, "perhaps, with your gracious permission we can start?" He was perched on a higher level than me and he was in a big oak chair that I assumed was normally reserved for whomsoever it was that discharged the duty of running the council. The back of the chair was carved, a gargoyle, a griffin, or something, and, unlike HMC, it was clearly visible behind an old fashioned desk. In stark contrast to the back of the chair, HMC, you see, was not very noticeable at all. Indeed, from my vantage point, only his decaying face with grey complexion and sallow cheeks, was on plain view. "Hurry up and get the jury sworn!" He had shouted his order at a female clerk and, he had not just shouted, but he had shouted in a very aggressive way. Indeed, his manner led me to believe that here was a little squirt with a Napoleon complex.

A jury of seven having been sworn, HMC explained that it was their duty and theirs alone to decide the reason, by accident or otherwise, why it was that the deceased had acquired his title and why he was to retain that title for the whole of eternity, unless, or, until, the computer records found themselves expunged, as happened in Kidshore when the clerk of that parish had had cause to inform the Almighty that he was on the way up to see him and chose that magical moment to reposition his secretary's bottom so that it rested on the delete button. And it weren't only dozens of dearly departed's and never forgotten who, in a mad moment of ecstasy, had found themselves forever forgotten, for a decade's worth of marriages went the same way with the causative effect that, for all of eternity, Kidshore became known as the single mother's capital of Worcestershire.

Anyway, HMC started the inquisition by reading from a pathologist's report. He told the jury that they could take it from him that the deceased had definitely earned his title having been killed, dead, outright. There was an elderly couple sat in the back of the court. "Your son did not suffer at all," he told them. They hugged each other and appeared to be comforted by what HMC told them until, that is, he added, "you see, death was instantaneous because decapitation does that." As the parents of the dearly departed rushed from the courtroom, sobbing uncontrollably, HMC turned his attentions on the leather-clad individuals. "It could be one of you lot next if you don't have a care. There are too many cars on the road and too many careless drivers to make motorcycling at all safe." He proceeded to address a man who I had hitherto taken no notice of. He was sat at the other end of the table. "Motorcycling was an altogether safer pursuit in our day wasn't it, Mr. Grantora?"

"I hesitate to interrupt," I said, getting to my feet, with no hesitation at all. "Those are wholly inappropriate remarks to make in the presence of a jury. And," I added, "I say that with the utmost of respect," although in truth the proviso was uttered with no respect, utmost or otherwise.

HMC looked fair fit to give a tongue-lashing and he opened his mouth so to do, but thereupon Mr. Grantora popped up. "May it please you, sir, I am here, of course, to represent the interests of the family of the deceased." He stopped for a mo' and glanced towards the jury, as if he required self-assurances that, as mere laypersons, each and every one had understood the point that he had made. On presumably being so assured he continued, "I am quite certain, sir, that your observations are of great comfort to those relatives and friends of the deceased who are here today." Thereupon, Mr. Grantora hitched up his stripy solicitor-type trousers, a waste of time bearing in mind that, in solicitor-type fashion, the said trousers were already worn and baggy at the knees. With a self-satisfied, solicitor-type grin, he proceeded to return the equally worn and baggy seat of his trousers to the chair that it had just left.

"Thank you, Mr., Grantora," said HMC, and, ignoring the fact that I was still on my feet, he stated to the jury, "You may be assured from the report of the autopsy that the deceased died as a result of massive injuries." And looking at those in the public area who were dressed in leather, he said, "You see, it doesn't matter how careful you are these days. If you're hit by a car you stand no chance." He looked Mr. Grantora's way, and added, "it's true isn't it?"

I coughed, politely. "I would be most grateful, sir, if you could refer the attention of the jury to that part of the report which refers to the blood alcohol level in the deceased."

"Irrelevant," said HMC, "there was, I grant you, a reading of alcohol but it was below the legal limit." He looked once more at the jury. "That is why I did not require the pathologist to attend in person." He looked once more, Mr. Grantora's way. "These doctors are very busy people, you see."

I coughed politely, once more, lest it be that he had forgotten that it was me doing the submitting of the submission. "This accident occurred at eight o'clock in the morning and the blood alcohol level was just below the legal limit. . ."

"Precisely," said HMC, addressing the jury, and not me, who I must state, for the avoidance of doubt, was doing the submitting. "The deceased was within the limit deemed by Parliament to be safe to drive. We," he then said, addressing Mr. Grantora, "do not see the point," and, with a nod of his head, Mr. G concurred.

"The point," I said is that the post mortem occurred more than twenty-four hours after the time of death. We have no evidence when the blood sample was taken and we have no evidence whether, as a result of the delay, the alcohol dissipated"

"Huh!" said Mr. Grantora, rising, and so, out of politeness I sat down. "Counsel is trying to twist things and suggest that this wretched man was under the influence of alcohol," (He was quick, I was prepared to give him that.) "Counsel," he went on, "is not a doctor and he's trying to besmirch my client by suggesting that the level of alcohol could have dropped during the twenty-four hour period between death and the post mortem."

"Or gone up," I said, without bothering to rise.

"Pardon?" said HMC

I deduced that by some remarkable phenomena my voice had failed

253

to carry due to me being in the sitting position. I therefore got to my feet and said again, "Or gone up!" and I said those words both slowly and loudly lest it be the case that by further phenomena HMC had been rendered deaf. "In the interests of justice," I added, "if it's the truth that we want, who knows whether the stomach contents had fermented with the result that the reading of alcohol was artificially high."

One of the members of the jury began retching. Another member of the jury said, "That's disgusting that is!"

"You're not medically qualified," said HMC. "He's not a doctor," he told Mr. Grantora

"Precisely, sir," I said, "and neither are you."

"Well," said HMC, once more addressing the jury, "its pure conjecture," and turning to Mr. Grantora, once more, he said, "This is my court and I decide who will be to summoned to give evidence, and," the head swivelled back towards the jury, "I'm going to ask a police officer to give evidence now."

Sergeant was the rank and Page was the name of the officer who took the stand and took the oath. He told us that he was on duty riding his pushbike that fateful day and was first on the scene. Sergeant Page was a giant of a man which led me to believe that his cycle must have been made of sturdy stuff. It was necessary for the officer to place a large folder on one side whilst he had held the good book high above his head. Indeed, Sergeant Page was a giant of a man so much so that the good book had been held at such high altitude that it was a wonder it hadn't come down with snow on it. Anyway, with the oath done with, Sergeant Page put down the Bible, though I could have sworn it was actually a copy of the electoral roll, and, with that hand thereby free, he flipped open the folder, and began to fumble with a pile of photographs. The other hand, I should mention hereabouts was temporarily redundant. You see, the arm to which it was attached was being used to clamp a policeman's helmet firmly to his side.

"Here," said Mr. Grantora, who was nearest. "Let me take your helmet. It will make your task easier if I do."

"It will," said HMC eagerly to the jury. "It will," he reassured both the officer and Mr. Grantora.

Thus, with both hands free, Sergeant Page began the task of distributing photographs of a blood-splattered road and a mangled motorbike.

"Goodness gracious!" exclaimed HMC on flicking through the photographs. "It's a Harley- Davidson!" he told the jury. "It really is!" he told Mr. Grantora, thrusting the album forwards whilst repeatedly jabbing his forefinger on the relevant image.

"From the skid marks," said the officer, slowly and precisely, "I estimate that the motor vehicle was travelling at forty miles per hour . . ."

He was interrupted by HMC. "And, from the photos, tell the court where you found the deceased."

"Here," said the officer, pointing to a spot that appeared to be a drainage ditch, "is where I found Mr. Medway's body. He was laying in a northerly direction and he was quite obviously dead . . ."

"Well how did you know he was dead?" It was HMC interrupting again. "You are not a medical man, Sergeant."

"I had reason to believe that the deceased was dead, sir, because here," and the sergeant pointed to a spot in the center of the road, "is where I had found the deceased's helmet." The officer paused, rode up and down on his heels, as police officers, and particularly police sergeants, tended to do, then he coughed and said, "And his head was still inside it."

"Ah, yes, of course," said HMC. "Do continue."

"Well that is all really, sir,"

"Very well, Sergeant," said HMC. "Do you have any questions, Mr. Grantora?"

"No thank you, sir," said the solicitor, half rising.

"Thank you, Officer," said HMC, efficiently, "that will be all."

I coughed and stood up. "Well, with respect," I said, without a modicum of respect, "I have some questions," and, as it happened, I had.

HMC proceeded to sigh, heavily. "Very well," and, addressing the jury, he said, "Mr. Gatehouse, here, represents the driver of the motorcar that killed poor Mr. Medway and he apparently intends to ask some questions, but," he paused for a moment and looked at Mr. Grantora, and then added, "I cannot think why."

"Officer," I said, loud, and bold, "it's actually a Honda Goldwing isn't it?"

"It is, sir."

HMC's head jerked backwards and it let forth a loud gasp. "Well, what on earth possesses you to think that?"

"Because it says so in the officer's written statement, a copy of which," I said, "is here." And I held the thing aloft. "In addition," I said in addition, "if you would care to observe photograph four you will see the words Goldwing on the side of the bike, which tends to suggest, sir, that it was a Honda because Harley-Davidson's don't make Goldwings, but," and now it was my turn to look at the jury, "Honda does make them," and then it was my turn to look Mr. Grantora's way. "It's true, you know, they're made by Honda, as the word Honda on the fuel tank tends to suggest."

"Very well," said HMC, "do not labor the point. Kindly continue."

So, I continued. "There is only one set of skid marks, Officer."

Mr. Grantora pounced. "That is a leading question."

"Of course it is," I said, addressing HMC. "I'm cross examining, and besides," I added, addressing the jury, "this is not a trial, and as such the strict rules of evidence do not apply. This is an inquisition, you see."

"Which is the only reason why," mumbled HMC, "I regrettably granted exemption for you to appear before me."

"The skid marks," said Sergeant Page, still talking slowly and still talking precisely, "are from the motor vehicle that I ascertained was being driven by Ms. Stoser from Kidshore in the direction of the City of Worcester."

"Aha!" said HMC, and he began scribbling in a notebook, "which all tends to suggest that the motor car was going so fast that it skidded," and he spoke those words without addressing the jury, nor, for that matter, his chum, Mr. Grantora.

"Which suggests," I suggested to the sergeant, "the motorcycle did not brake at all?"

"That appears to be the case, sir."

"And additionally," I said, in addition, "the skid marks merely suggest that the driver of the motor car was obliged to brake heavily?"

"Er? Yes, sir."

"And there is no evidence to suggest that the vehicle was being driven too fast?"

HMC dived in at that juncture. "How on earth can the witness answer that?"

Sergeant Page coughed. "By reason of the skid marks not

suggesting that the vehicle was travelling at a high speed." He pointed at one of the photographic images. "You see, I will explain . . ."

But that's as far as his explanation went because HMC cut-in. "Yes, yes! I do not require a full explanation! Proceed, Mr. Gatehouse, if you must."

I did feel the need and so I duly proceeded. "Did you remove the severed head from the helmet?" I asked.

A female in the public section stood up, and, before dashing out, sobbing, she shouted, "That's sick, that is!"

Mr. Grantora, whose presence I had clean forgot, smiled. "She does have a point, Mr. Gatehouse."

"Well, Officer?" I said.

"Well," said the officer. "No I did not, sir."

"What," said HMC, "is the relevance?" His face not only went pink but he squinted so severe that I swore his eyebrows were in danger of meeting his cheeks.

"The relevance," I said, "is that, according to the pathologist's report, there appears to have been a bandana wrapped around the head . . ."

"Yes?" said HMC.

"Of the sort associated with kamikaze pilots."

"That is outrageous!" said Mr. Grantora, rocketing up, so forcefully that the loose specie in his trouser pockets jangled like the Prestwick parish church bells on Easter Sunday.

HMC's head began going up and down which led me to believe that his torso was bouncing about in the chair. "What on earth are you implying?"

"That before losing his literal head, he had lost his metaphoric head."

At that juncture, HMC, Mr. G, and Police Sergeant Page, as one, uttered the words, "What? Outrageous!"

"Sergeant" I said, above the noises coming from the public area. The sounds were of threats to my health, thus far fair, save and except for the spot of bother. "Sergeant," I said again. "The photographs depict that there was a hotdog stall at the top of the road."

"They do indeed, sir."

"Then tell me this," I said. "Did you ask the stallholder whether he, or she, had witnessed the accident?"

"That's it!" said HMC, and he flung his pen on the desk before him with such force that it bounced off to that part of the room normally reserved, according to a little brass plaque, for the planning officer of the District of Kidmore whose job it was to advise the elected members whether it was right or whether it was wrong to permit the construction of two hundred more cardboard-walled houses on the flood plain in exchange for a few thousand readies and a dinner date with her who danced exotically at the Kidshore Conservative and Unionist Club, but only on Sunday lunchtimes, mind. "There will be no more questions, Mr. Gatehouse. The object of this inquisition is to ascertain the cause of death and not whether any one was to blame!"

"Which is why," I mumbled under my breath, "inquests serve but one purpose, namely to drag out in public all the gory detail just at a time when the relatives and other loved ones are getting accustomed to their loss."

"Did you say something, Mr., Gatehouse?" said HMC.

"Nothing at all, sir," said I, sitting down, "except," I said, rising up again, "I was wondering whether that Goldwing badge comprised at least ten parts silver, in which case it might be treasure trove. And," I added, because as I was on my feet anyway and thought it might save a bit of time, "my client won't be giving evidence so there's no point warning her about the dangers of self incrimination."

Well, at the end of it all, HMC told the jury, "It is, of course, a matter entirely for you, but I suggest that you deliver a verdict of accidental death. So, are we all agreed?" So, sod-all coming from the jury, HMC continued, "Well, that's all agreed, then. Benjamin Medway died by reason of accidental death. Court adjourned." HMC shot out of his chair and made for the exit, that on Tuesdays was generally reserved for the Lord Mayor and the Lady Mayor, but only on market days when the travelling hairstylist with raven-curly locks and snake hips was in town, but before he disappeared from view, he said, "Mr. Grantora. I need to see you on a matter of some urgency concerning the conveyance of Easleton Farm House and all appurtenances attached thereto, including the stable block that lends itself very nicely, thank you, to conversion into a four bedroom apartment and a jackoozie in the walled garden."

As for me. I dashed off to the conveniences with the specific intent of attending to the spot of bother with the so on and so forth, whereupon I found myself face to face with a skull and crossbones, the owner of which was, himself, addressing Mr. Armitage and Mr. Shanks. When the individual was done with the addressing, I heard a zipper zip-up and he turned and the skull and crossbones disappeared from view.

"I'm only the mouthpiece, you know," I said. "So, don't you go trying anything funny, like?"

"No, No, mate," said the huge man in a soft sort of a voice that didn't all together go with the leather jacket, oily denims., and tank top with 'live hard die young' emblazoned on the front. "I only wanted to say that Benny (Benjamin Medway, deceased to you lawyer-types) was suffering from an aberration of the mind whereby he was intent on self destruction and he deliberately drove at that Ford Capri."

"Well, how do you know that?" I said, passing alongside, intending myself to have words with the before-mentioned makers of fine porcelain.

"Mr. Gatehouse," said the biker, woefully, "on that fateful day, I told Benny that me and his girlfriend, you know, her who rushed out of court earlier screaming that you're sick in the head, were going to run away together, but not till after the Worcestershire Wolf Bash."

"What?" I said.

"The Wolf Bash. It's a biker's festival . . ."

"Yes, yes, I know that." I hadn't meant to snap at him, especially since 'live hard die young', was at my eye line, meaning that in terms of the height of the mountainous biker, I was no taller than base camp, if I stood on my toes.

"I happen to know," said the mountain, "that Benny was screaming 'hissatsu!' when he came bombing around the corner on that fateful day."

At that stage I began groaning on account of the bit of trouble. Having managed not one driblet, I proceeded to ask, "Who told you all this?"

"Why," said the mountain, "the woman who runs the hot dog stall, of course." He proceeded to take a shufty over my shoulder, tweaked his droopy tash, and said, "Heavens above! You can get cream for that, you know."

"Listen up," I said. "I think the driver's insurance company may wish to obtain a statement from you."

"No problem at all, mate. They can contact me anytime at Kidmore General or simply leave a message with my dad at the police station. My name is Page. Doctor Gabriel Page."

CHAPTER TWENTY-SIX

Later that very same day, I strolled down the lane to Prestwick where, in the fields all around, the combine harvesters were whirling and sending rabbits scattering and chucking out dust in abundance. When I arrived at The Fly in the Ointment I was greeted by yet more whirling and, just like the rabbits, Colin and the piglets were scattering. And, on opening the big front door, I found myself enveloped with yet more dust.

"Ian? Is that you in the corner?" There came no response so, bravely, I entered and followed the whirling sound, and, on finding someone's shoulder, I rapped it sharply.

"Good heavens!" It sounded like Ian's voice, but it was difficult to tell. He wore a dirty linen towel as a facemask, you see. And, furthermore, upon the figure turning around, I was confronted by the nozzle of a vacuum cleaner. Now that was odd; indeed it was very odd. And it was odd on two counts. The first count that was odd touched on the very existence of a vacuum, for not once during the occasions of my occupancy had I observed the performance of dusting, spitting, brushing, or, for that matter, any form of domestic chore. The second count concerned the fact that the vacuum in question was blowing and not sucking, the consequence being that, from out of the nozzle, there came spewing into my face, bits of tinsel, a toy trumpet from a Christmas cracker, and dog hair, the latter having presumably come from Dave, deceased, the misunderstood bulldog, all of which provided forensic evidence of the time, or approximate time, when it was that the vacuum had last seen the light of day.

"Ian! For pity's sake, man!"

"Gatehouse, old chap! Just a moment! I can't hear a word!" Ian gave the cord of the vacuum a sharp yank, whereupon the socket that had connected it with the recently reconnected electricity supply came flying out of the wall, narrowly missing both our heads. "That's better," said Ian, as the incessant whirling, whirled-down. "You gave me quite a scare, Gatehouse, old dear," and Ian shrugged, winced, and chuckled.

"What on earth are you doing, Ian?"

"Distressing, old boy."

"It ain't half distressing, Ian, especially after I've had the mortal remains of Dave shot in me face."

"No, no, Gatehouse! I mean that I've been distressing the tools of my trade," and, with that, Ian produced from behind his back a barristers wig. It was full of dust, cobwebs, and hairs from Dave, dearly departed, for nigh on nine months. "This thing was as white as the driven snow," said Ian, scornfully, "I doubt whether the previous owner spent much time in the higher courts."

"Oh, good God, Ian! Where has that thing come from?"

"Gatehouse!" Ian proudly plonked the wig atop his head. "Providence has shone upon me this fine day!" He winced, just a little, and chuckled.

"You've nicked it, you have!"

"Gatehouse!" Ian reached towards the better of the two armchairs and he copped hold of a black gown. "Seek and you shall find!" He winced and chuckled. "That's Matthew, chapter seven."

"Ian," I said, "permanently depriving the lawful owner. That's the Theft Act, section one."

"And see here!" Ian scooted to the other armchair where there lay a blue robe bag. It was a bigger version of the school pump bag that I had for all the games lessons that I skived. "It's got my initials," said Ian, picking up the bag by its thick drawstring. "Do you see? IP! Gatehouse, old dear! It was clearly meant to be."

"Ian," I said, taking the place left absent by the bag, "It was clearly meant to be, all right. It was clearly meant to be returned to Igor Patterson."

Down at The Case I declined to partake of the fruits of the end barrel. "Gatehouse, old chap, you're the color of the devil's nutting bag. It's obviously a woman." Ian proceeded to clamp a brand spanking new clay pipe between his teeth.

"Ian, I'm going away on important business tomorrow and . . ."

"Business? Important?" Ian withdrew the pipe from his lips, peered into the bowl, shrugged, winced, and went up and down on the balls of his feet. He reached into his trouser pocket and pulled out a large bodkin. "Spill the beans then, Gatehouse. What business and where?" As Ian spoke, he poked and prodded the pipe with his bodkin.

"Ian," I said, curtly, for in my book Janie's honor was sacrosanct until our coupling was official, "I'm going up the cut in a coal boat."

"I beg your pardon, old chap?"

"Ian. It's private, but . . ."

"Fair enough, fair enough." Ian casually put the pipe to his lips and blew hard. "Clear at last," he said, with a satisfied grin.

"But, I was about to say, Ian, that I'm worried on account of the bit of trouble . . ."

"Not another word, Gatehouse, old dear," said Ian, interrupting. "I simply know that a woman is behind it all." Ian pointed with his pipe in the direction of a sports-jacketed individual who sat with a rustic at one of the cribbage tables. "Jacob!" hollered Ian. Jacob stopped his game and glanced up, confused. "Jacob!" said Ian, once more, because, what with all the tobacco smoke, Jacob was plainly having difficulty in identifying the source of the calling of his name. "It's me Jacob! Only we need your help, old boy! Gatehouse has a problem with his todger and I require your expert opinion!"

"For pity's sake, Ian," I said, as all eyes within the bar focused on me and my loins in particular.

"Gatehouse," said Ian, "for your information, Nurse Stringer has told half the parish about your trip to the cottage hospital. You see," and Ian proceeded to nod but once, "I told you that her conduct is unbecoming. But providence has now shone on you too, old chap. Jacob, you see, is a retail purveyor of pharmaceutical products."

"Aye?"

"Jacob runs the chemists shop in Shipsford."

"There's no need to involve half the county, Ian. Tell you what. Let me borrow that bodkin thingy."

"What on earth for? My God, you surely can't be that desperate, can you? Here," said Ian, after a brief pause, and a double wince, and he handed over the pin.

"Ian," I said. "Where Nurse Stringer failed, I shall succeed."

"Service, please!" shouted Ian, while, at the same time hammering

263

the top of the bar with his fist. "One double brandy, if you will be so kind. And make it snappy!"

"Gosh, thanks, Ian, I think I need it."

"It's for me not you, you fool." No sooner had the double measure been measured than Ian wrestled the tumbler from the bartender. He insisted that the cost of the same be chalked up in the name of the pair of yuppies recently arrived from London and living in Rosemary Cottage, and swallowed the lot in one.

I made my way outside, and, after the only other incumbent had finished what he was about and had departed, I fished out the bodkin.

Moments later, Ian bounded in and he was quickly followed by Jacob. "Good heavens above, Gatehouse! I thought you were being murdered. Not even The General screams like that! Come on, Jacob. We'd best get him to that shop of yours before he does himself some serious mischief."

In common with the proprietor, the chemist's shop was old but exceedingly smart. Lined up against the back wall were tiny drawers, many in number, wooden, and each had its own label.

"It'll take no time at all to find what I'm after," said Jacob, in a quasi rural tongue. "Here you go, Mr. Gatehouse," he said, discharging his undertaking, for Jacob had located two tubes in next to no time. He leaned against the glass counter and beckoned me over. Ian, meanwhile, stood with his back turned, eyeing jars of barley sugars, humbugs, and such-like, on a far away shelf. "The secret," said Jacob, "is to moisten the old, you know," and he looked south.

"Yes, I know, the old block," I snapped. It weren't like me to react like that. And Jacob, being so amicable, it made me feel bad. But I was at close to breaking point by now.

"Mix, this," and Jacob handed me one of the tubes, it was red in color, "with that," and he handed me the other tube, and it was of the color blue. Jacob stood to attention. "Two to one in favour of the red ought to do it, Mr. Gatehouse, plus," he added, with a knowing wink, "plenty of whiskey and paracetamol."

"What on earth for, Jacob?"

"It may keep the pain at bay," answered the pharmacist, to the background noise of chuckles coming from yonder.

"But Jacob," I submitted, "I shall end up with the stuff everywhere. What color are these creams, by the way?"

"White," he answered, "both white," and he did so to further chuckling from the other side.

"But Jacob," my submission went again, "I shall end up with cream all over my trousers, sort of thing. I'll be locked-up for indecency."

"Bhonny!" came a cry from the far end, and, thereupon, he who had cried out came over. I reached down for a wastebasket and proffered it to Ian. Thereupon, he spat out an enormous gobstopper. It was a wonder he hadn't choked. "Gosh, that's better," said Ian. "I knew I should have opted for a mint humbug. Anyway, as I was about to say, johnny, Jacob. That should do the trick."

"You are nothing short of a genius," said Jacob, excitedly, and both he and Ian fell about.

"Would anyone care to share the joke with me?" I said, and, I said it with indignance.

"Gatehouse, old dear. Must I spell everything out?" Ian shrugged and winced. "After you have slapped on the old cream from the red and the old cream from the blue, you simply have to slap on a . . ." He paused for a chuckle. "Condom!" he managed to splutter, before he fell about, once more.

"What?" I said. "I don't know how to handle them things." And I spoke the truth for I had been reared on the streets of Dudsall where family planning had consisted of shutting one's eyes and thinking of the ugliest of clippie's on a corporation bus, all the time hoping that the ten o'clock out of Wolverhampton wouldn't come rattling over the viaduct, just at that vital moment.

"Jacob," said Ian. "Ignore the fellow and fetch out your finest johnnies. Our friend, Gatehouse, here, must be gone before the cock crows . . ."

"Except that you killed the cock next door and had it for dinner, last Easter."

"Stop splitting hairs, Gatehouse," and Ian spoke abruptly which I thought was a bit rich considering that I'd only tried to put the record straight. He proceeded to clamp the brand spanking new clay between his teeth and produced the howitzer.

"I'll see what I can do," said Jacob, and he copped hold of a chair, clambered up and onto the same, and he reached for the highest of the little wooden drawers. "Whilst you're about it, Jacob, you may as well get one for me. I have to be elsewhere tomorrow." Then, Ian turned towards me. "Unlike you, old chap, I am only gone for the day, but." He shrugged, winced, and chuckled. "I may get lucky, you know."

Jacob came down from the perch and opened his palm and revealed an oblong packet. It was pale, and fresh scrubbed clean looking; the palm that is, just how you'd imagine a respectable pharmacist's palm to look. As for the packet, it was dark and dirty looking, with a use by date that was long gone, and it wasn't what you'd think a respectable pharmacist would go hawking especially as the label disclosed that the content of the packet was Black Tickler, one in number.

"Jacob," I said, "I can't go swanning around for the best part of five days with that as a permanent fixture and fitting. What happens if I'm in a road accident or sommut?"

"Five days?" said Jacob. The fresh scrubbed palm copped hold of a pocket calculator and the fingers attached to the other, equally fresh scrubbed, palm started tapping away. As Jacob tapped, he began to mutter, all to his self. "Awake on average sixteen hours each day, with a need to attend the lavatory every hour." At that juncture, Jacob ceased tapping and looked up. "On second thoughts, Mr. Gatehouse. I think we'll work on you going every thirty minutes. Oh. And, as an aside, Ian, I must warn you that the jars on the middle shelf where you are pointing that lighter are filled with methyl alcohol." And, with that, Jacob's head went back down, with a recommencement of the tapping and of the muttering, thus. "Add four per day in case he strikes it lucky (tell a lie, he stands no chance) although, add two per day for breakages (that's more like it) equals thirty four, times the number of days." Jacob stopped his tapping and muttering, and, once more looked up. "Good," he said, boldly, "that's settled then."

"How many, Jacob?"

"One hundred and seventy, Mr. Gatehouse."

Ian shrugged, winced, and bit the stem of his clay pipe so hard that he snapped it clean in two.

"Jacob!" I cried. "You have to be joking!"

"I'm being deadly serious," said Jacob, sounding deadly serious. "It will be a health hazard if you go with any fewer in number."

"Righty-ho," I sighed, "you'd best make it the round two hundred. Just in case, sort of thing."

"Very wise, Mr. Gatehouse, except." Jacob's caveat sounded ominous, and I weren't far wrong because the pharmacist only went and imparted, "I have nowhere near that number of Black Ticklers in stock. However," he said, on eyeing my look of desperation, "I do have a box out back that I've never been able to shift. You can have the whole contents for fifty quid and, Mr. Gatehouse, that's cheap at half the price."

While Jacob went to his back room, Ian winced, shrugged, and chuckled so much that anyone peering through the bull's eye glass windows could have been forgiven for assuming that he was convulsing. "You won't be wanting that bodkin, either," I told him, and, to prove the point in issue, I plucked from the counter a bit of broken clay pipe and wafted the same before his eyes. "And besides," I furthermore told him, "I'll need a bodkin if the creams don't work."

Ian was still wincing as Jacob returned bearing a very large cardboard box. I eagerly dove into the same and, after rummaging about for a tick, I pulled out a sample that comprised packets of the same shape and size as the one from the top drawer. But, whereas that one had borne the trade name Black Tickler, dodgy enough in itself some might have said, the packets I pulled out were found to contain one of each of Spiked Sensation, and Screaming Thrusters.

"These are disgraceful, these are," I said to Jacob.

"Take them or leave them, Mr. Gatehouse."

"I'll take 'em."

"I'll swap my Black Tickler for one of your Spiked Sensations," said Ian, eagerly.

Well, mid morn the following day found me and my busted suitcase at the railway station. I was kitted out in twenties type gear for the occasion. To be frank, it hadn't been too difficult a thing to do 'cause twenties clobber was still in vogue as far as Dudstall and surrounds went. Mind you, I could have done without hitchhiking down in clobber of that sort but one hundred and ninety nine condoms crammed within my case had meant that there was very little room for anything else.

Anyway, I went to the platform where a row of smart, chocolate Pullmans were parked, and, I awaited the arrival of my beloved Janie. *This is it,* I thought, *no more cat and mouse games for you malady. Before the night is out, I'll be down on one knee, providing black tickler remains in situ.*

Ten minutes or so passed and there was no sign of Janie. I began to experience that stood-up sort of a feeling. You know the score. You spend what's left of your week's wages on back row tickets, center aisle, and then spend the whole of the films running time on the front steps of the Odeon wondering whether she's had an accident or something, *'cause the rumors about her and the DJ down at The George are scurrilous.*

Well, twenty minutes went by and those passengers who had begun to arrive were looking at their wristwatches, eagerly awaiting embarkation instructions. Then, amongst all of the unfamiliar faces, I saw one that I recognised.

"Ian!" I said. "What the hell are you doing here?"

"Gatehouse, old chap! I could ask the same of you."

"I'm here by invitation, I am. What's your excuse? And," I added, for good measure, "you look ridiculous in those two tone shoes and spats."

"Gatehouse," said Ian, with a shrug and a wince, "I too am here by invitation. Here," and he reached into his inside pocket and produced some crumpled paper. "To coin your phrase, take a deco, if you don't believe me. And another thing, Gatehouse," he said.

"Yes?"

"You look more ridiculous than ever I do, sporting a green felt jacket, white flared trousers, and a crimson kipper tie. In fact, Gatehouse, old dear, you greatly resemble a glam rocker, save and except that I doubt very much whether even the likes of him, the dead one, from T Rex strolled about town with a johnny strapped to his todger."

I snatched the paper from out of Ian's hand. "This is my invite, this is!"

"No it jolly well is not!" said Ian snatching it right back again.

"But I found it in the kitchen where you left it for me."

"No I did not." He sounded assertive, as though he meant what he had said. "I left it there for me. Janie and her family and friends always invite me to their work's annual day out. I am, you see, a conduit between them and the ordinary folk of Prestwick, many of whom work at the processing plant. Last year it was a matinee followed by a slap up nosh at an exceedingly posh hotel. This year's jolly is a trip to the

268

coast and another slap up nosh, only in a Pullman carriage."

"This is dreadful, this is, Ian," and I rocked my sole asset, to wit the case. Having, in that fashion, made certain that it was safe to sit upon, I proceeded to sit upon the same. Then, I placed my head, complete with black trilby hat, the "I heart Blackpool" band having been removed mind, into my hands.

"Gatehouse!" barked Ian. "In heaven's name, show some dignity. And," he added in a manner most cruel, "you've positioned that tiresome case on a broken paving slab right where the lions and tigers are likely to attack you."

"It's all right for you," I blubbered. "I thought Janie was taking just me and her to Venice where I'd propose."

"You? Janie? Venice?" Ian shrugged, winced, and then chuckled. Indeed it would be fair and accurate to state that he chuckled so hard and he chuckled so loud that everyone on the platform stopped what they were about and stared at we two. "And what's with the proposal nonsense? It is public knowledge that if you approach Janie Jetty within fifty yards a power of arrest, appended to a non-molestation order, will be invoked. And besides," he cruelly added, "the poor woman has never, not once, seen you when you have not been sporting black eyes and severe facial bruising. Indeed, it is fair to state that Janie does not even know what you look like!"

"Ian," I said, pitiably, "I thought it was her and not Harry who'd sponsored my studies."

"Ha!" cried Ian, and he stomped one foot hard upon the platform surface. He thereby induced self- inflicted pain and I reckoned he'd done it to prevent himself falling about in convulsions of laughter.

"Ian," I said again, only this time I was a mite more assertive 'cause I'd recalled evidence of relevance; indeed it was evidentially so significant that it was certain to save the day. "Ian," I said with even more assertiveness, and I arose from my seat, my sole asset, a new man. "It happens to be a fact that Janie cannot hide her true love for me. You see, whenever I have been near, her chest and swan-like neck glows crimson with raw passion, they do."

"Gatehouse," said Ian. He sounded rather dismissive considering the weight of the evidence in favour of that racing certainty that Janie and me were meant to be. "If you are to make a career as an advocate in the highest courts in this land, it might be altogether better were you

to pay attention to simple facts as opposed to diving head first into . . .."
"Aye?"
"Gatehouse. I suggest that you do not confuse signs of raw passion with signs of an acute allergy to cat hair."
"Aye?"
"Gatehouse, old chap." Ian placed one hand upon my shoulder that was sagging, despite all the padding. "Is it or is it not the case that Janie has had a domestic cat unleashed upon her whenever she has displayed these signs of. . ."He coughed before completing his sentence and, after the cough, he completed the sentence, "raw passion?" And I could have sworn he was about to chuckle, all over again.

I returned to the seated position on my sole asset, only I did it heavier than before. Indeed, I could have sworn I heard a hinge go. "Sorry, Ian," I said, "I'll go breach in hand, I will." It had dawned on me that Ian was right. Every time Janie blushed, she'd had a cat crawling up her. In Prestwick it had been Colin. Why, even in High Barnet, it had been Sixpence, deceased, killed by a car, dead. In fact, the only times Janie had not gone crimson was when *Felis catus* had not been in sight, dead or otherwise. "Ian," I sobbed like a babby, "I'm undone, I am."

"Pull yourself together," said Ian snappishly, "enemy approaching, at nine o'clock."

A whole flock of factory workers, done up to the nines, had just streamed off a coach. They were headed by Janie and her family and friends. And what really stuck in the craw was the sight of young Pinstripe, swaggering and strutting his stuff.

"Ian!" said Janie, as the gaggle approached. Her wonderful eyes glowered. "What is he doing here?"

That hurt, I can tell you because, though Janie had spoken those words to Ian, she had stared scornfully at me. And, as she had done so, I saw no glowing of crimson passion about her person. This was incontrovertible evidence, in my opinion most humble, that it was simulated fur around the collar of her twenties type tunic of cream and not the remnants of a skinned mammal.

"I'll have you know," said Ian, coming to the aid of one who was down for the count and very nearly out, "my esteemed, learned friend and colleague, Gatehouse, here, has sacrificed his weekend conference with The International Bar Association in favour of driving me here because I felt somewhat unwell."

Janie stuck her beautiful face into a huddle comprising her family and friends, and, naturally enough, her. But even young Pinstripe had a look-in. After the huddling was done, Janie came over again. "We should like Izaak to join us," she said to Ian. It had been a majority verdict in my favour, four to one, judging from Pinstripe's apparent cob on.

Ian shrugged. "Do you not think it fitting to extend the invitation to Gatehouse in person?"

"Yes, of course, sorry," said Janie. She was simply wonderful when she was flustered. Anyway, all-graceful like, Janie bent down to address me. The bending down was naturally essential on account of the fact that I had remained, throughout, perched on my sole asset. "Izaak." She spoke my name softly. "We would very much like you to accompany us to the coast."

"I'd love to," I said, calling time on my sulk.

"You know," whispered Janie, ever so sweetly, "you are rather handsome without all that bruising and those black eyes."

We were directed into the carriages by a blue suited guard.

"No thank you very much," I told him, "I'll keep hold of my case." I had no intentions of inviting a repetition of Venice airport. "Important case studies," I said to Janie as I lifted aloft my sole asset. In actual fact, the luggage rack onto which I plonked the same consisted of little more than a piece of fishing net strung between a pair of brackets. Anyway, with the case secured overhead, Ian and I took our places. And to everyone's surprise, not least mine, we found ourselves seated dead opposite Janie and the others. The disdain on Pinstripe's face was a sight to behold.

Even before we had rumbled out of the station, the fine wine was hitting the spot.

"Steady on, Gatehouse, old chap. It's a long way to Folkestone."

"Sorry, Ian. I have to keep myself anesthetised. Here, cop hold of my wine glass while I fish around for the paracetamol. I know it's about somewhere."

But before even the canapés had come our way, I was feeling woozy.

"Gatehouse, old dear. I think you ought to go easy on the Mateus."

"Sorry, Ian. I have to have a crack at going. Wish me luck."

Now, the littlest room on the Pullman may have been luxurious but when all was said and done, it was located within a railway carriage. And, in common with most, if not all, railway carriages, especially when they are being towed to the coast at high speed, this one tended to shake and rattle a bit. So, shoulders hunched, legs set firmly apart, I fetched out the red cream and the blue cream. Then, I gingerly removed Black Tickler and tossed it in the lavatory pan. *Now, then,* I thought, through the alcoholic haze, which had, at least in some part, numbed the pain, *two parts red to one part blue. Or is it two of blue and one of red? I'll go to the foot of our stairs! All the spare johnnies are locked in the case!*

I deftly reached into the bowl and recovered Black Tickler. He may have been well past his use-by date but he were a plucky chap. You see, he was none the worse for wear despite the half drowning. I proceeded to dry him off with the hand towel but, thereupon, the train lurched and speeded up and, trousers around my ankles, I stumbled forwards. And the last that I saw of Black Tickler was when he sprang back down the toilet pan. I tried my best to recover the little fellow but it was to no avail. In a flush, Black Tickler was halfway down the Maidstone Line.

Undaunted, I proceeded to mix and spread the red cream followed by the blue cream. Or was it the blue cream followed by red cream? Well, either way, it didn't much matter because in the absence of the retaining qualities of Black Tickler, as guaranteed on the packet, but only to the extent of seventy-five per cent, I'll have you know, the creams found themselves plastered everywhere on everything, save and except the old block.

The half gallon of Mateus, by then, had worked its way through the system and was complaining something rotten that it needed to be let out. So, I swallowed a brace of paracetamol, took a deep breath, and fetched out Ian's bodkin.

Well, fair-do's, I give the train driver the benefit of the doubt that he was no sadist and that the pile of house bricks and rubble on the line was as bigger surprise to him as it had been to everyone else and he'd consequently had no option but to perform an emergency stop.

Next, came a hammering on the door. The proprietor of the pounding fists had a quid in his gob and could only have been Pinstripe. "Open the door this instant! Miss Jetty demands an explanation for the blood curdling screams!"

"Hold your horses, Anker! I'll be out in a bit!" And, moments later, I emerged from the littlest room with Pinstripe pacing up and down outside.

"What have you been up to in there, Gatehouse?" And that was a far as his enquiry went because, on noticing nowt but circumstantial evidence, notoriously misleading, unless it is so compound as to be more probative than prejudicial, Pinstripe had passed judgment. "That's disgusting, that is!" he cried, whilst simultaneously pointing at the white cream splattered about my flares. "You need locking up! Miss Jetty and the others will hear of this!"

I grasped the wretch by his pink and white cravat and reeled him in and I thereby thwarted his escape to the dining car. "You breathe a word of this, Anker, and I'll shove your head down the jankhole!"

But on observing evidence that Pinstripe was in danger of asphyxiation, I loosed my hold and let him up from the lavatory pan. Thereupon, the abominable wretch tidied his cravat and squared up. "You don't frighten me, Gatehouse. But listen to me now, and listen to me good. I mean to have Janie Jetty and there is nothing my dear guttersnipe that you can do about it. But . . ."and weirdly, he began to smile, "all may not be lost because I have a proposition that should serve you well."

"I wouldn't accept a brief from you if it were the last brief on earth," I said, proudly.

"You're hopeful ain't ya, Gatehouse?" Pinstripe sounded cocky and he looked cocky. "Gatehouse," he sneered, "I would not trust you to conduct a corporation bus, let alone conduct one of my management buyouts."

"What sort of a proposition are you talking about then?"

I made my enquiry with suspicion, and I was right to do so, 'cause then, with a leering smirk, he proposed that I keep my distance from Janie for nigh on eighteen months. "By then, Gatehouse, I'll have her whipped into shape and I'll have my share of the assets. After I've done with the little filly, you can shag her all you like, as long as you're discreet. I'll be in London during the week, and, while you're amusing yourself with sweet Janie Jetty, I'll be amusing myself with . . .," he paused and coughed, "more worldly girlies," he went on, all of the time smirking. "In fact," he said. "Give me the phone number of Michaela and we'll shake on the arrangement, right here and now!"

"Why, you . . .!"

"He's gone totally mad!" Pinstripe screeched, as he made a bolt for the dining car. "He's pulled a sharp instrument from out of his trousers and has threatened to gouge my eye out!"

I determinedly strode after the chancer, though not before secreting Ian's bodkin behind the lavatory. Well, be fair, going equipped with an offensive weapon constituted an offense for which I could have been imprisoned, notwithstanding that it was only a solicitor, and a city solicitor at that, with whom and on whom I'd intended to be offensive.

I spied Pinstripe hiding behind a woman's petticoat, as all cowards do, except that, in the particular instance, Janie wore a flapper dress and not a petticoat, and, permit me to state that it was extremely fetching and went well with the cream tunic.

Janie had a stern expression as she stood over her salad of prawn and avocado. "Izaak," she said. Janie not only looked stern but she sounded stern. Indeed, it would be fair to state that never had I heard a woman sound quite as stern. "Is it true that you have attacked William?"

It was now or never. This was my Rorke's Drift, even though the opposition only fought with sticks. In fact, this was more of a Donoghue versus Stevenson situation 'cause who'd have thought anyone, not least a Scot, would prove that drinking ginger beer was a pursuit so hazardous as to warrant the award of substantial damages, well, substantial for 1932, that is. *It's true,* I thought to myself, as I approached Janie. *I do want to shag you till you beg me to stop, but I must tell you right here and now that I love you with a passion and want you as my wife.*

"I'm waiting for an answer," said Janie, arms folded, fingers fithering the sleeves of her tunic.

I marched right up and stood nose to nose, toe to toe, with her for whom I'd lay down my life; give up watching Dudsall FC when drawn against better opposition in the cup, even. *Janie,* I thought to myself, *I love you with a passion and want you as my wife.* "Janie!" I said aloud, "I must tell you right here and now that I want to shag you till you beg me to stop!"

The ensuing silence was at last broken by Ian. "Top marks for speaking your mind, old boy, but there is a time and a place."

"Janie," I protested, as she sat down aghast, hand to mouth, tears swelling. "It weren't supposed to come out like that."

Janie removed the hand. "Izaak," she said, "I think you have said . . ."

Suddenly the Pullman jolted forwards, and, from the waving of fists from people on an allotment whose glasshouses seemed strangely to have been smashed to smithereens, I adjudged that the driver had removed the obstacles from the line, thereby affording free and uninterrupted passage. Normal service having thereby been resumed, I thought it best in the circumstances to postpone my proposal of marriage until we'd had the main course.

Now, with Janie seated, young Pinstripe found himself with no place to hide, no metaphoric petticoat, sort of thing to hide behind. So, by way of alternative, he made a grab for the emergency cord.

"You'll be fined for improper use," I cautioned him, in vain.

"You're a homicidal maniac, Gatehouse!"

The Pullman juddered to an abrupt halt.

I next recall looking up at the carriage ceiling. I was lying on a stretcher awaiting transportation to men's surgical. I reckon that I'd blacked out on account of the misuse of Mateus as an anaesthetic, the damned good slapping from Janie, the white creamy substance on which I'd skidded, or, a combination of at least two of those things. However, Ian swore that my unconsciousness came about as a result of being hit on top of the head by my airborne case that had then bust open despatching in all directions one hundred and ninety nine packets of assorted Spiked Sensations and Screaming Thrusters.

Well, either way, as I was carried past Janie, I reached up and, on stroking her soft mousey hair, I gently removed a packet of condoms. The use-by date was so very far gone as to render the purveyor liable for prosecution by the Health and Safety Department of Shipsford District Council. In fact, Jacob was lucky never to have found his self ordered to pay child support in a paternity by proxy suit.

"Oh, Izaak," said Janie.

"Oh, Janie," I said.

Lightning Source UK Ltd.
Milton Keynes UK
14 March 2010
151373UK00001B/28/P

9 781608 60036